FREEDOM OR DEATH

a novel by
NIKOS KAZANTZAKIS

Translated by Jonathan Griffin

PREFACE BY A. DEN DOOLAARD

A TOUCHSTONE BOOK
Published by Simon & Schuster, Inc.
NEW YORK

This novel is a work of fiction. Names, characters, places and incidents are either the product of the author's imagination or are used fictitiously. Any resemblance to actual events or locales or persons, living or dead, is entirely coincidental.

Library of Congress Cataloging in Publication Data

Kazantzakis, Nikos, 1883-1957.
Freedom or death.

(A Touchstone book)
Translation of: Ho Kapetan Michalēs.
1. Crete—History—Fiction. I. Title.
PA5610.K39K33   1983   889'.332   83-17571
ISBN 0-671-49260-8 Pbk.

Preface

By A. DEN DOOLAARD

HOLLAND knew the Greek author Kazantzakis from only one book: The Greek Passion. Within three years of publication almost 40,000 copies were sold—a record for a literary work in Holland. Many people, from reading this book, gathered the impression that Kazantzakis was a Christian author, be it of little orthodoxy. But the well-known habit to classify, which automatically urges many Dutchmen to surround everything with partitions and to label it once and for all, here caught only one part of the many-sided figure.

Kazantzakis escapes simplifying definitions as a continent rejects them. A continent like Asia is tundra, steppe, and desert, fertile river valley and jungle. Kazantzakis is Christian and heathen, anarchist, humanist and stoic sage, alternately and sometimes simultaneously. He belongs to no school, and he cannot found a school, no more than could El Greco, who was also born in Crete. Kazantzakis is, before everything else, Cretan; and as such he is more than European only. When one takes a compass, pricks one leg in Mount Ida and swings the other one along the Greek coasts, one touches—before the circle has been completed—Phoenicia and Israel, Egypt and Libya. Crete is as far removed from Europe as from Africa and Asia. The ancestors of Kazantzakis came from a group of Cretan villages to which a Byzantine conqueror had banished his Arab mercenaries, amongst whom were many Bedouins. As Africa's flame scorches Crete in summer, so it burns in the blood of this man who strove, for many long years, to build a synthesis from Greek and Oriental thought.

But the Byzantines were not the only conquerors of the island which was once the most bitterly fought-for place in the Mediterranean. Libyans and Greeks, Saracens and Arabs, Venetians and Turks, in the course of fifty centuries, have overpowered, destroyed and fertilized Crete. What they left behind was silt layer after silt layer on the primeval soil of the Minoan civilization (3000–1500 B.C.) which worshiped life and the life force, and which looked death in the eye without troubling itself about personal immortality. Unlike the Egyptians, the ancient Cretans hardly bothered with eschatology; their worship of life contained an undaunted acceptance of death. "This heroic view, without hope and without fear, serenely directed upon the precipice, that is what I call the view of Crete," Kazantzakis wrote. And to this primeval soil of his being in later years he returned, after long wanderings through both the physical world and the world of thought, which carried him through Russia and Spain, India and China, Africa and Arabia, and during which the spirits of Homer and Dante, Buddha and Confucius, Nietzsche and Bergson were his guides.

Hence the great diversity in his work. For sixteen years he worked at a sequel to the Odyssey, in 33,000 verses. This work is now being translated in America. One of his earlier novels, Zorba the Greek, is dionysian and apollonian at the same time, as well as a struggle against the suctional force of the Buddhist Nothing. Besides this book, foaming with heathenish joy of life, he has written profound Biblical dramas, whose value for the stage, however, seems doubtful. In his novel The Last Temptation he arrived at an interpretation of Christ which is as original as it is bold but which remains unacceptable for every dogmatic Christian, even though it shows Kazantzakis' belief in a personal God.

And now we have a novel in front of us which, at first sight historical, violates the ordinary framework of the historical novel with as much indomitable force as Captain Michales, the hero of the book, angrily smashes his host's glass by putting two fingers into it and spreading them.

In a philosophical essay written during his youth, Kazantzakis wrote: "You are not one; you are an army. Are you angry? One of your forebears foams on your lips. Do you love? Deep inside you whinnies an ancestor. . . ."

In this book the Proteus of contemporary novel writing shows hundreds of persons (amongst whom are many of his own ancestors) from his native land, and he shows them with as much love as ruthlessness. Indeed, in his artist's mind there is no contrast between these two conceptions. Briefly summarized, this novel tells the story of the revolt of 1889 by the suppressed Cretans against their Turkish oppressors, as well as a love intrigue in which the two Cretan heroes, the captains Michales and Polyxigis, fight with each other and with the noble Turk Nuri Bey about the same Circassian woman. But this skeleton gives only a vague idea of the wild and luxurious outward form. Half of the time the action takes place in the city of Megalokastro (nowadays Neraklion); and the reader receives the strong impression (which becomes a feeling of happiness, in spite of the repeated shocks he has to undergo) that he knows this town and its inhabitants better than his own place.

Every mask is torn down; everyone's virtues and vices are brought to light. In the spirit we float with the author over towers and minarets; and Kazantzakis not only raises the roofs from the houses with his magic wand, but also the trapdoors from the dark caverns in which man hides secret wishes and passions.

All this is bathed in an eternal light, like an El Greco. And that makes even the most horrible scenes supportable. It is this fourth dimension of a supernatural forgiveness, never described in so many words but always audible as a floating overtone, that makes these wild sinners into children of God—never for these people the God of Love but the Old Testament God of Revenge.

Much of the action in this book may seem unbelievable, however stirring the author's narration is. But whoever knows a little about the Cretans and their history will realize that the people in this book are real, even if the author makes some of them bigger than life—which is a condition for a true epic. And one should also remember where and when the story of the book is laid: on an island, after a long century of oppression by the Turks. No power lifted a finger to help them. The Cretans stood alone "and with their rifles called to God. They stood before God's gate and fired their weapons, that He should hear them." It was the Crete where for two days and nights 200 rebels and 65 monks defended their monastery Arkadi against 15,000 Turks. When, at last, the enemy finally rammed in the gate of the monastery, a young fighter fired off his pistols into the open barrels of an underground powder vault, where 600 women and children were hiding. *They all perished, together with the hundreds of defenders and attackers inside the crumbling walls.*

Freedom or Death! Crete is an island in which burns a flame. Even in peacetime the many people in this book are driven by a demonical fire. They do not fear death, and they love life in the sensual way which, in a somber and sunless North, may seem sinful to ascetic spirits. But over Crete blows a tornado of light. And this book, epic, heroic and tragic, is a world in itself, above which, with wings outspread, floats an eagle: Kazantzakis.

FREEDOM
OR DEATH

1

CAPTAIN MICHALES gnashed his teeth. He usually did so when wrath took charge of him. "Captain Wildboar" was his apt nickname in Megalokastro. With his sudden rages, his deep, dark eyes, his short, stubborn neck and jutting jaw, the heavy, broad-boned man really was like a wild boar rearing for the spring.

He crumpled a letter in his fist and stuffed it into his wide corduroy belt. He had been a long time spelling it out and seeking for its meaning. . . . He won't come (he understood) this Easter either, and so his ill and dying mother and his poor sister won't see him, because, so he says, he's still studying. . . . What the devil is he studying? Will he always go on studying? He doesn't say that he hasn't the courage to return to Crete because he's married a Jewess and not a countrywoman of ours. That's what that favorite son of yours has come to, Brother Kosta! If only you were living! If only you were there to lift him by the ankles and hang him head downward from the beam like a sack of seed!

Captain Michales stood up—a fine giant of a fellow. The crown of his head nearly touched the ceiling of his shop. The black tasseled band that bound his hair behind had fallen loose on his back, and Captain Michales grabbed at it and pulled it tighter round his thick-boned skull. Then he strode to the door to get some air.

Charitos the apprentice, a wild shoot of a brown-haired village lad with frightened, blinking eyes and protruding ears, crouched behind a coil of ship's rope. His glance swept over the sails, planks, pots of paint and tar, heavy chains, iron anchors—all sorts of ship's gear and tools. But in his fear he saw nothing but the

3

Chief, now standing on the threshold, filling the whole of the doorway and staring out toward the harbor. Captain Michales was his uncle, but Charitos called him the Chief and trembled before him.

"As if I hadn't enough trouble already this evening," Captain Michales muttered. "What does the dog expect of me, sending word to me that I must go over to that miserable house of his this evening? And now, on top of it, the vexation with my nephew! His mother would have me write to him, and I did write to him. But he doesn't even show up!"

He gazed leftward at the harbor—at the steamers, the sailing ships and the sea. Sounds rose from up on the mole: dealers, sailors, boatmen and porters were swarming among oil and wine casks and piles of rubbish, shouting, cursing, loading and unloading. They were hurrying to be done with it by the time the sun went down and the fortress gate closed. The sea poised sultrily; the harbor stank of rotting oranges, turnips, wine and oil. Two or three middle-aged Maltese women sprinkled with spray stood on the walls and chattered hoarsely. They were waving to a broad-beamed Maltese steamer which was coming in with a cargo of bottles.

The sun sank in a red sky; the last day of March was ending. A sharp northerly breeze sighed, and Megalokastro shivered. Shopkeepers chafed their hands, stamped their feet and drank herb infusions—some even drank rum—to get warm. Up above, the peaks of Strumbula were covered with snow, and farther off Psiloritis* rose, dark blue. Frozen masses of snow glimmered in white streaks from deep hollows protected from the wind. But the sky shone crystalline, steel colored.

Captain Michales raised his glance to the massive Kule, a strong, thickly built tower to the right of the harbor entrance with the winged marble lion of Venice on its front. Megalokastro was entirely surrounded by walls and fierce, battlemented towers, which had been built by its Christian masters in the heyday of ancient Venice and had been slaked with Venetian, Turkish and Greek blood. Here and there remains of earlier taste were still left, as for instance the stone lions of Venice, carrying the Gospel in their claws, and the Turkish axes which had been carved on the fortifi-

* Mount Ida (Tr.)

4

cations on that bloody autumn day when the Turks had trampled Megalokastro after long years of hopeless blockade. And everywhere among the tumbled blocks there now luxuriated an undergrowth of fig trees, stinging nettles and caper bushes.

Captain Michales lowered his gaze and fixed his eyes on the base of the Kule tower. The veins of his temples swelled, and he sighed. There, in that dungeon, against which the waves beat, was the accursed prison where generations of Christian warriors had gasped out their lives, chained hand and foot. Truly the bodies of Cretans, strong though they are, do not come up to the strength of their souls, he thought. I accuse God of not having given us Cretans bodies of steel with which to hold out for the hundred, two hundred, three hundred years until we have set Crete free. Then we could turn to dust and ashes.

His anger rose again, and he thought of his nephew living abroad as a "Frank." He's studying, he says. What the devil is he studying? He'll come back like his Uncle Tityros the schoolmaster, a seedy creature with glasses and a hollow rump! A good pig, but, dammit, with worm!

He spat in a large arc and hesitated a moment longer before going to the small spice shop kept by Demetros.

You *have* come down in the world, bold race of Mad-michales the Turk gobbler! he said to himself, and in his mind's eye his fear-inspiring grandfather Mad-michales appeared in flesh and blood. How could he die, he who had so many children and grandchildren? Far and wide the old people still remembered him, the way he used to gaze along the coast of Crete, shading his eyes with his hand: he was watching to see if the Muscovite ships were coming out of the sea and sky. He would tilt his fez awry, saunter up and down the walls of Megalokastro, bow before that accursed Kyle and sing in the Turks' faces, "The Muscovites are coming!" His hair and his beard had been long, his boots high and hitched to his belt, and never—it was said—did he take them off. He had worn, too, a long black shirt, for enslaved Crete was in mourning, and every Sunday after Mass he used to swagger along with *his* grandfather's bow over his shoulder and a quiver full of arrows as well.

"Those were men," Captain Michales snarled, frowning. "Those were giants, not worms like us! So were their womenfolk. Yes, even wilder. Ah, time, time! Mankind's going downhill, going to the devil!"

A curtain rose within him and revealed, after his grandfather, a skeleton with loamy nails—his grandmother. When she had reached a ripe age she had left the rough-walled house and her heap of children, grandchildren and great-grandchildren to bury herself in a deep cave up above her native village, at the foot of Psiloritis. For twenty years she had stayed in that hole. One of her granddaughters, who had married a man in the village, brought her every morning a lump of barley bread, some olives and a small bottle of wine (there was water enough in the cave), and at Easter two red eggs in remembrance of Christ the Lord. And every morning the old woman appeared, crouched at the cave's entrance, plaster-white like a ghost, with her long hair and nails and her rags, gazed at the rising sun and flourished her thin arms at it for a long time, either in blessing or as a curse. Then she dived back into the maw of the mountain. Twenty solitary years. But one morning they did not see her come out. They understood. They called the village priest, climbed up there with burning torches and found her, a crooked trestle of bones in a little, bathlike hollow, with her arms crossed and her head gripped between her knees.

Captain Michales shook his head, took his eyes from the prison and let the dead sink down again within him. . . .

In the little spice shop Demetros sat sleepy and swollen-eyed on a narrow sofa. He held a fly whisk and moved it languidly from side to side to keep the flies from the little bags of cloves, nutmeg, mastic and cinnamon and the little glasses of laurel and myrtle oil. Yellowheaded, cucumber-nosed, perpetually morose. Now a scratch, now a yawn, now a blink of the sleep-heavy eyes. Still he had not dropped off to sleep, and it seemed to him as if, from over the way, Captain Michales swung round and looked his way. Demetros raised the fly whisk to bid him good evening, but his vigorous neighbor turned his head in the other direction, and Demetros sank back into his doze.

Captain Michales shoved his hand into his broad, twisted belt, found the crumpled letter, pulled it out and tore it into a thousand pieces.

"As if *one* schoolmaster wasn't enough to make our family look silly! Now we've got this one! And whose son? Yours, Brother

6

Kosta, and it was you who grabbed a torch, set fire to the magazine and blew the Arkadi monastery—saints, crucifixes, monks and all, Christians and Turks—sky-high!"

Vendusos, the well-known lyre player, came hurrying along to the harbor, wrapped in a woolen jacket. He had ordered a cask of wine from Kissamos for his tavern and wanted now to collect it. But when he saw from a distance that Captain Michales' headband was pulled down to his eyebrows, he understood and veered off.

"The dragon's in another of his rages this evening," he muttered. "I'd rather go a different way."

The sun sank over Strumbula's cliffs, the streets fell into shadow, the white minarets became rose-colored, and in the harbor dealers, carpenters, dockers and boatmen sought relief from their day's work. The men and the barking ships' dogs made a great din, but the world turned mild. Captain Michales pulled a tobacco pouch from his belt and rolled himself a cigarette. His anger passed away in smoke. He stroked his raven-black chin.

"My son, my Thrasaki, must live," he muttered. "He'll wash our faces clean again. He'll set a torch to his Uncle Tityros. And he'll set a torch, too, to that nine-times-wise nephew of mine, who isn't ashamed of mixing our blood with that of moneylenders. He'll take up the standard of our clan!"

And suddenly life seemed good to him, and God just. Captain Michales no longer had accusation against Him.

A Turk, a bald-headed old man in rags and clogs, drew near, trembling, raised quivering eyes and looked at Captain Michales.

Captain Michales looked down at him and shook his head. "What do you want, Ali Aga?" he asked roughly.

Ali Aga was his neighbor, but he could not bear the disgusting fellow. That slimy snail—half man, half woman, neither man nor woman—sat in the afternoons with the Greek women of his neighborhood and took part in women's gossip.

"Sir," the old man murmured, "I was sent by Nuri Bey. 'Greetings,' he says, 'and will you give him the pleasure,' he says, 'of coming this evening to his konak?'"

"All right, I've had the message already through his servant—the black one. You may go."

"He says it's very urgent."

7

"Go, I tell you." It annoyed Michales to hear the womanish eunuch voice.

Ali Aga bit his tongue, turned with a shiver to the wall and made off.

"What have I to do in Turks' houses? What does the dog want with me? Why doesn't he come himself? I shan't go!" He wheeled around. "Charitos," he called, "go in and saddle my mare!"

He had suddenly had the idea of taking a ride on his mare, to work off grandfather, grandmother, nephew and Nuri Bey—a ride on his mare, and he'd be rid of the lot!

Just as he raised his arm to take down the key and lock up, a fresh, joyous neigh rang out from the street. Captain Michales knew that horse's voice and turned. Black and shining, sleek and slim, the noble, frothing beast came forward, stepping proudly. A plump, barefoot Turkish lad held it firmly by the rein and was leading it at a walk and unsaddled through the streets of Megalo-kastro to calm it. It had certainly come some distance at a gallop, for there was foam showing at its mouth, on its chest and under the shoulders. But its strength was still unimpaired, and, snort-ing, it tossed its foam-flecked neck and dripping mane. Every now and then it pranced, stamped hard with its slender forelegs on the paving, and neighed.

"Look, children, here comes Nuri Bey's horse!" somebody shouted outside the barbershop kept by Paraskevas the Syran. Five or six unshaved men and one man covered with lather rushed to the door. With open mouths and craning necks they stood there and gazed at it.

"By my soul," shouted a lanky youth with a sparse goat's-beard. "By my soul, if someone asked me, 'Which would you rather, Nuri Bey's horse or his hanum*?' I'd choose the horse."

"You've got as much sense as my paintbrush," said Janaros the master painter, whom they also called Pitchfork because he had a bushy, bristling mustache. "You silly idiot, Hanum Eminé is beau-tiful, twenty years old and wild. Choose her, you poor thing, and give your thighs a bit of fun!"

"I like the horse, I tell you," answered the goat-beard. "I don't go in for dirt."

*Wife (Tr.)

8

"Not the horse, my good countryman, and not the hanum," Signor Paraskevas ventured to break in, in his high voice. He too had rushed out, scissors in hand. "Neither the horse, nor the hanum! They're all more trouble than they're worth!"

The goat-beard wheeled around. "Hey, you Syran titbit," he said, "the whole of life is trouble. Only death brings repose. I mean well toward you—don't talk like that to Cretans. We might misunderstand you and bury you alive. . . ."

The poor Syran shuddered. The friendly, decent chap could himself no longer understand why he had got to Crete to shave these wild beasts here. Every time a Cretan from the mountains came over the threshold of his shop, the Syran would jump up and examine him with dread. Where was one to begin on him? For months he had not shaved or washed, for years had not had his hair cut. He would arrange the towel, grasp the scissors and bustle around the chair, on which the Cretan sat wondering at his grotesque face in the glass. He looked to him like a wether, that monster did, or like Saint Mamas, the enormous herdsman, whom Signor Paraskevas had once seen in a holy picture. Altogether overgrown as he was with the rankest beard, whiskers and locks, ten barbers could not have made a job of him.

Signor Paraskevas' scissors suddenly became small. Where was he to set to work with them in this undergrowth of hog's bristles? Then the Syran would sigh, make up his mind at last and begin in God's name with the lathering.

"Alive?" he now asked, and drew back in alarm. "Why, my good friend, would you bury me alive?"

"Because do you know what we call people who talk like you? Dead!"

The Syran swallowed, pretended he had heard nothing, and went in.

At that moment Stefanes, the aged captain of the *Dardana*, which the Turks had sunk in the '78 rising, came hobbling by. A grenade from the Turkish ship that had holed her had smashed his knee. And since then all he had been good for had been to thump the dry land with his stick and to limp about the harbor. He had two sticks: one, straight as a dart, he used when things were going well in Crete, and the other, a crooked staff, when things went crooked and the air reeked of powder. Today he had

9

the crooked staff. He listened to what was being said, and stood still. "Don't quarrel, young fellows," he said. "That's easy to decide." "Tell us, Captain Stefanes, which you'd choose for yourself." "You idiots, Nuri's horse to ride, and Hanum Eminé to make sit behind on the rump—like Saint George!" "Me too, me too, me too. Captain Stefanes!" bawled the Cretans, shaven and unshaven. "May God hear what you say!" Captain Michales had raised his eyes. The horse was now close to him, graceful yet fiery, like a black swan with its neck arched high. It turned toward him and its eyes gleamed as if it recognized Captain Michales. It checked for a moment and neighed. Captain Michales took a step toward the beast. He could not restrain himself; he took another. He was near it now. His hand itched to touch it, to feel the heat of its body. The Turkish boy saw him and stood still.

Captain Michales' hand strayed over the broad, moist chest, with its necklace of light-blue stones clasped by an ivory crescent. He eagerly stroked the neck, the nostrils, the head, patted the damp mane. His hand traveled longingly over the back and rump, went down and along the steaming belly and was still not satisfied. The hand seemed as if it wanted to engulf the whole horse.

And the proud, graceful animal bowed its neck and seemed to take an insatiable pleasure in the man's caresses. It turned its huge plum-dark eye and with a snort sucked its hot breath in over the man's hair. And suddenly it decided to play. It snapped at Captain Michales' black headband, lifted it high and waved it in the air without letting it go. The horse's eye coquetted with the black beard in front of it. And the man himself felt his heart go soft. Never had he looked at a human being with such delicate delight. He began to whisper words of endearment, and the horse lowered its neck as though it listened, and rubbed gently against the man's shoulders. Unexpectedly Captain Michales raised his hand, caught the headband from the horse's lips and wound it, sprinkled with foam as it was, around his hair. Then he turned and made a sign to the Turkish boy that he could go on.

"I shall go there," Captain Michales muttered, still following the horse with his eyes as it now approached the main gate. "I shall go there."

He had suddenly made up his mind, and he now returned to close the shop and to set out on his way to the konak of Nuri Bey.

But Captain Stefanes, who had observed him as he stroked the horse with so much feeling, stood before him, leaning on his crooked staff, and wished him good evening. He had no fear of man haters. He was himself a real man, a sturdy sea dog. In each of the risings of 1854, 1866 and 1878, he had run the Turkish blockade in his *Dardana* countless times to land food and munitions for the Christians in remote natural harbors. And when they shelled him and sank his ship, his blood had flowed from his smashed knee. But he had swum into St. Pelagia's Bay, holding in his teeth, above the waves, the letters which the Athenian Committee had sent to the famous Captain Rabe, chieftain of the Mesara region. Since then he had indeed come down in the world: he limped, had grown poor, let his clothes go into rags, went on wearing those captain's boots of his that had been patched again and again, made his daily round of the harbor and admired, though with burning heart, the foreign ships. It did him good to smell tar and to hear the voices and greetings and the noise of anchors on the hard, deep bottom. His body was weak, his pockets empty, but his soul stood upright in his breast, and he gazed out over the sea like the Gorgon figurehead.

And so he leaned on his crooked staff, stood firm in front of Captain Michales, and spoke. "Hey, Captain Michales, did your ear catch the talk down at the barber's? If you had to choose, they were saying, between Nuri's horse and Hanum Eminé, which would you choose?"

"I don't care for shameless chatter," said Captain Michales, and went over to his shop without so much as looking around at the ship's master.

But the obstinate sailor did not give up. He behaved as if he had not heard, and overhauled the other.

"Nuri has brought her from Constantinople, and she's a Circassian, they say, with beauty for five, and wild—a real man-eater. My neighbors the Hags hear from her woman, the dark Christian she brought with her, what goes on behind the cage doors at the Bey's. And they spread it about. Bless their little tongues."

"Captain Stefanes," repeated Captain Michales with irritation, "I tell you I don't care for shameless chatter."

But the tough seaman stood his ground. No, he would not have his mouth shut. He had shown no fear in face of the powerful Turkish Armada. Was he to show fear in face of this man? He shall hear it all, he said to himself, whether he likes it or not.

"Nuri Bey," he held forth, "is your blood brother, Captain Michales, and don't you forget it. And so it's right that you should know what goes on in his house. The Bey, that terrible wild beast, sits, so they say, tied to her feet and gazes into her eyes. And she presses her lighted cigarettes against his neck and giggles. And sometimes, they say, her thoughts stray back to her own country—to the tents, to the smell of dung and milk, the neighing of horses—and then it takes hold of her, and she smashes the porcelain cups, empties the scent bottles on the floor and whips her black woman. . . ."

Captain Michales, growling like a dangerous sheep dog, held the key out in front of him and shoved the old sea wolf from the doorway so as to be able to shut the shop. But the sailor could not hold his tongue. It would have been better not to engage in any conversation with such a wild beast, but now he was well and truly involved. . . . So hoist sails, whatever comes of it! He therefore made haste to finish his story:

"The hanum is jealous, so they say, of Nuri's horse. The evening before last, when the Bey tried to embrace her, she pushed him away. 'First you must do me a favor,' she said. 'Anything you wish, mistress of my heart. Everything is yours.' 'Bring your horse into the yard. Light lamps, so that I may see, and slaughter it in my presence.' The Bey sighed, bent his head and ran out of the room. He shut himself up in his room. And all night long he could be heard pacing up and down and bellowing. I'm telling you so that you may know. He's sent for you to come to his house. He needs you. Don't deny it. Ali Aga told me. So it's as well you should know how the loving couple are at loggerheads."

Stefanes rubbed his callused hands, glad that it was over and that he had finished his say without being overcome by fear.

"Yes, Captain Michales, that's how it is. Well, if it's lies, the Hags had better look out!"

Captain Michales gave a jerk; the door banged and he locked

it. He stuck the key in his belt and turned to the castaway captain. "You seafolk," he said contemptuously, "have no respect for women!"

And he went off.

"You dry-land captains," Stefanes retorted peevishly, "know all about that! Always paddling in horse dung!" Shouting this, he hobbled quickly around the corner, as if fear had suddenly got hold of him.

Captain Michales pulled the black headband over his forehead so that the tassels covered his eyes. He wanted to see no one and be seen by no one. Breathing heavily, he stumped through the Turkish quarter.

The sun had gone down. Trumpets rang out, and the police picked up their keys and double-locked the four city gates. Till sunrise no one might stick his nose outside Megalokastro or come in. Turks and Christians remained fenced in together all night.

Darkness broadened out and spread its shield over the alleys. Women no longer appeared in the streets. The lamps were lighted in the houses, the tables laid. Respectable men hurried home to dinner, the gayer ones lingering in the taverns for another drink or two. Megalokastro, as dusk hid it, felt hungry and addressed itself to the evening meal.

That was the hour when the triplet sisters, known as the Hags, would be standing behind their door, close against one another. They had bored three holes in the door, high up, and pressed their faces to them. They studied the passers-by and commented on each one's ugliness or good looks. All three old maids had snow-white hair, eyebrows and eyelashes, and red rabbits' eyes from birth. They never went out all day. It was said that they could not see well in sunlight, and longed for evening when they could stand at the three little holes and gape at the passing world. Nasty, poison tongues. Through the peepholes not a fly escaped them. Their house lay at the corner of a shopping street, at the point where the Turkish quarter left off and the Christian houses began. They saw everyone and gave everyone his nickname, from which in a lifetime he could not shake free. It was they who had called Captain Michales "the wild boar." They had christened his brother, the schoolmaster, "Tityros." For once, when his father brought back a big cheese from the village, his learned son had

13

asked him in classical Greek: τί τυρός ἐστιν αὐτός, πάτηρ? (What sort of cheese is that, Father?) The Hags had heard, and he became Tityros.

All through the day they cooked, sewed and swept in the half-dark. They had nothing else to worry about. They had no menfolk or children to look after, and God had created for them an excellent brother, a man of gold, Mr. Aristoteles the chemist. The poor man, though unmarried, worked from morning till night making up powders and ointments. Sallow, patient, with feet swollen from long standing, and with bad breath, he carried the loaded market basket morning and evening for his sisters.

When he was still young a pretty maiden with a dowry and of good family had been found for him, but he had never married. Mr. Aristoteles would have made an ideal son-in-law. His pharmacy was in the heart of Megalokastro, on the main square, full of bottles and phials, scents and soaps, and every evening teachers and doctors gathered there to take to pieces and put together the major world problems. And melancholy, shriveled Mr. Aristoteles listened, said nothing, merely looked at them with his small, blue, tired eyes and wagged his plucked head, as though to say to each one, You are right, you are right. But his one thought was that his life on this planet was going to rack and ruin. He had wanted to marry—not because he cared about women. God forbid! No, he merely wanted to beget a son who would take over the pharmacy. But where was he to put his sisters? They must marry first—that was the custom.

The years went by, his hair became white, his teeth became loose, his back became bent and his firm red cheeks sagged and shriveled. Mr. Aristoteles had grown old. His life was drained away. He took to mastic. Not the kind you drink, but the kind you chew. And so the grinder of ointments chewed and chewed all day, and when evening came he listened to teachers and doctors debating about free will and the immortality of the soul, and whether the stars are inhabited. And he himself wagged his bald head and said to himself again and again, Even if I do get married now, I can't have a son now, I can't have a son now, I can't have a son now. . . . He held the pestle upright on the table, chewed his mastic and ground his medicaments in the mortar till the late hours, deep in care.

14

Today the Hags were early at their posts. It was cool. Their hair was untidy, their hands and spindly legs had gone to sleep, but they kept manfully on their feet and waited. They stuck their ruby eyes to the peepholes and kept them firmly aimed at Nuri Bey's green, arched doorway.

"Keep your eyes fixed on that," said Aglaja, the middle one. "Something is cooking there. Think what the Moorish woman told us yesterday!"

"The Bey came in from his village this evening in a rage," said Thalia. "I saw him. He banged into the door and sent it flying open, and immediately afterward I heard shouts and cries. I'm sure he beat the servants again."

"Who else is there for him to beat? The horse? Eminé? No fleas on him." Phrosyne laughed.

But just as the Three Graces were whispering, the street seemed to them suddenly to grow dark. They drew back and looked at one another.

"Captain Michales!" they muttered, and pressed their eyes again to the peepholes.

Breathing hard, but light of foot, the sturdy man with the raven-black, curly beard went slowly by, and the tassels of his headband were over his eyebrows. He was keeping close to the wall, and his hand rested on his broad belt, grasping firmly a knife with a black hilt.

He brushed against the door through which he was being observed, wheeled around for a moment as though he felt the six eyes upon him, and the whites of his eyes flashed in the twilight. The three sisters trembled and held their breath, but the heavy man went slowly on and stopped opposite the big doorway. He took a quick glance around: solitude; not a soul about. Then in one spring he crossed the narrow alley, pushed Nuri Bey's door open and went in.

The triplets yelled. "Kyrie eleison," said Aglaja, and crossed herself. "Did you see the way he went in? Like a robber."

"What's Captain Wildboar after with the Bey? The bean has a maggot in it. I bet he wants to sell him the horse."

"Or Eminé." And the Three Graces—Aglaja, Thalia and Phrosyne—began giggling again.

Captain Michales, who had stepped over the threshold with his right foot, glanced in all directions. He stared at the Negro who awaited him behind the door. An old, worn-out slave whom Nuri Bey had inherited from his father, this Negro lolled like a mangy dog behind the street door every day till midnight. Captain Michales touched him on the shoulder with his fingertip, and the old man sank back and let him pass. He walked slowly forward between huge pots filled with roses. Somewhere there must be a lemon tree in blossom, for the air had a scent of lemon blossoms. The freshly watered earth smelled of dung. In the depth of the garden, where the old residence glimmered in the twilight, a partridge in a cage was still cackling. Light came through the high wooden lattice. Feminine laughter could be heard.

Captain Michales breathed in the Turkish air against his will, with head bent. What am I after here? he thought. Turks' stink?

He stood still and gazed about. There was still time: no one had seen him, except the Negro; he could still leave. Charitos had by now saddled the mare. He would ride, race up and down the big square to quiet himself down. But he was ashamed. "They'll say I'm afraid," he muttered. "Forward, Captain Michales!"

With swift strides he went on. There was the central door. It stood open. A large, burning lamp with green and red glass hung in the door space. Under it stood Nuri Bey, all red and green. He had heard the outer door, recognized the step. He came forward to welcome his guest.

He was a stately, rather stout man with expansive gestures. From his round face a pair of dark almond eyes peered out, and the light from the lamp brought out a steely glitter in them. His thick mustache was smeared with black pomade. The Bey had a serene Oriental handsomeness: he was like the moon-faced lion which Turkish women of the past used to embroider on costly Persian stuffs. He wore long blue woolen stockings, but his belt was blood-red and the turban that enclosed his hair was snow-white. His shoulders were perfumed with musk, and he smelled like a wild beast in heat in the spring.

He took a step forward and stretched out his short-fingered hand. "Don't be angry with me, Captain Michales," he said, "for bringing you to my house. It was necessary. You'll see for yourself."

Captain Michales growled and, without a word, followed the

16

Bey to the men's quarters. For a short moment he remained on the threshold, as though in angry thought. He cast a stolen glance backward. Nobody. The big lamp in front of the divan was lighted. There was a fire of coals burning in a large bronze brazier. In the hot atmosphere it gave out a smell of burned lemon peel. On a round table in one corner there stood a long-necked porcelain jug full of raki, two glasses and some sweetmeats.

They sat down close to each other on a small divan. Captain Michales was near the closed window which gave onto the garden. Nuri Bey took from his belt his dark iron tobacco box with a mother-of-pearl crescent in the middle. He opened it and held it out to his friend.

Captain Michales rolled a cigarette, and Nuri Bey did the same. They smoked. For some time they remained without speaking. The Bey cleared his throat. He did not know how to put the matter to prevent his guest from taking it amiss and losing his temper. He knew that he was not the man to let a fly run up and down his saber. And what he had to say to him this evening was difficult.

"Shall we have a raki, Captain Michales? It's a nice mature one. It's made from lemons. I ordered it for you."

"What have you to say to me, Nuri Bey?" asked Captain Michales, and held his hand over both glasses. He did not want to drink.

The Bey coughed and crushed his cigarette into the cinders in the brazier. As he bent his face over the burning coals it glowed copper-red.

"If I have to speak out," he said, "don't take it in bad part, Captain Michales."

He waited a little for the dark Greek to say something and rouse his temper. But he kept silent. The Bey stood up, went to the door, opened his shirt at the neck, returned and sat down again. Suddenly the slippers he was wearing were too tight. He kicked them off and placed his naked soles on the ground. This refreshed him.

He turned to his dumb companion. His mind was now made up. He raised his hand to twirl his mustache, but let it fall again. Careful! The irascible captain might take that too in bad part.

"Your brother Manusakas," he said, and sighed. "Your brother Manusakas, Captain Michales, scoffs at Turkey. The day before yesterday, March twenty-fifth, he was drunk again, hoisted an ass onto his back and went into the mosque to pray. I came in from the village and found all my people beside themselves. Your people were armed. There was serious trouble brewing. I'm telling you this, Captain Michales, so that you may not make a fuss later. It was my duty to tell you and yours to listen. Do as God directs you."

"Pour out the drinks," said Captain Michales.

The Bey filled the glasses; the world smelled of lemons.

"To your good health, Nuri Bey."

"And to yours," Nuri Bey answered quietly, looking him in the eyes.

They clinked glasses.

Captain Michales stood up and brushed back the tassels of his headband. "Is that what you wanted to say to me, Nuri Bey?" he asked. "Is that why you sent for me?"

"If you are Godfearing," said the Bey, and caught him lightly by the belt, "don't go. This is a spark, but it can cause a fire in which our village would burn up. Order your brother not to put our government to shame. We're of the same village, the same soil. Sit down and let's set this right."

"My brother is older than I—sixteen years older," said Captain Michales. "He has children and grandchildren and years of discretion. He's strong enough for seven. What he wants to do he does. No words of mine would do any good."

"You're the captain of the village. People listen to your words."

"Words are dear, Nuri Bey. They don't easily get past my teeth."

The Bey bit his lips, but his heart hardened. He examined Captain Michales, who had already got up and was looking at the door, ready to go out. This giaour comes of a savage, upstanding stock, the Bey thought, and my race has some old scores against him. Was it not Kostaros—may pitch defile his corpse!—his brother, who slew my father against a rock? I was still a mere child, and I possessed myself in patience till I should be ripe to take blood for blood. But I had no luck. The accursed man got himself killed at Arkadi—blown sky-high. And his son was still a sapling; it would have been shameful to kill him. I waited for him to grow up. But as he was just growing a mustache, he escaped me. He went back, so they say, to the Franks to study. . . . When will he come back? My father's blood cries out!

He stood up and placed himself in front of the door. Within him rage rose and sank. He did not know where to begin. Captain Michales' tangled beard of prickles flashed in the soft glow from the lamp. He had taken an oath, it was said, not to cut it off till Crete should be free. Nuri Bey's eyes sparkled with scorn. Let him wait for that, the giaour, if it doesn't bore him. Let his beard flow down to his knees, to the ground. Let it lay hold of the earth and strike roots there, but Crete, no, it won't see freedom! For twenty-five years we got ourselves killed in front of the Venetian walls of Megalokastro before it fell into our claws. We're not letting it go, it's not letting us go. It's become part of our flesh.

Nuri Bey groaned. He thought of his father and of the Mussulmans who had met their death in the trenches around Megalokastro. Between him and Captain Michales a stream of blood rolled.

"Let the bellows rest, Nuri Bey!" Captain Michales said, raising a hand to push him out of the way and get to the door. "It's no good puffing and blowing. What you want can't be done."

Nuri Bey was a strong man. He restrained his rage. "Don't go, Captain Michales," he said, softening his voice. "Don't go like this, with wild thoughts, as though we had had a quarrel. If it seems hard to you, I take back what I said. I have said nothing, you have heard nothing. Are we not friends? I sent for you that we might have a drink and taste a dainty morsel. It's a partridge from our village—I've just brought it in from the village. I thought we would eat it together and remember old times, Captain Michales. When we were young. When we used to play together, in the good old days, in our village."

"I'm not eating. It's a fast day for us," Captain Michales answered.

Full of commiseration, Nuri Bey took him by both hands. "If I'd known," he said, "by Mohammed, I'd have got you some black caviar."

He filled the glasses. "Your health, Captain Michales," he said, raising his glass. "I'm glad you've consented to come to my house and drink a raki with me. There, may my blood be spilled like this if I wish you any harm."

So saying, he sprinkled a couple of drops of lemon raki on the floor.

Captain Michales yielded and sat down again on the divan near the window. "I too wish you no harm, Nuri Bey, but it's a matter of honor to weigh our words."

With those words, he emptied his glass.

They fell silent again. The Bey felt hot; he got up and opened the window.

A small fountain outside in the garden made a cool and friendly plashing. The scent of the roses and lemon trees came in. Laughter was again to be heard from the women's quarters.

The two men remained in silence. Nuri Bey exerted himself to find a way of starting the conversation afresh. And Captain Michales listened to the water and the laughter, breathed in the fragrance of the garden, and again his heart began beating hard. Is that Crete—laughter and scent, and you drinking raki with the Turks? So he brooded. Suddenly he shut the window.

"Don't be angry, Captain Michales. I opened it without asking you," said the worried Bey, and filled the glasses again.

Captain Michales came back and stared at the Turk. They were born in the same village, the one a bey, to be all rich acres, and the other a raia—an underdog. His father, Captain Sefakas, owned the stone house. At that time he had not had permission to ride a horse. He sat on his little ass, and whenever he saw the enemy of Christians, Hani Ali, father of this same Nuri, old Sefakas had to jump down to let the great man pass. But one afternoon Captain Sefakas was in a bad mood and did not dismount. So Hani Ali raised his whip, and the defiant head streamed with blood. The old man said nothing; he held his heart in and waited. A Christian is no Albanian, he thought; he's a right-thinking Christian. The day will come when he'll pay me back my due. Hardly a year had gone by when the 1866 rising broke out. His eldest son, Kostaros, ran into the bloody Hani Ali one night outside Megalokastro and slaughtered him like a lamb, on a rock in the Cave of Pendevis.

But now just look at his son: he's come and taken up his throne in Megalokastro, in this huge residence, with the goods and the fountains and the wooden lattices. And he eats and drinks and kisses, and rides on his horse every fine afternoon through the Greek quarter as far as the Three Vaults, striking the sparks from the roadway.

Captain Michales took out his tobacco box, rolled a cigarette and lighted it. His nostrils filled with smoke. Did he hate this Turkish fellow here beside him, or was he fond of him? Was he disgusted by him? He had often asked himself the question and could come to no conclusion. And when by chance the two of them met in the narrow alleys of Megalokastro or on horseback outside, Captain Michales would look at the clear, lovable face of Nuri Bey and his heart would rejoice. He did not know what to think. Should he kill him or no? Ought he to embrace him as an old friend well met?

As small children they had played together on their village threshing floor, had run races for bets, had wrestled, thrown each other, laughed, fought, made up. And one afternoon, when they were grown men, they had met, both of them on horseback, on this side of Nuri Bey's estate, an hour from Megalokastro, quite close to the Cave of Pendevis. For a while they had ridden side by side in silence. Both were sullen, for in those days Turks and Christians had been killed, Crete was again catching fire, the raias were again raising their heads.

They rode without a word. The famous Venetian walls came in sight, blood red from the glow of the setting sun.

This dog, Captain Michales had thought. I can't bear the sight of him any longer, the way he rides for fun through the Greek quarter and bewitches the women.

I can't bear the giaour any longer, Nuri Bey had thought. Every time he's drunk he comes out from his house on horseback and insults the Turks. Last year he caught me by the hips, lifted me up like a sack and tossed me onto the roof of his shop. People came thronging, placed a ladder for me to get down, and laughed at me.

Nuri Bey's cheeks had burned. Angrily he had turned to Captain Michales and said, "Hey, Captain Michales, either I must finish you off, or you me. There's no room for both of us in Megalokastro."

"Choose the weapons, friend Nuri Bey! Shall I dismount so that we can start?"

Nuri Bey had not answered. His glance had rested on the Greek at his side, and his eyes had filled with that heroic figure. What a man! he had thought. What pride and what courage! He never says a superfluous word, he never boasts. He doesn't quarrel with those beneath him. He knows no fraud. He has no respect even for death. Happy the man who has such an enemy!

At length he had opened his mouth: "Not so fast, Captain Michales. It would be a pity . . . I take back what I said. Yes, by my faith, neither my Mohammed nor your Christ wants that. You're a good palikar*, I think, and so am I. We ought to mingle our blood, but in a different way."

"In a different way?"

"Become blood brothers."

Captain Michales had spurred his mare and ridden on. His heart had swollen, risen to his throat. For a while all he could hear was the blood throbbing in his jugular vein. At length it had subsided and his brain cleared. A strange agitation had taken possession of him. Perhaps it was pleasure at the thought of mingling blood with this young Bey, brought up amid the scent of musk, of no longer being obliged to kill him, of banishing the temptation which, every time he saw him, pushed the knife into his fist.

The man was splendid, even if he was a Turk. The pride of Megalokastro, and nothing false about him. He was kindly, generous, noble, a man through and through. Curse him!

He had tugged at the reins. The mare had pulled up short. Nuri Bey had spurred his horse and drawn level with him.

"All right," Captain Michales had said without looking at him. They had ridden back without a word to the Bey's estate. As they came into the courtyard a laborer had run up, taken the horses and led them to the stable. The Bey clapped his hands, and an old daily servant appeared and bowed.

"Kill a cock, the big one with all the feathers," the Bey had ordered. "Get out some of the old wine. Yes, and get two beds ready—spread the silk sheets on them. We're eating and sleeping here tonight. Go and shut the gates."

*Young warrior (Tr.)

They had been left alone. They had knelt down, close together and facing each other under the hollow olive tree which, still heavy with blossom, stood in full glory in the middle of the courtyard. The sun had gone down; the evening star shone large and bright between the olive leaves.

Nuri Bey had risen, gone out and fetched from the well the bronze cup which hung there for travelers to drink from and bless the name of the builder of the well—Hani Ali. Then he had sat down cross-legged on the ground.

"In the names of Mohammed and of Christ," he had said, and pulled the knife out of his belt. Captain Michales had rolled the right sleeve of his jacket up high. The muscular arm had shown sunburned and firm. Nuri Bey had bent forward and with the knife's tip slit a powerful vein which stood out from the flesh. Dark, hot blood had gushed out, and Nuri Bey had pushed the cup underneath. He let a finger's breadth flow in. Then he had undone his white headband and tied it tight around the cut arm.

"Your turn, Captain Michales," he had said.

"In the names of Christ and Mohammed," Captain Michales had said, and pulled out his knife. He slit the Bey's stout white arm, and its rich blood flowed into the cup. Then Captain Michales had taken off his black headband and tied it tight around the Bey's arm.

They had placed the cup between them and begun slowly mixing the blood with their knives—without a word.

Evening had been well advanced. Smoke rose from the manor chimney: the laborers were at their meal in their quarters. The two men had wiped their knives in their hair and hidden them once more in their belts.

Nuri had seized the cup and raised it high. His voice had rung deep and solemn, suitable for an oath: "I drink to your health, Captain Michales, my blood brother! I swear—yes, by Mohammed—that I will never harm you, not with word and not with deed, whether in war or in good times. Honor for honor, manhood for manhood, loyalty for loyalty! I have more than enough Greeks, you have more than enough Turks. Take your vengeance among them!"

So he had spoken, and pressed the cup to his lips. He had begun drinking the mingled blood slowly, drop by drop. He drank

23

half of it. He had wiped his lips and offered the cup to Captain Michales.

And he had taken it in both palms: "I drink to your health, Nuri Bey, my blood brother! I swear—yes, by Christ—that I will never harm you, not with word, not with deed, whether in war or in good times. Honor for honor, manhood for manhood, loyalty for loyalty! I have more than enough Turks, you have more than enough Greeks. Take your vengeance among them!"

And he had drunk the blood to the bottom without a pause. . . .

Now Captain Michales opened the window and threw his cigarette out. It fell like a small red star into a pot of roses and was extinguished in the freshly sprinkled manure. He stood up. His face darkened. The Bey shrank back. He too stood up.

"I've not forgotten. That's why one of us is still alive."

Like a flash of lightning, that evening on the estate under the olive tree darted through his mind. The glad drinking bout with the old wine. The deep sleep in the silk sheets . . .

Captain Michales took the bottle, filled his glass and drank. He filled it again and drank again. He sat down.

"Haven't you a dwarf in your house?" he asked. "A karagios?* Call him and let him dance for us or play the drum or sing. If not, I shall explode."

Nuri was glad. The rage was taking a good course; it would dip into raki and be smothered there. It must be conjured away!

His heart longed to do something big, something unheard of, for his blood brother, something that would surpass friendship and love, so that this gloomy, pitiless man might be a little tamed, a little cheered. He racked his brain, ransacked his house from top to bottom to find something for his blood brother. Old gold pieces out of the chest, silvered weapons off the walls, stuffs of fine wool and silk, casks from the cellar—what should he give him? And suddenly his mind rose up to the wooden lattices; he found his costliest treasure, and laughed.

Nuri turned to his guest. "This evening I am going to do something to gladden you," he said, "something no Turk has ever done for anyone except his brother."

*A jester (Tr.)

24

Captain Michales looked at him but said nothing. He filled his raki glass again.

Nuri went to the low door leading to the women's quarters. "Maria!" he called.

An old Moorish woman came hurrying down the stairs. She was broken, toothless, arid as bean straw and had a little golden cross hung around her neck.

"Tell your mistress she should get her mandolin and come here."

Amazed, terrified, the Moorish woman raised her blinking eyes and stared at him.

"Go!" he shouted, and pushed her out.

Captain Michales took away the glass he had already set to his lips and turned to Nuri. "What's this mean?" he snapped.

"To gladden you, blood brother. I trust you."

"There's nothing gladdening here. Only shame for you as a man, shame for your wife too, having to show herself before a stranger. Shame also for me, raising my eyes to look on her."

Nuri stammered, "I trust you." He was already sorry, but was ashamed to go back on his decision.

He placed a cushion of down upon a small sofa in the corner and another against the wall for the hanum to have something soft to lean against. Captain Michales rose and turned the lamp lower, so that it cast a gentle half-light over the room. He took from his belt a small rosary of black ebony and began to play with it nervously, staring at the floor.

Feminine voices rang out upstairs, with sounds of rapid footsteps, doors opening and shutting, a tap running, water being poured, then silence for a while.

Captain Michales looked up. The bitch won't come, he thought. She's wild, a Circassian. She's refusing. So much the better. Far better. What evil spirit is keeping me here? I'm going!

At the moment when he decided to get up, the staircase creaked. One stair after another gave out its sound. A gay tinkling of little necklaces and pendants was audible. Nuri Bey ran forward, opened the low door and in greeting put his hand to his chest, lips and forehead.

25

"Welcome, Hanum Eminé," he said tenderly. "Welcome, welcome."

In the doorway, in the half-light, there appeared a young woman whose face was moon-round like Nuri's. It suggested the plumpness and whiteness of her body. Huge, slanting eyes, painted cheeks, lips, eyebrows and lashes. Her nails and hands were stained red with cinnamon. She was holding in her arms, as if it were a child, a small, glittering mandolin.

She advanced an elegant little foot in its tiny red slipper, craned her neck, saw the shadow of the man near the window, gave a display of terror and a sharp cry.

"You needn't be ashamed, mistress of my heart," said Nuri, catching her under the arm. "It's my blood brother. How often have I spoken well of him to you! Captain Michales. The hearts of both of us are heavy this evening. Come, do us the pleasure of playing the mandolin for us and singing a song of your country to cheer us. That's why we asked you, mistress of my heart, to come downstairs."

Captain Michales listened, his eyes lowered. He clenched the rosary in his fist as though he might break it. He had heard much of the beauty of this Circassian girl, of her wildness and her singing which sometimes, during the feast of Bairam, pierced through the thick wooden lattices and disturbed the neighborhood. Then Turkish and Christian gallants would creep in the darkness to the street corners to listen to her. All sighed like young calves, and Nuri would keep her well away from the lattices. He would clasp with his hands Eminé's bosom and feel proud, as though he were clasping the whole world.

Captain Michales caught the heavy smell of musk, which spread abroad as the hanum stepped forward to the corner where the Bey had prepared her place. She came past him; her eyes flashed and she looked at him. At that same second Captain Michales also raised his eyes. The two glances met—and broke away at once, both of them wild.

The hanum sat down on the cushions and crossed her feet. "What darkness!" She giggled. She wanted to be seen.

Nuri Bey screwed the lamp wick higher. Light flooded the room, and the Circassian's cheeks, hands and delicately arched, red-colored soles shone.

26

Captain Michales looked at her stealthily. But immediately he lowered his eyes, and two beads of his rosary cracked in his fist.

"Good evening, Captain Michales," said the Turkish girl, and her nostrils trembled.

The voice came from the man's throat hoarsely: "Good evening, Hanum Eminé. Excuse me."

The hanum laughed. Far away in her own country the women worked with unveiled faces beside the men and rode astride their horses. There a man enjoyed a woman and a woman a man till they had had enough. But as a small child she had been taken away, and her father had sold her to an old pasha in Constantinople. Later this Cretan Bey had come and stolen her, and Eminé had never managed to live with men and have enough of the atmosphere of men. And so her nostrils shuddered like those of a hungry animal every time she met a man.

All day long she crouched behind the wooden lattice and watched young lads go by, Turks and Christians, and her bosom hurt her. And when she went out walking, thickly swathed in her silken veils and with her nurse, the old Moorish woman, gliding behind her, she liked to go past the coffeehouses, which were full of men, or down to the harbor with its robust porters and boatmen, or out through the fortress gates, where shaggy, unwashed, sweating peasants came in. Then the Circassian would draw deep breaths; she could not have enough of the stench of men.

"By God's love," she had said one day, turning to her old nurse. "By God's love, Maria, if they didn't stink, I wouldn't go running all over the place to see them."

"See whom, my child?"

"Men. How did you manage when you were young?"

"I believed in Christ, my child," said the old Moorish woman, and sighed.

She looked at Captain Michales in silence. After all, how often and with what pride had the Bey spoken of this man who now sat before her? What had she not heard of his heroic deeds, his drunkenness and wildness? Also that he would never say or listen to a word about women! And there he was now before her; her husband himself had brought him.

"Eminé, mistress of my heart," said Nuri Bey, "sing us a

Circassian song for our pleasure, to make us forget the cares of the world. We are two men here. Have pity on us."

The hanum giggled. She laid the mandolin on her lap, struck a couple of loud chords and threw back her head.

"What are you going to sing us, wife?" asked the Bey happily.

"You'll see," she answered.

The notes of the mandolin became faster. She swayed in the half-light like some wild beast, and drew a deep breath. And suddenly there shot from her pulsing throat a fountain out of the bowels of the earth—the woman's voice. The house shook and Captain Michales' temples were pierced. What an uproar there was! What ecstasy in his fists, his throat, his loins! The mountains laughed and the plains turned scarlet with Turkish soldiers. Over them stormed Captain Michales on Nuri's charger, behind him thousands of Cretans in black headbands, before him no one. The villages shouted, the minarets snapped like felled cypresses, the blood rose as high as his horse's belly. . . .

Captain Michales clutched his temples. The Circassian's throat fell silent. Suddenly the world stood firm again. Crete was again there, and Megalokastro, and the Bey's konak. The Bey too gazed at Eminé and sighed and drank. The soul had forgotten its flight and gone back to prison.

For a while no one spoke. At last Eminé stirred, stroking the mandolin on her knees. "That was an old Circassian song," she said. "The men sing it when they ride out to war."

Nuri got up. His knees trembled slightly. He walked over to his wife and raised his glass. "Your health, Eminé," he said. "Three things I was told by our muezzin, three things Mohammed—God's mercy be upon him!—loved: sweet odors, women and song. You, my Eminé, bring us all three. May you live a thousand years—a thousand, two thousand!"

He emptied his glass at one gulp, smacked his lips and turned to Captain Michales. "Drink, blood brother! You too drink to her health," he said, and filled his glass for him.

But Captain Michales stuck two fingers into the overfilled glass and pressed them apart, hard. The glass broke in two, and the raki spilled over the table.

"Enough," he growled heavily, and his eyes grew troubled.

Eminé gave a cry. She leaped up from the sofa and stared at

28

Captain Michales with tears in her eyes. Never had she seen such strength in a man's hand. She turned to her husband challengingly.

"Can you do that, too, Nuri Bey?" she asked breathlessly. "Can you do that? Can you do that?"

Nuri turned pale. He gathered all his strength into his right hand, stretched it out and was about to insert two fingers into the other glass to split it. But he broke out in a cold sweat and drew back. He felt put to shame in front of his wife, and cast a dark look at Captain Michales. Once again he's made a fool of me, he thought. I won't stand it any longer.

He seized Eminé by the arm and shook her like a madman. "Go up to your room!" he shouted.

"Can you do that too?" she repeated, and her cheeks were burning. "Can you do it too? Can you do it too?"

"Go up to your room!" the Bey ordered for the second time. He seized the mandolin and smashed it into a thousand pieces against the wall.

The Circassian gave a dry, contemptuous laugh. "Yes, that you can do—smash a mandolin. Yes, *that* you can do, Nuri!"

She grazed past Captain Michales, her dress brushing the back of his hand. Once more the air was stifling with musk. Captain Michales felt his hand burning.

Smiling, mockingly, she described a circle around Nuri—once, twice—gave him a playful push and laughed. And suddenly she ran to the stairs and vanished.

The two men were left standing opposite each other in the middle of the room. The Bey rolled his mustache. His chest rose and fell violently. Captain Michales bit his dry lips sulkily and watched him. Both laid their hands on the hilts of their knives, which stuck out from their belts.

At last Nuri half opened venomous lips. "Go, Captain Michales," he said.

"Nuri Bey," he answered, "I'm going when it suits me. Take the unbroken glass and give me a drink."

The Bey clutched the hilt of his knife and glanced quickly at the lamp. He had the idea of putting it out and leaving them in the dark, to wrestle until one of them was dead. Yet his heart was undecided.

"Take the unbroken glass and give me a drink," Captain Michales repeated quietly. "Otherwise I'm not going."

Nuri turned toward the table and advanced a foot. It was heavy as lead. Bathed in sweat, he reached the table. He filled the glass too full. His hand was shaking; the raki spurted over the remains of the partridge.

"Drink," he said, and pointed to the glass.

"Hand it to me," said Captain Michales.

The Bey groaned. He seized the glass and pressed it into Captain Michales' fist.

And Captain Michales raised it, gravely and somberly, saying, "To your health, Nuri Bey. I'm going to do what you asked and tell my brother not to scoff at Turkey."

With those words he moistened his lips. Then he tightened the black headband around his head and strode across the threshold.

The lamp threw a shaft of green and red light over the now quite dark garden. Captain Michales went quietly and slowly out to the street door without looking about him.

Darkness reigned. Megalokastro had now had its evening meal. It yawned, shivered, shuttered first one window and then another, crossed itself and went to bed. A few belated people still moved in the streets, a few pairs of lovers embraced under the shuttered windows. Here and there subdued talk could be heard from lighted cellars: night workers.

The Hags became frozen in their effort to keep up the watch behind their door. Captain Michales was taking his time about returning. The darkness, too, had become impenetrable, and their brother, monosyllabic and morose as usual, came home. So they laid the table and exchanged a few words: what the meals would be tomorrow, how there was no more coal, no oil for the salad, no oil for the lamp. How Aristoteles must pull himself together. They talked, served the meal, cleared it away, prepared their nightly camomile tea for digestion, donned their night dresses which reached to the ground, and crossed themselves; but their thoughts were on the green door.

Captain Michales went home by the longest way round. He felt he could not contain himself within four walls this evening.

His heart was swelling, overflowing. There was not enough room for it in his body or in his house. Suddenly even Megalokastro was too small for him. He strode on. Houses, alleys, human beings stifled him. He went with long strides and with his teeth clenched—like a hunted wild beast. He came to the main street. It was empty. Spaced-out petroleum lamps threw pale-red glimmering shafts on the pavement. He passed through the Bazaar. A Turkish cookhouse was still open, a coffeehouse, two or three taverns. Someone called him. It seemed to be the voice of Captain Polyxigis. He quickened his stride. He came past the pasha's door, past the Venetian marble fountain with the lions. He raised his eyes and saw the tall plane tree—accursed tree! He moved nearer. Nobody was coming. He crossed himself.

"God bless your remains," he muttered. "Till we meet again in joy, my fathers!"

From this magnificent plane tree, for generations and generations, the pashas had hanged the Christians who had dared to raise their heads; and winter and summer on its strongest bough there hung the rope with the noose ready.

"As I'm a Christian, one night I'll rise up, take an ax and cut you down. Curse you!" he muttered, and gazed furiously at the old plane tree as though it were a Turk.

He resumed his way and plunged into a long, dark alley. He came out by the Three Vaults. Not a soul! He unbuttoned his shirt—it was stifling him. He breathed deeply and looked around him. There, to the north, the sea gleamed and roared. About him in the air the dark-blue mountains were visible—Iuchtas, Selena, Psiloritis. Above, in the sky, the stars flared. Like a wild horse he went in circles, ran back and forth. He reached the moat which girdled Megalokastro. Up above, on an isolated hill, some mud huts lay apart—Meskinia, the lepers' village. By the sea there was another, lower hill, called "Seven Axes." From it, two hundred years ago, the Turks had stormed out and occupied Megalokastro. And seven of their axes were still embedded in the ground. Ahead, out to sea, far off and vaulted like a tortoise, appeared the uninhabited island of Dia.

Behind him he heard women's voices and a soft rustling of silk. There emerged an aged Turk with a stoop, holding a huge,

31

flaring lantern. Tittering and chattering, two Turkish ladies with black veils and open parasols followed him. The night reeked of musk.

Captain Michales growled, "All the devils are on my track." He turned his eyes away toward the sea, so as not to see the hanums. "All the devils—but they shan't succeed!"

Now he longed to get home. But he wished to see no one. They would hear his stride a long way distant. He would cough. They would understand and hide. That would be all right. Once he had kicked open his door, he would be quite alone. No wife, no children, no dogs—quite alone!

And then he would make his decision.

Bent under the lamp, his wife, Katerina, and his daughter, Renio, sat and waited. Behind them, at the window end of the long narrow divan which went the whole length of the wall, was the place where Captain Michales and nobody else sat. And when he was absent, a weighty shade sat there, and neither the wife nor the daughter dared go near it. They felt as if they touched his body, and shrank back with a shudder.

The mother was knitting a stocking. The lamplight fell obliquely on thick, straight brown hair, proud eyebrows and firm cheeks; it revealed a bitter mouth and a broad, obstinate chin. The woman had a strange charm—charm and strength and independence. As a girl she had been a defiant captain's daughter. Since no son hàd been granted to her father, Captain Thrasybulos Ruvas, Katerina had enjoyed a son's masculine freedom and favor. But with her marriage she fell into the claws of a lion. In the first years she showed defiance and put up a resistance. But in time she bowed her head. He was Captain Michales. Who could fight him? Strength and independence slackened. She grew softer.

She knitted—knitted and thought. Her whole life was flowing past her like water. Sometimes she looked up. High up around the four walls were ranged, in wide, dark frames, all the heroes of 1821—wild beasts, iron-beards. In the middle, in front of one of the warriors, burned a small silver lamp.

Katerina silently shook her head. Her whole life, in her father's house and in her husband's house, had been lived under arms. When she was still unmarried, during the 1866 rising, she too had put on a cartridge belt, taken a musket and fought to keep the Turks from trampling her village. Even as a child she had cut up old books which the monks had brought from the monasteries and, along with other girls, had made cartridge cases out of them. Katerina knew the smell of powder well, and loved it. Captain Michales was good, a real man, and she loved him. And yet a life like hers was hard on a woman, and somewhere inside her she was unhappy.

She left off her knitting and raised her eyes again. Above the divan hung a huge old lithograph: Samson, bound and being insulted by the Philistines. The unbowed young hero was in the middle, trussed hand and foot with nets, thongs and chains, and behind him was a rabble of youths, tugging at him, hitting him and mocking him. And up above in the tower Delilah was leaning out of a little latticed window—a malevolent, full-bosomed, scornfully grinning woman.

Katerina's glance darted from picture to picture, as though she saw them all for the first time. She sighed. Then without a word she bent over the stocking again.

Her daughter, a plump, blooming thing of fifteen, with her father's thick, bushy eyebrows and her mother's broad, obstinate chin, looked up from her knitting. She stroked the savage, lanky cat which lay in a ball at her feet.

"Why are you sighing, Mother?" she asked. "What are you thinking about?"

"What should I think about?" her mother answered. "My life. And you, you poor thing, who've fallen into the claws of a wild beast. I'm thinking, too, of the baby. I've lulled him to sleep again, so he shan't cry and rouse the evil spirits again in your father. Thrasaki is the only person he's well disposed to—because he's like him."

She looked at the coverlet and listened. "He's gone off to sleep," she said. "Bless his heart!" And after a moment: "His father all over—the image of him! Have you seen the way he gets angry? The way he puckers his eyebrows? The way he hits his friends? The wild way he has of looking at women?"

Renio said nothing. She was afraid of her father, but she loved him and was proud of him. What he did seemed right to her, and if she had been a man she would have done the same. She too

33

would have wanted to see only her son; the girls could just creep away as soon as they heard the door open and him coming. From the day when she had completed her twelfth year and her bosom was becoming full, her father had forbidden her to come into his sight. For three years he had not seen her. She always stayed in the kitchen or concealed upstairs in her little room, when he was in the house. The girl could scent his footsteps far off, and would hide at once. The cat too would scent him, and she too made off, even sooner, with her tail between her legs. It had to be so. Her father was right. Renio could not unravel the "why." But she was sure her father was right.

Her mother felt the same, but she was not reconciled to it. Her husband was the same as her father and would do the same. How many years had old Captain Ruvas, her father, let pass without seeing her. She was already twenty, and still unmarried, when one night the Turkish soldiers fell upon the old captain in his home. He killed as many as he could, but there were too many. They took him prisoner, brought him out to the yard, and were given the order to hand him over to the pasha in Megalokastro. And so Katerina came out with her mother and saw him. His clothes were all torn, and there was blood all over him. He raised his hand. "Farewell," he called to them, "and don't be sad, you women. Bake the funeral cakes for me in the proper way. I'm dying for freedom. Don't cry! Look after yourself, Katerina! And bear a man child. Then you'll have a Thrasos, one like me!"

He was taken to Megalokastro and placed in front of the pasha's door, under the tall plane tree. Then a Turkish barber came, took his knife and beheaded him. Mustapha Pasha had a tobacco box made for himself out of the skull.

All this went through Katerina's head now, and she knitted her stocking and sighed. She got on well with Captain Michales; she had nothing to complain of. He was a palikar, honorable and honored, a serious man. He did not run after other women or play cards; he was not niggardly. He got drunk only twice a year, to calm himself down. He was a man; no harm in that. Others did worse—he merely got drunk. And yet, this year, life was really too hard. The girl she had borne at this time last year—Captain Michales refused to look at her eyes.

"I won't see it, I won't hear it!" he shouted at her each morning as he opened the door to go to his shop. "Where the devil did she get those blue eyes?"

No one of his stock had blue eyes. And this infant had. As though some black sheep had strayed into his house, as though his blood were defiled. Captain Michales could not endure the thought.

The unfortunate mother swallowed her tears and said nothing. What should she say to him? She possessed herself in patience, knelt down in front of the great icon of her house—the Archangel Michael with the golden wings, the flaming sword and a new-born soul which he held curled up in his hand like a trembling infant. . . . She fell on her knees before him and implored him —was he not the protector of her house?—to speak with her husband, to stride in upon his dream in the night and to chide him, that his heart might become a trifle gentler. . . .

The captain stayed in his shop all day. She sent him his meal by the apprentice Charitos. And the mother let the baby shriek and cry and rocked it on her knees. But toward evening she gave it something to make it sleep, so it would not wake till morning.

From the other room they heard little Thrasos, dreaming and crying out in his sleep. The mother laughed. "Bless him, he takes no rest, even asleep!" she said. "He's always dreaming that he's hunting and in at the kill, or in command of soldiers and slaughtering Turks. . . . When he's grown up, he'll do what he now dreams. Like his father, like his grandfather. Ah, the woes of Crete have no end. . . ."

They sat silent. Renio looked out of the window into the night. A north wind was still moaning; one of the shutters was creaking. In a remote house a young woman sang a lullaby to her little son. Renio shut her eyes, listened, and her bosom trembled.

"He's late this evening," she said after a moment, to change the path of her thoughts.

"Nuri sent for him, they say. What does that dog want with him?"

Renio laughed. "Father will lift him up again by his red belt and pitch him onto the roof!"

The mother shook her head. "But then Nuri will lay hold of ten Christians to get his revenge. The woes of Crete have no end, I tell you."

"As long as Father's alive, I'm not afraid."

"I said the same about my father, but one night . . ." She stopped. Gevatter—that was the name of the cat—jumped up on Renio's lap and pricked up its ears. The two women also listened. Renio hastily cleared away the twine, the needles, the scissors. The cat vanished into the kitchen.

"He's coming," said the girl. A dry cough was heard outside the door.

"There he is!" said the mother, and stood up. "I'll go and warm up the supper. He'd prefer to come in and see no one. That's why he coughed."

The street door rattled. Captain Michales opened it, stepped over the threshold and pushed the bolt to. He crossed the yard, went in and looked around—no one. He unwound his headband and pulled off his jacket, which was soaked with sweat. He sat down in his place at the corner of the settee, near the window giving on the garden. He took his handkerchief out of his belt and wiped the sweat from his forehead, neck and chest, then opened the window to get some air.

He heard the two women in the kitchen lighting the fire to warm his supper. For a moment he thought he heard the boy, and his blood at once warmed. He listened. Silence. He pulled out his tobacco box and rolled a cigarette. He took the tinderbox and lighted it. But his mouth was bitter, full of poison. He threw the cigarette out the window.

His wife came in with the supper dish. Without raising his head Captain Michales said, "I'm not hungry. Take the dish away!"

His wife said nothing. She took the dish away and was gone.

A heavy silence weighed on the house. Captain Michales got up, pulled his jacket on again, wound the black headband twice around his head and went to the door. He pondered his decision as he stood there. He cast a quick glance about him. The warriors of 1821 glimmered all around the walls with their weapons, their cartridge belts and pistols. Their mustaches were twirled into needles, their hair fell to their shoulders. . . .

For a while Captain Michales forgot his own thoughts. He gazed at them and greeted each one. He was not very sure of their faces, of where they had fought, which manly deeds they had carried out, and from which region they came: Rumelia, and Morea, the Islands or Crete. One thing only he knew for certain: all these men had fought against the Turks, and that was enough for him. The rest was schoolmaster's stuff.

He went out into the yard. The well, the vines overhead, the flowerpots round about, all constricted him. He approached the small stable adjoining the yard. The white mare gleamed in the half-dark. She pricked up her ears, turned her head, saw her master and whinnied with pleasure. Captain Michales went up to her. With wide-open hands he stroked her neck, belly and rump. She was a warm, cherished creature, always ready whenever he ordered. Proud and obedient. Never did she disturb his mood—she was with him always, like his own flesh, until death.

He stepped back from the mare's warm body and groped for his boots. He pulled them on over his knees, over his thighs, up to his loins, and his chest braced itself for the spring with strength from within.

He vaulted into the saddle.

"Charitos," he called.

His wife came out. "He's asleep," she said.

"Wake him up!"

Once more he rolled a cigarette, and waited without moving. He smoked, and no longer felt any poison in his mouth. He blew thick smoke through his nose and waited tranquilly.

Charitos came out, rubbing sleepy eyes. Shaggy hair, long neck, bare feet—like a wild twelve-year-old goat. Charitos was his nephew, son of his brother, Famurios the shepherd. He had come from his village, sent by his father, he said, to learn his letters. But Captain Michales thought book learning stupid.

"Do you want me to make you into a starving nobleman?" he would say. "Or a schoolmaster? Can't you see the misery of your uncle, the schoolmaster Tityros, whose life is made a burden by the school louts? You'll ruin your eyes, you poor child, wear glasses and get yourself laughed at. Stay in the shop and you'll grow big and your brain will get solid. Then I'll give you an advance, and you can set up a shop of your own and become a man."

He had said the same to Famurios. "Do as you please," the brother had answered. "The bones are mine; the flesh is yours. Lick him into shape, make a man of him."

Captain Michales caught Charitos by the nape and shook him.

"Go to the trough," he told him, "wash yourself and wake up. Then I'll give you your orders."

Charitos drew water from the well, washed himself and combed his unruly hair with his nails. He went back to his uncle.

"I'm awake," he said.

Captain Michales clapped him on the shoulder. "Go to the five houses you know," he commanded, "and knock on the doors till they open. Take a stone, and knock till they open. Understand?"

"I understand."

"Vendusos', Furogatos', Kajabes', Bertodulos' and the teke*, where Efendina lives."

"Horsedung Efendina?"

"And tell them, Greetings from my uncle, Captain Michales, and tomorrow, he says, is Saturday. On Sunday good and early will they please come to his house. Understand?"

"I understand."

"Go."

He called his wife. "Kill three hens and cook them. Clear the cellar, set out the big table, the benches and the glasses."

She wanted to say to him, "It's the time of the fourteen fast days; have you no fear of God?" But he held up his hand. His wife sighed and said nothing.

"We're having another feast, curse my luck!" she said to Renio, who was standing at the sink washing up. "We're to kill three hens, he says, and clear the cellar."

The stairs were heard creaking. Captain Michales was going up to bed.

"What's come over him? The six months aren't up," said Renio, but her heart leaped with pleasure. She liked it when the house was in confusion, when the dainties were passed to and fro, when the men sat in the lower room and drank.

"Her heart has swelled up too soon," muttered the mother. "The evil spirit has awakened in her again."

She crossed herself. "I am a sinner, O God," she said. "I'm saying things I shouldn't, but I can't bear it any longer. He tramples on the great fast times now. He no longer fears God!"

Her thoughts turned rebelliously to the Archangel Michael up

* A Moslem shrine (Tr.)

there in the icon. How often have I confessed repentance before him, she reflected. How many prayers have I addressed to him. How often have I filled his lamp with oil and lighted candles to him. All in vain. Even He is now on his side!

"Ah, if only I were a man!" she muttered. "By my soul's salvation, I'd do the same. I too would have five or six friends, and, when my heart was smoldering, I'd invite them to the cellar, make them drunk, let them sing, play the lyre and dance, and so be lightened. That's what it is to be a man!"

2

HEAVY NIGHT, full of sultry spring air, lay over Megalokastro. Shortly before midnight the crisp breeze from the north had dropped, and now a warm, damp wind took its place, making the trees belly. It came from Arabia, crossed the Lybia Sea, swept the plain of Mesara from Tybaki and Good Harbor to Saint Barbara, left behind it the famous vineyards of Archani, leaped over the fortress walls and, through the chinks of doors and windows, fell upon the women like a man and upon the men like a woman, allowing them no sleep. Malignant April came to Crete like a thief in the night.

Even the Pasha of Megalokastro, a hard-bitten elder, started from his sleep, feeling hot and lascivious, and clapped his hands. Suleiman, his Arabian, appeared. "Open the window, Suleiman, or I shall faint. What's the matter with me? What sort of a wind is this, Suleiman?"

"It comes from Arabia, Pasha Effendi, and it's hot. But it means no harm, have no fear. We Cretans call it cucumber wind, because it ripens the cucumbers."

"Cucumber wind—well I never! Go and call the slave Fatuma —she's to be ready if I need her. And bring me a jug of water from the basin and a fan, to give me some cool air. . . . This Crete may yet be the death of me!"

Even the Metropolitan of Megalokastro, a God-fearing octogenarian with a wavy, snowy beard, was all on fire. He threw off the bedclothes, got up and leaned against the window of the Bishop's Palace, to get some air. Profound stillness! The houses were slumbering in deep darkness. The old lemon tree stood blossoming in the square before the church, and, all around, the world smelled sweet. Above, in the vault of Heaven, numberless lamps were burning before God's throne. With awe the Metropolitan lost himself in the starry sky. For a moment his heavy stately body hung high up in the night air, surrounded by God's deep stillness; then he fell back to earth and found himself leaning on the window sill once more. The Metropolitan crossed himself, the warm spring wind was banished, and now the old man felt his whole body cool and light. He went back to his bed to sink sinless into God's embrace.

Captain Michales tugged at the sheet and sat up angrily in bed. It must be after midnight. He grabbed at the jug which stood near him, pressed it to his lips and took two or three deep gulps, to wake up, to drive away the shameless dream which had been weighing on him all night. But it clung to him like a woman and would not let him go. "Damn sleep!" he growled, "damnation take it. It opens the door to evil spirits, and in they come."

He sprang up, went downstairs barefoot and out into the yard, drew water from the well and plunged his head into the bucket to extinguish the blaze. But the sweet saliva remained in his mouth and the folly upon his eyelids. He went back and sat down again on his bed. He opened the window near it: pitch dark. He listened. Megalokastro was sunk in sleep; its breathing could not be heard. A strange, hot wind, reeking of earth and water, sighed, and the leaves of the trellised vine by the stable rustled.

Captain Michales leaned with his back against the wall and began to smoke. He did not mean to yield to sleep again. It was a Turkish creature, a mad one, and he did not trust it. He smoked and gazed up at the icon of the Archangel Michael, protector of his race: Heaven's fury with his quiver on his back. On the right of the picture, hanging in a row, shone the silver pistols he had inherited from his father; on its left, the crown of honor from his wedding, made of waxen lemon blossom. From the next room he heard his wife Katerina sigh briefly. Above, in the rafters, a mouse was nibbling, and all of a sudden the cat rushed soundlessly and stealthily up the stairs. Then profound stillness.

Captain Michales smoked. Neither the agitation nor the shame had fled from his brain. Breathing heavily, with his gaze fixed on the window, he waited for day to come.

41

At the other end of Megalokastro, near New Gate, Barba* Jannis was going home bathed in sweat, with his sleeves rolled up and a flaring oil lamp in his hand. He was a miserable little old man with a bald head, gray, round, bright little eyes, and a long stork's neck seamed with wrinkles and cavities. He stumbled along the narrow alleys and cursed his fate. People would not even allow him the one thing left to him after the death of his wife: his sleep. From early morning he toiled, bringing drink to the inhabitants of Megalokastro—in winter the sweet barley water, *salepi*, to warm them; in summer sherbet to cool them. Did he ever take a nap? One of the neighbor women, or a relative, would be taken with child: "Quick, my poor Barba Jannis, deliver her!" He had learned midwifery from his regretted father, who had been a blacksmith and had delivered people's mares and she-asses. Barba Jannis had transferred his father's art from the mares and she-asses to women. Yesterday evening he had delivered poor Pelagia, his niece. It had not been easy. Three hours the pangs had lasted, but he had brought the child forth—a lusty, pitch-black boy.

And now, talking to himself as he walked along, he caught the sound of a horse's hoofs behind him—but not a horse like any we know, which eat barley, neigh and make dung. Barba Jannis recognized it by its hoofbeats, which were soft, as though muffled in cotton, and by the holy scent of incense which pervaded the air. . . . Barba Jannis understood. This was not the first time. He pressed close to the wall, crossed himself and waited. The light, onward-sweeping step drew near, the fragrance grew stronger.

"Remember me, O Lord," he muttered, "Saint Menas, my saint, good evening."

He opened his eyes joyfully. In the roadway there appeared, glittering out of the darkness, on a gold-harnessed bay and in a silver coat of mail, with his red lance at rest upon his shoulder, the gray-haired hero and protector of Megalokastro, Saint Menas. This evening, as usual, he was riding on his rounds. Always at midnight, when the town lay lost in sleep, Saint Menas stepped silently out of his icon-shrine and struck out over the walls and through the Greek quarter. Where anyone had left a door open, he

*Uncle (Tr.)

42

closed it. Where a light showed in a window and a Christian lay sick, he paused and prayed God for a cure. Men's eyes had not the strength to recognize him. Only the dogs wagged their tails. Yet there were two men in the town who did see him: Barba Jannis and Horsedung Efendina, the hodza who was weak in the head. As soon as Saint Menas had finished his round in the gray of dawn, he went back into his icon-shrine, and no one would have suspected what secret things had happened in the night if Murzuflos the lamplighter had not noticed, as he cleaned the church in the morning, sweat on Saint Menas' horse.

Barba Jannis watched the saint till he was out of sight in the darkness, and crossed himself. "Tonight I've seen him again. Great is his grace, my affairs will go well," he murmured, and pulled out of his jacket a round grape tart, which he had been given as payment for his trouble over Pelagia. He began to eat it contentedly. Then he reached his hovel and put out the lantern.

Captain Michales smoked and paced up and down. His mind droned like a beetle and flew over all that he had seen and suffered, loved and abhorred in his life—his village, his father, his house, human beings, Turks and Christians. He gathered together the whole of Crete, from Grabusa to Toplu Monastery, from cliff to cliff, from insurrection to insurrection. But nowhere would his thoughts pause; they kept running on and sliding back to a shameless red mouth and would not leave it.

Captain Michales wandered up and down in agitation and cast wild glances at the Archangel Michael, as though he were asking him to abandon his inactive existence in the picture-shrine and restore order. Then he turned around and glared through the window at the sky, now not so utterly dark. "It's getting light now," he called out. "It's getting light, and I'll be able to see where I'm going."

He strode to the yard, plunged his head again into the bucket and calmed down a little. Then he crouched on the threshold and waited.

Like a bull, Captain Michales fought with himself; but Nuri Bey, too, had spent the whole night rushing up and down in the men's quarters, going out into the garden to get some air, coming in again, smoking one cigarette after another, drinking one raki after another and bellowing. He raised his eyes to the wooden lattice. The Circassian had bolted it and would not let him come near her.

"I don't want you!" she shouted at him through the keyhole. "You've disgraced yourself, you're no use to me."

She too had not been able to shut her eyes. Half naked, she went to the window and ardently stretched out her arms toward the Greek quarter. She saw in the dark the eyebrows, beard and strong hands of Captain Michales, and whinnied like a mare.

"The woman's right, she's right," murmured Nuri Bey, and began to weep. "I shall go to the dogs, like Efendina. The giaour will call me too, whenever he gives a feast, to play the karagios for him."

In the morning the Moor found his master in a heap on the threshold, dead drunk. His mustache, chest and jacket were covered with vomit, raki and cigarette ash.

At the moment when Nuri Bey was thinking of him, Efendina was asleep on his back and smiling happily. He had received the news late in the evening. There was to be another feast, eight days long! He would eat pig's flesh and sausage—they would go down like butter. He would get wine as well, and forget his misery for eight days—yes, and to hell with it! To hell, too, with holiness! He shut his eyes, stroked his small, fair beard and fell asleep. And behold, just when Nuri Bey thought of him, Efendina had a dream: The door opened, and a pig came in, well grown, well nourished, with a fez on its head like a Turk, and with a knife slung around its neck like a talisman. As soon as Efendina looked at it the pig stood up on its hind legs and greeted him Turkish fashion. Then it took the knife and stuck it into its own thick neck. The pig rolled to the ground, and Efendina bent over it; it was freshly roasted, wrapped in lemon leaves, and smelled lovely. Efendina gave a shout of joy and woke up with his mouth full of saliva.

While below on earth the poor human beings were catching fire and seeking to put it out in torments and embraces, the vault of Heaven was turning, the stars going their way, and suddenly behind the peaks of Lasithi the Morning Star sprang forth and clanged in the wind. The thickly feathered cock in Captain Michales' yard opened his round eyes, took in what was happening in the sky, beat with his wings, puffed out his chest and began to crow. Up above, in the rich farmer Krasojorgis' yard, the lewd Cyprian ass sniffed the air, smelled the dainty, dew-fresh grass, and the Cretan she-ass raised her tail bolt upright and began to bray.

Megalokastro awoke. From one end of the street to the other, from Idomeneas' well to Tulupanas' bakery, a stretching and a stirring began afresh in Captain Michales' quarter. First of all, the wife of Mastrapas untied her husband, that holy man, from the bedposts, to which she tied him fast every evening out of jealousy, to prevent him from going secretly downstairs and finding the fat maid Anesina, with her cow breasts, in the kitchen below. She bound him fast every evening and only loosened the bands a little if he woke her up to make water. But even then the cord remained around his ankles, and his wife held him fast lest the prisoner should contrive to slip away.

Captain Polyxigis had been back some time from his nocturnal adventure, very tired and reeking of musk. Mr. Demetros yawned by the side of his wife Penelope, who was again in a bad mood. She had thrown the bedclothes aside and was muttering: "Why am I twenty-five? Sometimes my body catches fire, and sometimes the fire goes out and makes me feel like a tortoise." At that moment, at gray of dawn, her body had caught fire. She sat up fiercely, cast a sidelong glance of hate at the yawning Demetros and went out.

The sky became pale, the songbirds awakened under the eaves, and up above, in Krasojorgis' house, the blackbird was singing in its cage.

"Krasojorgis' wife is lucky," muttered Penelope, and sighed. "Krasojorgis is a rich farmer, and he's still got his strength and vigor. And he doesn't disappoint his wife."

She listened. A rattling and grunting came from the house farther up. Fat Krasojorgis was lying on his back and snoring. His mustache reeked of wine and onions; his breath came heavy as from a cellar. By him his young wife Katinitsa was still asleep—Barba Jannis' daughter, a merry, well-fed, drink-loving creature. She was smiling and cooing, for she was dreaming that she was engaged and had gone for a walk in a walled garden, holding her young man by the hand. He put his arm around her shoulders,

45

and it was not Krasojorgis, the fat fellow, but a slim, spruce palikar with a fine waxed mustache, long raven hair and silver pistols
in his belt; his breath smelled of cinnamon. He was the image of
that picture which all visitors to Captain Michales' house admired. Written under it was the name of Athanasios Diakos, a
well-known hero of the fight for freedom. . . . Well, he put his
arm round her shoulders; sleep lay over her like a tendril heavy with
dark clusters, and she walked along in bliss, smiling and cooing
like a dove.

But as the devil would have it, Krasojorgis heard her in his
sleep, gave a start and opened his eyes. "Hey, wife!" he called out.
"What's all this simpering and cooing early in the morning?
Is it a bit of gingerbread you're munching? Give me some of it!"

But she turned her back on him angrily. "Don't disturb me,
leave me alone!" she said, "I'm sleepy!" And she closed her eyes
and tried to find her young dream man again.

From Tulupanas' bakery rose cloud on cloud of the first thick,
pale-blue smoke. The old baker, always gloomy and taciturn, was
awake and all alone in his bakehouse, beginning his work in order
to forget his worries. But how could he forget? He had a dear and
only son, a lad of twenty, fair haired and handsome, whom he
had always clothed and looked after devotedly. Suddenly, three
years ago, the boy had begun to have swellings, his face had become covered with boils, his finger tips had rotted and his nails
fallen off. And now his lips were beginning to fester. Father and
mother were unwilling to take him to Meskinia, to the lepers'
place. How could they part from their son, since they had no
other? They kept him shut up in his room, that no man's eyes
might see him. How then could old Tulupanas sleep happily now,
and why should he open his mouth to speak? He bent down to the
kneading, pushed the dough into the oven, pulled out the baked
bread, made his round of the streets selling ring-loaves and
spinach-pastries. He wore himself out with work, to forget. But
how could he forget? Each morning when he went in to see his
only son, he was forced to see how the rot progressed.

Old Tulupanas worked at the oven and sighed. As he looked up
for a moment and saw a light still burning in the window up
above, he shook his head and sighed. "Poor Frenchwoman!" he

muttered. "You too are suffering, you too are suffering under your fate. . . . No, the hearts of men find no rest."

All night long, in fact, the light had not been put out; the Frenchwoman had not closed an eye. She coughed, spat, groaned. Kasapakes the doctor had brought her back with him from Paris as his wife and had transplanted her to this nest of Turks at the end of the world. At first she had sighed, later she had coughed, and now in the end she was spitting blood. And the doctor, it was said, would have none of her now, and was carrying on with his maid, a filly from Arkalochori.

"Where's the railway you said ran past our house?" the Frenchwoman had wailed during the first weeks. That's what you said in Paris."

And the fat doctor had laughed. "In Megalokastro we call the donkeys our railway," he had answered.

Captain Michales crouched, limp and silent, in the middle of his yard, and still waited for the sky to get light. When he heard the cock, he raised his eyes. The sky was changing to a bright glow. He sprang up, strode into his room, put on his clothes in haste, wound his wide sash tightly several times around his body, thrust the black-handled knife into it and took the little bottle of oil which hung before the icon-shrine. He filled the little lamp— it was already beginning to flicker—and gazed at the Archangel Michael, his chief.

"I'm going," he said to him. "What we have to say to each other we've said—so I'm going. Watch over the house!"

He went down to the yard, opened the street door, saddled the mare, mounted and rode to the Hospital Gate. It was light. The soldiers took the keys and made ready to open the four fortress gates. The houses were still shut, but some hearths were smoking. Barba Jannis was already up and about, already crying out, at this early hour, his hot, thick barley water liberally laced with pepper. Captain Michales spurred his mare on, rode quickly past the big plane tree, eater of Christians, turned off at the market place, reached the Three Vaults and stopped for a moment, looking around. The whole arc of mountains glowed rose-red—in front of him Cruel Mountain, a naked precipice; behind him Psiloritis the great lord, serene, with his snowy head; on his right the marble dragon Iuchtas, standing on its head. Over there, the sea shimmered pale blue, flecked lightly here and there with blue-green foam. The Maltese ships' boats, black with red sails, had already begun their work on the sea. The sun rose out of the waves in glowing mist. The mare turned, saw the sun; her eyes sparkled, she threw back her neck and whinnied to greet it.

The trumpets pealed, the Turkish flag went up on the flagpole, and, grinding, the iron fortress gate opened. The peasants, who had been waiting outside since the first gray of dawn, all rushed in at once, treading on one another's feet. Their asses and mules were laden with wood and charcoal, bottles of wine and oil, baskets of vegetables and fruit and brass jars of honey. To get into the fortress they had to pass through the dark tunnel which traversed the whole thickness of the Venetian walls. Inside, under the stone vaulting, voices and curses mingled with the neighing and tramping of beasts and men, and their echoes clashed. The whole dark subterranean gullet clanged with the din.

Captain Michales forced a way through the raving horde, came out among the fields and rode down to the coast. Megalokastro lay behind him, and he took the beach path toward Cruel Mountain and past the Red Hills. To his right the dark green land gave forth its fragrance, to his left was the sea. The sun hung low like a gold talisman on the breast of the town.

"In the name of Christ and of the Archangel Michael," muttered Captain Michales, turning to the east and crossing himself.

Megalokastro had filled itself with sun. First the minarets seized upon it, then the light blue cupola of Saint Menas' and the roofs of the houses. Soon it sank lower and hung there in the damp alleys. The young girls opened their windows to it, and in it came, and the old gray women went into the yards to warm themselves. They crossed themselves and praised the Lord that March, that month accursed of God, which plagues the aged with sudden cold, was over. Now their limbs would sun themselves. Welcome April and Saint George.

Through all the fortress gates the Cretan donkeys streamed in; nimble and always gay, they raised their tails and brayed at the inhabitants to announce the advent of spring.

Penelope went back into her yard; she yawned so wide that

48

her jawbones creaked. Middle-aged, with breasts and haunches of double girth, she ate well and had a good digestion. She washed and scrubbed her husband Mr. Demetros, fed and groomed him like a horse, and every evening tried hard to animate him. She had no children, and loved cats, canaries and spring meadows. This morning she had strange pins and needles in her back, and, if she had had a tail like an animal, she would have raised it high and brayed, to announce the spring to Katerina, to the wives of Krasojorgis and Mastrapas, to the doctor's wife and all the neighbors. Why were they still lying in bed? They ought to get up and let the sun touch them to make them all bray together and roll in the fields! Spring has come! Today her four walls could not contain her. She cooked quickly and sent the little maid to knock at the door, opposite, of Katerina the Captain's wife, and say: Greetings from my mistress Penelope, Demetros' wife, and if you would like, she says, we're taking our meal and going out to the fields to eat it there. Spring has come, she says.

But how could the Captain's wife leave her house, since it must be cleaned to let the five boon companions tramp in, early next morning? She was preparing hens for the feast: one to be boiled, another stuffed with sweet corn, the third roasted on the spit.

"We can't. Tell your mistress we can't today, and please will she excuse us. But if she would like to come here this afternoon with her sewing, the neighbors are coming too, and so is Ali Aga, to amuse us. Captain Michales will be absent all day today. She need have no fear."

Penelope frowned and sent the little maid to the other neighbors: to Mastrapas' wife, to Krasojorgis' wife, to Polyxigis' sister. But the first said she was expecting Manoles the pope, who was to exorcise the house; the second said she had a headache and giddiness; and Polyxigis' sister was doing the baking early for supper. Besides, her feet had swollen and she could not move.

"Perish the lot of you! Addled idiots!" growled Penelope, enraged. "Don't you ever open your peepholes to look out? Or would that make you feel naked? Come, Marulio, go to the doctor's wife, Massella—she will understand, even if she is French, what spring is. She'll come!" Marcelle was her name, but Penelope called her Massella. Penelope made fun of her because she talked broken Greek and had many big-town airs. According

49

to the Frenchwoman, "Parisia" was bigger than Megalokastro, and a big river flowed between its streets; also, the women there went to the coffeehouses, talked boldly with the men and showed their feet up to the ankles. These were fairy tales, certainly, but the heretical Frenchwoman had a pretty way of telling them, and you could see she believed them herself. . . . I've often noticed her eyes go dim, she thought. And what she has to put up with from that impudent husband of hers, with his airs and graces— for shame! To hell with him! He has no shame, carrying on with a girl from Arkalochori . . . the poor woman must come out into the country. We'll go as far as Saint Irene of the Four Springs. That'll wear her out.

But the little maid came back with downcast face. "She can't, she says, she can't. She coughed all night and had no sleep— another day. And will you excuse her?"

Penelope swore. In her mind she ran through the whole neighborhood. Should she—God forbid!—invite Kolyvas' wife? Her husband's a gravedigger, and she herself's a hypochondriac and sees ghosts. All the dead flutter past her pillow. Serves her right! Why does her husband strip them of their clothes and dress his wife and his own bag of bones in them?—And the dead are left naked in the damp of the earth and are angry, and quite right too. No, she wouldn't have Kolyvas' wife. . . . Should she send again to Archondula, that bitter nut, to ask her to be so kind as to go out with Penelope the grocer's wife? Archondula's father, so they said, had been a dragoman in Constantinople and had played cards with the patriarch; now that he was dead, she received a bag of gold pounds from the patriarchate every year, and ate caviar by the spoonful! No, the food of ordinary people was not good enough for her! The visits of the Metropolitan and the pasha were not good enough for her! When she was still young, she found that one man reeked and another stank. The conceited creature! Let her now stew in her own juice, left sitting there on the trunk with her trousseau. Serves her right! Serves her brother right too, the deaf mute. Sins of the fathers. . . . Once a Christian had been brought to Constantinople to be hanged, because he was supposed to have killed a Turk. The dragoman—curses on his bones!—knew the truth: the murderer was not the Christian but a bey. But would anything make that blackguard of a dragoman open his mouth to speak? He was afraid and remained dumb. So his only son too became dumb. No, you're not going out with Miss Archondula, no, not even if she were willing.

Her mind swept away from the snob's grand house and wandered further: should I ask Vangelio? But she won't come either, because she's in such a hurry. She's getting her trousseau ready and is set on marrying Tityros, the schoolmaster, at Easter. . . . Why the devil has the unfortunate girl chosen *him*? That yellow-head, that half-helping with glasses? Did I hear it said she loves him? But there's a curse on her, poor thing! Her brother, the pretty ne'er-do-well with the gold watch, has frittered all her money away on finery and debauchery.

After long searching up and down, Penelope came to a decision. She climbed into the trough, cut a bunch of vine leaves from the trellis, went into the kitchen, wrapped the food in the leaves, filled a basket with bread, olives, a couple of oranges, a small bottle of wine, a spirit-lamp, coffee, sugar, a knife and fork and a cloth, and came out into the yard.

"Come with me, Marulio," she said to her little servant girl.

She shut the street door and trotted down to the harbor. Thickset and broad-shouldered, she suggested, with her rocking gait, certain fat-tailed sheep recently imported into Crete from Asia Minor. The poor woman was embarrassed, for she could feel how her bottom wagged. But what could she do about it? Even those dumplings are God's work, she said to herself, and felt consoled. Luckily for me my legs aren't swollen like Miss Chrysanthe's, Polyxigis' sister. I can still get about, God be thanked, and I order that pig of mine about. I manage him; he doesn't manage me. I'm a match for ten girls, ten lads can't put me down, I'm rightly called the Strong Woman.

After much pitching and tossing she crossed Broad Street. It was swarming with porters, artisans, farmers. What a shouting and squabbling! What great coarse asses' throats these Kastrians have, thought Penelope, pursing her lips; she herself was from Rethymno and proud of it. Kanea for weapons, Rethymno for books, Megalokastro for mugs. Scarcely were the Kastrians done with their work in the evening when they were all lolling in the taverns and swilling away, chewing dried fish and gobbets off the spit, and reeking of wine, ouzo and meat—How unlike the Rethymniots with their slow, dignified gait, deep bows and lordly ceremony! Only her Demetros was different from all the rest of Megalokastro; but he, bless him, was half a corpse! Why couldn't she bring him to life at night? All my efforts in vain, she thought. Yes, if he were only from Rethymno. . . .

She sighed. She walked on until she was near the harbor. He will be sitting there as usual, flapping his fly whisk, she thought. Yes, he can do that all right.

But Demetros had got tired of flapping his fly whisk some time ago and was now immersed in a large volume in which he recorded in two kinds of ink—red for the meat, blue for the rest —the food he consumed each day. He was deep in study, reading the dishes and savoring them till his mouth filled with spittle. He had got as far as the last few days, and was spelling them out slowly, with relish, as though chewing. *"The Year 1889, March 20:* Fresh broad beans with artichokes and green onions; lots of oil; well blended. *March 21:* Baked cucumbers with garlic; burned by that wretched Tulupanas."

A little girl came into the entrance of the shop. "Mr. Demetros, sir, Christofakas' wife has sent me. You're to give me six ounces of Chios mastic for cooking."

"I see what you want, my child, I see. But it's there, high up!" And he drawled the words out as long as he could, to show that the mastic was somewhere on the peak of the world.

The girl departed, and Mr. Demetros again plunged into his studies. *"March 25, the Annunciation:* Boiled cod with lemon; cod with parsley; roast cod with garlic; cucumber salad. Very tasty."

But now he had had enough of his studies too. He took up the fly whisk again and sighed. "I, the son of the famous Captain Leanbottom, what have I come to?" he muttered, and slapped his good-natured face with his open hand. "My grandfather owned a warship and set the Turkish frigates on fire. My father owned a gun and killed Turks. And I've got a fly whisk and kill flies. Curse this face of mine!" And as his warrior father came into his mind, the shop became too small for him. He stretched out his arms and touched the walls to his right and left. Like Samson he wanted to burst the walls, to make the world wide, so that he, Mr. Demetros Leanbottom, should not feel confined.

Just at the moment he was vowing to burst the walls asunder, the shop darkened. On the threshold towered Penelope, tall and round and fat and out of breath. As Mr. Demetros saw her, his face grew troubled. *What the devil does she want from me now?* he asked himself. *Isn't the night enough? Where does she get the energy, the shameless woman? Has someone put petroleum in her buttocks? Ah! the respectable women of Rethymno!*

"Welcome!" he said aloud, and hastily opened the book.

"Up you get, Demetros," his wife called. "Up you get! We're going out into the country together! Don't molder away; give those bones of yours a chance to warm up, bless you! Here you are, stuck in a swamp like a frog. Pull yourself together! I've brought our meal with me—your favorite dish."

She bent down and whispered into his ear: "Eggplant wrapped in vine leaves, with lots of pepper. . . . You'll see how good they taste, out in the country!"

Mr. Demetros shuddered. "I'm not coming!" he shouted, "I'm not coming!" and clung to his bench.

"Come, Demetros, poppet, come! To please you, I promise not to scold you."

But he flapped hard with the fly whisk, as if Penelope were a fly, a bluebottle that he wanted to chase out of the shop.

"I'm not coming!" he shouted again, "I've got lots of work to do today, can't you see? I'm doing accounts. What I owe, what I'm owed, so as to see how we stand. Go alone, there's an angel."

"Let's be off, Marulio," said Penelope, taking her little maid by the scruff of the neck. "I'll take you as my neighbor and husband! Let's be off, we'll have our meal together out in the sun." And she turned her towering back on Mr. Demetros and went.

"Curse my fate," she muttered, striding along. "I ought to have taken a palikar for husband, a guzzler and swiller and wencher who'd have begotten a dozen children on me ere I was tamed. And I should have lived in Rethymno, where the best people live, and not here with the Kastrians—the asses!"

She muttered to herself and moved on, raging. She was already hungry. She saw the sun getting higher, and her nostrils quivered —she could smell the fresh grass. She was still holding the diminutive Marulio by the scruff and powerfully pulling her along. The girl dragged, gasping, with the loaded basket. She kept losing her trodden-down slippers; then she took them off and laid them on top of the vegetables. After that she trotted on, barefoot, beside her mistress.

Near Saint Menas' church Penelope stopped. She crossed herself. "Dear Saint Menas," she murmured, "you know what I want—help me!"

Shrieks and laughter rang out. The alley filled with children. The bell had rung, and they were rushing to school. Penelope's heart leaped. She remained where she was, admiring the children. "Ah!" she said, "if only the lot were mine! And not all by Demetros, God forgive me!"

In an instant her eyes went dim, and before her mind there passed the young men she had seen in the streets and villages and in dreams. God forgive me, she said to herself, but I think Barba Jannis' wife, with her thousands of men, is right. How many men has she had children by! God alone knows—*and* by whom she had my neighbor Katinitsa, Krasojorgis' wife! Barba Jannis did try to be hard of hearing, but a flea got into his ear all the same. He saw his horns, groped for them and felt them. But what was he to do? Once only, when he was ill, he called his wife. "Ah, wife," he said, "in God's name, in Whom you believe, tell me the truth. Are all the children we've got mine?" But his wife said nothing. "Tell me the truth, wife. You can see I'm dying. What are you afraid of?" "And suppose you don't die?" the creature answered. "Suppose you don't die?" . . .

Penelope laughed as she remembered, and drew to one side to let the schoolchildren by. She looked at little Thrasos, the son of her neighbor, the captain's wife.

"Thrasaki, Thrasaki!" she called, and looked in the basket for an orange to give him.

But how could Thrasaki hear her? He had his arms round the shoulders of his two friends; on his right, Manolios, Mastrapas' son, on his left, Andrikos, Krasojorgis' son. They were running, chattering, laughing, as they went over, again and again, how they had strewed small shot about the threshold of the school door at the moment when Tityros had turned his back and was preparing to teach them the song they were to sing on next Sunday's outing: "Spring has come, the flowers are here again . . ." They had all begun shouting, and Tityros too had joined in the

54

fun: he raised his birch and said, "Children, let's go out into the yard, all of us, and sing out there. Then, the day after tomorrow, when we're outside the Three Vaults, we shan't disgrace ourselves. Forward!"

He had led the way, with his head in the air, but as he set foot stoutly on the threshold he slid and fell to the ground like a jar. His glasses were smashed to bits.

"Didn't he break any bones too?" asked Andrikos, worried lest they should be whole.

But Thrasaki reassured him. "He did, I tell you, he did. Didn't you hear the crack? That was his bones."

"And did you hear the way he yelled 'Oh!'?" said Manolios, rubbing his hands contentedly. "He must have broken his hip— he couldn't get up. He yelled 'oh! oh!' and groped for his glasses."

"That means we're rid of the outing and can do what we planned. Agreed?"

"Agreed!" cried his two companions.

A dog came by. They picked up stones and chased him away.

By the teke, next door to Saint Menas', they heard shrieking and brawling. They stopped. "Hamidé Mula is beating Efendina," said Thrasaki. "Let's wait. Might see some fun."

They stood on tiptoe, to see through the grille in the wall. The big weed-grown yard stretched before them, and in the middle was the Saint's tomb, decked with strips of colored fabric. Near the tomb the old barefoot mother, her hair coming down and her nose standing out like a spear-point, was holding her son by the neck with one hand and a forked stick in the other. "Have you no fear of God?" she screamed. "You'd go again to the house of those Greeks, where they stuff you with swine's flesh and make you drunk with wine and defile you! I'll lock you in, you damned blockhead, I'll beat you senseless. You shan't go!"

Efendina made a movement to escape from his mother's claws. He shrieked as though she were trying to murder him.

"You shan't go," she screamed, and shook him. "You shan't go! Have you forgotten the shame you bring on yourself every time you do? When you're sober again, you're sorry and you howl. Then you tear off your cap, and your scab shows. And you smear it with horse dung and run out into the streets and bray like an ass. . . . And the Greeks pelt you with lemon peel and give you a woman's name. They call you Efendina—Efendina Horsedung! Aren't you ashamed, in front of this saint, your grandfather?" So she abused him shrilly and pointed at the tomb with its bright-colored shreds.

"Day and night I think of him!" shouted Efendina, raising his hands high. "I swear it, day and night I think of him!"

"Then why do you defile yourself?"

"Don't you want me to become a saint? A saint, like my grandfather? How the devil do you expect me to become a saint if I don't sin? If I don't fall into sin, shall I repent? shall I weep? cry to God? show my scab to men? No! How then can I become a saint?"

Hamidé Mula stood with open mouth. Now she stared at her son, now at the tomb, and fell silent. Perhaps her idiot of a son was right. Perhaps, too, it was true, what she had heard about the old man, the saint, Efendina's grandfather. He had spent his whole life getting ripe for the halter and the stake, and only when he shriveled up and could take no more wine, meat and women had he fallen into saintliness. He had climbed up the minaret of Aja Katerina and would neither come down nor eat and drink. He wept, struck himself and cried to God. He bellowed for seven days and nights, and then he gave a mighty cry, so that the hair of the people of Megalokastro stood on end and the ravens flew up into the sky. God had pity on him and sent him food to prevent him from dying. . . . Was that perhaps her son's way, too, to become a saint?

Hamidé Mula felt bewildered. She did not know whether to beat her darling again or to squat down in the corner of their yard and sun herself, for she was shivering. She laid down the forked stick near the tomb and withdrew her nails from Efendina's neck. She raised her fist and shook it at him.

"There! Devil take you, do as you wish! Eat, drink, dance about—and then rub horse dung over your scab!"

So saying, she flung herself, full of anxiety, back into the sunshine in the corner of the yard.

"A pity," said Andrikos, "she hasn't sliced him up."

"Just wait, my father will see to that tomorrow," said Thrasaki. He gave his friend a nudge. "Come," he said, "tomorrow at sundown the thing's going to be done. I'm inviting you. Bring your catapults too. I'm bringing a rope."

"I'll bring a stick," said Andrikos.

"I'll bring a stake," said Manolios.

"We're letting Nikolas, Furogatos' son, come in as well. He's got strong hands."

"But what happens if her father sees us?" asked Manolios, and stood still.

"Pff . . . what's it matter if he does see us," said Thrasaki contemptuously. "Is he able to beat anyone? He's not a Cretan, he's from Syra."

"But shall we be able to hold her up?" said Andrikos. "She weighs a ton. Suppose she shrieks?"

Thrasaki frowned. "Listen, Andrikos," he said, "these affairs need a stout heart. Haven't you got one? If not, get out, and I'll find someone else."

"Me?" said Andrikos, injured. "My heart's like a mountain."

"We shall see tomorrow," said Thrasaki, and ran faster. They were nearing the school now. "Be quiet now," ordered Thrasaki. "Don't let a word out, or it'll be the worse for you! Tomorrow my father will be drunk, and I'm free. And you sneak out. Say it's for the evening service. Then your mother'll give you a copper to light a candle. We'll buy roast peas with it."

"And take them home to her," suggested Manolios.

"Idiot, why should we take them home to her?" shouted Thrasaki. "We eat them."

Meanwhile Captain Michales was riding past Cruel Mountain. His headband was down to his eyebrows. To his left foamed the sea, to his right was rock, iron-bearing rock, the wild, bare mountain. An accursed mountain. Passing it, a Christian makes the sign of the cross and abuses Turkey. For in whatever hole, whatever cranny of it you search, you find the bones of slaughtered Christians.

Captain Michales crossed himself. Among those cliffs, ten years ago, his brother Christofes had been killed with both his sons. For many days afterward people had followed the ravens, and at last had found, in a gully, the three corpses, piled on one

57

another. Their tongues were missing. As they had gaily ridden by in the evening, they had been singing the Moscow Song. It was the day of Thrasaki's christening, and the brothers and nephews were on their way home, drunk and pleased with life. They waved at the sea's horizon and called on the Muscovites to come. The Turks had lain in wait for them; they fell on them from an ambush, and cut out their tongues.

"Forsaken Crete!" Captain Michales muttered, and spurred his mare. "For how many generations have you cried out, unlucky land, and who has heard you? Even God needs a threat for His miracles. The mighty ones of the earth want a good threatening. Grasp your gun once more, you fool: that will be your Muscovite. There is no other!"

He sighed and rode slowly away from the sea into the plain, and from the plain into the mountains. His nostrils dilated; the Cretan precipices were fragrant with thyme and sage.

"How beautiful Crete is," he murmured, "how beautiful! Ah! if only I were an eagle, to admire the whole of Crete from an airy height!"

And truly an eagle would see beauties to admire in Crete—the way her close-knit body rose and poised, sun-browned; the way her coasts gleamed, now with white sand, now with blood-red, sheer promontories. He must needs rejoice over the villages, the big farms, the monasteries and the little churches glittering against the iron-dark rock or planted deep in the soil. And sorrow over her three tormented, Turk-oppressed towns with their Venetian walls and their Turkified churches: Kanea, Rethymno and Megalokastro.

God too, higher than the eagle, must have the same view—if He had not forgotten Crete, generations and generations ago, and delivered her, soul and all, into the hands of the Turks.

No, without the soul. For the Cretans resisted, boiled with rage and refused to place their seal under God's seal. It was injustice! They raised their heads to Heaven and shouted "Injustice!" and bestirred themselves like good Christians to put right this intolerable divine injustice. God too is a fighter, they reflected. He must be waging war somewhere else, on some other star, against other Turks. We will call Him till He hears us.

There are peoples and individuals who call to God with

prayers and tears or a disciplined, reasonable self-control—or even curse Him. The Cretans called to Him with guns. They stood before God's door and fired rifle shots to make Him hear. "Insurrection!" bellowed the Sultan, when he first heard the shooting, and in raving fury sent pashas, soldiers and gangs. "Insolence!" cried the Franks, and let loose their warships against the tiny barks that fought, braving death, between Europe, Asia and Africa. "Be patient, be reasonable, don't drag me into bloodshed!" wailed Hellas, the beggar-mother, shuddering. "Freedom or death!" answered the Cretans, and made a din before God's door.

At first this happened only once in a generation, but later, after the great rising of 1821, the clamor grew hotter, indignation quickened its step. Crete's heart swallowed for a time its contempt, its sense of injustice, its suffering, until it swelled and at length overflowed. It burst out against the dreadful beast whose claws held it prisoner. It consumed its own flesh, burned its villages, trampled down its olive groves and vineyards, piled the corpses on its naked plains as high as God's threshold—and fell back, bleeding from a thousand wounds, into the beast's claws. It exploded in 1866, the time of Arkadi, rose again in 1878, and fell to earth once more. It began afresh to swallow injustice and misery, and now, at the beginning of the year 1889, the heart of Crete was again near to overflowing. In the villages the Christians were clenching their fists and gazing north toward Greece and, farther afield, toward Moscow. Their grandfathers were awake in them and making them itch. They could no longer endure staying quietly in their homes and in their villages. They were losing their sleep. Every Sunday they would call for the schoolmaster, the pope or the lyre player: he must tell them or sing them of the woes of Crete, to make their rage rise and come to a head. Always at the onset of spring, as the spring fields began to warm and surge, and the superfluous force of life stoked them up, the hearts of the Cretans grew wild. The Turks knew it and sent orders—and soldiers—to hold them in.

Captain Michales' heart swelled, it could bear the misery of Crete no longer. He drove the spurs into the mare's belly and rode past Cruel Mountain. He came to the red soil, then took the shore way. He felt hungry and dismounted at the widow's inn. The owner came—a gay, capable widow, rank and fat. She smelled of onions and caraway seeds. Captain Michales looked past her: he did not like coquettish women, waggers of buttocks. He stared at the road before him and at the sea.

"Welcome, Captain Michales! We don't see you often!" said the widow, and winked at him artfully. "If you're not fasting, I've hare stewed with fresh onions and caraway seeds."

She bent down to get him a dismounting stool, and the cleft of her hospitable bosom was visible, downy and cool.

"You should eat meat, Captain Michales," she said, giving him another wink. "You're on a journey, and it's no sin."

But Captain Michales was angry. He hated the woman and the food and his own hunger.

"I won't have anything," he said. "I'm not hungry!" He leaped on the mare again and rode farther.

He left the mountains and came out onto the plain—peaceful, gracious green, with the hum of bees, the twittering of birds, come trustingly back to their Cretan nests of the year before. Today, on the first of April, Crete was sparkling under the soft spring sunshine. But Captain Michales saw nothing. He hurried forward. Where was he going? Why had he started off this morning at gray of dawn? Whom was he hunting? Who was hunting him? A cloud covered his senses. The sunlit coast was overcast, the path rolled onward like a river; above, the Lasithi mountains steamed and wavered like smoke.

Two hefty peasants, who passed him on their asses, raised their hands to their chests and greeted him: "Long life to you, Captain Michales!" But he made no reply to their gaze and greeting. His mind swept to Nuri's konak, slunk around it and surveyed the high walls like a thief. He was calculating how and where he could spring over them and get in. But then his mind became troubled, and he could not think of his next move, once he had jumped down and penetrated into the garden.

Sweat broke out on his brow. He thrust his hand into his sash and fingered the knife-hilt. "The dog's right," he muttered, "one or other of us is one too many."

As he gripped the knife and in spirit climbed over the high wall and slid down into the garden among the pots of flowers where the lamp with the red and green glass still burned, he heard above him, behind the wooden lattice, a laugh. At once the sweat poured in heavy drops from his brow, his neck and his shoulders. A light burst upon him, and he realized—he was not breaking into that house to kill! A demon had got into him, a new, unsummoned one that had nothing in common with the demons of his stock. This one was scornful, shameless, fragrant with musk, and its face was—oh, shame!—a woman's face.

"Aren't you ashamed, Captain Michales?" he groaned. "What have you come to?"

He saw his forefathers raising their tombstones to curse him. He shrank back and clenched his fist. "Hey, grandfathers, stay in your holes in the earth! I'm alive, I'm in command, don't shout!"

He wiped his brow with his headband and pulled himself together again. The mountains stood firm once more, the coast glittered, under his feet the river straightened and became a road again. Once more he remembered why he had ridden out to the Hospital Gate and where he was bound. He had given the Bey his word yesterday and must keep it. He meant to go and see his brother Manusakas at Ai-Janni.

To this small village, wide with gardens, an hour from the large village, Petrokefalo, where his family came from, fate had blown his brother Manusakas like a grain of seed, some years ago. He had taken root there and flourished. Now, as an oak has its branches and twigs, he had children and grandchildren sprouting all over the village and drawing nourishment from the soil.

One unforgettable day—it was September fourteen in the year 1866—Manusakas, sweeping along with his palikars in search of Turks, had stormed into Ai-Janni and found there, in a peasant's house, a young woman with her hair down, keening. They had just slain her husband on the threshold. She was newly married and she was cursing God: He is unjust, He is no Christian, He loves the Turks. Manusakas, who was forty and had lost his wife two years before, gazed at the young widow, and his heart was lost. He left his palikars to rest and feed in the yard, and himself went into the house, a powder-blackened, long-haired savage. When the widow saw him, she was terrified. "Holy God!" she shrieked, and hid her face in her lap.

But he did his best to look gentle and approached her. "Weep,
61

woman," he said, "weep yourself out and lighten your heart. I too had a wife, and those dogs of Turks killed her. I too yelled and shed tears and lightened my heart."

He squatted down close by her; he watched how she struck herself and howled; he waited. He stared at her and his heart shuddered with longing. Ah, if only he could seize her and clasp her in his arms! So, with her neck bare, hot and convulsed as she was with the keening—never had Manusakas felt such a yearning for a woman. He laid a hand warily and softly on her shoulder.

"That's enough," he said to her tenderly, "that's enough. You'll destroy those eyes of yours, woman. Aren't you sorry for them? Lovelier ones, by my soul, the world never brought forth. And remember, I've been about the world—I, Captain Manusakas, now kneeling before you. I won't boast to you, but you can ask anywhere from Kissamos to Sitia, and they'll tell you who I am."

He fell silent. He was afraid a word too many might escape him and the widow be terrified again. But he could not bear it. He drew still closer, bent over her and began to tell, in a soft singsong voice, of the things he had seen and suffered, how many widows and orphans were left in the same anguish as she, how many streams of tears had been shed, from one end of Crete to the other. These were the trials of Crete; and whoever was born a Cretan had to know them and must not flinch.

Slowly the widow raised her head. She longed to hear of the trials and sufferings of the world, and it consoled her. She wiped her eyes, cleared her throat, and began in her turn to tell how they had killed her husband; and raising her hand, she pointed at the blood, which was still on the threshold. She meant never to wash it off, she said, so as to have it before her eyes, to think of it and bewail it.

And he touched her gently—very gently—now on the shoulder, now on her hair, now on her knee, and said to her, "You're right, woman. I too did the same for my dear one. They murdered her in my yard, for revenge, because she had a leader for a husband. The yard was full of blood, but the rain came and washed the blood away. The stones were again white."

He sighed and bent over the widow. "The soul of man, too, is like stone, woman. Slowly, slowly, the blood will be washed away —all will be forgotten."

As he saw that the woman grew angry at such words, he took his warm cloak, which reeked of powder, and placed it around her shoulders. "It's turned cold," he said. "Don't catch cold."

And she looked and felt ashamed, as though a man had placed himself on top of her. She wanted to throw off the cloak, but she was afraid to hurt him. She bent forward and felt, at first with shuddering, but gradually with sweet agitation, a warm male smell arise from the woolen cloth and stealthily penetrate her body, from her shoulders to her back, her thighs, her flesh. . . . She thought of her husband, his first embraces, his arms, and how softly and supplicatingly they had held her body on the first night. . . . She grew warm under the cloak and found a little comfort. She felt the man's breath upon her, panting violently. A sweet sympathy overcame her. She turned to him.

"I can't get you anything to eat," she said, "and you must be hungry. You're straight from the fighting. But those dogs of Turks have robbed all my stores."

"I don't want anything to eat, woman," he answered. "God forbid! How should I eat and let you go hungry? Either you have courage, and we eat together, or by God in Whom I believe, I die of hunger with you."

He dreaded lest too strong a word might have escaped him. He coughed and could not think how to put it right again.

"Don't be angry with me," he said, "for speaking to you so boldly. But what am I to say to you? How am I to say it? You won't believe me!"

He sighed again. He began to roll a cigarette, but gave it up. He was bewildered and at a loss. The widow raised her long tear-wet eyelashes and gazed at him. She wanted to question him, but was afraid. She longed to hear what he would say, but was ashamed.

"It's shameful," Manusakas began again, "but I can't hold out against it. I'm going to tell you the whole truth honestly. Don't take it amiss, for God's sake! If I'm lying, may God hurry with His lightning and burn me up! As soon as I came in here and saw you weeping, a knife went through my heart. I'm telling you the truth, woman, I was undone—never in the world have I seen such beauty! I mean well. Don't be angry. Don't get up and run away. There, I'm not touching you. Listen, though, to what I've got to say: your dear husband is dead; he's gone. My dear wife is

63

dead; she's gone. Both of us are left alone in the world. Come and let me look after you."

The little widow cried out, reeled, and sank on her knees. Her teeth were chattering; she was trembling. Manusakas rose and went to the door, to leave the woman alone for a moment and give her the chance to pull herself together. He saw his palikars stretched out in the yard; they had opened their sacks and were eating. Beyond the yard he saw the fertile fields, the fruit-laden olive trees, and the windmills turning and creaking peacefully. "I'll strike root here," he muttered, his mind made up. "This soil is good and fruitful, and I like it. The widow, too, is good and fruitful: she'll bear strong children, I like her. By the all-seeing sun above me, no, I'll not stir from here!"

When he went back to see how the young widow was, he found her with her bodice laced and her hair tidy. She had bitten her lips and licked them to make them red. She was still wearing the warm cloak.

"Captain Manusakas," she said cunningly, rolling her eyes, "what you said was not proper, forgive my saying so. And if it's true, it's a great sin. The blood of my dear husband is still warm on the threshold."

Manusakas sighed. He paced up and down.

"If only I had a bit of bread," he said at last, renouncing the conversation, "and a mouthful of wine! And if you wouldn't mind, woman—I can't do it myself—sewing on this button that's hanging loose on my waistcoat."

The widow said nothing; she was sorry for the man. She found her needle and threaded it, and the man knelt down in front of her. She wiped her eyes, to see better. Then she began sewing the button on tight. As she sewed, she could feel the heart of Manusakas beating hard within his waistcoat and his fiery breath upon her knees.

She was ashamed, sewed hurriedly and stood up. She opened the chest. It wasn't true, she said, the Turks hadn't stolen everything. She took out a woven tablecloth and spread it on a table. It was snow-white and lighted up the house. Then she started a fire and began cooking. Manusakas lighted a cigar and, taking a footstool, sat down at the threshold, as though he were the man of the house. He looked out but his ears were attentive to the sounds inside the house. He heard the woman busily going up and down, poking the fire, cooking the food, getting knives and forks and plates and laying the table. . . . He heard, and his heart rejoiced. Never had he felt so comfortable, so hungry, so patient. He knew now, he was sure: this young powder-stained widow, now cooking for him and with whom in a moment he would sit down to a meal, would, after the prescribed period of mourning for the dead, share food and bed with him for life.

That was how Manusakas won his Christinia and struck root in her village. She fulfilled her promise and gave him children. She bore them by twins, and his yard became full. In due course he even had his first grandson—and got drunk to celebrate. He hoisted his ass upon his shoulder and lugged it into the mosque of the big village at prayer time, late in the evening.

"He did right," muttered Captain Michales. "I would have done the same—the same and worse. But I've given my word, and I must keep it, even if he is older than I. I'm the head of the village."

On the mountain slope, Petrokefalo showed in the distance, and farther up the defile, surrounded by green, Ai-Janni, Christinia's village. He spurred the mare hard. She too recognized the village and whinnied and began galloping along the road.

Manusakas' door stood open. Captain Michales ducked his head, rode in, and halted in the yard.

"Brother Manusakas," he called. The whole family was seated indoors around the low table, eating. Manusakas was leaning against the wall and had hung the whip near him. Opposite him, with her legs crossed under her, sat his wife, Christinia, happy and grateful. She had got rather fatter, and her breasts sagged: she had suckled too many children. But her face still glowed like a rose in full bloom.

Manusakas heard his brother's voice and sprang up. He came out into the yard.

"Welcome, brother," he said, stretching out his huge hand. "The table's laid, your sister-in-law loves you, get down."

"I'm in a hurry," said Captain Michales. "Shut the door. There's something I must say to you."

"Good news? Bad?"

"Depends how you take it. Shut the door, I tell you."

Manusakas shut the house door, to keep his sons and daughters from hearing. He went over to his brother.

"Listen to what I'm saying, brother Manusakas," Captain Michales said. "If you can't carry your wine, don't drink any."

Manusakas' face darkened. "Why do you say that to me?"

"God didn't make the ass to ride men, but for men to ride. Understand?"

"I understand. Your blood brother, Nuri Bey, has been upset by it and has sent you to do his dirty work. Has it upset you too, on your own account, Captain Michales?"

"I wasn't upset. And don't throw my words in my face. You know what I feel. But it's no service to the Christian cause. The moment hasn't come yet for us to raise the banner."

But Manusakas had become angry. "When you get drunk and sing the Moscow Song, burst into the Turkish coffeehouses, insult beys and send them sprawling on the pavement, do you think of the Christian cause? And do you now come to me in my own yard and play the schoolmaster?"

He bent down, picked up a stone, threw it to the ground violently, and gripped the reins of the mare. "What have you to say, Michales? Am I right? Don't play Saint Onufrios with me!"

Captain Michales was silent. What was he to say? Manusakas was right. As soon as he himself got drunk, he gave no thought either to Crete or to Christendom. To the devil with sweet reasonableness! At those times he rode out on his mare, and the whole world seemed to him small and trifling, a nutshell, and he rode up and down and felt like trampling it under his mare's hoofs. The devil take it!

"You don't answer," said Manusakas, looking hard at his brother, who frowned and stared up at the mountain. "You don't answer. Now for what's worrying you—I can see what's going round inside you. Make up your mind: you're a palikar, aren't you? Make up your mind, I tell you. That is Crete's destiny. Let me too have my revenge, and the world can go to blazes! At their feast of Bairam I'm going to take a mule over my shoulders and bring it into the mosque. There it can pray alongside the ass. They can kill me if they like."

"I don't care if they kill you, I care only if Crete is smashed."

"Idiot, it won't be smashed, have no fear. We men are smashed, but not Crete the immortal. Wait a minute," he said, thoughtfully. "Brother," he went on, "here's the truth I'm telling you. I'm stifling in this village, don't you understand? For a long while I didn't understand it myself, but when I drink wine my mind clears, and my heart overflows like yours. I can't go to Constantinople and kill the Sultan—so let me work it off in my own way and prove myself a hero in my own small village."

Captain Michales tugged at the rein and steered the mare toward the outer door. "Weigh what I've said to you, brother Manusakas," he said, "weigh it well, when you're alone. And do as God enlightens you. Do what's best for Crete. I've nothing else to say to you. Farewell!"

"Get down, I tell you, have something to eat, don't be in such a hurry. What demon's after you? Stay in my house tonight. It's big, thank God, there's room for you. And see your nephews and Christinia, and my first grandson. I'm going to call him Lefteres*, so that he may see freedom."

"Greet them all for me. I'm in a hurry."

"Won't you even ride into the village and visit our old father?"

"I haven't time. I'm in a hurry, I tell you. Tomorrow morning, early, I've something to do. Health and happiness to you!"

"You're an obstinate, pigheaded fellow. Whatever you get into your head to do, you do, and the world can go hang. All the best . . ."

Captain Michales spurred the mare, rode through the main door and galloped out onto the plain. He was happy. Manusakas had spoken well, had stood up to him well and like a man. But for his horror of sentiment, Captain Michales would have flung his arms round him. *Yes, you're right, Manusakas. Act on what you believe, the devil take it! Even if the water boils over!*

He rode like lightning and came back to Megalokastro with his heart leaping. He had put his stock to the proof once more. And he found it as he would wish.

Noon was already past; the sun was beginning to sink. When the women of the quarter learned that Captain Michales would be absent all day, they gathered in his yard with their sewing, their spindles and their vegetables to be peeled: Penelope,

* The Free (Tr.)

67

Chrysanthe, Polyxigis' sister, Krasjorgis' wife Katinitsa and Mastrapas' wife, all in a Saturday-evening good humor. The week was at an end. Tomorrow meant leisure, good food and plenty of society. Praise be to God, Who created Sundays.

"Have you heard the sad news, Aretusa, my dear?" began Katinitsa in a singsong voice. "Last night there were shouts and screams in the neighborhood, from Furogatos' house. Furogatos was being beaten by his wife again."

"Pity my Demetros hasn't Furogatos' mustache," remarked Penelope. "Looking at it you feel deliciously afraid—he's twirled it so tight, and the wax he uses makes it stay so stiff."

"Why don't they change places, I wonder? He ought to give his wife his mustache and put on her dress," said Mastrapas' wife —the one who kept her husband tied by the ankles all night.

Miss Chrysanthe laughed. "Last night, about midnight," she said, "he was yelling again, so loud that he brought all the neighbors to their feet. My brother was passing by and heard him. In the morning he went to see him. 'Brother Furogatos,' he said to him, 'why do you let your wife slash you to ribbons? You never raise a hand to lick her into shape. You're making all us men look like fools. Aren't you ashamed of yourself?' And what do you think he answered? 'I am ashamed, Captain Polyxigis, I am ashamed, but I *enj-j-j-joy it!*' "

The women shook with laughter. Renio got up and brought the food and drink—coffee, preserves and sesame biscuits. Just as she was serving them, lo and behold, over the threshold came their neighbor Ali Aga with his stocking and knitting needles and with the green bag given him by Renio slung around his shoulders. He was bald—without a single hair—and he shone from much washing. His shabby many-times-darned shirt was shiny, his thin little legs in their clogs were shiny.

Katerina greeted him politely. "Welcome, Ali Aga," she said, "dear neighbor. Come and get a cup of coffee."

"I've just drunk some, thank you," answered Ali Aga, as he made a bow to each of the women. "And I've had a biscuit too and some excellent cherry jam. Many thanks, all the same."

"Oh, what's it matter, Ali Aga? Might as well be hung for a sheep as a lamb. Drink another to keep us company," the women called out with one voice, for they knew his pride and his pov-

erty. He was as poor as a church mouse and had had nothing—
neither coffee nor biscuit nor jam. All his life he had been hungry,
and food was his one thought. He was always talking of good
things to eat, and he dribbled as he talked. The women seized at
once on his favorite subject, for the fun of it.

"And what good things did you have to eat at lunch, Ali Aga,"
said Katinitsa, starting the ball rolling and winking at the others.
"You're such a connoisseur, God knows. I expect you had chick-
en's breast."

Ali Aga smiled contentedly. He smacked his lips and stuck the
knitting needles into his sash. Then the washed-out old man
greedily began describing how tender today's chicken had been,
with what he had seasoned it, what sauce he had devised and how
nicely the oven had browned it. He talked and talked, smacked
his lips and sighed.

The women, suppressing their laughter, plied him with questions and led him on.

"Won't you ever stop eating meat and sauces, Ali Aga? You'll
ruin your health. Eat some vegetables, too, from time to time.
Too much meat is bad for you, you know."

"I'll give you a plate of cabbage this evening, neighbor," said
Mastrapas' wife. "You'll see how it helps your digestion. All that
white bread you eat must be heavy on the stomach."

"And too much caviar, neighbor, does a man in," Penelope
added quickly. "I'll give you a dish of chopped olives. You'll
see, they're bitter, and they sharpen your appetite."

The proud old man, sadly unprosperous in a Greek neighborhood, lived on such good-humored charity. Thus the women
whiled away their afternoon. Now that Ali Aga's evening meal
had been taken care of, there began a long conversation about
the signs of spring in the countryside, and about men, who were
all libertines and, sighed Mastrapas' wife, had no taste for any but
unlawful flesh. And Katinitsa complained that her husband ate
too much and snored and prevented her from sleeping.

Murzuflos, the stocky sacristan up there on the bell tower of
Saint Menas', had, for a long while, been holding his hand to his
ear and listening to Megalokastro as it hummed like a hive of
bees. Murzuflos could distinguish the wild shouts of men crying

their wares, the blows of the blacksmiths' hammers, the gray-headed beggars singing pitifully and knocking at the doors, dogs barking, horses neighing and the little bells the kids wore, as they were driven in to Megalokastro on Saturday evening to be slaughtered.

Suddenly he felt scornful of the voices and the tumult. "Quiet! It's time for me to speak!" he growled, and gripped the bell ropes of the three bells which hung above him. "Five and seventy years have I now been listening to you. I've had enough."

It was seldom that Murzuflos opened his mouth to speak. What was there to say? What he himself did not say he uttered by means of his three bells. They were mouths, they had tongues, they shouted. Secretly he had christened them and given them names: the middle one, the largest, was Saint Menas, the protector and lord of Megalokastro; the one on the right was Elefteria (Freedom); on the left was Thanatos (Death). The voice of Ai-Menas always rang out deep and commanding. Immediately afterward Elefteria spurted forth gaily and playfully, like cool water. Last, dragging heavily after, came Thanatos. These three voices came out of the entrails of that gray-haired church servant—out of the entrails of Crete. Fearlessly they announced, over Christian roofs, Turkish streets and the pasha's palace, the longing for revenge and the yearning of the oppressed.

The soul of Murzuflos with its three voices of silver and bronze rang out triumphantly and encouraged Kastro, though enslaved by the Turks, to celebrate the four festivals of the year: Christmas, Easter, Saint Menas' day (the eleventh of November) and, above all, Saint George's day, the name day of the King of Greece. In his imagination Murzuflos decked himself with laurels to welcome Saint George as he arrived in Crete, riding on a white steed, wearing a fustanella and white silk waistcoat, a leather belt and silver pistols. He wore pointed shoes, too, with red tassels. Behind him on the horse sat a little girl, a King's daughter, Elefteria. She came from Athens. And every year, on the twenty-third of April, Saint George landed at Megalokastro, and Murzuflos, hanging on the three bells in the dance, was the first to see him as he came up from the harbor and the first to greet him by rapturously swinging Saint Menas, Freedom and Death.

But today Murzuflos was depressed. For today, the first of April, seventy-five years had gone by—how, though, had they gone by?—since he was born. Suddenly, for the first time, he felt that he was growing old, and he was afraid he would die without witnessing the liberation of Crete. Will someone else, then, ring the bells on that holy day? No, Murzuflos' soul could not endure that. No, even if the devil has got hold of me, on that day I shall run away out of the bottomless pit, hang on my bells and get started with the din!

A cold sweat bedewed his wrinkled, tight-skinned forehead. His hands trembled, and he began with noisy gasps to ring the evening bell.

In Captain Michales' yard, where the Greek women were chatting, and Ali Aga was explaining to them the words of Mohammed, the evening bell was heard. At once the women broke off their work, gathered their sewing together, crossed themselves and got up to go home. In every house, on Saturday evening, the fire was made up to warm the water for washing. The flushed, barefooted girls scrubbed the doorsteps, scoured out the cobbled yards, and watered the pots of flowers. The old women took down the censers of the icon-shrines and censed the house. Murmuring, with their eyes half-shut, they thought of the dead.

At the moment of the bell's first stroke, Manoles the pope strode breathlessly into his house. From early morning he had been busy visiting all the houses around and blessing them for the first of the month. In each house, after drinking an ouzo, he had snatched up dainties proffered from the dish and stuffed them higgledy-piggledy into the depths of his pocket. Now he was bathed in sweat but in a good mood.

"Hey, wife," he called, clapping his hands.

Contented and well-nourished, toothless and dragging her log-like feet in worn-out slippers, the pope's wife trotted out from the kitchen. In her youth she had been beautiful, a great enchantress. A tiny olivelike wart on her chin had bewitched the pope at that time. Now the little olive had grown fleshy and hairy. But her eyes still sparkled with roguishness and zest for love. She observed her pope's bulging cassock.

"Welcome, old man," she said. "Shall I unpack you?"

The pope raised his hairy hands above his head. "Unpack," he said. "Bring the dish."

71

The pope's wife brought a huge dish and began to empty the inexhaustible pockets, which sagged from the hips about his legs. She worked and worked, heaping the dish with the sweetmeats, sausages, rissoles, cucumbers, almonds, dates, nutcakes, medlars, roast peas, cheese tarts. . . .

"Just listen to that damned Murzoflos, he's deafening me. Hurry up, wife!"

The dish was full. "You're unpacked, old man," said the pope's wife, raising the dish greedily against her chest. "Now run along, for the good of your soul!"

Lightened of his burden the pope stretched his legs and set out for the evening service.

Meanwhile Chrysanthe, Polyxigis' sister, had gone home, thrown her best shawl of Indian cloth over her stout, bowed shoulders and put two small votive offerings, a little bottle of wine and a little bottle of oil, into a basket. At the moment when Pope Manoles, with his cassock still stuffed, was passing by, Miss Chrysanthe stepped over her threshold and started with heavy steps for church. She too had been supple and slim in her youth, but now she was heavy, her eyes were troubled, and long hairs sprouted on her upper lip, chin and cheeks.

"Ai-Menas be good to you, Miss Chrysanthe," said the pope in greeting, casting a greedy look at her basket.

Miss Chrysanthe was gasping under her fat; her feet were swollen and heavy, her seventy-two joints too were clogged up. Her mind swept on ahead. Ai-Menas, she said silently within herself, you see how, every Saturday evening, I bring you your gifts, your wine and your oil. Do me, in your turn, the favor I've asked of you for so many years. Let me die before my brother. He's generous and, if he's still alive, he'll give me a fine funeral. He'll even have the grand lanterns carried before me.

Not long before, the grand lanterns had been brought from Constantinople by the wardens of Saint Menas' church. They were magnificent, hung on chains, silvered, with glass of several colors and black silk cords. They were carried only at rich funerals. The unmarried, friendless Miss Chrysanthe, grown old in toil,

72

had now no other demand to make of life than a funeral with the fine lanterns.

When she was young she had prayed Saint Menas to send her a good husband; he was to be handsome and a hard-working family man. Later, after long hoping and hoping against hope, she had asked the saint to help her brother in his business. During peacetime, when Polyxigis was unemployed, he had opened a shop by the Kanea Gate and had bought wine, oil, grapes, lemons and turnips from the peasants. He then sold them again to the wholesalers—the whole-hoggers, as he called them—and filled his cashbox with Turkish pounds and gold napoleons. "Help my brother's trade, Saint Menas, to go well," she had then prayed. "For the service I'm asking of you, you shall never lack gifts: candles, wine and oil—all that a saint needs. Let us also have plenty to eat. Plentiful, good food, you know, is as good as a husband and children: a great consolation for mortals. It's all very well for Ali Aga to say, 'I won't get stout and lay up fat for the worms.' Ah! my poor Ali Aga, that servant of God, fasts because he's got nothing to eat."

She had sacrificed her whole life for her sturdy brother. For him she washed, sewed, scrubbed, cooked and yearned. What a vigorous man, what a real master he is! she used to think. No one would think of calling him a good-for-nothing. Women are made for men—let him have his fun! She was one with him, they had been born of the same flesh on the same day, and if she was growing into an old hen, that didn't matter at all, if only he stayed young and slim! Yes, I'm happy with him, she thought. Poor me, I sit up for him at night and it gives me something to live for, even if I do sleep all alone.

Every time he came home at dawn from his gadding, Miss Chrysanthe gladly started up out of her sleep, pulled off his boots for him, warmed water for him to wash in and made him a cup of coffee, very bitter, to refresh him. And when she came near him, she sniffed secretly and longingly at his mustache and hair for the heavy fragrance left there by the women.

So even poor Miss Chrysanthe enjoyed love in this world.

But lately, now that she was really aging and her legs were getting more and more swollen, she prayed Saint Menas for only one

73

thing, as every Saturday evening she brought him her present to put him in a favorable mood: to arrange, out of his goodness, for her to die before her brother, that he might hire the grand lanterns for her.

When, at the other end of Megalokastro, at the Kanea Gate, Polyxigis heard the evening bell, he made the sign of the Cross on his silk waistcoat, sketchily and without thinking, in the midst of playing the mandolin. Then he sprang up nimbly to shut his shop.

He was a handsome man, well built and untroubled-looking: a dandy, always dressed like a youth of twenty, in woolen breeches, a knitted silken waistcoat, a broad silk sash and cream gaiters as worn by Turkish and Christian fops alike. The gaiters were slit down the middle from top to bottom and laced with red laces, to give full value to the smart masculine leg.

Polyxigis now put on his big fez, tilted it to one side so that its tassel fell saucily over his left shoulder, and set out on his way, striding from stone to stone, to the good barber Paraskevas.

Every Saturday he had himself shaved. On the way to the barber's shop he would stop frequently to greet friendly shopkeepers. Here and there, too, he cracked a joke, here and there drank a raki, and went on his way with his fez still more to one side and his step still lighter. He enjoyed the sense that his body was so brimming with strength, and all his internal organs going like clockwork. He enjoyed, too, having not a care in his head. He had once read in a pamphlet something that had made a great impression on him: Kanares, the fighter for freedom, was asked one day how he managed to perform so many heroic deeds, and that fisherman and commander of munitions ships had answered: "Children, I always tell myself, Kanares, you've got to die sometime."

Since that day, Captain Polyxigis had worn his fez to one side, and whether it was a war or a party that faced him, he would say: "Polyxigis, you've got to die sometime," and he was always the first to step forward. He had also engaged workmen and had them build for him a roomlike monument of stone and marble in the churchyard. It was an underground vault, with ledges and cushions all around, with a low table in the middle and a cupboard sunk in the wall, where full bottles and raki glasses were always kept. When he was in the mood, Captain Polyxigis would fill a

74

basket with dainties, take a few bold friends with him, and go with them to the monument. There they would set to, seriously drinking and discussing war, women and death.

So now Captain Polyxigis walked along, and two red feathers adorned his temples. First, it was going to be a lovely evening: not a leaf was stirring, from the courtyards came the scent of April roses, the gutters were moist and the earth was fragrant. But this pleasure was not all. Soon Signor Paraskevas would lather him, shave him and anoint his hair with good pomade, and then Polyxigis would emerge from the shop looking like a lad of twenty. Then he would turn into the shadowy alleys to have a look at his boon companions and his wenches.

Captain Polyxigis sighed. "Ah, if there is a God, let Him make a miracle! I want it now! I'm in my prime, now's when I want the miracle! A few years back I was a clown and understood nothing. How was I to understand what women and wine and war meant? A few years more and I shall have shot my bolt. How will I still enjoy the world with no teeth or digestion? I'll go and have a look at the women and talk like the fox about the grapes. . . . Saint George, I think you are the saint who understands me best. I always admire you in the icons, the way you ride there and have a woman sitting behind you. Ai-George, my name-saint, my cousin, help me and have no fear. For I'm stirring my stumps already."

So saying, he pushed his fez over his forehead and turned into Broad Street.

Broad Street was one of the two chief arteries of Megalokastro. It ran from the Kanea Gate on the west as far as the Hospital Gate, where the large square, the Three Vaults, and the pasha's gardens were. There under a group of dusty trees stood a wooden kiosk where, every Friday, a military band played. The other chief artery ran from the New Gate down to the harbor. At their crossing was the main square, the heart of the town. On Broad Street were the cobblers' shops, the glass and china shops, the stores, the Greek coffeehouses and the grocery shops. From the shops, which extended without a break, there came always the sound of loud conversation: shopkeepers, assistants and apprentices joking, chaffing each other, chattering and bursting into laughter. And woe to him if Efendina or any bowlegged, squinting or half-witted creature came by! The cobblers would all bang on their lasts at once, the apprentices would whistle—and where did they find so many bits of lemon peel and rotten tomatoes?

On Saturday evenings love was in the air. Today, as usual, Broad Street was bubbling. The bell for evening service had brought it to tumult pitch. This week, too, was over, God be thanked. Artisans' lads and shop assistants pulled off their aprons and bent down to the gutters to wash their work away. They washed and tidied themselves, twirled their mustaches and brought out the chairs, to sit down. They ordered their coffee the way they liked it, and their narghiles. Soon, too, on her way from the main square, Ruheni the Moorish woman would pass by: a mountain of dark, glowing flesh, with a necklace of thick glass beads—the kind usually worn by horses—around her neck. Her breasts drooped right down to her belly. She always had a friendly laugh and used her eyes roguishly. Her teeth flashed, and on her head she balanced a dish of sesame cakes. And lo and behold, from the direction of Idomeneas' fountain came Tulupanas also, silent and sad as always, with a tray in each hand, the one full of spinach pasties, the other of sesame rings with cinnamon. It was no longer Broad Street. It was a great manor house where the dainties were just being passed around.

For a moment Captain Polyxigis paused and felt proud of the Greek street: the full shops, the plentiful merchandise, the pure air and not a Turk in sight. The Christians were laughing and joking, the bell was ringing. This is Paradise, thought Captain Polyxigis, there's nothing missing, except the flag with the cross on it. But that too will come, we Cretans will bring it about. So he told himself and moved on. He gave greetings right and left and entered the barber's shop.

The shadows were broadening, the muezzin had now climbed the minaret to call the faithful to evening prayer. But before deciding to send his voice up to the sky, he paused for an instant, wound the green cloth around the white cap he wore, and glanced down and around at the world.

"Allah, Allah," he murmured, "try as he may, man will never be able wholly to fill the eyes Thou hast given him, when he looks upon the world."

He leaned out upon the lattice of the minaret and rejoiced over Megalokastro—how it spread below him, many-colored and many-voiced, with its white minarets, with the copper domes of the saints, with the flag of the Prophet, with the pasha's gardens. Overcome with the sweet fullness, he sighed, and said: "Blessedness includes all, all, all! Women are there, and handsome palikars like Nuri. When I see him storm in on his charger I become twenty years old. There are slender youths, too, white as little rolls of bread, who sing in the coffeehouses in the evening, and you feel giddy and don't know where you should go to praise God—to the mosque or to the coffeehouses. And even the stench here, by Mohammed, enchants me. When I go out to the Hospital Gate and take a deep breath and smell the dung cast out by our little Cretan donkeys, my heart becomes a garden and I believe it too is about to be manured. And I wouldn't trade this stench of Megalokastro for all the patchouli in the world. To others it's a stink, but it pleases me!"

He breathed deeply and put his hands over his ears. And suddenly from the depths of his body his voice thundered, deep and pure, bearing all love and prayer in its impetus. What sweetness there was in it, and what might! And how far this voice of the muezzin surpassed all the bells of Murzuflos! Like a lark, it climbed up toward the sun with outstretched beak, struck into the sky and called God. Then it fell suddenly upon Megalokastro. It had drunk its fill of God and was intoxicated.

At the moment when the muezzin was praising Nuri so lovingly, Nuri was returning moodily from his estate. He had gone there to wear himself out. But shame still clung to his face and neck and exposed chest and burned him. His horse was puffing yellowish foam: it too had something wrong with it today, it was weak at the knees and kept stumbling. The sea had a glow and foam and a swell, yet there was not a breath of wind stirring. He crossed the River Jofyro. The first leaves were sprouting on the vines, the almond trees were already in blossom, the fig trees were heavily fragrant.

"Nothing, nothing," groaned Nuri Bey, "nothing can console me. Curse the sea, the trees and the sun!"

Before him stood Captain Michales again, just as when he had stretched his two fingers in the glass. Nuri Bey heard the glass crack, and—Eminé fell on the captain's neck.

"Shame on me!" he said aloud. "The earth ought to open and swallow me. Since you're no longer the best man in the land, what do you still want of life? Anathema upon it!"

He went over the whole of last night in his mind. What a turmoil it had been, what a drunken orgy—so much so that he had lain on his own threshold, dead drunk in muck! Then, he remembered, sleep had overcome him, and in it what a wild shrieking there had been, what a howling! Who had come into his sleep and called? When the Moor had come to him in the morning and washed him, the dream had turned to smoke and vanished. Yet a knife remained stuck in his heart.

Today he had ridden through the Turkish cemetery, where the gravestones with the tortuous lettering and painted stone turbans stood upright like a marble people that had risen from the ground and was striving to get free, to wrench itself away from the monuments and come home to Megalokastro.

Up there in the corner away from the sea and between two cypresses, he tried to make out the grave of his father. As he found it, his temples began to throb. It seemed to him that the marble turban moved and leaned back, just as the blear-eyed Hani Ali had always done when wrath possessed him. The world spun; he was giddy, and the horse stumbled. It blundered against a tomb, and the Bey seized its mane to prevent it from falling. He tugged hard at the reins, and the proud steed reared, trembling. This was the first time it had stumbled, the first time in so many years. A bad omen.

The Bey gave a cry. He wanted to dismount, to kneel at his father's grave, but he was afraid of the dead. Like a flash of lightning it went through him. He remembered now, perfectly clearly, his last night's dream: His father had stood over his pillow, shaggy, dirty and barefoot—he who never deigned to touch the earth with his foot! He raised his long, blackened hand. "How many years already," he roared at his son, "have I been wandering around your damned konak? Since eighteen sixty-six! Twenty-three years! Count them! I fondly believed my son, my only son, would think of me day and night and sharpen the knife to avenge my blood. I glide about your miserable house, but all I hear is

78

laughter and mandolins and song. And you abandon me, to wander in shame up and down the streets and fields! Why do we get sons? That they may avenge our blood. And you've not been ashamed to become blood brother to the brother of my murderer! And you show him your wife without a veil! Damn you, you giaour!"

When Nuri remembered the heavy curse, he was overcome with anger. He wanted to shout: What, old man? Are you trying to go on ordering me about, even from the grave? But the words had stuck in his throat. He dug his heels into the horse. The sun had still not set. He returned by the Kanea Gate and stormed into the Greek quarter.

At the same moment Captain Michales reached the Hospital Gate, at the other end of Megalokastro. He had ridden his mare hard. The sun was just sinking, it still shone on the open fortress gate. From afar he could see the lepers getting up. All day long they lay on each side of the gate in the dust and dung, stretching out their stumps of arms and begging. At sundown their day's work was ended. They stood up and moved off in line, one after the other, toward Meskinia, the lepers' village. They did not look at one another, but hurried forward, not uttering a word. Their cheeks were eaten away, noses and ears were missing; many were blind, some seemed always to be smiling because they had no lips and so showed their teeth. All ran as though the Last Judgment had begun and they had heard the Angel's trumpet, as though they were breaking away from earth and had forgotten some part of their flesh in their haste.

Captain Michales turned his face away. He hated to see illness. Only healthy people ought to live, he thought. What use are these?

He spurred his mare and came through the fortress gate just as the military guard blew the trumpet for sunset and the Turkish flag was hauled down.

3

NIGHT LAY HEAVY and dead upon the town. The air was sultry. Captain Michales slept badly. The damp weight was oppressive. Kastrians, men and women, opened their windows, went out into their yards and unbuttoned their nightshirts to get some air. Several old women scented disaster and sat on their doorsteps, but dared not open their mouths for fear of betraying their thoughts. They were afraid the evil destiny of Megalokastro might overhear them and put into action what, they suspected, was not yet finally decided.

And so they whispered together and tried to keep small talk going—yet their speech kept returning to the secret, unavowed anxiety: "Do you remember the last time? Not a leaf was stirring. . . ." "Be quiet!" "Can't you hear a humming under your feet?" "Be quiet!"

And they bolted themselves inside their souls again and waited for the relief of sunrise.

Veiled in copper-colored shreds of cloud, a darkly wrathful sun came up behind the Lasithi mountains. The minarets caught fire, the sea flushed, Murzuflos rang the trinity of bells. The Greek quarter awoke from its stupor, doors opened, and out stepped the householders, all washed clean, in their Sunday suits and shirts with collars. Husband, wife, behind them the mother-in-law and in front of them the children, the boys with folded white handkerchiefs in their hands, the little girls with ribbons in their hair.

They were on their way—the noble, gray-haired guardians of Megalokastro—to honor the mounted saint, Ai-Menas. They wanted, too, to hear today's sermon by the Metropolitan and to receive nourishment at his hands. Today was Sunday. There was no business, the shops were shut; for this one day the great trader Satan was asleep. People were glad to accept the word of God—it cost nothing, one lost nothing by it. Tomorrow there would again be weights and measures and haggling, and each trying to eat up the other. Six days belong to the Devil and one to God: light the lamps for both, then you'll surely be in favor.

The church twinkled like the starry sky and smelled of candles and incense. It was warm. There was a humming, as in a hive, of angels, saints and human beings. There was not room enough for all the Christians—many were standing in the narthex, others in the aisles. The stout Metropolitan stood by his throne with his gigantic body and snow-white beard, with the golden crosier and the kingly miter, like some terrifying beast from Heaven, come down to earth to haul men home and scare them.

At the gate of the iconostasis, Pope Manoles had taken his place, with solemn countenance and caparisoned in gold, and was intoning the Gospel for the day as Kajabes opened his door to proceed to church with his wife. Their wedding had been last Sunday, and, as custom required, the young couple must for eight days pray in their wedding garments to Saint Menas, protector of the country, and bring him a large cake made with cinnamon, mastic and sugar.

Their little house was near the harbor, just where the Jewish quarter began, in a welter of narrow, winding alleys plagued alike by sultry winds and cutting sea air. Garufalia took her husband by the arm and hung upon him. They walked slowly and proudly, and both greeted with friendliness the newly wedded world. How the myrtle-decked streets shone and gave out sweet scent! How the cliffs smiled! How the world, beyond all hope, had advanced to the married state! Yes, some thorn bushes in one of the garden hedges had brought forth white blossoms. Was this Megalokastro, enslaved by the Turks? Were these the alleys of the poor quarter and the odors of refuse? Was that the Cretan Sea, savage and far from tender toward men? Garufalia stealthily raised her sleepy eyes and gazed at her husband. "God, what is all this talk put out by the popes? Paradise is here, my good man. God, give me no other paradise!"

They had now reached the market place and were about to turn

81

into the street leading to the church. Kajabes turned and looked at his wife. His heart was joyful. Suddenly it seemed to him as if the world was no more, and in the chaos nothing was left except this living creature at his side, warm and perfumed, delightfully swathed in blouse and petticoats and skirts, with lots of buttons and laces, and her mouth fragrant in a sweet, warm, human way. . . . He had been put out, ever since the evening before last, when he had heard that he was bidden to Captain Michales'. He would have had just eight days with his wife. His blood grew hot. He stopped still in the market place. What was the Kastrian Ai-Menas, with his local customs, to him, the wild man from Sfakia? And why should he waste his time in church, instead of going back home as quickly as possible? *We're newly married, God forgive us.* . . . He had only a little time left. Captain Michales, that ferocious beast, was certainly in his cellar already, waiting.

"Shall we not go home, wife, to our little house?" he asked, and his breathing stopped with longing.

The woman blushed scarlet, her eyelids grew heavy. "As you decide, my little Jannis," she murmured, her eyes shut.

They turned back as though someone were after them. Quickly they crossed the market place, passed the plane tree and the pasha's palace, entered the narrow alleys and reached the harbor. Kajabes opened the door with a kick, they went in, bolted the door and flung themselves on the bed.

Meanwhile Captain Michales sat in his cellar, having gone down to it at dawn. On his right stood three casks of wine on two stout boards, on his left, two jugs, one of oil and the other of flour. Suspended in rows above his head were figs, pomegranates, quinces and canary-yellow winter melons with green veins. On the wall hung bundles of potherbs, sage and marjoram. The cellar smelled of wine and quinces. Soon the hot chickens, cuttle-fish and sausages would overlay this smell.

He sat on a high stool and leaned his heavy head, bound tightly in its dark cloth, against the wall. His eyes stared at the low door opposite him and saw nothing. He thought of nothing. He sat without moving. Only from time to time his claw of a hand pressed the edge of the table in front of him and made the wood bend.

His mind was inert and heavy, but his heart was simmering.

82

Life had been kind to him, he lacked nothing; he was a strong, healthy man, with a good wife and a family, and the world took him seriously. His son was like him—he too had no fear of death. As soon as he died his son would step into his footsteps. His son, too, had a birthmark on his neck; thick, bushy eyebrows, also, like his, and eyes, like his, small and pitch black. What the devil was the matter with his heart, then, to make it boil so? He could feel no pleasure, force no smile, bring no joke or friendly word to his lips to relieve him. He was always reserved, taciturn, fierce.

One evening his wife's brother, kindhearted Manolakis the tailor, had come to his house and had said something and laughed. Captain Michales had frowned, and poor Manolakis was as though paralyzed, and soon got up and left.

Then Captain Michales had turned to his son. "He's got no pride," he had said contemptuously, "he laughs!"

When Crete is set free, he sometimes thought, my heart too will be free. When Crete is set free, I shall laugh.

And yet, not long ago, he had had an extremely lifelike dream: Because Crete was set free the bells were ringing; the streets were strewn with myrtle and laurel, a white warship had anchored in the harbor, and the King's son from Athens sprang onto the mole, bowed down and kissed the soil of Crete; and on the mole he himself, Captain Michales, was standing, holding the keys of Megalokastro on a silver platter, to hand them to the King's son. Crete was set free—but his heart was not relieved. "What the devil's the matter with me," he growled angrily in his dream. "What the devil do I lack? I shall come a cropper yet!" His blood came in waves, his brain seemed to grow too large, his eyes became bloodshot. Crete rose and fell within him—it was no longer an island, it was a wild beast gazing out to sea. It was the Gorgon, the sister of Alexander the Great, lamenting and slashing with her fish tail and stirring up the sea. As Captain Michales heard her lament, she again changed her aspect, and a shudder went through his brain. Crete struck root in him like a plane tree and began to feed on his vitals. From its branches there dangled gray-haired, barefoot forefathers; their heads looked bluish and they bit their tongues. A powerful wind moaned. As Captain Michales stretched out his arms to pray to them, all vanished. His mind was empty. There remained only a lantern with red and green glass, and under it Nuri and the lemon raki and the cooked partridge. Suddenly there was a tittering—two Circassian women. . . . Captain Michales leaped up, and struck the wall heavily with his fist so that the house trembled. He raised his eyes to the low doorway and suddenly began to curse furiously because his boon companions were late.

At the moment when Captain Michales was striking the wall with his fist, the boon companions were setting out from the four ends of Megalokastro. The first to get up had been Vendusos the tavern-keeper. He crossed himself, stood in front of the icon-shrine with the ever-burning lamp, and prayed his protectress, the Holy Virgin of the Vineyard, to give him the strength to hold out. He was setting out for the great tournament: eight days it would last, from Sunday to Sunday, and eight nights, and if the Virgin did not help, they would be wasted. Some years ago he had commissioned the monk Nikodemos to make for him a Virgin, not as the painters depict her, like a mother, but as he himself had seen her in a dream: a woman like the grape-pickers in August, mad for men, thick-lipped, with a white Cretan headband around her head, and in her arms, instead of a child, a bunch of grapes. The monk had been unwilling at first. Nothing of the kind existed, he said, there was nothing of the kind in the Scriptures, it would be a sin. She must hold Christ in her arms, not a bunch of grapes. But Vendusos gave him a bottle of raki and several pounds of cod as payment, and the monk was pacified. He crossed himself, took up his brush and painted the Holy Mother of the Vine Tendril.

And now Vendusos stood in his stockings, without shoes, before her and entreated her: "My lady of the Vineyard, who protectest taverns and tavern-keepers, I greet thee. I am going, I am going off to Captain Michales' cellar. Thou knowest what that will mean—I need thy help! As thou knowest, I gave money and cod and raki to have thee painted. Help me! Help me to hold out and not to get drunk and not to be sick this time, and make a mess of the walls. And enlighten, O Maiden, that unruly beast of a Captain Michales, so he lets us go quickly. Eight days and eight nights are a lot, Holy Virgin, a lot, really they are!"

He washed and dressed, took down his lyre from before the

icon-shrine, went out into the yard and took leave of his wife Marusio and his two daughters. He bade them come every two days and see what was happening. He left them money to buy their food for the whole week, and told his elder daughter, who, being a schoolteacher, was good at writing, to write down for him on a piece of paper a notice that his tavern would be closed, and this he put in his pocket. He looked around him at the whole house as though he were saying farewell, crossed himself and stepped over the threshold.

First he went to the tavern, pulled out the piece of paper and stuck it on the door so that people might see it: "The proprietor is obliged to be absent for eight days on private business." This satisfied him somewhat, and he hurried off toward Captain Michales' house. He was late. The dragon would make no remark, but would frown, and that was enough.

As he passed the house of his elder brother, the wholesaler, he quickened his pace. He mustn't see me, he thought, he'll suspect where I'm going, and I shall get another scolding. To hell with the old ass! He rubbed his cucumber nose which drooped every month a bit more and was already nearly touching his mouth. "Ah! to hell with him!" he muttered. "He'd like to give me lessons, would he? But the day before yesterday I gave as good as I got! I knew what was the matter with me, damn it, and was pitching and edging along by the walls, when here comes our fat father of a family and sticks his mug out of that damned fine house of his. 'You ruined lyre-player!' he says to me, 'haven't you done yet, always drinking and drinking?' Then I stood up straight as a candle—close to the wall—and opened my little mouth. 'You wholesaler!' I said. 'Haven't you done yet with not drinking and not drinking and not drinking?' One or two people, who were just passing, stopped and laughed loudly. And the old ass—he vanished, he vanished."

Talking to himself, Vendusos went on his way. "It was God's will, since I was born on Good Friday, and my father was a pope, for me too to be made into a pope—even perhaps one day (the Devil has such a lot of legs) into a bishop. But how was I to be kept always at school, how was I to put my neck under the yoke? From the time I was a small child I was always playing the lyre, and the stones listened and danced. Wherever there were fes-

85

tivities and fun, there was I, and there I stayed; I was not to be torn away. Gradually I got used to drinking freely and couldn't live any longer without the whiff of wine. So I started a tavern. And I ordered my own Holy Virgin, who suits me, and no one else in Christendom has one like her. When I call her she comes, and never minds running up and down for all sorts of odd things. When I need her she doesn't leave me in the lurch. She belongs only to me, and I'm not lending her to any silly idiot. Last year that blasphemer Captain Polyxigis wanted her from me, so as to order one like her for himself. But how could I give her to him? 'Would you give me your mare, Captain Polyxigis?' I asked him. 'No—so I won't give you my Virgin either.' "

At this point in his monologue he suddenly ran into Furogatos and Bertodulos by Idomeneas' Fountain. They too were on their way, breathlessly, to the dragon's den. They were all in such a hurry that Vendusos' lyre missed by a hair's breadth being smashed in the collision, and Bertodulos' cloak fell off and his hat almost toppled.

"Hey, Vendusos," cried Furogatos, "why are you running so hard into the lion's jaws? Stop! Let's roll a cigarette to give us courage."

They sat down on the marble steps of the fountain and pulled out their tobacco boxes. Furogatos sat throned and towering in the middle; he had grown stout in his old age. He had a giant's long legs—when they went out to dance, the soil of Crete rejoiced. If he had not had those legs, nobody would have bidden him good day, for you do not bid good day to a man who beats his wife. He had bushy eyebrows and a bristling mustache that stuck straight out, so that he really did look like a furious cat (Furogatos).

He bent affectionately over his comrade Bertodulos and wrapped him again in his cloak. He also arranged his small, stiff, decayed nobleman's hat firmly on his long gray hair.

Bertodulos was a blameless, friendly little old man with a thin, prim mouth, a jutting, freshly shaved chin and two short side whiskers reeking of pomade. He was the first man in Megalokastro, perhaps in the whole of Crete, to defy God and Man—and shave off his mustache. At first the Cretans had supposed that smooth skin natural and were not angry. But when they realized that he shaved, they became furious. It was not possible! He was

86

destroying the order of things! He was mixing up women and men. Some threw stones and lemon peel at him, others, more enlightened, ceased to greet him.

"Such freaks won't do for Cretans!" Barba Jannis shouted at him one day, twirling his mustache. "Here in Crete, Bertodulos, there are two kinds of human being, not three—men and women. We won't have men-women!"

One Sunday, as Bertodulos went past the Three Vaults, elegant, light-stepping and smiling, with his guitar, the drunken Furogatos caught hold of him and tried to pull his breeches off in front of everyone, to see, so he said, whether there was a Bertodulos inside them or a Bertodulina. But one or two sober people came between them, and Furogatos burst into tears. He embraced Bertodulos, clasped him to him, caressed and kissed him. Bertodulos cried out, "You're cracking my ribs! Let me go!" and gave him a powerful kick. Since then the two had been inseparable friends.

It was Bertodulos' fate not to be a Cretan. It was his fate to be from Zante and to be a count. He himself no longer remembered how he had got to Megalokastro among the wild beasts, and how he had there become a teacher of the guitar. His name was not Bertodulos, but Count Mangiavino; but now, because he shivered all through winter and spring, wrapped himself in a thick green cloak or "berta," was shriveled and bowlegged, said odd, comical things, and was easily frightened, the Kastrians called him Bertodulos. The name stuck.

With each year the number of his pupils diminished. What should Kastrians do with a guitar? And those asses' voices of theirs were not suited to the love songs of Zante. Poor Bertodulos went hungry. He would go to the coffeehouses and tell, with touching charm, of his life, of his sometime brilliance, of the distinguished ladies and the serenades and mandolin concerts in Zante. He would take his instrument on his knee and hum some old melody. Then the owner of the coffeehouse would feel ashamed and treat him to a cup of coffee and a biscuit, sometimes with Turkish Delight or sugared orange peel as well; thus the count charmed his hunger away. Sometimes he even obtained permission to wrap the Turkish Delight in a clean piece of paper and take it away with him. He was ashamed to revel in sweetmeats alone, and as he was fond of his gray-haired landlady, a woman old as the hills, he would share them with her. He knew how much the poor thing loved Turkish Delight, because you needed no teeth for that.

He'll do for my cellar, thought Captain Michales one day, as he heard him recount truth and fable in Trialonis' coffeehouse. That day Bertodulos was speaking of Zante, the Flower of the East, which no Turkish foot had ever trodden, where, too, the poet of the Greek spring song had been born. Captain Michales called him over. "Listen, Mr. Bertodulos," he said, "you're a superior person. It's a disgrace to Megalokastro that it can't give you a living. So I'll pay you a monthly salary, and you shan't suffer. But you will come to my cellar every time I send for you."

"With pleasure, sir," answered the count, doffing his hat to the floor. "Thy slave, renowned Captain Michales."

Furogatos wrapped the little old man up like a baby. Bertodulos giggled gratefully, as though he were being tickled.

"Courage, my Bertodulos," said Vendusos. "We're bound straight for a great storm, my poor friend. In that cellar Greek freedom will be born."

"Don't worry, Signor Vendusos. For better, for worse, I've taken my precautions!" he said proudly, and pulled out from his cloak a parcel he was carrying under his arm.

"What have you got there, Signor Bertodulos?" asked Vendusos, fingering the parcel.

"A change of shirt," answered the clean little man, and blushed.

"Eh, that's enough," cried Furogatos, throwing his cigarette end away. "We've had a breather. Now up, children! On into the labyrinth! With God's help, forward!"

All three linked arms, Bertodulos in the middle, and off they went to Captain Michales' door.

Middle-aged, with a thick, fair beard, wild goggle-eyes round as eggs, and with his head swathed in the many windings of a broad, white Turkish turban, which he had also earmarked as his winding sheet and now regularly wrapped around his head, so as always to be ready to enter Paradise in it—such was Efendina. Years ago he had been to Mecca, and ever since those holy, agonizing days, his brain had reeled with their heat, thirst, dirt and God-filled delirium. His mind had been filled with flames and terror. He had returned to Megalokastro and spent all his time in the teke where one of his forebears had become a saint. For a time several Turkish children came, and he taught them to read and write. Sometimes he hit them, sometimes they hit him, until one day young Braima, Nuri's nephew, broke his head for him, and the school came to an end.

The teke was near the church of Ai-Menas—an oblong, flat yard overgrown with cabbages. At the far end were three small dilapidated vaults and in the middle of the courtyard the saint's tomb: the wooden coffin with an upright marble slab topped by a green turban. The gold lettering had been worn away by rain and sun. Around the tomb stood large and small benches where the faithful took their places each Friday, gazed at the saint and talked, smoking narghiles meanwhile and drinking coffee, which the exorcist, Hamidé Mula, Efendina's mother, prepared for them. The turban was hollow inside. The faithful threw small coins into it to secure the saint's help for their affairs in this world and the next. They did not ask for such a variety of things as the Christians did: good food, good women and good courage, in this world as in the other, were enough. So they threw into the turban presents for the saintly intercessor.

Each morning at sunrise Efendina sat down in the courtyard with his legs crossed and placed on his knees a huge Koran. He swayed backward and forward until he was giddy, and then began intoning and howling. If it was cold, he would spring up, stretch out his arms, wag his head as low as his shoulders, dance like a dervish, whistle, spit, and stamp with his feet to get warm. Each noon, when his hunger became acute, he ran madly from one end of the yard to the other, wearing nothing but his turban and his sackcloth pants, puffing like a bellows and dripping with sweat. The neighbors would pass by and watch him through the latticed window which gave on the street. Some would laugh at him, others were sorry for him and called out, "In God's name, Efendina, what's the matter with you?" "I've flames inside me, neighbor," he would answer, without pausing.

Whenever he gave the slip to his mother and got out into the open, the Greek children threw stones at him. Then he would run quickly on, and would try to jump across from one gutter to the other. But he could not. The street appeared to him like a river; he wanted to plunge in but dared not. He drew back trembling, unable to swim.

Captain Michales invited Efendina each time he had a drinking bout in preparation, for he liked to include this Turkish abortion. Efendina received the news with fear and eagerness. He would count the months that passed before Charitos came again to the teke and piped stealthily into his ear: "Greetings from my uncle Captain Michales, and will you, he says, please come to his cellar."

All the year long he yearned for pork, white bread, sausage and wine. But the Prophet would not let him drink wine or eat pork. Nor would he let him look into the eyes of a woman. If ever this did happen, a trembling came over him, and one day, when an impudent young thing teased him and pretended to be in love with him, he fell to the ground and foamed at the mouth. One pleasure only remained to him in life, a sinful but very precious pleasure—Captain Michales' invitation, every six months, to drink wine, to eat pork and fill up his poor frame for the next six months.

"By my faith, Captain Michales, threaten me," he would say to him, "hold a knife to my throat! Shout at me: 'Guzzle pig's flesh, swill wine, or I'll kill you!' Force me, Captain Michales, so I shan't be sinning." And so he would eat and drink and utter every blasphemy that he had bottled up during the past six months, because the Prophet forbade him to relieve himself by saying them.

Also he would betray what he knew about "his neighbor," for so he called Saint Menas. Only a wall divided them, and he could hear him ride forth from his church every night. Then Efendina was frightened, buried his head in his pillow, and in the morning stole the oil from his grandfather's lamp and secretly filled the lamp of the Christian Saint Menas.

Twice eight—sixteen days in the year—Efendina drank and blasphemed in Captain Michales' cellar like a real man. Then his brain worked like clockwork, he carried no flame about in him and could jump across from pavement to pavement without fear. But the good days passed like a flash, and sainthood and martyrdom began again.

All last night he had been unable to sleep for joy. He had got up in the dark, slipped barefoot out into the courtyard, opened the door softly so that his mother might not hear, and darted out. He had kept close to the wall of Ai-Menas', passed the Greek school and reached the mosque of Saint Catherine. There he stopped. A cold sweat dripped from him. Now he must cross to the other pavement, to take the turning toward Captain Michales' house. He put one foot forward, but at once drew it back and began to tremble. That was not a street in front of him, but deep water whirling boulders and balks in its course and raging between the two pavements.

Efendina leaned against the wall, wiped the sweat away and gazed up and down the street. "Will nobody come by, will nobody come by—Turk or Christian, or even a Jew—and have pity on me?"

He waited, breathless. Over there, on the other footpath, the wine, the pork, the sausages. Courage, my heart, jump over!

He began to run, but as he bent forward and saw the street he shrank back and clung to the wall once more.

Above him the minaret of Saint Catherine gleamed brightly. Sunlight was already falling on the steps, and over there Tulupanas' oven was giving out a smell. From Ai-Menas' there sounded sweet, sustained intonings.

"Will no Christian on his way to church pass this way and have mercy on me? Will nobody come by? Is the world deserted? What desert is this? I am lost!"

Suddenly he shuddered and cried, "Hey, Christians, help!"

The door opposite opened—a high, ornate door with a heavy bronze knocker. Mr. Charilaos Liondarakes, the avaricious money-changer, came out—a dwarf with enormous buttocks, a wild beard and short hairy fingers. He had shoes with triple soles, a short coffee-colored overcoat and a walking stick with a silver handle in the form of a lion's head. Mr. Charilaos Liondarakes belonged to an important Venetian family which had become Greek. His ancestors had had a lion on their banner and carved in relief on their palace.

He was on his way to church. He stared at Efendina and began laughing scornfully. He liked to see half-wits, lepers, blind men, beggars, and other unfortunates. It consoled him for his own appearance.

"Efendina," he shouted across, "courage, you poor idiot! Jump!"

"Have you no faith in God, Mr. Charilaos?" the poor man cried. "By the day that's above us, come nearer! Give me your hand, help me to get across! I want to go to Captain Michales', and I can't!"

A girl with full lips and a dark little face came out of the door. Mr. Charilaos was in the habit of making love to her and climbing on a footstool into her bed. One night she had given him a piece of advice: "Swallow a fresh egg, sir, every morning, on an empty stomach! Swallow that, and God will help you!" So the little gnome swallowed an egg to make him strong.

"Sir, you've forgotten your egg! The hen's just laid it," said the experienced baggage, and pressed the egg into his hand.

Mr. Charilaos Liondarakes took out his pocketknife, made a hole in the eggshell at one end, then at the other, threw back his short, obese neck and swallowed.

"Help me, Mr. Charilaos, if you believe in God!" Efendina shrieked again.

The little gnome laughed. "You'll go eating pig's flesh again, my poor fellow, and defiling yourself!" he said, playing with his stick.

"Even if the Devil gets me, I'm going! Poor me, it's the only pleasure I've got in this world. You'll be rewarded; stretch out your stick, Mr. Charilaos, so that I can catch hold."

God had pity on Efendina, for at the corner there appeared a bald old man wearing clogs. He had come from the public garden, where he had filled his bag with wild turnips. Efendina stretched out his arms.

"Dear Ali Aga," he called, "dear Ali Aga, you're a good man, a believing Mussulman! A lot of water lies in front of me, a lot of fire! Help me through it!"

Without saying a word the kindhearted old man took Efendina by the hand and led him slowly and carefully to the other pavement. He turned to him to say something, but thought better of it—what should he say? He tucked the bag under his arm and made off. Allah is merciful, merciful and mighty, he thought. He can turn pork into lamb in your mouth, and wine into water. He does what He wills. Eat and drink, Efendina. And trust in God.

When Efendina arrived panting at Captain Michales' house, all the guests had already descended into the lion's den. Charitos was running to and fro between kitchen and cellar, fetching the dainties. Efendina's nostrils quivered eagerly; he heard glasses clinking below in the earth. A smell of sausages hung in the air. Efendina leaned against the doorpost in order not to faint. In that moment he caught, within him, the voice of the Prophet:

"Efendina Horsedung" (that was how the Prophet addressed him), "will you sell your soul for a morsel of pork? Think of Mecca, of the voice, the desert, the camels, the incense, the black stone on which I mounted for my ascension. Think of your ancestor, who, for so many days and nights up on the minaret without bread, without water, ever fasting, called mankind to prayer. And you should see him now: he sits in the midst of a cave of pilaf; before him flows a river of milk and cream; and on each knee he holds a boy worth seven maidens and often changes boys. You are from a saint's family, do not forget! Efendina Horsedung, in this hour you are going to Hell. But the door is still open. Flee!"

Poor Efendina heard the voice of Mohammed with trembling and glanced now at the street door, now at the little door to the cellar, through which the sausage fragrance came. And as his understanding wavered, Katerina came out into the yard and saw him.

"Are you here, Efendina?" she said. "Go down quickly or there'll be trouble."

"Is the food already down there, Mrs. Katerina?"

"It is. Hurry up."

"It's God's will," muttered Efendina. "God has sent me Mrs. Katerina. I mustn't resist: that would be a great sin. Am I to contend with God? Allah, Allah, I beseech Thee for one grace: let me commit all sins, let me too—poor me—enjoy this world above, and then, half an hour before my death, give me time for repentance! Is half an hour not enough? It is enough. I beseech Thee!"

He gave a leap forward. He pushed open the little door and went down.

On a high stool opposite the door, weighty, frowning, in a cloud of cigarette smoke, sat Captain Michales. His whip hung

93

from a nail above his head. To right and left on two long benches were the four guests: on one side Vendusos and Kajabes, on the other Furogatos and Bertodulos. On the high table the food steamed. The wine sparkled, dark red like blood, in large glasses.

Vendusos had placed his lyre on his knees. He held his ear close to it, and was twisting the pegs and tuning it. Bertodulos, wrapped in his cloak, trembling and happy under the protection of Furogatos, nibbled ceaselessly. Kajabes ate and drank; his thoughts were with his wife.

Captain Michales kept filling and refilling his glass and drinking. The wine gave him not the slightest pleasure. He hated it. Each time he raised his glass to his mouth, his lips resisted and refused. Against his own will he forced the wine into his stomach, to quell the demons within him. Neither woman nor war nor God could overcome them. His demons were afraid of wine alone, and he drank of it freely whenever he felt their rage rising in him. These demons were savage voices; most of them were not human voices, but bestial ones, bellowing inside him as soon as the portcullises below opened, letting ancient images spring forth: a tiger, a wolf, a wild boar, and after them the hairy ancestors out of the caves of Psiloritis.

But now for the first time a new demon announced itself within him. This one did not bellow, did not threaten; it laughed. Its breath did not stink, it smelled sweet. For the first time Captain Michales was afraid, and he kept filling his glass and refilling it and drinking.

When the door swung open and Efendina appeared, he raised his head. Efendina rubbed his hands distractedly, jerked a foot forward, but dared not come down the steps. His words, too, fled in confusion. He wanted to say, "Greetings, Captain," but he could not get it out and merely stuttered.

Captain Michales raised his hand and pointed to a low stool opposite him. "Sit down!"

"What am I to play, Captain Michales?" asked Vendusos, without taking his ear from the lyre.

Furogatos had already stood up. He shoved the benches aside to make room for himself. He was eager to start. His soles had caught fire, they were tickling him. For others wine led to song or joking, or to weeping and slumber. For this long clumsy fellow,

wine led to dancing. He drank, danced and became sober—or
rather, the drinking fit merely changed its form. It became a great
and fruitless effort to give the body wings, to make it the conqueror of unconquerable laws. And Furogatos began drinking
afresh, to win fresh power to soar.

Captain Michales took in each of his five guests in turn with a
circling gaze. Neither song nor dance nor lyre could lighten his
heart today. His gaze rested on Efendina.

"Sir," cried Efendina in alarm, "don't ask me to smile and
utter blasphemies against the Prophet. Threaten me first! Compel me against my will to eat and drink, then I'll have the
courage!"

But Bertodulos, who had eaten and drunk and acquired
strength, chimed in. "Most noble Captain Michales," he began
in his drawling, singsong speech, "to pass the time, may I tell
you a famous old story from Venice? I saw her with my own eyes
on the balcony, and since then my heart has been able to find no
rest. How often have I forgotten the bitternesses of life, because
I bore in my imagination Dysdemona, the nobleman's daughter,
ignominiously murdered.

"Who?" asked Captain Michales, frowning.

"Dysdemona, my respected capitanio, the nobleman's daughter from Venice—haven't you heard of her? A Moor loved her, a
tremendous palikar he was, but he was jealous and he killed her in
the heat of love. He took a handkerchief . . ."

Captain Michales raised his fist, to stop the shameless mouth.
"In my presence," he said, "there will be no talk of women,
Bertodulos."

Bertodulos shriveled, and the Venetian tale remained stuck in
his throat.

"Well?" asked Vendusos, raising in the air the lyre, which had a
pair of bells attached to it.

"Play what the devil you like!" replied Captain Michales and
leaned his head heavily against the wall.

Kajabes emptied his glass and wiped his lips. And Furogatos,
with his eyes fixed on the lyre, had already raised his right foot to
let fly. . . . But he did not. The house shook, the walls cracked.
The quinces, pomegranates and melons piled on the shelves
rolled all over the place and bounced as far as the table.

"Earthquake!" cried Vendusos, and started to run up into the open. Kajabes had already made for the door. His thoughts rushed to the harbor, to a certain poor hut, in search of Garufalia. And Efendina had fallen on his nose on the floor and was twitching.

On the ground above, confusion and running and the shrieks of women were heard.

"In God's name," Furogatos whimpered, "open the door and let us out!"

But Captain Michales grabbed for the whip above his head. "Aren't you ashamed?" he shouted.

"Why should we be ashamed?" Furogatos had the courage to retort. "That's an earthquake, Captain Michales. It's not a human being that you can overcome."

As he said this there rumbled from out of the earth a dull, rolling, long-drawn-out thunder, like the bellowing of a bull, and the bells of Ai-Menas began ringing of their own accord.

"Saint Dionysios, help! I am Count Mangiavino!" cried Bertodulos, and hid his head in his cloak.

Captain Michales swung the whip in the air.

"No one's to stir!" he shouted. "Lift Efendina off the ground. Lean him against the cask."

He whisked the cloak away from Bertodulos.

"An earthquake, Bertodulos, is nothing. Crete is a living thing. It's moving. One day you'll see the way it'll join Greece."

Suddenly he was in a good temper, and he began to talk. He had been a youngster when the great earthquake destroyed half his village. Women and men too were bewildered; they shrieked and cried and were buried in their houses. Only his father, Captain Sefakas, had quietly and without a word braced his hands and arms against the door frame and held his elbows high, until his wife and children and the two pairs of oxen and the gray mare had got through. Then he himself had sprung out in one bound, and the walls had collapsed. Since then Captain Michales had lost the fear of earthquakes. He knew that a proper man could hold them within bounds.

He filled the glasses. They drank, and their hearts returned to their places.

But up above, the women of the neighborhood had rushed out of their houses, buzzing about and screaming. Even Archondula, that stiff, acidulous old maid, had run out into the street with her deaf-and-dumb brother on her arm. She too had mingled with her neighbors and had become one with them. She was chattering and screeching just as though she did not come of an important family.

In the church, at the same moment, the Metropolitan had been preaching. At first he spoke of God. But soon his discourse swooped away, left Heaven in the lurch and sank downward to Crete. The priest stood upright in front of his gilded throne, and his deep voice soared into the cupola, on which was painted the Lord Christ. From the cupola, his voice seemed to gain power. It sank down and boomed about the church. And the Christians pressed close to one another, as though it really were the Lord Christ sending His voice down to them from high up in the dome. Trembling they bowed their heads.

"My children," the old man said, "now comes a great time of fasting, the sufferings of Christ are approaching; fear must dominate Man, and he ought to direct his thoughts only to the blood which was shed upon the Cross. And yet, God forgive me! I speak of the sufferings of Christ, and I am thinking of Crete."

He raised his hands toward the vaulting of the church, where Christ, the rainbow of hope, gleamed, watchful.

"How long, O Lord?" he cried. "How many generations, how many thousands of Cretans have, like me, raised their hands toward Heaven with the cry: 'How long, O Lord, how long?' We are not stones or pieces of wood, O Lord, we are souls. Souls hast Thou given us. We are men and women. How long yet will the blood of Crete flow? The whole sea from the Cretan shore to the Hellespont and to Constantinople is red."

And behold! As the old man, standing upright and gazing up at the cupola, fell silent for a moment as though awaiting an answer, the whole church shook, the lights swayed, and the bells rang without being touched by human hand.

"Earthquake! Earthquake!" the cry arose. The women ran from the women's side of the church and pressed, trampling on one another, to the doors. The Metropolitan stood stiff with terror, motionless. He still gazed at Christ with staring eyes. Murzuflos came running, threw his arms round him, and led him from the throne through a side door into the churchyard.

"My lord," he said to him, giving him a friendly slap on the shoulders, "My lord, don't be afraid. It's an earthquake, it's passing."

"I have sinned, O my God," muttered the Metropolitan, and his eyes filled with tears. "I have sinned! I am guilty. Instead of speaking of Thy sufferings, I spoke of Crete."

Captain Polyxigis was gliding through the Turkish quarter. While the Christians were at their service, he had set out for his walk. Shaved, with plenty of lavender water on his hair, and with his roomy fez cocked on one side, he swaggered along. His boots creaked as they touched the ground, and he felt throughout his body a deep happiness. He was at the height of his strength, like a horse, like a glittering bullock wandering through the fields in spring. His heart, his stomach, his bowels—all his organs were working without friction. Each was fulfilling its duty without quarreling with its neighbor; and all together in obedient and glad community made up Captain Polyxigis.

He murmured to himself: It's really a shame that youth in human beings doesn't last a thousand years! Is God perhaps afraid that we'll take His throne away from Him? Is that why He craftily dismantles us, piece by piece? He pulls out our teeth, screws our knees up stiff, wears out our kidneys, dims our eyes and dribbles slime and spittle out of our noses and mouths. . . . Death doesn't worry me—by my soul, it doesn't worry me. There's something to be said for getting it over once and for all. But I can't do with this way of turning gradually into a caricature . . .

The phrase was still hanging on his lips as the whole of the Turkish quarter began to stagger. Doors flew to pieces. Screams of women and the clattering of clogs rang out in the courtyards. Ruheni, the stately Moorish woman, who was coming round the corner at that moment, shrieked out "God, have mercy!" and the round platter on her head swayed. The sesame cakes rolled in the dirt and horse dung.

Captain Polyxigis braced his legs, so that he would stand firm and not fall. He pressed his hand against the wall, quite close to Nuri's door, as his fate would have it.

"Earthquake!" he muttered, and his face became covered with fine sweat. He could fight against anything—against sickness, against enemies, even against women. But how was he to fight against an earthquake? Captain Polyxigis turned pale. He wheeled round and saw that he was standing in front of Nuri's green door. He could hear high-pitched voices within, and pricked up his ears. He waited: was the earth going to open and swallow up mankind, or was this only a passing terror? All Megalokastro waited, with held breath. Even the dogs, which had begun to howl, stuck their tails between their legs and waited, with their hair standing on end and their necks craning. A dim, yellowish light was spreading, and then an uncanny sound like a piping came from under the ground. Suddenly the houses were again shaken, the minarets reeled like cypresses, and the wall against which Captain Polyxigis was leaning split right down the middle. In Nuri Bey's house there was a crash of glasses, dishes and lamps, as they fell to the ground and smashed.

Suddenly the arched green door flew open, and Eminé Hanum burst out screaming, with her hair down and her feet naked. She fell in a faint in the middle of the street. Behind her the Christian Moorish woman came running, carrying her mistress' small red slippers. She knelt by her and called to her. But Eminé lay on the stones, with her head thrown back, white as wax.

Captain Polyxigis's eyes flashed. "Eminé Hanum," he muttered, and moved away from the wall. He came closer. His pale face suddenly flushed. For a long time he had yearned to see the wild Circassian. And there she lay before him—what did he care for the earthquake?—with her hair down and her feet naked, just as he wished her to be.

Eagerly he bent over her, but the Moorish woman seized him furiously and pushed him away.

"That's Nuri Bey's hanum," she shouted menacingly. "Don't you come near!" Then she pulled hard at her mistress' scarf, to cover her face.

"If I don't give her lavender water to smell, the poor thing will die," said Captain Polyxigis, and he pulled out of his waistcoat pocket a small bottle of perfume which he always carried on him. He opened it and, kneeling, held it to the Circassian's nose.

The earth was now firm again, the heart of Megalokastro was beginning once more to beat in its proper rhythm. The dogs, too, took courage again and barked at the earthquake.

99

The Circassian took a deep breath and opened her eyes. She saw an unknown man bending over her. She gave a cry and with both hands covered her unprotected mouth.

"Go away!" said the Moorish woman to the man, "go away if you value your life. Nuri Bey will be out in a moment."

But Captain Polyxigis was gazing at the Circassian's eyes. How could he decide either to live or to die?

At first the black sparkling eyes were fierce and scornful. But the Circassian slowly softened, as she let the man's tumultuous breathing and provocative smell flow over her. She turned to her maid. "Who is the giaour?"

"Captain Polyxigis," he himself replied. "Thy slave, mistress. Keep the perfume to remember me by."

But the Circassian threw the bottle in his face and stood up. Her eyes were furious again.

"I'm going," said Captain Polyxigis, and sighed. "Don't be angry."

At that the Circassian tittered contemptuously. "Are you afraid?" she asked.

"I? Of whom?"

"Of Nuri Bey."

"You are the one and only person I'm afraid of, my mistress. If you tell me now to kill myself, as truly as I'm a man, I'll kill myself and never come near you again."

But he was scared at his own words and took them back.

"If there's a God in Heaven, I shall come near you one day, Eminé Hanum," he said defiantly, "one day I shall come near you, perish the whole world!"

The Circassian measured him with half-closed, angry eyes, as if she were reckoning up his value, as if she wanted to reckon up his value and buy him. And Captain Polyxigis stood stiffly, with his right hand on his silken sash, and waited.

"My God," said the Circassian at last, slowly covering her face with her scarf, "thinks Greeks are loathsome."

"My God," replied the man, "loves Circassian women and is almighty."

He heard voices and turned. Two Turks were approaching from the corner. Doors were opening. The Moorish woman seized her mistress around the waist and hurried her into the house. The green door slammed behind them.

Captain Polyxigis wanted to leave, but his knees were paralyzed. "I'm lost, I'm lost," he muttered. "It's as if I'd never kissed, never had any fun, never touched a woman."

He looked about him. He felt giddy. The streets were changed, people's faces were changed, Megalokastro undulated beneath his feet like some mottled net for snaring partridges on which houses and minarets and gardens and seas were painted.

He walked forward over the net. Anxiously he went home. As soon as he reached the entrance, his fat, spongy sister fell into his arms and cried, "The earthquake!" With all her quivering mass of flesh she longed to hear a kind word from her brother.

But he pushed her aside and flung his fez onto the divan. The house was too small for him.

Meanwhile the party in the cellar had progressed. At the beginning of the afternoon, Renio had looked stealthily through the peephole, to see in what waters her father's foolish guests were swimming.

Furogatos had taken his boots off—his soles were burning, and he danced alone, thoroughly drunk and possessed. At each big leap his head hit against the ceiling. Blood was already trickling over his ears and neck, but he went happily on with his leaping dance. Efendina had forgotten all shame, and had undone his turban so that his scab showed white. He was leaning against the middle cask. Kajabes was leaning over him, adorning his skull with artichoke leaves. There were still some eggs left in the clay dish, and Vendusos was nerving himself heroically to consume them, shells and all. He coughed, and his eyes filled with tears from the effort of swallowing the shells. Poor Bertodulos had taken up his position in the corner behind the jugs, with his thin legs braced and his cloak thrown back to avoid soiling it, and was now cautiously shoving his finger down his throat to make himself vomit. After each flood he turned to his companions and bowed.

"Excuse me, most noble captains," he kept saying in his sing-song voice, "excuse me."

Renio was delighted to see how all these toadies demeaned

themselves to amuse her father. She looked toward the far end of the cellar for Captain Michales.

With his head thrown back, he was leaning in silence against the wall and staring into emptiness. The wine had not affected him. He was neither drunk nor talking, nor was he gay. Only his upper lip quivered slightly, and between the raven hairs of his mustache his teeth flashed.

Renio smiled. She liked her father. She was proud of his fierceness, his silence, his pride. If I were a man, she thought, I'd be like him. If I take a husband, I want one like him!

The sun sank. Megalokastro forgot that it lived over an abyss, and glowed, rosy and happy, under the farewell beams.

The Three Vaults were full of people. As after a rain the ants come out in swarms into the sun, so men and women came out onto the streets, to see and be seen. They had escaped from a great danger. For a moment the grave had opened under their feet, but it had closed again. God be thanked, they were still alive and could behold the upper world. They came out with their families for a walk. They greeted one another, raising their hats or heartily shaking hands. A sudden love united them this evening. They observed one another tenderly. They gazed, too, at the sea as if they had never seen it before. A honeysuckle creeper had blossomed on the pasha's kiosk in the middle of the square. All stopped and sniffed the air, as though stupefied by so much sweetness.

"What's that, friend?"

"Honeysuckle."

"Lord bless me!"

Tired of walking to and fro, they gradually sat down at the big coffeehouse of Leonidas Babalaros and clapped their hands. Wasplean, barefoot waiters came. People ordered cherry syrup and soda water, lenten pastries and grape tarts. Turkish children with pumpkin pies and jasmine came by. Ruheni too, that gleaming black mare of a Moorish woman, appeared, with her broad drooping breasts and the glass beads round her neck. She had brushed the sesame cakes clear of the horse dung in which they had been thrown by the earthquake, and now wandered, all laughter, up and down, swaying and bending. The setting sun drew gleams from her snow-white teeth and roguish eyes.

"What happiness this is," thought the Kastrians, "what a paradise it is. And there comes Ruheni too, with the sesame cakes!"

While more and more people from the neighborhood streamed together and made the Three Vaults gay with their new clothes, the sun had vanished behind Strumbula, leaving a soft violet glow in which the faces of men and women were transfigured.

What man of Kastro was not sought and found, in his Sunday suit, at the Three Vaults? What woman of Kastro of any consequence did not sit at Leonidas Babalaros', buy pumpkin tarts, push back her glass and gossip about all the world?

There was Tityros with his fiancée Vangelio, and with them Chrysanthe, all combed and powdered and wearing a hat for the occasion of a visit to the Three Vaults with her niece and her new nephew. She glanced stealthily at Vangelio and smiled, relieved. I'm better, she thought, nicer to look at, and I've got something a man can lay hold of. But this poor creature! Skin and bones! Tityros will find no flesh to get a grip on. But what do I want with marrying? I've got my brother, I don't need anybody!

The doctor, too, came in sight, with Marcelle. He was a stout, self-satisfied poseur with a stiff hat from Paris, a stick and black gloves. Poor Marcelle was thickly painted and smeared with powder, to cover up her misery. She had reddened her lips too. The women of Kastro turned mocking looks upon her. *What a mask, my dear, what airs! Serves that doctor-dandy right! Should have got himself fitted out in his own country!*

The sea sank into the dusk, and on its horizon the island of Dia disappeared. A breeze from the shore sighed; it set the women's hair waving and made them shut their fans. A group of Maltese fishermen came by with their concertinas. They wore earrings, and their open shirts showed their broad, hairy chests tanned by the sea and sun. They sang in raucous voices and did not turn to look at the women of Kastro, but pushed on toward the harbor where, stretched out among trawling tackle and fish baskets, the Maltese women were waiting for them.

In the darkness the young men gained courage and began to rove. They approached the girls and caressed them with stealthy glances. Over their faces a warm wind of love flickered. On one side the mountains, on the other the Cretan Sea, and up above a dim sky, glimmering blue. And over every unmarried head there danced with a thousand rogueries the evening star, Venus.

While the men and women of Megalokastro were gathered at the Three Vaults, Captain Michales' son Thrasaki and his three friends were slipping along toward the Pervola. The Pervola was an unfenced, unkempt garden at the end of Megalokastro, full of spindly cactuses and nettles. Thrasaki was carrying a rope coiled round his waist, Mastrapas' son Manolios a cudgel, Krasojorgis' son Andrikos a birch and Furogatos' son Nikolas a whistle.

"If we see her father come out," Nikolas explained, "I'll blow the whistle, and we all run for it."

"Did you say that Pervola's always on the doorstep?" asked Andrikos.

Pervola was their nickname for Paraskevas' daughter; the young rascals called her that because she was stout and lush and always smiling.

"She stands on the doorstep every Sunday with ribbons in her hair," said Thrasaki. "Give me your whistle, Nikolas. I'll whistle when we're to attack her."

He seized Nikolas and took the whistle from him.

"You take the rope," he said. "Aren't I the captain? Well, I must have the whistle. Let go!"

A few wretched houses were scattered about in this out-of-the-way quarter where poor Turks and Armenians lived. The Armenians ground coffee in large stone mortars and then sold it. The Turks were porters and laborers by the day.

The four friends began to move more cautiously. They kept close to the walls, in single file, led by Thrasaki with the whistle. Suddenly he stopped. At the door of her house stood the cheerful, lush Pervola with a red ribbon in her fair hair. She was chewing mastic.

Thrasaki turned to his companions. "Watch out! There she is!" he whispered. "I'll whistle and rush in first. There's nobody coming."

They advanced a little farther. The full-blooming Pervola now towered in front of them, still and enormous. She had her face turned away from them and was watching two cats which were having a noisy fight on the wall above her.

The four boys pressed against the wall and held their breath. Thrasaki glanced up and down the street—not a soul. He clapped the whistle between his lips, blew it, and rushed at the girl. Behind him the other three screeched like cats. Thrasaki caught hold of her on one side, Nikolas on the other, Andrikos by the feet, while Manolios held her mouth to prevent her from crying out. She did not struggle. Gasping laboriously—for she was heavy—the four lifted her up and did not know what to do with her.

"Into the Pervola!" Thrasaki ordered. "Hold her fast, so she doesn't escape us! Come on!"

They stumbled through the broken gate and a few steps beyond. Soon they had no strength left and threw her down on the grass. Then they stood around her and looked at her. The red ribbon had come untied and her hair was falling over her shoulders. Her dress was torn to above the knee. Her plump breasts rose and fell frantically under the revealing bodice. At first the girl had been frightened. Now, when she saw who had made off with her, she began to giggle. Stretched on the grass she looked at the children with half-closed, teasing eyes, and waited.

"What shall we do with her now?" asked Nikolas, examining the outstretched "Pervola" curiously from head to foot and unable to make up his mind.

"Let's spit on her," proposed Manolios.

They all began spitting on her. Yet that did not relieve them. That was nothing. Discouraged, they left off, and stared at her. They must do something else, something else, but what?

"Let's thrash her," said Andrikos, and raised the birch he was holding. They all rushed at her and began beating her with the birch, with the rope, and Nikolas, the strong one, with his fist. Now the girl was frightened and cried out.

"Let's stamp on her," Thrasaki proposed, "to stop her screaming."

"What about the cudgel?" asked Manolios. He took out from his belt the thick cudgel he was carrying.

"That comes later," said Thrasaki.

They jumped on her back and on her stomach, while she rolled on the grass to escape their feet. At length she got up and tried to escape, but they fell on her again and dragged her to the ground.

They were now sweating and tired. Once more they paused and looked at the girl and were at a loss to devise other torments. What else should they do to the girl? They had expected to feel pleasure as they kidnaped and maltreated her. For a whole month they had been thinking over the plan. And now, when they saw the girl lying before them, they got no satisfaction. They gazed at her with hatred.

"We ought to have brought a pocketknife," said Thrasaki, "a knife to stick into her and make her bleed. That's it!"

"Shall I bite her?" suggested Nikolas. "I can tear off a bit of her flesh."

"Yes, let's take turns," said Manolios.

"No, all together!" Thrasaki again ordered.

Nikolas unwound the rope, and they all threw themselves on the girl to tie her up. Manolios also pulled out the cudgel. But they got no further. From the broken gate there came a shrill, furious voice: "You damned ruffians!"

They wheeled round. Signor Paraskevas was standing at the gate of the Pervola, half naked and armed with a broomstick. Saturday-evening haircuts and shaves for so many Cretans had worn him out. Today he had slept all day, to get up strength for the coming week. Never had scissors and razor blades seemed to him so blunt as on this devil's island. . . . Suddenly in his sleep he had heard his daughter's cries. He had jumped up, grabbed for the broomstick and rushed out, clad only in his breeches, into the street.

"You impudent ruffians!" he yelled, making his voice as manly as he could and raising the broomstick. Then he started back; among the four figures he had recognized Captain Michales' son. "Oh, that means trouble," he muttered, "be careful, wretched Paraskevas!" And he contented himself with brandishing the broomstick threateningly in the air.

"Let's go," said Thrasaki. "Follow me."

He turned to Paraskevas. "Hey, Mr. Paraskevas," he said, "keep away from the gate and let us through. And throw away that broomstick!"

"Sorry," said the man from Syra, and he threw the broomstick away.

4

How NEATLY God has arranged things in the world! During six days of the week the hunt for money; the seventh day belongs to God, good food and amusement. Monday broke, the wheel took another turn, and yesterday's mannerly God-fearing Kastrians forgot the earthquake and God and plunged into "give and take" and "eat or be eaten."

The sun rose, the soldiers took the fat keys and opened the three gates to the outer world. From afar the peasants streamed in, shouting, with their laden asses and mules. The Harbor Gate too was thrown open, and down went porters, boatmen and dockers. Over the mole the din of many human beings rose once more. The same din filled men's ears in the market place, while in the neighboring gypsy quarter the smiths' hammers began banging. The crier stood in the middle of the square, and his voice was like a bell. It announced that a calf would now be slaughtered at Ismaili's butchery. Its meat would be as tender as Turkish Delight, and those who came in time could choose the best cuts.

In Broad Street the cobblers' shops were opening, one after another. The masters took their places on their high benches and began to cut the pieces of leather. The assistants and apprentices brought out their stools and their tools and set to work. Meanwhile they kept looking out at the street in case any deformed or half-witted person should come by for them to make fun of. That was the best way of passing the time.

The first to come was Captain Stefanes, leaning on his crooked stick. He had heard that the small ship belonging to his friend

Captain Jakumes had arrived yesterday evening from Smyrna, and he was going down to greet him. He wanted to know what was happening over there in Greece, what the King was doing and what people were saying about the Union. In Syra there was the Cretan Committee, which thought of Crete day and night. It was collecting money, buying muskets and cartridges and waiting. If there was no progress, so they said, Crete would revolt again. So Captain Stefanes hobbled along to embrace his friend and to learn from him in a tavern something of what was happening in the world.

One of the cobblers' boys whistled—it was the sign. All looked up and stared out. But immediately they turned aside, furtive and embarrassed. Were they to get across that dogfish who, the day before yesterday, had given a cruel beating to an apprentice who had laughed at him? "You young louse," he had bellowed, "would you snigger at me? Do you know, idiot, where I got this limp— where, when and how? Very well then, find out, you snot-nose!" and struck at him with his stick. The master had not defended his apprentice. On the contrary he had even said, "You're quite right, Captain Stefanes. You are Crete's Miaulis*. Hit him again!"

So the cobblers' boys kept their heads down, made not a sound, and let Captain Stefanes pass by.

"That's a hard nut, children, by all that's holy," said one of the journeymen, when the captain had gone out of sight in the direction of the harbor. "A hard nut to crack!"

While he was still speaking Mr. Charilaos appeared—that bow-legged dwarf with his slender stick, his little twirled and waxed mustache and his triple soles. He swaggered past the shoe shops, striking the pavement with his stick. The masters raised their hands to their chests to wish him good day.

Every time the Kastrians saw Mr. Charilaos pass by they felt respect and dread, as though he were not a human being, but something between human and demon. The children would stop dead and stare at him in terror. He was a guardian of treasure, who kept gold hidden underground. He had command over dark forces. He had the evil eye, and if he looked at you for any length of time your skin might become green and swell as though a snake had bitten you. The story went that one day in Archondula's gar-

* A Greek pirate hero (*Tr.*)

den he had stared at a blossoming lemon tree, and the blossoms had at once faded.

So the cobblers bowed their heads in silence and let him pass by.

"A bad beginning to the day, children! Nothing to laugh at to-day!" said the one who had spoken before. "Where's Efendina got to? Where's Barba Jannis? Are they dead?"

"Talk of the devil!" cried a journeyman from a shop opposite. "Here is Barba Jannis!"

They all leaned forward contentedly to watch him. Crying out his sherbet with a hoarse croaking, carrying the bronze can in his right hand and in his left the little basket with the snow in it, Barba Jannis approached, hideous with his pointed head. Everyone at once got into position. The intention was to bellow and catcall systematically to drown Barba Jannis' voice. Then they would pelt him with lemon peel, and make fun of him into the bargain. One of them would ask, "Hey, little wife, are all the children in my house mine? Tell me the truth. Think! I'm dying, dear wife." And another from the opposite side of the road would answer in a high-pitched voice, "And suppose you don't die, Barba Jannis?" And the whole of Broad Street would shake with laughter.

But now the journeyman stood up so that all should hear him, and called out. "Children, this time we'll play him a new trick. We won't make a sound, and when he goes past we'll act as if we don't see him at all. That'll send him quite mad. That'll be real fun!"

Now at last Barba Jannis reached them. He looked to right and left at the shoe shops, stopped still for a moment and waited— What's going on here? Lord, have mercy! Does nobody raise his head to look at him? Does nobody open his mouth to yell at him? Has he sunk so low? Is it all the same whether a dog or an ass or Barba Jannis passes by? Why don't you make a noise, children? What's become of the lemon peel? I am, after all, Barba Jannis. . . .

Silence. Bent over their leather without a word, they all hammered away, dyed laces, threaded needles, sewed. Barba Jannis trembled. He rubbed his eyes. Was he dreaming? He put his can and snow-basket down on the ground.

"In God's name," he shouted, "say something, children! You're driving me mad! No, no, I can't bear it. Where's the lemon peel?"

But no one looked up; no voice was heard. Barba Jannis again implored them. "Have pity on me, children! I'm a dying man, and you don't spare me a look! Indeed, am I still alive? Or am I already dead? Say just one word!"

Nothing. The stillness of death. Barba Jannis was seized with dread. "Magic!" he muttered. "The world's coming to an end, death is upon us! Either the cobblers are dead, or I am." With a cry of "Help, feet!" he clutched violently at his can and basket and banged them against his feet.

And now Broad Street shook with roars of laughter.

It could be heard as far as the Bishop's Residence. The Metropolitan rose from his bed, where he lay with a cold. Murzuflos had just taken away the cupping glass and was now rubbing him with raki.

"What can that row be?" he asked, pricking up his ears. "Is there a storm approaching, or is it another earthquake?"

"It must be the cobblers, my lord. They're having their fun with some poor unfortunate," answered Murzuflos angrily. "They're a shameful lot! The world's going to the dogs, but they will bawl away. Curse them, they've interrupted our conversation, most reverend Bishop."

The Metropolitan had been telling him about Russia—about Kiev, where he had been archimandrite for many years, about the snowstorms, the golden cupolas on top of the churches and the subterranean monasteries filled with saints.

"As long as Russia survives," he said, "have no fear, Murzuflos: the true Faith will live forever and reign. That is where Christ has now taken refuge. That is where I once saw Him with my own eyes, Murzuflos, in the depth of winter, at evening. He was striding through the snow. He wore a long leather coat and high boots and thick gloves. He kept knocking at the doors, but no one would let Him in. I saw Him through the window and dashed downstairs to open to Him. 'O my Christ,' I cried, but He had vanished."

Murzuflos made the sign of the Cross.

"I have never seen Him," he said dolefully.

"Go to Russia and you will see Him," answered the Metropolitan, and turned his face to the wall and dozed off.

The pasha too had waked up in a bad mood this morning, for he was not feeling well these days. Out of a clear sky there had suddenly descended on him the feeling that he was growing old.

The day before yesterday, near the Three Vaults, as he was smoking his long pipe in the Pasha Kiosk and the soldiers were blowing their trumpets and beating their drums, he had noticed among the crowd of Greeks who were streaming idly past the band a girl with luxuriant hair and a voluptuous mouth, who delighted him. He had turned to his groom, the Arab, Suleiman, and asked: "Fellow, who's the Greek girl over there in the red dress?"

"Does she please you, Pasha Effendi? She's no Kastrian. She comes from Kruson, the savage village. Last Sunday she married the grocer Kajabes, who's such a good singer—you've heard him. In the devil's name, let her go!"

"Is she a respectable woman? May she perish if she is!"

"Very respectable, Pasha Effendi, very respectable. And her husband's from Sfakia."

"A respectable woman, a respectable woman," muttered the pasha, wagging his bald head. "She's respectable because I'm growing old. It's coming to an end. What do you expect of life, when you can't misbehave any more, when you can't do away with a man when you want to, or kiss any woman you want to? What sort of a pasha am I? This damned growing old! Ah, what a time I had in other Greek places! I used to send my executioner along with an apple wrapped in a cloth for the bride and a bullet for the bridegroom. I would tell them that they must choose. How could they be expected to choose the bullet? They always chose the apple, and that same evening the bride would come, all tearstained and dolled up, and would struggle as I like women to do, and then sit on my knee. But now I've grown old. The State, too, has grown old. And it's the fault of this damned Crete!"

He turned to the Arab. "What about it, Suleiman?" and winked at him.

"Act as if you'd never seen her, Pasha Effendi. This is Crete. Here we shall have trouble. Don't sigh. Shall I fetch the Armenian girl?"

The Armenian girl, Marusia, was famous in Crete. She had
even been celebrated in a song. Her husband was an uncouth
broad-boned Armenian, whose shop was situated in the main
square. There he stood all day, bent over the deep stone mortar,
and pounded the coffee, whose smell spread all around. From the
constant pounding his arm had become as thick as a thigh, so that
with the heavy pestle he could break through a wall. His wife, a
small Armenian witch, looked from behind as if she consisted
merely of two half-spheres, which wagged as she went. Late in the
evening the youths would slip out to her hut near the Pervola. It
was as though they caught her scent, as sensual as a beast's. She
would stand on the doorstep, quietly, her eyes almost closed, with
her bodice half undone, her cheeks thickly powdered and her delicate little mustache damp with sweat. And late at night, when her
husband was asleep, she would open her own shop and sell love by
weight, while in the next room the Armenian snored. She left the
bedroom door open on purpose, for it enchanted her, at the moment when strangers—Turks, Christians, Armenians, Jews—were
embracing her, to feel her husband close by and to shudder with
fear.

Every time the pasha was depressed, every time the vizier repri-
manded him, the Arab brought him this Armenian woman, and
the bad mood passed.

"Wouldn't you like me to fetch the Armenian woman?" Suleiman asked again.

"Fellow, I don't want any women," roared the pasha, and spat
with disgust. "The hypocrites, they are as bad as priests; they
make me sick. For sixteen—seventeen years I've done nothing else.
Now I'm sighing because I've grown old and Turkey's grown old.
We're both of us going to the devil. . . . What's the name of that
one, anyhow?"

"Garufalia."

"May her dead body rot! Tell Barba Jannis the salepi vendor
to come to me in the konak this evening and amuse me. My heart
is very heavy, my dear Suleiman. Efendina's to come too."

He knocked out his pipe against a stone. "She loves me, she
loves me not," he murmured softly, that the Arab might not overhear. "Allah make me a liar, but I believe Turkey too has reached

the stage of saying 'she loves me not'. . . . Fill my pipe, light it, and don't speak to me!" he said to the Arab.

A horseman came by: fierce, with a black beard, his forehead hidden by a headband. He struck his mare with a whip, galloped past like a flash and disappeared through the Hospital Gate into the fields.

"Who was that giaour, Arab?" asked the pasha with surprise. "He often plays the hero, it seems to me. Where have we seen him before?"

Fascinated, the Arab stared after the horseman, who was now circling the fortifications.

"Where do you keep your wits, blockhead?" asked the pasha, flourishing his pipe. "Didn't you hear my question?"

"Who was it, Pasha Effendi? Don't you remember summoning him to the konak last year and dressing him down for having made a fool of Nuri Bey? He never opened his mouth to apologize, and as he went he caught hold of the stair rail and nearly wrenched it out."

"Captain Michales!" said the pasha. He fell into thoughtful silence for a moment. Then he went on: "Listen, Suleiman. One day I shall stand you up by the Three Vaults in front of all the people, Turks and Greeks, and let you fight with him and strike him down. Then we'll be rid of him. . . . Are you listening?"

The Arab looked out toward the sea. The whites of his eyes were yellow, with a network of red arteries. He did not answer.

The pasha had made a sign. The trumpets stopped. He got up to go and turned once more to his groom: "If you're afraid of the giaour, Arab, then we're lost. You mark my words!"

He had said no more. But for three days now his mind had dwelt on the woman in the red skirt and on the chicken heart of Turkey. And today—Monday morning—he had waked up full of agitation. He had had a bad dream. In the middle of the market place two raging beasts were fighting: Captain Michales and Suleiman the Arab. Both were naked and anointed with grease. Each had in his hand nothing but an ax. The whole of Megalokastro was gathered around them: on the sunny side the Christians, on the other, in shadow, the Turks. They were standing and looking on. No one spoke; all watched with pale faces and open mouths.

He himself was squatting under a red canopy. His heart was shuddering like a reed. *If Captain Michales wins, Turkey falls. But if Suleiman the Arab wins, Christendom falls.*

The two fought and roared. The earth trembled under their tread and the hollows in the ground filled with blood. The sun went down. Turks and Christians were lost in the darkness, and now the pasha could only make out the two wild beasts as they roared and staggered and rose again, with the strips of flesh hewn by the axes hanging from their bodies. Suddenly the pasha despaired. "Allah, Allah," he murmured, "it's only a dream. I'm going to give a cry, to wake up and not see the end."

He cried out and woke up. And now he sat, depressed and sunk in thought, on his wide bed with its horsehair stuffing. He clapped his hands, and Suleiman appeared.

"Go and fetch Captain Michales!" he said.

He did not know what he wanted with him. But he must come! Perhaps some insolent word will escape him, he thought, so that I shall get angry and make up my mind! He's not to indulge in any insolence in my realm. I am the pasha! And he goes riding out on his mare when I'm listening to the soldiers' music!

"Captain Michales?" asked the Arab, scratching his head. "But I hear, Pasha Effendi, that he's gone down into his cellar with his idiotic drinking companions and there he's drinking. . . ."

"And suppose he is drinking! Have him get sober and come here!"

The Arab still hesitated. He lowered his voice: "Pasha Effendi, do you want to drown Crete in blood? Have you had orders from Constantinople?"

The pasha put both hands to his bald head. He felt giddy. "What's that?" he asked.

"Well, suppose he says to me: 'I won't come.' What do you propose to do with him then? Are you going to send soldiers after him, and have him give them a beating? He's no man, especially when he's drinking—he's like an earthquake. When he was drunk last year, didn't he seize hold of the Harbor Gate, to pull it down? . . . And if, after all, you arrange things so cleverly that he gets killed, then the whole of Crete catches fire! Leave him alone and let him go to the devil, Pasha Effendi."

"Let him go to the devil because he's a palikar, and let her go to the devil because she's a respectable woman—yes, what sort of pasha am I?"

He pondered this way and that: If the wretched island catches fire again and fresh soldiers come from Anatolia, with guns and gallows and fresh pashas, the Franks will again mix themselves up in it—curse them too! And it won't do me any good—I shall simply have more trouble.

"Quick, bring me a pot of cream and sugar, and fill me my pipe, you Arab scoundrel," he said at last, tugging angrily at his mustache.

"And Captain Michales?"

"May the devil take him!"

While the pasha was talking of him, Captain Michales was observing the coming of daylight through the small window of the cellar. His headband had fallen on his shoulders. His forehead gleamed like bronze in the light, and the hair of his head and beard glittered. His round, deep black eyes were motionless, gazing at the window. All night he had not slept, but had watched, listened and drunk. Each time his heart had tried to calm itself, he had given a fierce, hot cry that made it contract again. What the devil do I want? he asked himself again and again. The wine I pour down is wasted: robbing Peter to pay Paul.

He was not drunk. It was his secret pride that wine could never bring him down. From time to time he stood up, paced up and down the cellar and again sat down. He despised the wine-bibbers who reeled about the place, stuttered, made much of their unwashed thoughts or set up a howling. At one moment he turned to Bertodulos. "Who was that she-demon you were talking about?" he asked, suddenly.

"Dysdemona, Captain. A prince's daughter in Venice. Her hair was honey-fair and wound in plaits three times round her head, like a royal crown. She had a little olive birthmark, too, on her cheek. . . ."

"Go on!"

". . . And so, Captain, not to beat about the bush, this delicately bred prince's daughter—what a thing it is, the human soul! —fell in love with a Moor, a powerful fellow with giant limbs! But, to give the devil his due, a doughty palikar! And how do you think it came about that she fell in love with him? One night the great big rascal sat down beside her and told her about his life, like a book. And the girl was so stirred, she was filled with such a strong sympathy for what he had suffered, that she began crying and fell on his neck. 'Ah, dear Moor,' she said to him, 'don't be sad. I will console you. I will bring a smile to your lips.' "

Bertodulos drew breath, emptied his glass and sighed.

"Go on," ordered Captain Michales again.

"I'm sorry, Captain, my head's gone blank," said Bertodulos, scratching his pointed skull to bring the memory back. "Remarkable things happened," he said at last. "They didn't stay in Venice, they journeyed to Cyprus. They got married, I think, and a white officer with gold stripes got mixed up in it. And later. . . . I've forgotten again. It had to do with a handkerchief."

"A handkerchief? Now you're making it up, Bertodulos."

"No, no, I'm not making it up, my lord. A handkerchief, a handkerchief really. But it was properly poisoned, bewitched—how should I know? And the Moor became furious with jealousy, and one night—ah, that night brings it all back to me—he stuffed the handkerchief into Dysdemona's mouth and . . ."

A sobbing took hold of him, he pulled his scarf off, wiped his eyes and forehead and gave a loud cry:

". . . and he throttled her!"

The four drunken men, who had been craning their necks from all sides to listen, burst out laughing. But Captain Michales angrily shouted, "Quiet!" Then he turned to Bertodulos. "It's not your fault. It was my fault for asking."

He leaned his head heavily against the wall and closed his eyes. The Moor was right, he was thinking, he acted properly.

Meanwhile those around him had forgotten strangers' sorrows. "Don't cry, my little Bertodulos," said Furogatos. "Those are all fairy tales. Only we are real. Here, Vendusos, play your lyre, my legs are twitching, I want to dance."

The lyre with the bells on it was itself drunk and it sprang onto Vendusos' knees like a living woman, a newly wedded one; Kajabes looked at her with a sigh, leaned his utterly fuddled head on his hand and began a long-drawn-out intoning.

And Efendina, with his scabby head wreathed in artichoke leaves and his belly swollen with wine and pork, clapped his hands and sat up straight as a candle. Suddenly he jumped to his feet, flung his arms round Furogatos' shoulders, and danced like a madman—to the devil with sainthood!

"Turn Christian, Efendina," Furogatos implored him, "turn Christian, and come to Paradise riding on a pig!"

"I can't, friends," he replied sadly. "I can't, and you must forgive me. Turk I was born, Turk I shall die."

The eggs had already been eaten, shells and all. Now Captain Michales with a blow from his fist, smashed the pottery eggcups and distributed them to his guests to eat. Bertodulos, terrified, took his piece and clung breathless to a cask. With goggling eyes he watched the Cretans at his feet bite their bits of clay and chew them until they became sand and grit, which they swallowed with a snigger.

There are three sorts of men, Bertodulos slowly explained to himself: those who eat eggs without the shells, those who eat eggs with the shells and those who gobble them up with the shells and the eggcups as well. The third kind are called Cretans. Oh, oh, Count Mangiavino, what has brought you here? he asked himself, and glanced toward the door.

By dawn they had all laid down their arms. Some sprawled on the floor, snoring, some leaned with their heads against the casks and strained, groaning, to vomit. Bertodulos, who had already done his vomiting, found some water and washed. Then he hid his head in his cloak, which he wrapped twice round him, and stretched himself out in a corner. He lay there like a soaked hen with its feathers all over the place. Only Captain Michales, full of drink but unaffected, held his head high and stared through the little window at the breaking day.

As the light entered the cellar and lit up debris of food and pools of wine and vomit, Captain Michales turned and gazed at the five beaten nincompoops as though he saw them for the first time. And suddenly his heart gave a start of scorn. He pricked up his ears. He could hear his wife in the yard—she was up already, drawing water from the well. He could hear the cocks of the neighborhood crowing. The noise of humans and animals awakening rose from the face of the earth. From afar the unending roar of the sea surrounded him. The mare whinnied in the yard. It was time for Charitos to bring her her bucket of cold water and her fodder. The whinny mounted into the air as fresh as dew, it spurted like spring water. Captain Michales' soul was refreshed by it.

"I'm beginning to think," he muttered, "that I can only be friends with horses. Human beings seem to me to be nothing but pitiful idiots. Yes, if Crete had wolves and boars. . . ."

He stood up, and stretched himself till his bones cracked. He gave each of his companions a kick and threw wine from a jug over them.

"Forward!" he shouted. "Get up! To work!"

All through the new day and the following night the carousing went on. The whip whistled when anyone tried to slack. Charitos ran up and down the stairs with dainties. Like brothers, Efendina and Bertodulos crammed each other full. In their mutual tenderness they marveled that they had lived so many years in the same town and only now had got to know and love each other.

"I'll teach you to play the guitar," said Bertodulos, "and then you'll forget your worries. Then you'll play and you'll cross the streets without turning a hair."

"And I'll teach you," replied Efendina, "how to carry flames about with you, Bertodulos my dear, and you'll cool yourself at them."

The count had got used to the Cretan atmosphere. It made him happy to love and embrace them all. Only before Captain Michales he remained shy. He, the witty gentleman of Zante, would have liked to crack a joke with the captain, but at the last moment the story would not pass his lips.

He turned to Vendusos. "We two, Signor Vendusos—have you ever realized?—we two aren't men, we're artists."

"Artists? What the devil's that?"

"A sort of angel. Well, not exactly. There's a little something lacking. Look here: there are animals—asses, mules—and there are human beings. And then, above them, there are the artists, and higher still the angels. We two, my dear Vendusos, are artists."

"And so—?"

"And so, if you die a peaceful death, don't forget to take your lyre into the grave with you, as I'm taking my guitar. Yes, let's die together, Vendusos, my little Vendusos! The angels too play

lyres and guitars, and at the gate of Paradise we'll give the great
Maestro, whom the unmusical call God, a concert. I'll sing canzone and you'll sing Cretan mantinades, until the great Maestro
comes out to clash the cymbals for us and admit us into His immortal choir."

Vendusos laughed. "You've said a mouthful, my little Bertodulos," he said. "How do you propose that you should play the
guitar, and I the lyre, without hands, without fingers? Have you
seen what becomes of hands and fingers in the earth?"

"Be quiet, you wretch! You're making my hair stand on end!"
cried the count, and wrapped himself tighter in his cloak. "Do
you mean that even the hands that play guitars . . . ?"

"All, all, my friend in misfortune, all!"

"Well, let's get drunk, while we've still got hands and throats!"
shouted Furogatos, filling the glasses. "And women, Vendusos? Do
they too turn . . . ?"

"All of them, all. . . ."

"Even if they're beautiful like the sun?"

"Even then. But what's up with Captain Michales?"

Captain Michales was frowning. "Better let your hands do the
talking, Vendusos. And you your feet, Furogatos. Your tongues
should keep quiet."

"At your orders, Captain Michales."

Furogatos jumped up. What more could he ask for? Vendusos
placed the lyre on his right knee, Kajabes raised his hand to his
cheek, and dance and song began again. Outside, the day was enveloped in the fire of the sun, but the life of the boon companions
played itself out in that cellar. Noon came and went. The sun
sank, night took possession once more. In the middle of the table
and on the casks the fat candles burned. At the next daybreak there
the men lay again on the floor like abortions, exhausted, saffron
yellow. Corners and walls were again bespattered, and their clothes
were a mass of wine and grease spots. A stench rose from their
mouths and hair.

Motionless, Captain Michales watched over them. At last he
turned his face to the little window, not to have to look at them
any longer. He was thinking of nothing, he was only feeling, as
he had been now for two days and two nights, how his entrails

wavered and no longer found firm ground. As he sat thus with his head leaning against the wall, sleep like a flash surprised him—a flash, no longer than that. But long enough for the demon to master him.

At first it seemed to Captain Michales that he was walking into a cool, vernal cloud. Still dazed from the heat, wine and suffering, he wandered into it, and the cloud embraced him, held him under the arms and raised him, and from below caressed his body and thighs. But slowly the cloud changed, thickened, became a face. First there emerged two feminine lips, then the twinkle of two wild, shameless eyes, full of mockery and disdain. And last, two tiny feet with red-stained soles and two snow-white hands. The lips moved and a voice rushed forth like gurgling water: "Captain Michales, Captain Michales!"

Captain Michales wrenched himself out of the dream with such a jerk that the table capsized, and everything on it—glasses, plates, candles, tobacco boxes—rolled all over the room. The five sleepers sprang up. Daylight had reached the cellar. They looked about them and gazed at Captain Michales, who had grabbed the whip from the wall and now made a rush at them.

"Get out! Get out!" he shouted, as though possessed. "Get out!" He wrenched the door open. "Get out!"

Kajabes was first: he sprang over the threshold with one bound and ran across the yard to the street door. He was soon outside. Only the third morning! Garufalia was surely still asleep. His feet acquired wings and he ran to the harbor. The other four tottered out of the cellar one after the other, clinging to the walls. As they came into the daylight, their faces showed greenish yellow, sunken, smeared and begrimed. Half tipsy still, they stared across the yard at the well, the vine trellis, the street door, and could not think where to go. Furogatos, his mustache drooping, went first, making efforts meanwhile to get his belt straight. But the belt kept escaping him and sliding to the ground, so that Vendusos, who was following him with his lyre on his shoulder, tripped over it. Behind Vendusos came Efendina, one hand holding up his sackcloth breeches whose cord had broken, while with the other he attempted confusedly to hold his companions back.

"Stop, you fools! Where are you off to? The captain's only joking. He'll soon call us back. Just count, if you've any faith in

God: Tuesday, Wednesday, Thursday, Friday, Saturday, Sunday —six days still to go!"

It seemed to him unjust that they should be dismissed so quickly, just as one had begun to sink up to the neck in sin. Sins only began to bring real satisfaction when one was well and truly up to the neck in them. Then one began to have something to repent. Sin should be a mountain of pork to be mastered, a lake of wine in which to swim—not just a titbit!

He kept counting the days on his fingers, over and over: Tuesday, Wednesday, Thursday, Friday, Saturday, Sunday—a pity so many days should be lost. "No, it won't do, Captain Michales. Don't do us this injustice. Call us back!"

A hand touched him. Surely it was Captain Michales. He turned joyfully. Bertodulos had plucked him by the shoulder. He was whimpering and reeling.

"Efendina, my dear," he said. "I've left my purse behind. Would you go and get it for me?"

Furogatos had reached the street door. His belt still kept slipping down and trailing behind him. His hands and feet were heavy, as though paralyzed, and they refused to serve him.

"I'll get my wife to give my arms and legs a rubbing," he said. "Good-by, friends. We've got off lightly!"

"Where are you going? Don't leave me alone, Furogatos!" screamed Bertodulos. "Wait for me!"

"Come, little Bertodulos, you support me and I'll support you," said Furogatos, putting his arm round him.

The Maestro clung to the dangling belt. "I've left my purse behind," he said imploringly. But Furogatos pretended not to hear.

The sun was now reaching into the alleys. The voice of Barba Jannis could be heard, crying, "Salepi!" The peasants were shouting, "Logs, good logs!" as they drove their laden asses. Now the two approached Tulupanas' bakery. Two trays, covered with sesame rolls, were steaming in front of the oven.

Bertodulos looked at the sesame rolls and stopped dead. Furogatos stuck his hand into his waistcoat pocket and pulled out a small coin. He took a roll. "Eat," he said to his companion. "I don't want any myself." He had thought of the lepers, and felt sick.

With his head scratched bloody by the artichoke leaves, Efendina meanwhile was creeping back to the teke, stealthily, so that his mother should not see him and beat him.

Vendusos went home with his lyre over his shoulder, still out of breath and yellow in the face. His wife ran to meet him and supported him under the arms. His two daughters also came to his help and the three of them laid him on the settle. They rubbed him with oil from the lamp of the Holy Mother of the Grapes. They swung luck-bringing incense over him. They piled on him all the rugs they possessed, for he was shivering. Finally they ran to their neighbor, old Flamburiarena, and asked her to come and cup him.

Captain Michales had meanwhile saddled his mare and stuck his black-hilted knife into his belt. His wife came out into the yard to ask him where he was going and to remind him of the affairs of his house. But when he turned and she saw his face, her voice failed her.

"What do you want?" he asked hoarsely and angrily.

"Should I make you some coffee?" his wife asked.

"I'm going to the coffeehouse, I'll have some there. Get in."

Alarmed, Katerina went back into the kitchen. Renio had lighted the fire and made coffee.

"He's going," said her mother. "He's saddled the mare and is going to ride through the Turkish quarter. He's a wild beast, he is, a wild beast. He has no feelings."

Renio laughed. "He's going to ride into the Turkish coffee-houses again," she said proudly.

Both were silent as they listened. They heard the mare trample over the threshold, then whinny in the street outside. "May God hold His hand over him," murmured the mother, crossing herself.

"Did you see the way the fools ran for it?" asked Renio, laughing. "I was looking out of the window upstairs. One after the other, screaming and reeling. And Father standing there, sober and scornful with his whip raised, brandishing it in the air. Why are you sighing, Mother? Would you like to have Bertodulos or Vendusos as your husband? You ought to be rejoicing over your luck, Mother!"

"It's possible to be a decent husband and a good earner without needing to behave like a fool."

122

"Yes, it's possible," Renio answered, pouting. "But I don't like either earners or fools. I like captains."

Captain Polyxigis strode past Idomeneas' Fountain, and Ali Aga followed him with the heavy basket on his back. He was bringing the wedding presents to his niece Vangelio in good time.

Since the day before yesterday Captain Polyxigis had been out of order, as if the earthquake had upset his mind. He kept running about the streets, would neither eat nor drink, and from time to time he groaned like a sick buffalo. His wanderings always brought him before a green door. There he would stop, measure the high wall with a glance, stand on tiptoe as though he meant to fly over it, go away, again make his rounds and come back.

To remove the suspicions of the neighbors (he was afraid of the Hags, with their wicked tongues), he visited a Turkish coppersmith in the quarter and bought first a pan, another time a handbasin and a coffeepot, and again bowls, and coffee cups. At first he could not think what to do with them; then it occurred to him that his niece was getting married. He filled a basket with the copper, loaded it onto Ali Aga's back, and set off for Captain Michales' quarter, where Vangelio's house lay.

As he passed Idomeneas' Fountain, Captain Michales appeared, riding his mare, with his whip hanging from his wrist and the tassel of his headband hiding his eyes.

Captain Polyxigis stood still in astonishment, for he knew that on Sunday morning Captain Michales had begun another of his weeks of swilling. Yet here he was again on horseback, and it was only Tuesday. Evidently he had broken away from his drinking party and was now making for the Turkish quarter, running straight into the cannon's mouth. Captain Polyxigis shook his head. One of these days, he thought, he'll pay for his audacity with his life, and one of the pillars of Christendom in Megalokastro will come crashing down. But who can restrain him? Neither God, nor the devil. A man who's not afraid of death—even God is afraid of him.

Captain Michales drew nearer. He caught sight of Captain Polyxigis and spurred his mare on. He wanted no conversation with him. Polyxigis' foppishness got on his nerves, along with his silly jokes and his frivolous way of living. He was one of those men who whistle and sing every morning when they wake up. Captain Michales had no taste for such men. Yet they were honorable comrades when trouble came, when the Christians rebelled and picked a quarrel with the Turks. Then both captains were leaders; both of them felt themselves responsible. But as soon as times grew calm, they ran apart, in opposite directions.

He's like a wild boar, thought Captain Polyxigis, I don't like him.

He's a barber, thought Captain Michales, not my taste—and he urged the mare on.

At the sight of that darkened face, Captain Polyxigis guessed that he was up to no good and that nothing but trouble for the Christians would come out of it. So he whipped up his courage and called out:

"Where are you off to so early, Captain Michales?" With that he stretched out his arm, as though to bar the way.

"Get out of the way, if you don't want the mare to trample on you, Captain Polyxigis," growled Captain Michales.

Captain Polyxigis stood in the middle of the street with arms outstretched and did not budge.

"In Christ's name, brother," he said, "don't throw away your strength. You're a pillar of Christendom. Crete needs you. Your life doesn't belong to you, it belongs to Crete. She may soon want to use you."

But Captain Michales had never felt such a disgust for this *capitanio* as now. Yesterday Furogatos had escaped from the cellar for a moment to get a breath of air; he had stood at the street door and there had exchanged a few words with their neighbor, Krasojorgis' wife. In this way he had heard of Captain Polyxigis' new prank in the Turkish quarter. Furogatos had gone back to the cellar and had poured the story into Captain Michales' ear. Captain Michales had pretended scarcely to listen, but it had been like a blow to his heart.

And now he could hear it no longer. He bent down from the mare. His lips were bursting with wrath.

"Go and seduce those women of yours! Leave me alone to ride head first at the Turkish coffeehouses."

Captain Polyxigis went scarlet. "When we're at peace," he retorted defiantly, "I seduce hanums. When we're at war, I kill agas. That's what I call being a man."

He turned to Ali Aga. "Go ahead to Vangelio's house and unload there," he said, and drove him away. Then he took a step nearer and laid his hand on the mare's hot neck.

"Captain Michales," he said, lowering his voice, "as true as you're a baptized Christian, speak out; what have you got against me? I don't like that look of yours today, it bores through me as though I were a Turk."

"Get out of the way if you don't want the mare to trample on you," growled Captain Michales again, turning away.

"Tell me, what have you against me?" Captain Polyxigis asked again. "Why do you turn your head away?"

"Get out of the way if you don't want the mare to trample on you," growled Captain Michales for the third time.

"No one can talk with you, there's no knowing how to approach you!"

"Very clever, Captain Hanum," roared Captain Michales, furiously. He put spurs to his mare, and she reared high. By a hair's breadth she missed knocking Captain Polyxigis down.

"What can I do against him? After all, he's a Christian and a palikar," Captain Polyxigis muttered, biting at his mustache. "If not, I'd know, you madman, how to handle you!" He spat three times, as if to get rid of the evil meeting, and pushed on to the house of his niece.

Vangelio was sitting at her loom. She was just finishing work on the last double width of nubby cloth from which were to be made breeches for the bridegroom and nightdresses for the bride that would never wear out. She sped the shuttle through in haste. She was in a hurry, for the wedding was getting near. It stood over her like a great dark animal. And Vangelio herself was crouching like an animal to defend herself against it, against that repulsive animal—for so this marriage seemed to her to be—with this half-helping of a bridegroom, with his glasses, his soft priest's voice and his disgusting sheeplike gentleness. Was it then for this bit of a man that she had been born? Was it for his pleasure that she had fattened for so many years, till her breasts and hips grew full and her hair reached to her knees? All this for Tityros? "Marry him," Uncle Polyxigis had whispered in her ear, "say yes, Vangelio, a husband's a downy cushion and keeps you warm." Ah, where was God, that her voice might pierce through the seven heavens and cry to Him: "I won't have him, I won't have him"? For how many years had she seen in her sleep a heroic youth with a woolen cloak about his shoulders, a slim-hipped buck loving wine, women and strife, throwing his money about superbly—somebody matchless like her brother Diamandes! Ah, how often—indeed every time she lighted the lamps in front of the icon-shrines her parents had dedicated to them—had she begged Saint Nicholas, who looks after orphan girls, and Saint Famurios, who supplies bridegrooms, to send her a husband like her brother! Like her brother, not like her Uncle Polyxigis, that little, dark babbler; and not like Captain Michales either, whose breath reeked of sulphur and before whom even the dogs of the neighborhood trembled. He should be just like her brother Diamandes: a body like a cypress, hips like a boxer's, chest like a fortress. Otherwise she would rather stay unmarried, a thousand times rather grow old living with her brother. He too should not marry—a wife would ruin all the sweetness for them. If only they could die at the same time and be buried together; and over their grave two cypresses should grow—one a manly one, slender as a candle, and the other a womanly one with spreading branches. And under the earth their roots should intertwine.

But then Uncle Polyxigis had come and said she must take Captain Michales' brother Tityros and marry into an important family and have a man to keep her. For Diamandes had already spent the olive trees and vineyards which their parents had left them, so that this house was now all that remained to her, her only dowry. But in a few months her greedy little brother would guzzle and swill the house away too. And then?

"It's all the fault of Polyxigis," she muttered resentfully as she went on weaving. "He has got me into this soup. It was he who persuaded me to say yes. But God is just. He will punish him. And if He doesn't, then the unmarried man's sighing will come upon Polyxigis like a flash of lightning. May it strike him and burn him up!"

Captain Polyxigis kicked open the street door and entered. He

126

turned to Ali Aga, who was waiting outside, and signaled to him to come in and unload.

"Bless you, Ali Aga! Here, have a good time with this!" he said genially, throwing him a silver coin. Ali Aga caught it, held it tight in his fist as if it were a bird which might fly away, and bent down to kiss the lavish hand. But Polyxigis drew it back with a laugh. "I'm no pope or imam, Ali Aga!"

He strode across the yard followed by Ali Aga. The dog jumped up in its corner, sniffed, recognized the newcomers and curled up again on the ground.

Through the open door into the house Captain Polyxigis saw the loom—that docile domestic creature with feet, legs, pedals, metal feathers, tongues and combs. Its delicate rigging of warp and woof was like that of a frigate under full sail.

Vangelio turned. She saw her uncle and summoned all her strength to fetch up a smile of welcome. But from her lips, nose and chin there seemed to drip nothing but poison. She was now perpetually monosyllabic and sour. Some concealed worm was surely gnawing at her vitals. She was growing yellow, and her bosom had begun to turn flabby.

Behind her uncle she noticed Ali Aga with the basket, and she understood. "You've been extravagant for my sake, Uncle George," she said, with a stealthy glance at the basket. She made out the copper things and for a moment her face lighted up.

"Everyone's got to marry sometime. If the vineyard's lost, it's lost. People say, Vangelio, that there is no greater pleasure," said Captain Polyxigis with a laugh, trying to set his niece's blood in motion.

"People say——" Vangelio burst out, and broke off.

Captain Polyxigis sat down on the small sofa, took off his fez (for he was hot) and put it on the window sill. Vangelio went down on her knees and took the shining copper objects out of the basket, one by one. The house became filled with pans, dishes and jugs, and as Vangelio bent over them a reddish warmth gleamed for a moment from her yellow face.

"Bless you, Uncle," she said listlessly, "you take the place of a father."

"You say that halfheartedly, Vangelio! You're getting married and yet, my child, you're on the verge of tears. Raise your eyes

127

and let me look at them. . . . Here, smile just for once, let out a shout to make your breath come faster! When brides are weaving their last bit of cloth, they sing and make the house tremble— why, the whole neighborhood trembles as in an earthquake! It's called 'bride's time'! But you behave as if you were weaving a shroud."

Vangelio was furious. Such words in the mouth of a man who had all he wanted outraged her. She thought again of her fiancé. Was she to sing for that pallid face? She felt a foul taste in her mouth. She was on the point of losing her control, but immediately hesitated. What should she say? It was all one. If one was happy, why should one cry out? And why cry out if one wasn't? There was no help for it. So better keep quiet.

But Captain Polyxigis could not bear his niece's dumb complaining. The day of the wedding was drawing near; at Easter the crowning would take place. Before that he had to make something clear to her. He could feel that his niece, ever since he had fixed up her engagement, had looked at him with resentful eyes. He must let her know, before she married, that it had cost him something to induce the bridegroom to say yes. Up to the last moment Tityros had wavered. And so one day Captain Polyxigis had opened his money chest, taken out five gold pounds and given them to him. "Here, schoolmaster, take these as an extra dowry," he had said. "No one need know—neither Captain Michales, nor the bride, nor my sister. I'm gilding my niece and giving her to you." That was how he had managed it. And now, if you please, Miss Bride makes a face as if she were drinking quinine. Her bridegroom stinks! She'd like a prince!

Vangelio came out of the kitchen with a round tray on which were coffee, a glass of cold water and a spoonful of preserved cherries. She put the tray down on a chair in front of her uncle.

"Listen to me, Vangelio," he said with a glance at the door, "isn't Diamandes back yet? Is that swilling brother of yours still gadding?"

"He's young," replied Vangelio proudly, "he's handsome. It's right for him."

"Right for him? What? Was it right for him to ruin you, Vangelio?"

"Oh! He's ruined me, has he? But if he hadn't been there, I'd have died. What would I have had to live for? And let me tell you, Uncle: if I bow my neck now and accept the yoke you've found for me, I do it so that, even when I'm married, I shan't be separated from my brother. Otherwise, the devil take Tityros!"

Captain Polyxigis swallowed the glassful of water and suppressed his rage. He purposely took a long time munching the cherry conserve, to prevent himself from seizing his niece by the hair and swinging her against the wall.

"Dammit," he said finally, twirling his mustache. "He's your brother, not your sweetheart. He too should marry and found a family—and keep his mind away from taverns."

Vangelio straightened up. Her cheeks were glowing. "Pray God no such thing is written," she screamed. "And if it is written, may He rub it out!"

"What's happened to you, Vangelio?" cried Captain Polyxigis, shocked. "Do you love him more than your husband? But that's disgraceful! And after all the efforts I've made—"

"You've sold me for a bit of bread." Vangelio spat through her teeth.

Captain Polyxigis could control himself no longer.

"A piece of bread—dammit, that seems to you a trifle, does it, my princess? Very clever it sounds! And what, by God, should a bridegroom find to desire in you? Youth? Beauty? Riches? You're thirty-five, and shrunk to a dried currant, to an old maid with a mustache! And that hound of a brother has plundered you. A rag is all you are now! Who's going to look at you now, who's going to want you, you poor thing? God has struck Tityros with blindness to make him say yes."

Vangelio buried her face in her hands and began to cry, without moving. Captain Polyxigis's heart contracted. How could he have let such words out of his mouth? What was he to do now? How could he console the poor girl?

He laid a hand on her luxuriant hair. "There, there, Vangelio dear, don't cry. With God's help it'll all come right. A good man has been found to look after you. You'll see: soon your cheeks will be plump and rosy again. You'll grow young again! And then, if you have fine children. . . ."

"Bah! Little Tityroses!" said Vangelio scornfully, wiping the tears from her eyelids.

"Perhaps they won't just be little Tityroses. They'll have our blood in them too. Perhaps your sons will be like your brother!"

Vangelio was amazed. The blood rose in her faded bosom. "Be quiet!" she said, shuddering.

Captain Polyxigis stood up. He stretched out his hand to caress his niece, but drew it back. "We'll talk some other day, Vangelio," he said. "I'm going before that swilling brother of yours comes back. I've no wish to see him here!"

He crammed on his large fez and was about to cross the threshold when a heavy tread was heard and the street door burst open. Panting and worn out, with a yellowed sprig of basil behind one ear and a cigarette behind the other, the brother stood on the threshold, his woolen cloak thrown round his shoulders. He frowned and pursed his lips as he recognized his uncle in the doorway. Is he there again with his matchmaking? he thought. Devil take him! He jerked himself together, pulled off his cap and crossed the yard. He did not see the copper objects on the floor as he entered the house. He tripped over them and cursed.

Captain Polyxigis turned his face away. The sight disgusted him.

"Men drink wine," he said contemptuously, "but don't get drunk. Take me, for example. Men go hunting women, but don't make fools of themselves. Take me, for example."

Diamandes, who could not bear his uncle and knew his vulnerable spots, gave a contemptuous snigger. His tongue was out of control. He stammered out:

"Men drink wine and don't get drunk, and don't go to bed like infants but mount their mares and ride—not into the Turkish quarter to some hanum, but to the Turkish coffeehouses, to the agas. Take an example yourself, Uncle, from Captain Michales!"

These words pierced Captain Polyxigis through the heart, for he felt that Diamandes, drunk though he was, was quite right.

"Curses on you, you good-for-nothing! You're well on the way to squandering your sister's dowry on wine and women, watches and chains. If at least you could read the time! But you're not capable even of that, you good-for-nothing!"

Diamandes gave a yell and sprang forward over pans and cans to attack his uncle, but he tripped and fell thunderously to the floor.

130

Captain Polyxigis laughed disdainfully. "I wish you joy of your little brother, Vangelio," he said, and crossed the threshold.

"God grant I may have joy of him till my death, Uncle!" Vangelio retorted. She helped her brother up from the copper onto the sofa, brought him a cushion for his head and stroked him tenderly.

At midday young Thrasos came back from school in great excitement.

"Mama!" he shouted, throwing into the air the little red cap his sister had made for him. "Father's mare strikes sparks from the cobbles. I saw him ride along Broad Street, and the shopkeepers and cobblers stood up to gape at him. 'He's come from the Turkish quarter,' one of them said. 'He's going to the Turkish quarter,' another said. I stood where I was, took off my cap and waved to him. But how should he notice me? The sparks were flying from the cobbles, I tell you!"

"Signor Paraskevas was here and has been complaining to me," said the mother, frightened at her son's admiration for his father. "The day before yesterday, he says, you and your friends kidnaped his daughter. Aren't you ashamed of yourself?"

Thrasos laughed.

"Why did you do it?"

He shrugged his shoulders. "We felt like it. Yesterday we nearly pulled off something with Tityros. We'd planned to hide behind a door with rope, and just throw a noose round his neck when he came in, like they do to catch wild horses. He'd told us how, himself, the day before yesterday. So now we were playing horse-tamers."

His mother scolded, "Villains! What has that holy man ever done to you? Why did you want to kill him?"

"Kill him? Us? But we like him. It was a game. We wouldn't have tied the noose tight. We'd only have given him a fright, to see what he'd do!"

He took the clothesline from his shoulder and returned it to its place. Then he clenched his fist and frowned like his father.

"At the last minute the others were frightened. There were too many of them, and too many cowards among them. But it doesn't matter. Another time I'll pick them myself—fewer, and reliable. Perhaps I'll do it alone."

131

There was a knock at the door, and Ali Aga appeared.

"In God's name, Captainess," he said, "Efendina's playing the madman again. He's run out into the Greek quarter and is coming to your house. Bolt the door. Don't let him in."

He had not yet finished speaking when Efendina burst howling into the yard. It hurt Katerina to look at him. The poor creature seemed hardly human. His clothes were torn, his sackcloth breeches were showing. His eyes were red and swollen from weeping. He had taken off his turban, and his scab was thickly smeared with horse dung. He knelt down in the middle of the yard and began wailing.

"I have defiled myself," he screamed, "eaten pork, drunk wine, uttered wicked words. Men and women, forgive me! May God also have mercy and forgive me! Captainess, if God questions you tomorrow, tell Him that Captain Michales forced me to it against my will." He crawled on his knees toward her, to seize her hand and kiss it.

"Have pity on me, Captainess, I am hurrying to publish my suffering and my shame, and I am beginning with you. Afterwards I shall hurry to the pasha's door, and to the other Turkish houses. They must see my scab, and learn of my guilt; they must spit upon me. But in you I place my trust. If God questions you tomorrow, tell Him that Captain Michales forced me to it against my will."

Thrasos watched him and laughed. He had stealthily taken the clothesline down again and made a noose. Renio came out of the kitchen, glanced at Efendina and likewise laughed. But Katerina felt her eyes grow wet.

"Stand up, Efendina," she said gently, "stand up, I'll do as you say. I'll bear witness before God that I have seen with my own eyes how Captain Michales compelled you against your will."

"May you be blessed, Captainess! And now I ask you for a favor. Spit on me!"

"No, that I won't, Efendina. Stand up and go with the seven-fold blessing of God."

"Spit on me, or I won't go." He turned to Ali Aga: "Next, you will spit on me, Ali Aga—you, as a faithful Mussulman. And afterward, all Megalokastro. Before I left the teke, my grandfather

132

rose up from his coffin and spat upon me. You too must spit, Captainess! Spit on me, if you believe in God!"

The captain's wife turned away. "I can't," she said. "I won't. Go, good-by!"

"I won't go," bellowed Efendina. "Yes, by Mohammed, I shall stay here if you don't spit on me."

The captain's wife grew angry. "I shall do as I will, not as you will, Efendina!" she said, and went back into the kitchen.

"Here on these stones will I remain kneeling till dawn," cried Efendina and beat his forehead against the stones. Then he began his wailing all over again, and howled like a dog.

Thrasos made a sign to his sister. She understood and took up her position near him, behind Efendina's back. As Efendina beat his breast and howled, with his eyes on the kitchen, Thrasos threw the noose round his neck. Renio too caught hold, and they both pulled.

Efendina gave a strangled cry and fell over backward. His face went bluish, his eyes started. He wrenched at the noose to prevent himself from choking, but his hands were powerless with terror.

"In God's name, children, you're throttling the poor creature!" cried Ali Aga.

The captain's wife heard his cry and came running out. She snatched the cord out of her son's hands and loosened the noose. Then she pushed Efendina to the street door.

"Out you go," she said, "poor wretch, out you go! With my best wishes." Then she gave him a shove, so that he stumbled into the street. She bolted the door.

Thrasos and Renio burst out laughing. "You see, Mother, that's how they catch horses," said Thrasos and again hung the cord near the washtub. "Tityros won't be able to escape me now!"

Captain Michales stormed through the Turkish quarter on his mare. The wine had not clouded his brain. His knees pressed the mare's flanks powerfully, and in his limbs and muscles he felt a boundless strength that oppressed him more than the wine he had drunk. He did not know how to shake free of his oppression.

He did not clearly distinguish the men who went past; the

houses seemed to him to have got lower and the streets narrower. The Hags heard his horse and rushed to their peepholes. They recognized Captain Michales, but the sun was dazzling and they could not see the expression on his face. "What's up with the boar at the height of noon?" Aglaja asked. "Is he drunk?"

"Keep your eyes peeled, there's something going on here," remarked Thalia, sniffing as though she could smell it. "Why has Captain Polyxigis been hanging around our quarter since yesterday? I saw him, just when the earthquake started—when Eminé rushed out and pretended to faint. What a chance that he came by. But was it chance? Or was it arranged? And the person in question woke her up out of her swoon. And since that day our quarter has been smeared with honey, and he's stuck fast. And now Captain Wildboar as well—that damned bitch! Both those lecherous hounds can smell her a mile away!"

"Quiet, quiet!" said Phrosyne, "just listen to how Nuri's horse is neighing!"

From the precincts of the Turkish konak the noble steed could be heard greeting the lusty mare.

"Eminé's whinnying," said Thalia with a giggle. But immediately her tongue stuck in her throat, and both her sisters cried out; for as the mare heard the stallion's neighing, she reared, as if she wanted to dance.

"That's death for Captain Michales," cried the three.

But he gripped the rearing beast by the mane and fused with her to a single body. He put the spurs to her, and his power did not yield. She felt her pitiless master on top of her, lowered her head and moved on.

"Damn you, with that hot blood of yours!" he muttered, and struck the mare's head with his fist.

Outside, down by the sea, he gave her her head and let her run freely along the broad ramparts. His chest filled with sea air. High up on a bulwark overgrown with weeds he reined her in. He gazed out over the deep-blue foaming sea sparkling in the sun, and lost himself in the mist to the north, toward Greece. He sighed. "With Thee I can endure, my God," he muttered, "with Thee, not with men."

He rode on. Always when he thought of Crete, abandoned by all, he disputed with God. A violent blasphemy pressed on the tip of his tongue. He did not lament before God, he was angry with Him. He asked for no sympathy, he asked for justice.

A dark cloud, small as a water bottle, rose up from the south, became larger and larger, until it darkened the sky. The sun smoldered. A damp, sultry wind came sighing from the sea over Captain Michales' haggard face. He raised his eyes to the sky. "But I can't fight it out with Thee, my God," he growled between his teeth. "So I shall fight it out with men."

He dug his heels into the mare and shot along Broad Street again like a flash. The Christians stood up, the better to see him. He reached the Kanea Gate, where the big Turkish coffeehouse patronized by the distinguished agas lay. Every time there was a rising, the great consultations took place in this coffeehouse, and from here the Turks went forth with knives between their teeth to every slaughter. When, on spring afternoons, the sun's heat was diminished, the pavements sprinkled with rain and the earth fragrant, in this coffeehouse the handsomest Turkish youths sat enthroned on high benches and sang their languorous refrains. And here in winter the most gifted storytellers made the agas laugh. The muezzin, too, stopped here, searchingly examined the Turkish youths, listened to their seductive melodies and joined in their yearning. Sometimes he no longer knew whether this was a coffeehouse or Mohammed's Paradise. Nothing was lacking, neither good tobacco for his narghile nor a fresh little breath from the gardens.

Midday was already past. The agas had eaten and were sitting at ease, with legs crossed, on the straw mats of the coffeehouse. They had ordered narghiles and, half dozing with eyes almost closed, were sipping their coffee. They were happy.

Everything had arranged itself pleasantly for them. Generations ago their forefathers had divided up Crete, and its fat vineyards, olive orchards and acres were their heritage. The arid land had been left to the Greeks. From time to time the Christians raised their heads, but the soldiers from Anatolia struck at them and made them bow again under the yoke. Beautiful were the hanums, and each man could have as many of them as his purse allowed. Beautiful too were the Turkish boys, and if one only pampered them properly they acquired downy, blossom-white flesh. Also their Mohammed was no puritan: he liked what the agas liked. He did not worry them to become saints. He carried no cross and did not ask them to carry one. In his pocket he always carried a phial of scent, a small mirror and a comb. For the pleasure of Mussulmans he was no God, but a man. And death, for the faithful, had nothing about it of worms or stench, but was a green doorway to a wide, everlasting garden.

Nuri Bey appeared, freshly shaved, handsome as a lion, and his thinly pointed mustache, dyed with black pomade, flashed like steel. He bowed silent greetings to right and left and went to sit inside near the serving table, to be quite alone.

Since the day when his horse had stumbled between the tombs and his father had risen up before him in the air with wild and bloody hair, Nuri Bey had been able to get no pleasure from sleep or food or conversation. The blood of his father hankered for vengeance. The sons, brothers and nephews of the murderer were alive. They were marrying, breeding, carousing, swaggering. And had not one of them recently brought an ass into the village mosque to pray? How long were all these insults to be endured? How long was his father to wander barefoot up and down the underworld? The moment had come for him to make a decision, if he were a man.

"Pass me the narghile, Hussein," he told the proprietor, "and don't let anybody come near me."

In the distance dull thunder was heard. The agas turned their faces toward the door. The sky was now entirely covered. Sulphur-yellow lightning flashed. The wind hissed like rending silk.

"That's because of the heat," said one of the agas. "It'll rain; that'll be good for the crops," said another. "And for the olives and the almonds—make 'em ripen quick," said a third, and went as far as the door to observe the weather.

But as he reached the threshold he sprang back terrified. Captain Michales had appeared on horseback at the entrance to the coffeehouse. He saw the agas comfortably sitting around and sleepily smoking their narghiles. The blood rushed to his head and the world swayed. He spurred the mare and she reared and crashed into the coffeehouse. Inside, the mare smashed several stools and upset a table; there was a sound of china breaking. She got as far as the serving table, where the proprietor, as usual, stood in front of the coal fire, putting the coffeepots on and taking them off. There she came to a halt.

The coffeehouse was in a turmoil. The agas flung their narghiles aside and stood up. The bolder ones hastily felt for their knives in their red sashes. The old men raised their hands and cried:

"Be careful, Captain Michales, don't plunge us into bloodshed!"

But he remained unmoved by this and swung his whip in the air. "Out with you," he shouted, "I want to drink my coffee alone!"

The old muezzin jumped up from the platform where he had been sitting, cross-legged, and yelled, as loud as he could, "This time your game won't succeed, Captain Michales. You can't make fools of us every year. This time you won't get out of here alive, unbeliever!"

A Turkish hothead, sorry for the old muezzin, stepped forward to protect him. He wrenched from his sash a broad, two-edged dagger and rushed at the rider. But Captain Michales bent down and seized him by the wrist, so that the young Turk's arm was paralyzed and he let go of the dagger. Captain Michales stuck it in his pocket and again raised his whip.

"Out, out," he bellowed, "out!"

"Allah, Allah," cried the old men, and did not know what to do: send a messenger to the pasha for soldiers, or sugar the bitter pill and give in to avoid bloodshed.

Nuri Bey had not stirred. With bent head he smoked his narghile. But out of the corner of his eye he surveyed the coffeehouse, until everything before him vanished. Now he saw only the sweating chest and belly of the mare and Captain Michales' black boots. The first raindrops were falling outside. There were heavy claps of thunder and the glass of the doors tinkled. The muezzin screamed:

"If you believe in Mohammed, let me pluck him to bits like a sardine!"

But several old men seized him around the waist and under the arms, and dragged him out.

Nuri Bey bent his head still lower, smoked puff after puff and

137

blew the smoke through his nose. The hour has come, he thought. I have given my word to my father, I prayed for an occasion, here it is! The murderer's brother has come, my father has brought him, straight in front of the muzzle of my gun. Now for it!

He sought to rouse his heart to fury. "Now stir yourself, my heart, up, and strike! Or are you afraid perhaps?" His fists burned him, as if he were in a fever. He raised his eyes and saw Captain Michales' gaze directed at him. Nuri Bey put away the tube of the narghile and got up slowly and heavily. He walked down from the platform and took hold of the mare's reins. Then he turned to the proprietor, who had crouched down behind the serving table.

"Hussein," he said, "make a coffee for Captain Michales. I will pay."

He raised his hand authoritatively and signed to the young people, who were standing round the mare, to go.

"Nuri Bey," said Captain Michales, "I want to drink my coffee alone. I want no company. Clear the coffeehouse."

"Haven't I too a want? A small want, Captain Michales?" said Nuri Bey, and tried hard to make his face look gentle. "I ask you one favor. Don't insult me."

The white headband slipped from his head, he groped for it and set it swinging, so that the air smelled of musk. At once Captain Michales' nostrils quivered. The veins of his neck swelled.

The scent of musk pierced his vitals like a knife. It bewildered him: night, the lemon raki, the partridge, the laughter behind the lattice, the creaking stairs, and suddenly in the doorframe a body, which swayed and filled the air with the scent of musk . . . and this same Nuri . . . Captain Michales' brow spat sparks. He shoved Nuri aside, put spurs to the mare and very nearly rode him down. He came to the middle of the coffeehouse.

"Out, out," he shouted again, as though possessed. "Clear the coffeehouse!"

Nuri Bey wound the headband tightly about his hair. He bit his lips hard, drawing blood. The agas had left the divans and were pressing around him. A couple of them were waiting, crouched behind the door, with knives. The more prudent of the old men had already slipped out of the door. The coffeehouse was beginning to empty.

Nuri Bey felt ashamed. "Go out," he said quietly to the agas. "He's drunk. Don't argue with him. I'll stay. To see he doesn't go too far. To see we don't need to be ashamed."

The agas stood still. Selim Aga, who till now had been smoking his narghile, silent and unmoved, got up. He was the best-balanced mind in Turkey, an old man blessed with everything—rich, cultivated, of good family, the father of fine sons, still handsome in his old age as he had been long ago in his youth. He signed to the agas.

"Control yourselves," he said, weightily. "It serves no purpose to bathe Crete in blood. The hour will soon come—I see it already marked in Allah's book—when this Greek will have to pay. I can already see his head nailed up over the pasha's gate. Be patient. Let us go!"

He stepped forward with measured gait, and the agas followed. The coffeehouse was empty.

Captain Michales twirled his mustache and looked down at Nuri. He laughed, his jaw jutted out. His heart gave a bound of pleasure. He turned to the proprietor, who was now venturing out from behind the serving table.

"Hey, Hussein," he said, "put the pot on the fire and make me a coffee. Without sugar!"

5

THE STORM HAD BROKEN. The sky fell; Megalokastro seemed
to rise and become part of it. The falling water flooded the streets
and the world grew dark. Everywhere lightning played around
the minarets, and down below, in Broad Street, Captain Michales'
face flared harsh and undismayed as he rode home. The mare's
broad white chest glittered with wet.

It was a *bora* that lasted scarcely half an hour. Then came a
wind from the mountains, the clouds were rent, and through
them gleamed the deep blue sky, while slanting, newborn shafts
of sunshine fell upon the soaking town. The cobbles seemed to
laugh, and the sparrows on the roofs shook their soaked feathers.
Megalokastro emerged from the storm freshly washed and young
again. From the courtyards came the scent of rain-wet honeysuckle, marjoram and basil.

With one blow Captain Michales opened the door. His wife
took the mare by the reins without a word, while he himself
strode into the house and hung the Turk's dagger up on the
shrine, in front of the icon of Saint Michael. Captain Michales
was steaming with scorn, sweat and rain. Clean, dry clothes were
brought him, and he put them on. With his body refreshed, he
stretched himself on the bed, closed his eyes and was immediately
embraced by soft, merciful slumber.

While he rested, the Kastrians, Turks and Christians alike,
gathered in their homes early that evening. The men whispered
together, while the women sat about, listening and sighing, but
saying nothing. So Crete, abandoned by all, was once again not
to have repose? They pondered. Were the massacres going to

begin again? Would we once more have to lose our men? And where shall we go? With the infants, the pots and pans and the linen once more on our backs?

The most prudent of the Christians, the owners of shops and vineyards, cursed Captain Michales' drunken exploits which dragged so many men with him into trouble. The others on the contrary, the palikars, were proud of this fresh flouting of Turkey.

The Turks had gathered, some of them in the tekes, some in Nuri Bey's konak. They cursed and threatened, but could not think of a way to wash away the disgrace. The muezzin kept fanning the fire in them, and the more reasonable of the elders tried to put it out again, while Nuri Bey sat thoughtful in a corner and said nothing. At length they grew tired of the noise and of slaughtering the Christians in their thoughts. They chose three spokesmen to go next morning to the pasha and to urge him to tighten the reins upon the Christians. Is he a pasha or a piece of halvah? How long has it been since he stopped hanging Christians from the plane tree or putting them in the pillory? If this goes on, the giaours will venture anything and—God punish us if we are lying—that mad captain will soon ride even into the mosques and drive us out with his whip! He must hang or be stuck in the pillory, even if only to warn his followers to keep within bounds. That's how Turkey would act! But this pasha deals much too softly with the Greeks: the weak-witted creature talks of justice! He plays draughts with the Metropolitan, they drink mastic, eat baklava and sit up together all night whispering secrets!

Early next morning the three spokesmen proceeded to the konak. Their ears were still buzzing from the stormy instructions with which they had been charged. In the middle walked the muezzin, on his right Selim Aga, and on the left, sunk in thought, Nuri Bey. Their gait was measured, and they did not speak to one another. Each was weaving a web of his thoughts—what he was to say to the pasha and how. Selim Aga was for peace; he had a large yearly income in oil, corn, almonds and grapes. The muezzin was pressing the Koran to his chest, next to the skin, and it was burning him. Nuri Bey was undecided and he kept his head bowed.

That night his father had again appeared to him in his sleep, still in rags and covered with dirt, and had slipped his costly black-hilted knife under the pillow. But in the morning, when Nuri Bey picked up the pillow and found no knife, his heart was on the point of breaking. The old man doesn't trust me, he sighed, he's taken it away from me again. He's afraid I'll dishonor it.

Heavy and morose, the pasha sat waiting for them on the big divan. More trouble, the dogs and the cats are fighting again. These giaours want freedom—curses on them! The Mussulmans are pressing him to slaughter all giaours—curses on them too! Servitude, my respected giaours, is a thing ordained by God! The bondsmen too, my agas, are ordained by God: they till the fields, they keep trade going, they bring in taxes. Who wants to kill the goose that lays the golden eggs?

The Moor appeared. "Pasha Effendi, they've arrived."

"Show them in," replied the pasha, his voice rising.

They came in, one after another, made their bows, and without a word took their places cross-legged on the large divan.

The muezzin was the first to open his mouth. Lanky and bony, with sunken cheeks, sparse, whitish wisps of beard and a hairy wart as big as a horsefly, which sat between his brows and made him look three-eyed, he spoke and spoke. The longer he heard his own voice, the fiercer it made him. Foaming with wrath, he pulled the Koran from his bosom and began rocking to and fro as he read. The pasha felt faint; he raised his long pipe.

"Hodza Effendi," he said, "you've made me giddy. Speak simply, so I can understand. I'm an Anatolian, a slow mind. In a word: what do you want?"

"Action," the muezzin answered, and the hairs on his wart stood out.

The pasha sighed and turned to Selim Aga. "And what's your opinion, Selim Aga?" he asked. "Is that also your view?"

"We need peace, Pasha Effendi," replied the gray-headed property owner, "not a massacre, peace! We're having a good year: March has brought us plenty of rain and given the crops strength; the olives, too, are promising. We shall have a rich harvest and excellent oil this year, God be praised. So peace, Pasha Effendi! This Crete is a great savage beast. Let's not wake it up—it devours men! What does it matter that a madman broke into our coffeehouse? After all, he was drunk. Let's shut our eyes—it's in our interest to do so. If we pigheadedly give blow for blow, we're lost. Pigheadedness turns to wrongheadedness, Pasha Effendi. Open your records and enter the giaour in them: his name is Captain Michales. His hour will come. You are the pasha; you bear the scimitar, you strike off heads."

He turned to the muezzin. "That is my opinion, Hodza Effendi," he said. "I'm sorry. You own no trees, vineyards or fields, and you don't know the distress of the earth and of men and women. But ask me. Ask the trees and the crops. Do they want a rising? No, they don't."

"I don't ask among trees, crops and human beings," the muezzin bellowed, thumping the Koran, "I ask Allah." He again took the Koran out from his bosom and opened it.

But the pasha stretched out his hand. "The Koran says whatever its reader has in mind," he said with a yawn. "You want a slaughter? you open the Koran and find a justification. If Selim Aga opens it, he'll find another word—peace—and that too comes from God. Both are from God, so be quiet!"

He turned to Nuri Bey. "And what's your opinion, Nuri Bey?" he said. "Massacre or peace—which does your Koran say?"

Nuri Bey rubbed his fist several times along his hairy, crossed legs, as he sought the right answer. He took a long time to weigh his opinion. He certainly did not want peace. Turkey had already been patient too long, the Greek had grown too insolent. The moment had come to knock him on the head. But he also wanted no massacre—he was not bloodthirsty, nor was he a hodza who fetched his fire from the Koran.

"Well?" asked the pasha, annoyed by his hesitation. "I'm asking you again: do you want peace, Nuri Bey, or a massacre?"

"The straightforward, simple way has become lost to us, Pasha Effendi," said Nuri Bey, trying to gain a little more time.

"It's not lost, young man, but we've grown blind and can't find it. Or has your lordship found it?"

"I think so, Pasha Effendi."

"I hope so for your sake! Speak, then, and free us from our blindness."

"Neither peace nor a massacre. The guilty one must pay."

"Captain Michales?" asked the pasha. "Do you mean him?"

"Grant me the liberty, Pasha Effendi, not to say whom I mean. You are pasha. If you intervene, weapons will speak and we shall swim in blood. Let me undertake the vengeance on behalf of Turkey. Who the guilty man is you'll soon learn."

"Will you kill him?"

"I shall kill him, but no one will find out who the murderer was. Trust me."

The muezzin jumped up, furious. One man isn't guilty, thousands are. They all deserve the pillory. *That's* what keeping the peace means. The Greek understands nothing else. Cut off his head, if you like, then he'll be quiet."

Selim Aga's brain was full of trees and vines. He too jumped up and began to shout. But the muezzin's voice was like a bell—how was he to silence it? They came to blows. Nuri Bey stepped between them, to separate them. Unmoved, the pasha remained sitting on his divan. These Turks of Crete made his head whirl. All were right, all were wrong: how was he to unravel it? Above all, he was sleepy. He had not had a good night—he had overeaten and drunk too much. He was in a hurry to have done with the affair. He shook off his fatigue and shouted:

"Hey, you, aren't you ashamed of yourselves? Stop fighting, I tell you! Nuri Bey, you are right. That is the camel's way, the correct one. So do as Allah enlightens you. I give you freedom to do so!"

Selim Aga picked up his white headband from the floor and turned to Nuri Bey. "You have my blessing, Nuri Bey," he said in a tone of entreaty, "if you proceed cautiously, kill with moderation, don't make the Greeks wild, keep the peace for us."

"I shall not let my law be trampled underfoot," bellowed the muezzin. "I shall preach in the mosque and awaken Turkey!"

That brought life into the pasha, and he raised his fist.

"Hodza," he shouted, "I am in command in Megalokastro. By the beard of the Prophet, I'll make you wear a muzzle, like a dog that bites! Listen! There will be no massacre—get the idea out of your head—as long as I receive no orders from Constantinople."

He stood up, turned his face away (for he had a pain in his stomach) and yawned again.

"Go, I am busy. Do as we said, Nuri Bey, but be careful. Careful, children, for these are Greeks, damn them! If they had not been in our path, Turkey would already have swallowed up the world."

He clapped his hands, and the Moor came in. "Show the beys out," he said.

While this meeting was taking place, three other distinguished heads, Greek this time, were making their measured way to the Metropolitan. They were Hadjisavas, Captain Elias and old Mavrudes, known as Rose Bug.

The first, a pale hobbler and stutterer with a gray beard stained yellow by cigarette smoking, had in his time traveled into the land of the Franks to become a doctor, and had come back with his head turned. His madness consisted in paying workmen to dig up the earth for him in places where there were ruins, or on deserted parts of the coast and even in the caves of Psiloritis. He dug and dug, and found hands and feet of marble, dishes covered with odd lettering, and pottery vases. All this he took into the Bishop's Residence. He had already stuffed a huge room with it. That was now not large enough, and he had begun to spread out his treasures in the churchyard. The Christians grumbled that they could no longer send their wives and daughters to church for fear of their seeing those shameless ancient demons, stark naked.

It had been good advice that had been given to old Hadjisavas the father, not to send his son to the land of the Franks, for he would get his soul damaged there. Quite right! Back he had come with a shovel, and dug and dug and dug. It was said he was looking for the golden sow with the nine piglets. But how should he find her? All he possessed he spent on workmen's wages. Now he ran about in a shabby suit and worn-out shoes. He talked to himself in the street, and soon, for sure, he would begin throwing stones. Only—look—the Metropolitan respected him, gave him a seat near his own at church, and on Sunday handed him the consecrated bread before anybody else. And whenever the Christians found themselves groping in the dark, they sent him as spokesman to the Metropolitan and to the pasha. And once, when Frankish warships were anchored in the harbor, he had chattered with the Franks. He had talked and talked and none of the Greeks could understand him. Poor thing!—or did he really speak foreign languages?

Captain Elias was another relic of 1821, a crumbled, weed-grown tower without door or window. His body, pierced like a sieve with bullets, was square and big-boned, and his voice was like a clap of thunder—anyone to whom he said good day received a shock. His right eye had been put out by a Turkish pasha with a fork. But the Athenian National Committee had sent him a glass eye, the first glass eye to land in Crete. And Captain Elias wore it and shot sparks from it at those he could not hurt. On official occasions he took it out and put it in a glass of water. Then he came into the presence of Metropolitan or pasha with one eye, to remind them of 1821. The other two elders had now placed him in the middle and, bowed over his cudgel, he was on his way, one-eyed once more, to see the Metropolitan.

The third, Mavrudes, old Rose Bug, was a hideous, sour bachelor and miser who went hungry and moaned when he ate, shivered with cold and cursed when he bought himself a warm coat. He threw widows and orphans into the streets when they owed him money. He collected and collected: gold pounds, vineyards, fields, houses, steamboats. But if anyone asked him why he did not eat regular meals, he would whine: "What should I eat? Where am I to get it? Nothing's mine; all this belongs to the nation. I won't touch it!" In the 1871 rising he had gone to the Metropolitan with a sealed document. "Bishop," he had said, "take this paper. I am giving all my fortune to the senate of Megalokastro. An insurrection is an expensive thing, it requires money. Sell what I possess, and put it into arms." "And you—how are you going to live, Mavrudes?" the Metropolitan had asked with tears in his eyes. "Why are you worrying about me, Bishop? I shall knock at the doors and beg." The Metropolitan had taken care of him and had set apart a monthly allowance for him. But he had at once begun stinting again, would not eat, would not drink, would not dress respectably. He lent money at high rates of interest, and extracted their capital from widows and orphans. He had got together a new fortune. Old now and with one foot in the grave, he had made a will again leaving all to the nation. His brain was like an ax, and in difficult moments it hewed to right and left and opened up a way. So the Christians had sent him too as their spokesman.

The Metropolitan was waiting for them on a soft divan in the Bishop's Residence. Before him, on a stand of cypress in the form of a dove with outstretched wings, lay the silver-clasped Gospel. Above it hung three lithographs: on the right, the Patriarch of Constantinople, on the left, the Czar, in the middle, Hagia Sophia. The sun came in through colored panes and threw a blue and violet light on the opposite wall, which was crowded with photographs of living and dead Metropolitans and bishops. They had snow-white or pitch-black beards, miters and amulets and chains and crosiers. Some of them looked out with gracious and benevolent eyes and were as hairy as unshorn rams. Others had protruding eyes, wide mouths and stubborn necks, and clutched the crosier as though it were a police cudgel. Also among them was the present Metropolitan as a young archimandrite in Kiev. How powerfully he gazed out, what noble force he showed! This young hero had been created by God to be either a great leader or prophet, or a wencher and enjoyer of life. But Christ had wooed him for Himself, with words that to the young man were sweeter than honey, and had led him slowly on the way to what he was to become—a Metropolitan.

He glanced at his picture as a young man and sighed:

"I've grown old, I've got yellow as a cabbage, and the day is drawing near when I shall stand before the Judgment Seat with empty hands. How many Metropolitans of Crete will take their places before the Incorruptible Judge, bearing in their hands the gear of martyrdom—knives, axes, whips and stakes. And I shall stand there with empty hands. O God, grant me to die for Thy honor and for the honor of Thy poor daughter!"

Murzuflos came in with drawn face. "The elders have come, my lord," he said. "They're waiting."

"Show them in. And take the large silver salver to hand round. These are gentlemen, you know."

Murzuflos hesitated on the threshold. The Metropolitan looked at him in surprise. "Is there anything else you want, Murzuflos?"

"Do you forgive me, my lord?" said Murzuflos, and his face was anxious again. "Do you forgive me for what I've done?"

The Metropolitan laughed. "Don't worry, Murzuflos," he said. "The Crucified One will forgive you. Build on His mercy!"

"My guilt is great. . . ."

"But His mercy also is great. Go now!"

The three elders came in, kissed the Metropolitan's hand and sat down on the divan. They pulled out their rosaries and waited for the Metropolitan to speak first.

"Lovely weather, my children," said he, looking out of the window. "What pleasant days these are! What sunshine! God's own good cheer! The spring! Saint George! How goes it now with the crops, old Mavrudes?"

"God be praised," he answered.

"With the crops it goes well," said Captain Elias. "With men, not well. I'm for heroic deeds when they're needed. If not, they're idiocies!"

"The men of old used to say——" began Hadjisavas, but Captain Elias raised his hand angrily and interrupted him:

"Let the men of old alone, Hadjisavas, they're dead and done with. We're talking about the living. At the moment," Captain Elias went on, "the big agas are having a conference with the pasha. God alone knows what the dogs are up to now. Let's be on our guard. What do you think, my lord?"

"I too have heard of Captain Michales' new exploit," said the Metropolitan. "I'm sorry for the palikar, sorry for the man. Wine will be his ruin."

"He'll be the ruin of us! We must curb him. Otherwise . . ."

"In God's name, no rising!" said Hadjisavas. "We've much work to do in Crete. Our soil is blessed, it hides great treasures—statues, inscriptions, royal palaces. How can one carry on excavations in the middle of a rising? Therefore we must——"

"Leave the men of old alone, I tell you," Captain Elias interrupted. "Devil take them, let them leave us in peace! Speak, Mavrudes. My poor brain is blunt. Yours is an ax and cuts. Cut away!"

Old Rose Bug was pleased, and laughed.

"If you will allow, my lord," he said.

"In Heaven's name, what are you thinking of, that you laugh?" asked the Metropolitan. "Your brain's like a woman's. The welfare of Christendom is now in labor."

148

"Alleluia is a short psalm," replied old Mavrudes. "Now, this minute, rise up, my lord, and go to see the pasha. He's a kindly man, an Anatolian, good-natured. He doesn't like trouble. Tell him whatever truth and lies God inspires you with; soothe him, say that he must forgive us for Captain Michales' having been drunk, that we will call him to order and that he won't do it again. Take him some sort of present, too,—let's say a fine tobacco box, or a big piece of amber for his long pipe. The bishopric has precious things for difficult times. Give him something: he's a dog, throw him a bone to gnaw. Then he won't bark. And our renowned fighter here will have a talk with Captain Michales, and may God protect him as he does so!"

"At the deaf man's door you can knock for a long while," said the captain, wagging his scarred head. "He listens to no one, he's like a wall. All the same I'll speak with him. I'm an old man, fought in the 1821 rising: perhaps he'll listen to me. Apart from that, my lord, I think our respected councilor is talking sense. Take your crosier and go to the pasha. Quick, though! Before the blow falls!"

The round salver came with coffee, cakes, conserve. The elders fell silent. Through the window came the scent of the lemon tree in blossom. A bee flew in, circled round the four heads, saw that they were not trees in blossom, and made off. The three spokesmen drank their coffee in great gulps and smacked their lips. They had dispatched the business quickly, and had easily hit on what was to be done. The cream and the sesame cakes too came at the right moment. Hadjisavas asked the Metropolitan for permission to roll a cigarette. The other two did the same. They half shut their eyes, and clouds of smoke rose and veiled the Patriarch, the Czar and Hagia Sophia.

The Metropolitan stretched out his hand and opened a drawer. "My children," he said, "I'm going to show you a remarkable picture. Don't be carried away. You know our friend Murzuflos. It's his work. He is Godfearing, but a visionary. He sees things that we don't see—not because they are not there, but because God has put blinkers over our eyes, as we do to horses, so that they may not be distracted but may remain fixed straight upon their work. But God—who knows for what secret purpose?—has taken the blinkers off the visionaries."

He took out of the drawer a picture wrapped in a piece of white linen. He unwrapped it and held it out to the three spokesmen.

Captain Elias took it, placed it on his knee and stared at it with his one eye.

"That's the Crucifixion," he said, "the Crucifixion. But I can't quite make it out."

Mavrudes bent over it, looked at it, and gave a cry. "God forgive me, my eyes are flickering. But should . . . ?"

"Extraordinary," cried Hadjisavas, who had taken a magnifying glass out of his pocket and was eyeing the picture with it. "A wonderful idea! Bless those hands of yours, Murzuflos! It is the Crucifixion. By my honor, I tell you, if I were a bishop, I'd hang this icon up on the iconostasis in the church."

The Metropolitan gave a bitter laugh and shook his kindly lion head.

"But," said old Mavrudes, "that's not Christ on the cross. I am a sinner, my God, it's a woman, wearing cartridges and silver pistols."

"It is Crete, it is Crete," said the Metropolitan in a voice stifled by emotion. "The cross is raised upon a heap of skulls and bones. The sky is full of dark clouds, and a flash of lightning reveals a monastery in the background to the right. Look at its bell tower, the windmills in front of it, the domes, the walls with towers all around: that is Arkadi. And Crete is nailed to the cross in the form of a tortured mother in black, whose blood runs down on the remains of her children. And below the cross, one on each side, stand two captains, one gray-haired and the other a young man with a broad fez. . . ."

"There's a scroll coming out of his mouth," said old Mavrudes. "It says . . ."

"What does it say?" asked Captain Elias, and bent forward, but could not read it.

Hadjisavas moved his magnifying glass slowly along and read: *"Eli, Eli, lama sabachthani. . . ."*

"My God, my God, why hast Thou forsaken me?" the Metropolitan translated.

For a long while nobody spoke. The four men gazed at the new

Crucifixion and sighed. At last Mavrudes opened his mouth. "Isn't that a sin, my lord? Crete as Christ?"

"It is, it is," replied the Metropolitan with a sigh. "But . . ."

"But what?"

"But she is worth it," murmured the Metropolitan, gazing at the crucified woman, at Crete.

The way Murzuflos had painted her! The suffering that lay over her face! Her cheeks were furrowed, her huge, tormented, deep black eyes were overflowing. And her thin, half-open, twisted lips could be heard sighing. Her naked feet were sprinkled with shining blood, and at the bottom of the picture hung a pair of cream-colored boots.

Suddenly, with a fierce jerk, as though making a great decision, Captain Elias threw his black fez aside, seized the icon and pressed his lips to it. For a long time, as though he could not tear them away. His broad chest rose and fell violently. At last old Mavrudes could hold out no longer. With tears streaming from his eyes, he snatched the icon out of the hands of the gray-headed warrior, bowed over it and kissed it, weeping. Hadjisavas wiped his eyes, stood up and looked out of the window at the blossoming lemon tree.

The Metropolitan took the picture and crossed himself.

"We worship thy sufferings," he murmured, and kissed the blood-spattered feet of Crete. And all together they yielded themselves up without restraint to their sorrow.

The Metropolitan recovered first. He wrapped the icon in its white linen, pushed it to the back of the drawer and stood up.

"Go with my blessing," he said. "May God stretch out His hand over you."

"We must stretch ours out first, Bishop," said Captain Elias. "If God sees no human hand, He doesn't stretch His out either. Remember that!"

"Quite right, quite right, Captain Elias! I'm going to see the pasha at once. God grant I find him in a good mood!"

They bowed and kissed the Metropolitan's plump, white hand. They entered the churchyard. The captain shook his head. He saw, strewn all over the yard, marble hands and feet, severed heads, and dishes with unintelligible inscriptions.

"The men of old," he muttered angrily, "the men of old."
Hadjisavas bent down and began reading from the stones.

"Let's go," Captain Elias said to Mavrudes. "Leave him there.
There are seventy-seven sorts of folly. I'll go and look for Captain
Michales. And as for you, you've Turkish friends. Selim Aga especially. Have a word with them at once. God grant we don't
have another rising before it's time. Crete has already had too
many losses. . . .

At the Metropolitan's street door Barba Jannis stood waiting
for them. He had placed on the ground his basket with the snow
wrapped in straw and the copper can filled with sherbet. From
time to time, if anyone came past, he would cry his wares: "Cold
as snow, cold as ice! Buy the drink of Paradise!"

His piercing falsetto voice tore people's ears. Turks and Christians considered him daft, because he feared neither and openly
said what he thought. He cursed and blasphemed, now against
Christ, now against Mohammed, now against the Sultan. One
Easter, some years ago, he had stood in front of the bloodstained
Mustapha Pasha and had prepared a sherbet with plenty of snow
for his refreshment; and at that moment his spirit had become em-
broiled, and he had begun to bewail the Christians killed at Arkadi
and to leap into the air as though tormented by flames. The
pasha and the effendis sitting beside him in the kiosk by the
Three Vaults had smoked their long pipes and enjoyed the di-
version. People had heard the wailing and they ran up, Turks
and Christians together, and this excited him still more. He had
bent down, picked a blade of grass and brandished it about him
in the air, like one possessed. He wanted to provoke the pasha,
to tear his eyes from his head, to menace him. Suddenly he began
singing shrilly: "O my supple, gleaming saber, oh you'll slaughter
the Turks. . . ."

Christians and Turks were dumfounded; they did not know
how to take it, and gazed at the pasha to see what he would do.
Surprisingly, the pasha had clapped his hands and burst into peals
of laughter. What a piece of fooling—this human ruin who would
menace Turkey with a grass blade!

"Bravo, Captain Barba Jannis," he had called out. "Come here!"

The effendis, too, burst out laughing, and the people joined in. And Barba Jannis danced and sang and howled on.

"That's enough, now," the pasha had shouted. "Now you've done for us all: Turkey is lying on the ground! Come here, I tell you, you idiot palikar, I like you. I'm going to present you with a real saber, and pin a high decoration on your chest: the open hand, Mohammed's seal. And now listen carefully: I give you the freedom, every Easter, to gird the saber on, wear your decoration and strut like a pasha through Megalokastro from the Kanea to the Hospital Gate, and from the New to the Harbor Gate. And you've the freedom, every day, to say whatever comes into that silly head of yours, and even to curse me. You're a fool, your words are free of treason. For years, Barba Jannis, I haven't laughed so much as today, and for that I give you thanks."

So it had come about that Barba Jannis was the only free man in Megalokastro. When there was unrest in the air, Barba Jannis was the first to scent it. And what the Christians had in mind but dared not yet express, he shouted out loud with the sherbet in summer and the salepi in winter, and brought relief to Christendom. When he went too far, he sometimes got a box on the ear, and the Turks threw lemon peel and rotten tomatoes at him, but this did not stop Barba Jannis from letting his tongue work on.

Since yesterday he had smelled powder in the air. He had seen, too, the three elders going thoughtfully into the Metropolitan's residence in the early morning. That had put a flea in his ear. He took up his position by the street door of the residence and waited. He must find out what was going on. Easter was near. He would have to put on his saber and his tin decoration, and vent his rage outside the Three Vaults while the pasha and the effendis listened to the band. In that way he would give the underdogs, who might not say a word, some satisfaction.

As he saw the two elders emerge, he picked up his snow-basket and can and approached them.

"Good day, elders," he said. "Wait a moment. I'll make you a sherbet to cool you. It's getting warm."

"Leave us in peace, Barba Jannis," said Captain Elias. "We don't want your sherbet."

153

"Don't be so rude, Captain Elias. I'm not afraid of you. I'm a fool, you know, and I'm not afraid either of pasha or of sultan, while all you clever gentry and captains are pissing in your breeches. But Barba Jannis has his saber and his letter of freedom and his folly. What comes into his mind, that he says without fear."

"I wish you well, Barba Jannis," old Rose Bug said gently. "Curb your tongue, the time hasn't come yet."

"When will it come?" asked Barba Jannis. "I want to know."

Captain Elias raised his cudgel. Barba Jannis moved on.

The Metropolitan hung round his neck the golden talisman—one side of which represented, in many-colored enamel, the Crucifixion, and the other the Resurrection—and put in his pocket an old silver tobacco box from the celebrated workshops of Jannina, whose Metropolitan was his friend and had given it to him. He picked up his crosier and went on foot, with the deacon following him, to the pasha's entrance gate.

Meanwhile the pasha slumbered, stretched out on soft cushions. He was having a dream. He had gone for a walk in the garden of his home town, Broussa. The trees stretched their branches over him, some laden with blossom, others with fruit. As he smoked his long pipe and wandered about, he thought he was in Paradise, and that at any moment Mohammed, with his little mirror, comb and phial of perfume in his red sash, might come out to bid him welcome.

But as he turned for an instant, what should he see? A sturdy olive tree, scorched by lightning and twisted, without either leaves or blossoms. On its branches there hung fruit of a strange kind: guns and cartridges and daggers and black headbands. What sort of accursed olive tree was this, that bore weapons instead of fruit? cried the pasha in terror, and shrank back, to return again to his garden of blossom and fruit. But the garden had disappeared, and about him the pasha saw nothing but wild deserts and cliffs and, beyond these, bushes of muskets and silver pistols.

"Crete! Crete!" yelled the pasha and sprang up.

At that moment Suleiman the Arab opened the door.

"Pasha Effendi," he said, "the big pasha of the Greeks has come. He's coming up the stairs."

154

"I've had a bad dream, Suleiman," said the pasha, wiping the cold sweat from his forehead.

"Shall I tell the great beast to take himself off?"

The pasha reflected for a moment: "No, let him come in, you blockhead. These imams of the giaours are good interpreters of dreams. He'll explain this one to me. Let him come."

The Metropolitan entered, and the two highest dignitaries of Megalokastro greeted each other. They were like two gray-headed kings in this community, and their kingdoms were the Turkish and the Greek quarters. Cross and crescent were intertwined.

They sat down side by side on the broad divan. The pasha lighted his long pipe; the Metropolitan pulled out his rosary and began to tell its black ebony beads and to ponder how the conversation ought to begin. Through the open window were visible the buildings of the guard and the old plane tree with its young leaves. Near the plane tree could be seen the famous Venetian fountain with the marble lion. A warm wind was blowing.

The pasha yawned and began:

"Summer is here, Metropolitan Effendi. O Allah, how time passes! It is a wheel and never stops turning, and we turn with it. Summer comes and one says: 'How hot it is! I'm stifling!' and while one is saying so, the thunderstorms and the rains set in, and one wraps oneself in one's cloak. What does your religion say to these mysterious things?"

But before the Metropolitan could frame an answer, the pasha, in whose inside a worm was gnawing, asked him:

"Do you believe in dreams, Metropolitan Effendi? Where do they come from? Who sends them to us?"

"Some are sent by God," replied the Metropolitan, "others by the Evil Spirit."

"And how can you tell the difference? Which are from God? Which from the Evil Spirit?"

"You have surely had a dream, Pasha Effendi. It still lies on your eyelids, I can see it."

"Yes, that is why I am asking you."

"May it have been a good and blessed one, Pasha Effendi. Let me hear it."

"Do you understand something about dreams?"

"God sometimes grants me enlightenment. Well?"

The pasha sighed and recounted the dream. He added a little decoration to the olive tree. He said he had seen several heads hanging from its branches.

The Metropolitan lowered his lion head thoughtfully. He was seeking to use this dream to his own purpose.

"Well, is it from the Evil Spirit?" asked the pasha uneasily.

"From God," the Metropolitan answered. "But how can I interpret it, Pasha Effendi? Perhaps it disturbs you?"

"I be disturbed?" exclaimed the pasha. "Don't you know that a true Mussulman is never disturbed? For he knows that everything that happens in the world has already been written, and no one can strike it out. If at this moment the Sultan were to send me a firman demanding my head, I might well bewail, I certainly would bewail, but I would not be disturbed. It was written so. Shall I put my hand into God's plan? So speak out without fear, Metropolitan Effendi. But beware of lies. Tell the whole truth!"

The Metropolitan thought for a few moments, then said:

"The garden which you saw in your dream is the good man's heart. Your heart is a garden, Pasha Effendi: it is opened at night, to let you go in and walk about. What you saw in your sleep was what answers to your nature: to wander tranquilly and at peace beneath blossoming trees in Broussa, the town where you were born. . . . Your heart is a garden, but behold, for you it was written that you should become pasha and undertake this office here in Crete. . . ."

The pasha sighed. "What can I say to you, Metropolitan Effendi? It is true, as if you were reading my heart. But go on."

"When a man's village lies before him, Pasha Effendi, he needs no guide to it. The olive tree hung with weapons that you saw is Crete. You stood under the lightning-scorched tree, and your face darkened. Here your destiny begins to be troubled. It is a great pity that you woke up and do not now know what followed. Perhaps God wrote for you, further on, that He gives you freedom, from now on, to do as you will. The responsibility is yours."

"Yes, it may be as you say, Metropolitan Effendi," said the good Anatolian. "By the sun which shines over us, Christians and Turks could live as brothers; the Greeks work, the Turks eat, and both lead a happy life."

"It lies in your hands!" the Metropolitan exclaimed, having now found the starting point he had been looking for. "It is in your power to bring love to the island. God sent you the dream at the right moment!"

"What do you mean by that, Metropolitan Effendi? I don't understand."

"You have heard, no doubt, that Christians and Turks in Megalokastro are beginning once more to be stirred up, because, so they say, a drunken horseman forced his way into the Turkish coffeehouse."

"And does that seem to you a trifle? The giaour has put Turkey to shame!" the pasha exclaimed, his eyes coming to life.

"Turkey is not so easily put to shame. She is a mighty realm, Pasha Effendi!" said the Metropolitan in a studiously mild tone of voice. "Let's leave the drunkard hero. You were asking me about your dream. I believe that God is enlightening me, and I will interpret it for you. Though if it bores you—"

"No, by the Prophet!" said the pasha emphatically and placed his hand entreatingly on the Metropolitan's knee. "By your faith, go on."

"The seven heavens opened. God came down to you in your sleep, Pasha Effendi, and showed you the way."

"What way?"

"The way you will choose. There are two: one green and the other red. I can see them clearly marked in your dream. You can choose which you will."

"No, not as I will," protested the pasha, "but as it is written by God!"

"But it may be, I tell you, that God has written for you a free choice. You can decide on the red road and start the executions and set Crete in a blaze. Or you can decide on the green road, and then everything turns to milk and honey: Turks and Christians make friends again, and the world blesses your name. Now choose!"

So saying, and without giving the pasha time to think, he pulled out of his pocket the precious tobacco box.

"You are a connoisseur, Pasha Effendi," he said softly, "you know something about treasures. This tobacco box is a masterpiece from Jannina. On one side it has a two-headed eagle, on the other a crescent, engraved with the finest art. Just what you are working for: Mussulmans and Christians living together in brotherhood. Knowing your heart, I have long wanted to give it to you. The time has come. May it bring you luck!"

With that he laid the silver box in the pasha's open palm.

"By Allah," said the pasha, admiring the present, "you Greeks are an immortal race. You catch flies, sometimes with honey, sometimes with vinegar."

He bent forward and stroked the tobacco box delicately with his thick fingers.

"Yes, let me tell you, Metropolitan Effendi, what a rain of sweetness this box from Jannina brings to my heart. My first wife —may she be happy in the underworld, where she now is—possessed five-fold beauty like the Lady Phrosyne; she came from Jannina." With a sigh he added: "But how can you understand that? for you know no woman."

They fell silent. The Metropolitan played with his rosary and looked through the window at the great plane tree, which slowly moved its leaves under the blue sky. He brought the conversation back to earth:

"The crops promise well, Pasha Effendi," he said, and looked out of the window again at the green fields.

The pasha tore himself away from the sweet past and came back to Megalokastro.

The Metropolitan stood up. The pasha also stood up, and held out his hand. "Good-by, Metropolitan Effendi," he said. "Both of us are Godfearing men. We have deliberated wisely and have divided Crete wisely. You keep a tight hand over the Christians, and I will do the same with the Turks."

He was silent for a moment. Another sentence was on the tip of his tongue. He coughed, scratched his head and at length decided to say it.

"Noisiness at weddings is common—but even if, in these coming days, you hear a noise that sounds like a killing, pretend it never reached your ears."

"A killing, Pasha Effendi?" asked the Metropolitan, glancing uneasily at the gray-headed Turk with the deep-set eyes. "God forbid."

"Come, come, a drunken Turk might one day kill a Greek

158

palikar. Such things do happen. There's no lack of fools in the world. But you, Metropolitan, you act deaf, just as we acted blind, when we didn't see a certain Greek ride into the Turkish coffeehouse and flout us. So you act deaf now, Metropolitan Effendi. My best wishes."

A snake wound itself about the Metropolitan, but he pretended not to understand.

"God is great," he said. "He judges even sultans and pashas."

"And Metropolitans, Effendi," said the old Anatolian, and his lips smiled cunningly.

And on that they parted.

Days came and went. It was the middle of April. The trees were covered with blossoms; some were already bearing fruit. The spring sunshine enveloped Megalokastro. Within its walls men and women suffered. They had separated into two angry bands, each with its God. And men and Gods whetted their knives. They did not notice the cool sea, which smelled like a peach, nor the sun, which blossomed like a heliotrope every morning, nor the stars.

Taciturn and somber, Captain Michales went back to his shop. For the first time a carouse had failed to lighten his heart. The drinking bout had left him angrier, more disconsolate than before. Now he avoided every drop of alcohol and would eat only a piece of bread, then at once leave the table. At home he did not open his mouth all day long. He refused to sleep. He sat on his bed and smoked and looked through the narrow window at the night. He would not close his eyes, because he knew that in sleep dishonoring dreams would overcome him. No. One dream, one demon, which fell upon him every night. Was wine powerless to stifle this demon and his shame?

Nuri Bey also could not sleep. He was gnawed by the thought that he must keep his word to wash Turkey clean of disgrace and avenge his father's blood. To this was added the anxiety about his wife. Ever since the day when Captain Michales had been to his house, Eminé had refused to take him in her arms. "He's put you to shame," she said obstinately, drumming on the floor with her little slippers. "Captain Michales has put you to

159

shame, so I shall put you to shame. That's the custom among our women."

To distract himself, Nuri Bey had turned to his country estate. The weather was warm: soon the hanum would come out, as she did every year, to spend the summer among gardens and flowing water. And God is great: perhaps her thoughts would grow mild here and her love rise afresh. So he spurred his workmen on to paint doors and windows and to constuct little pavilions of brushwood. Also he ordered canaries from Smyrna and parrots from Alexandria to pass the time for Eminé. This would soften her mood, he hoped.

But she reclined on soft cushions behind the lattice of the balcony on the street, drinking sherbet, chewing mastic and eyeing the passers-by. She made no distinction between Greeks and Turks, they were all men to her.

"What's a Turk, a Christian or a Jew, Maria?" she asked her old nurse. "There are only two kinds of men—old or young, white beards or black beards. I like the black ones."

Every evening, as the sun sank and the alleys grew shadowy, a Greek with a large fez and jaunty boots walked back and forth, casting loving glances at the latticed balcony above.

"Who is that Greek, Maria? Where have I seen him?" Eminé asked the Moorish woman one day. "It seems to me as if I'd seen him in a dream."

"He's the one who roused you out of your faint, the day of the earthquake," answered the Moorish woman. "Captain Polyxigis."

"He looks handsome, by my soul. He has gaiety written in his face. He sways and stretches, and his boots creak. Listen, the poor man's sighing like a calf."

Eminé laughed, and felt eager for him. She half closed her long-lashed eyes and smiled contentedly. I'll do as I want, she thought. If I want, I'll fetch him into my bed. If I want, I'll leave him in the street, to wander about like a dog. Am I not a woman? I'll do as I want.

One midnight, when the street was empty of people, Captain Polyxigis took up his position beneath the latticed balcony. The moon was shining, honeysuckle and jasmine were fragrant, and in Nuri's garden the nightingale twittered a hopeless love-longing.

From the harbor, the sea, too, sighed and moved its breast against the fortress wall.

Eminé could not sleep. She was hot. She threw off her night-dress and peeped out, and saw in the moonlight a man, exhausted, leaning against the pillar of the street door. She recognized him at once. She laughed and nudged the Moorish woman, who was asleep, curled up like a hare.

"The poor thing," she said giggling. "Come, have a look at him. He's almost fainted, I think, and I should love to go down and rouse him. The way he roused me! What do you think, Maria? Nuri Bey is at the estate."

"Eminé, my child, it would be a great sin."

"For you," retorted the hanum, "for you, because you're a Christian. But I'm a Moslem. I've a different God and different laws. You eat pig's flesh and are not defiled. But if you nibble at a strange man, you are defiled. With us it's the other way round: pig's flesh defiles us, a strange man doesn't. Go, tell him to come up."

"Eminé, my child . . ." the Moorish woman pleaded, bewildered.

"See first if the Moor at the door is asleep."

"He's asleep," said Maria with a sigh. "I heard him snoring."

"Is the dog tied up too? Go on, you silly hen, stop shivering. Show some zest . . . God made men and women for this, you poor creature! Ah, what a moon there is tonight, what a warm wind! The jasmine is in blossom, and the nightingale is mad. Go on, fetch him up. I've often thought: in winter a woman can be respectable, but in the spring . . . ?"

Leaning forward, Eminé saw Captain Polyxigis still at his post, staring up at the lighted lattice. "I don't care for Nuri, and Captain Michales is not to be had: this one here is good enough for me!" She reached for her comb and mirror, hastily tidied her hair, rubbed musk under her armpits and gave the nurse a push. "Go on, I tell you!"

Holding her head, the Moorish woman stumbled down the stairs.

Eminé splashed the rest of the musk over her bosom and body. She stood up and pulled the lamp back behind the door. "I wanted another one," she murmured, "but he is wild and unapproachable. Doesn't matter, this one too suits me."

She pricked up her ears. She heard the street door slowly open. The dog barked once, steps became audible in the yard, in the men's part, on the stairs. . . . She leaned back on the cushions and started to put on her nightdress again. But she thought better of it and let the moon shine unhindered on her breasts and body. Boots squeaked on the floor. The smell of a man came in and Eminé's nostrils quivered. She passed her tongue over her lips. Then she half closed her eyes and waited.

Captain Polyxigis now stood on the threshold. She gazed at him through her long lashes. He raised his hand to his eyes as though he were giddy; his heart was beating wildly. The Circassian flung her arms wide in the moonlight and lay back. As if this were the agreed signal, Captain Polyxigis bounded toward her and extinguished the lamp.

April was nearing its end, and filled with fear, the Christians entered Passion Week. In the whole of Christendom there was no people that shared so deeply, so bloodily, in so special a way, in the sufferings of Christ as the Cretans during these decades. In their hearts Christ and Crete were mingled, the sufferings of both were the same: the Jews crucified Christ and the Turks Crete. The Christians felt in themselves how the sufferings of Christ mounted from day to day, as they grew weak from watching and fasting, until in their hearts an angry accusation sought to vent itself. They eyed the Turks wildly, and only with difficulty could they restrain themselves from striking down the few Jews—tinsmiths and money-changers—who lived huddled in the Jews' alley near the harbor. The Jews always bolted themselves in early during the sacred and dangerous time of Passion Week.

This time the atmosphere in Megalokastro was even more threatening than ever, for the Turks had not yet got over the injury done them by Captain Michales. At night they crowded to St. Menas' church, where the Christians were mourning for Christ. They hurled curses and tried with noisy singing to insult and dishonor the Christians. The Christians waited hourly to know where, when and how the agas would strike. The subterranean excitement grew stronger and stronger.

So passed, in incense-burning, watching and fasting, the Monday, Tuesday and Wednesday of Holy Week. The evening hours were soft and blue. Violets bloomed in all the courtyards; on Good Friday the girls would pick them, to place them along with the elder blossom and the last April roses on the cloth with the picture of the dead Christ. Immediately after sundown the Christians shut their shops, went home to their houses and rapidly ate the meal prescribed for a time of fasting: baked beans, lettuce, raw artichokes, red fishes' roes, olives and sesame soup. They paced around their yards, listening and waiting. St. Menas' bell rang out, hesitant and mournful, in the mild twilight. The Christians crossed themselves, opened their doors and streamed, bowed down and silent, through the alleys of Megalokastro, to learn once more, how God had suffered at the hands of men.

As the days of Passion Week went by, the excitement of the Cretans rose. On Maundy Thursday, as the reading of the twelve Gospel lessons began, and as the Metropolitan, Pope Manoles, and the Deacon in turn read, in harsh monotone voices, how Judas had betrayed Christ and how the Mohammedans of those days had begun to strike, mock and scourge Him, the people were affected as though they themselves were running breathlessly with Christ from Annas to Caiaphas and to Pilate, as Omer Vrioni had run to Mustapha Pasha and to the Sultan, to demand justice.

With growing impatience they managed to listen to the first seven lessons; then they rushed headlong out into the churchyard, where early that morning a Judas of daubed clouts and straw had been set up. They fell upon it with knives and burning torches, pierced it through and set it on fire. This relieved and cheered them all a little, so that they then went back into the church, to hear the remaining lessons.

On Good Friday morning the bells rang sorrowfully. Over the holy tomb in the middle of the church the cloth bearing the image of Christ was spread. The church doors stood wide open, and Christians went in and out.

In the churchyard stood Murzuflos, exhausted from watching and fasting. Round him stood Demetros, Kajabes, Vendusos, and Signor Paraskevas the barber. With bent heads they were all listening to the words of Murzuflos. He was telling them how yesterday the pasha had sent his Arab to the Metropolitan with the present of a hare. But the Metropolitan had been angry and had sent the hare back to the pasha with a message:

"We are fasting. The Jews have killed Christ, and we are mourning."

"He should not have sent it back," said Paraskevas. "That was an insult."

"The pasha shouldn't have sent it," said Kajabes; "*that* was an insult. Doesn't the dog know that we are in Passion Week?"

"It's pure madness," said Demetros with a sigh. "Are we now going to go against the pasha? Hit the egg with a stone and it goes to the devil. Hit the stone with the egg and again the egg goes to the devil. That's what I think."

During the holy days Captain Michales did not go to church with the crowds. He honored God and prayed to him, but could not abide the priests. His custom was to wait till the church emptied and the priests' vestments—women's skirts—were out of the way. When the place was pure he would visit it and light his candle. But always on Maundy Thursday morning, whether consciously or not, he would come to church when the popes were still there, and receive Communion. He would cross himself, open his mouth and receive the body and blood of Christ. He would feel the great fire die down within him.

But this year, for the first time in his life, he did not go to Communion. He rode aimlessly into the countryside on his mare. He got as far as the estate of Nuri Bey, but stopped short and turned. He breathed in the sea air. As long as the evil spirit is in me, he said to himself again and again, breathing heavily, as long as the evil spirit stays in me, I won't go to Communion.

There was no day in the year longer than Good Friday: it stretched over five afternoons, lost its way, stood still, took one step forward and two back and would not let evening come. The Christians, hungry from their fast, could feel themselves growing weak as they passed the fragrant bakeries. The women went about their housework as though possessed. They cleaned the rooms. Great fires were kept going. The courtyards were freshly scrubbed. Hearts were expectant, they were waiting for the setting of the sun, and then for the merciful, dark blue night to rise up, fulfilling the cry: "Christ is risen!"

Krasojorgis' wife kept looking up at the sun and measuring the time. The star of blessing, it seemed, would never come forth in the sky. The smell of the chicken cooking and of the custard cakes which her son Andrikos had brought from Tulupanas' bakery, made her nearly faint.

Penelope had been painting eggs since Maundy Thursday. They had turned out very well. Now she was gaily preparing the tripe soup in the kitchen. Mr. Demetros ran about at her orders with pots and pans, to and fro between house and bakery. "Up, my Demetros! Courage, my hero! This evening Christ rises; this evening I shall need you, my treasure! Are you listening? All this meat and these custard cakes must not be wasted."

God granted Krasojorgis' wife her prayer at last and made the sun go down. Easter smells spread over Megalokastro in the dusk. The Christian quarters filled with loud gaiety. The women began to adorn themselves. Vangelio too dressed carefully and sat in the courtyard waiting for her brother. Would he come? Or not? Would he take her to the Easter service alone for the last time? Next year they would have Tityros with them.

Midnight drew near. The Christians went out into their yards and listened for the chimes to begin. Already Christ was stirring in His grave, already He was gathering His strength to heave the heavy stone aside. All Christians stood on tiptoe in the court-yards and at their windows and waited. Only two in all Megalo-kastro were not with God in their thoughts. One of them, on this holy night, held a Circassian woman in his arms. The other sat upright on his bed in the dark and smoked one cigarette after an-other. Like a dog, his thoughts ran through the narrow alleys and stopped, barking, in front of a green door.

The Christians collected in the forecourt of the church gazed at their Metropolitan. They had not yet lighted their candles. The Metropolitan, in his Easter vestments, had gone up to the laurel-decorated platform under the blossoming lemon tree, and now opened the heavy silver Gospel. The faces showed light, and the night breeze played over them. And as the thundering cry rang out, "Christ is risen from the dead," the holy light flared up and all the candles were lighted and all Christians arose with Christ. The leaders fired their silver pistols, and Murzuflos, his joy over-flowing, set the three bells—Saint Menas, Freedom and Death—swinging, and they announced: "Crete is not dead. Crete lives!"

Barba Jannis girded on his long saber and his tin decoration and strutted up and down. This was his day of rest; today he sold no sherbet. Turks and Christians laughingly bowed before him, and he returned every greeting with the dignity of a pasha. He had hired a street boy and had daubed his face with soot; now he had a Moor, who followed him at every step.

The gnome Charilaos, with his mustache freshly waxed, went visiting in his carriage. He wore a straw hat brought from Athens. He supported his chin on his stick, and observed the people with spiteful looks. He could not forgive them for their shapely bodies.

Toward evening Christian men and women, dressed for Easter, milled around the Three Vaults. The silk ribbons in the girls' hair fluttered in the wind. To the north the rose-colored sea lay at peace, to the south the fields were green, the mountains glittered and the silvery olive trees shimmered. A violet, silken, very soft sky was a shield over all. Slowly the evening shadows grew darker, the faces of the Kastrians, now richly fed, became peaceful as they strolled and suddenly Venus hung in triumphant laughter high above the heads of the people.

6

RICH IN STRONG MANHOOD, Captain Michales' family rose at dawn in the four villages—Petrokefalo, Ai-Janni, Kruson and Redtower—in which it had been rooted since the times of his ancestors, and set out for Megalokastro, to be present at the wedding ceremony of the youngest brother, Tityros. They all came together in the mother-place of the family, Petrokefalo, where the hundred-year-old grandfather and father of them all, old Captain Sefakas, lived. He was to lead the procession. Some came on mules, some on horses, on which red cloths had been laid and wedding presents loaded: cooked lambs and suckling pigs, hard and soft cheeses, leather bottles of wine and oil, pots of honey, raisins, figs and little bags of almonds.

With a great stride old Sefakas crossed the threshold. He wore his best suit of heavy wool, black boots, a black headband and carried his long, double-handled stick. His beard streamed over his chest, his deep-set eyes sparkled under thick eyebrows, and from the wide sleeves of his snow-white shirt his arms showed, lean and furrowed as the stems of ancient olive trees. He looked about him. The street was motley with sons, grandsons and great-grandsons. He was glad.

"A thousand times welcome, children!" he shouted to them, throwing his arms wide open. "A field full of flowers and grasses!"

A single shout of joy answered him out of the human swarm that had come from his loins.

"We're happy to see you again! Rejoice in your kingdom, old man!"

Two grandchildren led an old mare up to him. One of them

held the reins, the other a stirrup. They placed the beast near the rim of the fountain in the yard, to make it easier for the ancient to mount. But with a laugh he shoved his grandchildren aside. "Do you think I've got old, that you must hold the stirrups for me?" He seized the mare by the mane and with one heave was in the saddle.

"Health and joy to you, old man! May you live a thousand years!" they yelled at him.

"A thousand years are a long time, children!" replied the graybeard, pulling his headband tight. "Five hundred will do!"

He had begotten eleven sons and four daughters, wild beasts all! Only the straggler was no good. He was lean and lanky, a fart. How the devil had such a product sprung from his loins?

"What are we going to do with him?" he had debated with his wife. "He'll be no good as a shepherd, he hasn't the pluck for stealing. He'll be no good as a farmer, he hasn't the strength for plowing. He'll be no good as a sailor, the sea makes him sick. He's no good for anything!"

"He'd make a good pope," suggested the old woman, to whom her youngest son was especially dear.

"A pope or a schoolmaster. In the village we've got a pope, but not yet a schoolmaster. So let's make him into a schoolmaster."

He had sent him to Megalokastro, to study—and so a son of Captain Sefakas had become the schoolmaster Tityros.

Old Sefakas had been relieved at getting him out of the house, for he was ashamed to call him son. His ten wild beasts remained on the large farm. He was proud of them. "When my sons are eating," he used to say, "the house trembles, so that strangers ask: 'Is it an earthquake? Oh no, Sefakas' sons are having a meal!'"

But Charos* had come, posted himself on the threshold and looked over the wide yard. Here, it seemed to him, were far too many palikars growing up. He sought out his share. Some he took honestly and in manly fashion, in war; others he stole cunningly from their beds. Yet enough remained, thought Sefakas, and they had given him grandchildren and great-grandchildren. One leaves

---

* One of the many survivals of ancient religion among the Christian Greeks. But as Nilsson—*A History of Greek Religion* (Oxford Press 1925), p. 303—points out, Charos or Charondas is greatly changed from the ferryman of the Styx. Charos is "the strong and cruel robber, who mercilessly snatches men away from their life in the light of day."

168

a hundred behind him, and then a thousand, and in the end Crete will be full of them. How many will Charos devour by means of the Turks? Yet enough yeast will remain to make the dough rise.

"In God's name, children!" he said, raising his hand, "forward, let's marry the last son."

At the head of the procession rode the old man. A step behind him, came the two eldest sons, with years upon them already, but still strong: Manusakas, the passionate farmer from Ai-Janni, and Famurios, the guerilla leader and great herdsman. Famurios was a man of the grasslands with a fierce face and smelling of cheese and ghosts. All the Lasithi mountains were his province. When the mountain loneliness oppressed him, he would come down from the bald heights to the plains. He would seek out the bull belonging to Hadjinikolés in Petrokefalo. If he found him tied up to an olive tree, he would untie him and fight with him to get rid of his depression.

He was afraid of only one wild beast in the world: his wife Despainia. She was a yellowish bit of flesh with light blue eyes. If you blew on her she would fall over. But the wild Famurios trembled before her. Every time he came down to the village to stay at home a few days to beget a child on her, he behaved decorously before her and adopted human manners. He wanted to drink and did not drink, wanted to curse and did not curse, wanted to spit against the wall and did not spit. He would wait for the night, till his wife had gone to bed. Then he would stick his paw out of the door, grab by the neck anyone who came by and drag him in. He would sit down opposite his guest and they would set to work drinking, without making a sound. Sometimes he would drag in more than one. They would lay their fingers on the rims of their glasses so that they could touch glasses without a sound. They drank until Famurios decided that they had had enough. Then he took them again by the neck and bundled them out. Only then did he visit his wife in bed. In this way his many children had been begotten.

The dust on the road whirled high, the sun was scorching. From time to time old Sefakas turned his heated face back and cast a swift glance at his followers. Behind Manusakas and Famurios came the grandsons—stately men, all of them. After

169

them the great-grandsons, with fair or raven-black down on their cheeks. And at the end of the procession the noisy, cackling womenfolk.

Then he looked ahead again, toward Megalokastro. He made no conversation with his sons, nor did he smile. His heart was satisfied and at peace. He no longer needed anything or anybody. Lately the words had remained within him. If any secret anxiety still gnawed at him, he could not speak of it with anyone else— only with God.

And recently, in fact, strange meditations had been revolving in his brain. For the first time old Sefakas was thinking of death. The day was drawing near when he would stand before God, and the gray-haired man of authority shuddered at the thought. He pictured death as a dark mountain, with rushing waters for which he was thirsty and wild beasts of which he was afraid. He remembered how once, during a rising, he had slipped out all alone at night onto Cruel Mountain, outside Megalokastro, where the Turks lay. He had gone forward slowly, bent double, with his knife between his teeth. Then he caught soft sounds of speech, saw cigarettes glowing, heard weapons clinking together and saw them gleaming in the darkness. Trembling he had crept away. God now seemed to him like that mountain.

Vangelio had had a hot bath. Renio was combing her hair with the ivory comb given her by her godfather, Idomeneas. She put rouge on Vangelio's cheeks to hide their yellow tinge, and powder on her nose to make it look less large, while the bride sat in silence before the mirror. Penelope and Krasojorgis' wife were decorating the bridal bed, strewing it with lucky lemon blossoms, as they trilled wedding songs. Both women were already slightly tipsy. Below in the kitchen those two good housewives, Katerina the wife of Captain Michales and Polyxigis' sister Chrysanthe, were preparing the wedding feast. Ali Aga was bringing all the plates, knives and forks in the neighborhood.

Diamandes entered with his cloak draped foppishly over his shoulders, gave offhand, sleepy, dissipated greetings and stared with his round eyes at the disturbed house. He pursed his lips and played nervously with his watchchain. All this was not to his liking. They had done very well without a brother-in-law. Why the devil was that fellow with the long coattails and the sagging glasses intruding on them? With heavy tread he stamped up the stairs. Krasojorgis' wife looked at him knowingly. She knew he had only bought his watch to show off and was quite incapable of telling the time, and that his friends teased him about it. So she asked him, mockingly:

"What time do you make it, Mr. Diamandes?"

"It's stopped, woman," he snapped back angrily. "It isn't going."

He turned away from her and saw how they were adorning his sister. They're preparing the victim for the sacrifice, he thought. His sister felt his gaze and turned toward him. Her eyes filled with tears.

Penelope broke in: "We're dressing the bride. Men are in the way here."

The handsome man pulled a hair out of his mustache and threw it onto the bed.

"May it bring luck," he said, and stumped downstairs, sighing.

The narrow street filled with horsemen and the twilight was alive with neighing and the clinking of harness. Captain Sefakas had arrived with his train. The doors of Vangelio's house swung open and immediately the smell of male sweating bodies, cooked meat and cheese poured through the house. The old grandfather took the bony Vangelio in his arms and kissed her. Then all her new kin fell upon her and enveloped her in the stink of sweat and goats and vinous breath. The bride's cheeks were rubbed raw by the bristling whiskers and beards that pressed against them. She ran upstairs into the bedroom to put on more rouge and powder herself afresh.

There was not enough room for the guests in the downstairs room, so the women went up to the bedroom, and some into the kitchen, and spread out the presents. Many of the men stretched themselves out in the yard. The house hummed.

"Don't make such a row, children," shouted Captain Polyxigis, as he ran up and down greeting his new sisters-in-law. "Don't make such a row, we're in Megalokastro here, not in the mountains."

Tityros and godfather Idomeneas soon got away from the embracings and greetings and began whispering together on a corner of the sofa. Tityros talked enthusiastically of the many old marriage customs still alive among the people. These Greeks were immortal. And he was glad, not because he was getting married, but because he was being married according to ancient custom. Idomeneas answered that he had yesterday sent a pressing ultimatum to the Queen of England. In a few days without a doubt he would have a reply, and a favorable one too. "God grant, godson," he said, "that your wedding may be a day of good fortune, and Crete may be set free."

Captain Michales appeared, with serious countenance, took off his cap and kissed his father's hand. Then in the courtyard he shook hands with his brothers and nephews, pretended not to see Captain Polyxigis and, going back into the house, sat down on the settle beside his father. The old man whispered in his son's ear, "The bride looks to me a right sorry sight, Michales."

"She suits the looks of the bridegroom," replied Captain Michales.

The old man shook his head and laughed drily.

But their conversation was interrupted. Pope Manoles with the capacious pockets, the deacon with the wild boar beard, and Murzuflos with the silver censer, entered. All rose. The freshly painted bride came down, her godfather took the bridegroom by the hand, Murzuflos filled the censer, and the intoning began. The bride kept her head bowed, and the wild clan, massive and breathing deeply, all full-bloodedness and mustaches, stood about and stared at her. This spindly woman was now entering their clan and would mix her blood with theirs. Would it work out? They were all herdsmen and plowmen, they knew a thing or two about cattle: which goat or bull to couple with which she-goat or cow to get the strongest young and make the herd thrive. And the women knew a thing or two about cocks, hens and rabbits; they sized up the young couple uneasily.

"The bride's very thin. She has no breasts. How's she going to nurse children?"

"Don't you worry. She'll give milk. Do you remember, last year, the she-goat Mavrada. Skin and bones she was, and you could hardly see her udder! But she was fruitful and had kids and yielded—you won't believe it!—a quart of milk at every milking!"

"She hasn't any hips either. How will she bear a child?"

"Don't get worried, she'll broaden out now. They all fill out when they marry."

The women went on whispering, and Pope Manoles sang the wedding words: "Isaiah danced. . . ."

When the service was over, the godfather carried out the exchange of crowns, and the relatives fell upon the young couple yet again, wishing them long life and an honored old age. Then at the loaded table the chewing and gurgling began. Later, the bridegroom could not remember when all this had happened. A cloud sank over his thoughts, and it was only dimly that he distinguished faces and voices—his father enthroned on the sofa, holding a roast suckling pig on his knee, Captain Michales on his right and on his left Captain Polyxigis. And later—he could remember this a little—in came Diamandes, his wife's brother, and greeted no one. His cap was drawn right down to his eyes. He went straight into the kitchen, to drink and celebrate there. Then Captain Polyxigis leaped up from the sofa and followed Diamandes; immediately after, there was the sound of disputing voices and glass breaking.

Captain Michales gnashed his teeth and started after them, but thought better of it. He remained seated, but his blood boiled. His daughter Renio came up to him with the salver and offered him fresh cherry juice. He became calmer as he drank. He gave the girl a friendly look. He had already seen her somewhere. Who could she be? All evening she had attended to him and had unobtrusively brought him whatever he wanted: water, wine, something to eat, a cigarette. He signed to his wife, who was carving the meat for the guests.

"Who's that nice girl?" He indicated Renio with a glance. "I've seen her somewhere. But where?"

Katerina sighed. "She's your daughter."

Captain Michales bent his head and made no sound after that.

Captain Polyxigis came back sweating. All eyes were turned on him. He managed to put on a smile, and said, "He's drunk. You must excuse him."

He sat down next to Captain Michales, to put him in a friendly mood and make him forget the behavior of the unmannerly Diamandes. Captain Michales' nostrils twitched: his friend smelled of musk. Captain Polyxigis went on trying to soften him. For days Captain Michales had been repulsing him roughly: why? After having several glasses of wine to give him courage, he burst out: "What have I done, Captain Michales, to make you dislike me?"

"You smell too Turkish for me," came the answer.

Captain Polyxigis blushed.

Captain Michales stared him straight in the eyes. Suddenly his heart leaped high in his throat and seemed about to stifle him. He seized the chair which Renio had brought him to put his feet on; the chair cracked as though its joints would give.

"Now I know," he said through closed teeth. "Aren't you ashamed? With a Turkish woman?"

"She's going to become Christian," said Captain Polyxigis.

Captain Michales jumped up. The house swayed before his eyes. "Instead of her turning Christian, why don't you turn Turk? Then we shall be rid of you," he said softly, and went out into the yard to get some air.

It was almost daybreak but everyone continued to eat and drink. Bagpipes were brought out and played, while in the yard the guests sang and danced the dance of the five rows. The newly married couple sat silent and listless on the end of the sofa, and neither was eager to go up to the flower-strewn bridal bed. The grandfather squatted near them with his eyelids lowered, but he was not asleep. He was listening to the noise of his grandsons around him, to the voices, the songs and the bursts of laughter, as though he were a huge plane tree in the rain, drinking up the water with happy roots.

Captain Michales, with somber eyes, signaled to his wife. "Let's go!" he said.

God began a new day. The sun shone over the wedding courtyard full of gnawed bones and bread crusts and men sleeping doubled up in their beards and wide woolen cloaks. It rose over Megalokastro where today, the Wednesday after Easter, the shopkeepers would put on their aprons and open their shops. Caressingly it touched the olive orchards and fields and the estate of Nuri Bey. It rejoiced over the newly painted window frames of his house and over the jasmine in bloom. Today, too, there had arrived from Alexandria four parrots, two dark-green ones and a pair that were sea green with yellow breasts. Nuri Bey had also engaged old Braimis, the blind drummer, that Eminé Hanum might not be bored. For two weeks the Bey had not been in Megalokastro. He had been preparing, like a lovelorn bird, the nest where the beloved was to spend the summer. He longed to see her. The day before yesterday he had sent her a message to say he was coming to her—he could bear the separation no longer. But she had answered by the Arab that she thought she was pregnant: she had attacks and could see no one. Every evening, she said, Hamidé the wise woman came and practiced her healing arts. Then the pain went away. If he loved her, he would not come before the birth.

This anxiety was not the only one. He had had to do without the sight of his beloved for two weeks, and now into the bargain the pasha had sent him word yesterday evening that he was taking too long to fulfill his word. The disgrace had still not been washed away, and the agas were murmuring. Whatever he had in mind to do he should do at once.

His father now visited him in his sleep regularly. He did not speak and no longer even remained standing over him. He did not turn to look at him, but went past him with bare feet and long, dragging steps, in his rags. He went and yet was never out of sight; all night he was there with averted face, inexorably present.

It chanced that, precisely that morning, the accursed tribe which had killed his father passed his house on its way back from the wedding. Furiously he shut the door, went upstairs to the bedroom and watched through the wooden lattice the hundred-year-old leader of the family proudly riding past, and behind him his following: a host.

As they rode past the door, Manusakas reined in his mare, pulled out a silver pistol and fired into the air.

"I'm shooting at your shield, Nuri Bey," he called out.

Behind the lattice Nuri Bey bit his lips and did not take up the challenge. Manusakas turned to his companions.

"The dog made a row because I took the ass into the mosque to prayers. The day after tomorrow, at their Bairam festival, as sure as my name's Manusakas, I'll take my sow!"

The wedding guests roared with laughter and vanished in the dust.

Nuri Bey's eyes grew bloodshot. He came downstairs, uncorked a bottle and sat outside, in front of the door, to quench his rage by drinking. He noticed the mess those accursed mules and horses had made of the ground in front of his door. He went to the middle of the road and looked toward the sun, where his enemies had vanished in the dust. He tipped the bottle and spilled wine on the ground.

"So may my blood be spilled," he muttered, "if I don't do what I have decided!"

He threw back his head and drank without pausing, splashing the wine over himself. Then he went in and loaded his pistols. He fired two shots: the pistols were in order. He pulled his large two-edged dagger out of the sheath and tested it against his wrist. It cut like a razor blade. He spent the day in running up and down his place or following the tracks of the mules and horses on the road. He returned full of renewed rage. At nightfall he killed a rabbit and had it prepared in his favorite way. He ate with appetite and plucked a handful of jasmine blossoms, which he strewed over his pillow. For the first time for a long while he fell into sweet, unbroken sleep. That night his father did not visit him.

In the morning he woke up cheerful. He whistled. The cocks in his yard greeted the sun. Light dropped from the sky onto the leaves of the trees, and on the fountain in front of the door. The stallion came out of his stable and neighed excitedly to the day, as though he saw a mare. And Nuri Bey, too, exulted in the young day.

He went into the yard. His old dog Kartsomis barked a welcome. The Bey stroked the horse in the stable. He ordered a groom to wash it with warm water. He himself brought the stallion a pail of water from the well to drink and shook out plenty of fodder. Back indoors, he told his cook to get ready some good things and to fill a bottle with lemon raki, quickly, for he must set out at once, before the sun grew hot.

"Are you going to Kastro?" the old woman asked, "and are you bringing our mistress?"

Without replying he went up to the bedroom. There he spread dark pomade on his mustache, put on his ceremonial suit, and dashed musk over his hair and ears. In his sash he stuck the silver pistols and the two-edged dagger. Then he went down to the yard again and stood at the door, radiant as the sun.

An aged Turk came by, with a sack on his back. He was Mustapha Baba, who collected herbs, prepared ointments for wounds and dealt also with jaundice, shingles and evil spells. He journeyed through Greek and Turkish villages crying: "Good doctoring, good medicines, long life!" From his sack he distributed, according to the illness, juniper berries, hellebore, rue, wormwood, mandragora: he was a holy man, who journeyed about as a healer and took no pay. He appeared to live on bread and water. As he caught sight of Nuri Bey he stopped dead and stared at him in terror.

"What's the matter with you, Mustapha Baba? Why are you looking at me like that?" Nuri Bey asked, holding the dog back by the scruff of its neck.

The old man bowed.

"You're very handsome today, Nuri Bey," he answered. "Handsomer than is right," he added in a subdued voice.

Nuri Bey laughed.

"Don't laugh, Bey," said the old man. "To men and women there are limits set, and to cross them means sin."

"Too great handsomeness, too great kindness, too much honor —is that sin?"

"It is sin, Bey," the old man sighed.

"Why? I don't understand that, Mustapha Baba."

"Neither do I, my child. But such is God's law. Be careful, Nuri Bey!" Once again he raised his hand to his chest, lips and forehead. "Farewell, Bey," he said. He took several steps and again stopped. Nuri Bey watched him and laughed.

"Would you like something, Mustapha Baba? Have some breakfast at my table."

"I'm not hungry, Nuri Bey. Excuse me. Only . . ."

"Only? Speak out freely, Mustapha Baba."

"I would like to say something to you, but you will laugh."

"You're a holy man. I'm not laughing. Speak."

"Rub smut upon your face, put on your everyday suit and your patched boots if you have any. Lay those silver pistols aside. Diminish your handsomeness, Nuri Bey!"

177

The Bey burst out laughing again, and sorrow spread over the kindly, thin, old face. "As God is above you, don't laugh, Nuri Bey!" he muttered and, bent double, passed on his way.

Proudly Nuri Bey went back to where his saddled horse glittered. The old servant was hanging a saddlebag filled with dainties and lemon raki from the saddle. Nuri Bey looked about him. The house shone, the olive, almond and pomegranate trees were bearing fruit, the fig trees were spreading broad, dark-green leaves and the parrots were preening themselvs in the cages between the trellised vines. Not a breath of wind stirred.

For an instant Nuri Bey's heart hesitated. Where was he going? Why was he going? Why was he leaving all these comforting gifts of God? His estate was a paradise; nothing was lacking here. The woman, too, would soften—she would come, and this courtyard would echo with her sparkling laughter. And the pomegranates would ripen and the figs grow sweet, and the parrots would lay eggs the size of almonds, concealing yellow, green and rose-tinted wings.

He sighed. The old servant observed her master. She had reared him, day by day, hour by hour. He had grown up under her hand. She had never married or known a man. She did not regret it. This man was her husband, her son and God. Never did she raise her eyes to him to question him. What he did was well done, what he ordered was right, and to obey him was a joy. She had no other joys. But today her heart was heavy.

"Where are you going, master?" she asked him again.

Nuri Bey turned in surprise. "What's the matter with you, little mother? Why do you ask?" He placed his toes in the stirrup and swung into the saddle. The old woman laid her shriveled hand on the horse's shimmering neck.

"Where are you going, master?" she muttered once more, fearfully.

"Look after the place!" he replied, and put spurs to the horse.

"God be with you, my child. . . ." She saw her master use the spurs again and vanish among the silver-leaved olive trees.

She felt a lump in her throat, and her heart was hard as a stone. "He's drunk the immortal water and knows no fear!" she said out loud, and bolted the door.

After the Easter days Manusakas had gone up to the pens on the slope of Mount Selena. The heat was already oppressive, the shearing had begun. This was a tremendous festival in the mountains. With their clumsy shears the herdsmen were shearing the goats and sheep and joking as they worked. The women too came up on the mountain, and kindled fires on which to heat kettles of water for cleaning the wool. Manusakas' sons had dug a hole that day, outside the pen, and had stuffed into it a dead lamb in its skin. They had covered it with plenty of glowing charcoal and were waiting till the meat was roasted in the earth.

Manusakas had got the big ram firmly between his knees and was clipping off chunk after chunk of the thick, matted wool. On his right stood about twenty sheep shorn to the skin, on his left as many unshorn. In front of him the mound of wool, smelling strongly of grease, was growing. Manusakas was humming. He was in a good mood. A little cool breeze was blowing from the mountain. It had been a good year. The flocks and herds were increasing. In the hut close by the pen his two eldest sons, Thodores and Jannakis, were arranging cheeses in deep copper jars, and in the cool cheese cellars there were masses, God be praised, of hard cheeses and soft. Down below, in Ai-Janni, the crops and vines were thriving. And his mare had brought forth a foal.

He let his shears rest for a moment and took a long look around him, and down as far as the plain. "Yes, the earth is like a rabbit," he murmured. "She's always bearing and bearing. The animals bear, the trees bear, the women bear. . . . Hey, Christinia, be a good girl and bring me a raki to cool me down."

His wife Christinia was poking the fire in the middle of the pen. She was still a woman with strong muscles and firm bones, but dried up. She could bear no more children, and about that she now complained to God. Only when a woman was over seventy should she be past bearing children—such was the advice she gave, in her monologues to God. Then one could manage to bring two dozen children into the world, and one's longing would be stilled. Two dozen children would be enough: twenty sons and four girls. And on the day when she received her first great-grandchild a pleasant giddiness, like a sleepiness, would come over her; then

179

she should cross herself and die. "My God, if only I had been at Your side when You were making the world! I would have revealed to You some secrets which only we women know. . . ."

She heard her husband call and answered at once: "With pleasure, Manusakas dear. Would you like something to eat as well? I've cooked some sheep's kidneys."

"Bring them over!"

And as he ate and drank and was content with the world, hoofbeats and rolling stones were heard.

What demon can be coming up the mountain on horseback? Manusakas wondered, and with his mouth still full he rose on his knees and looked over the stone wall of the pen. He shielded his eyes with his hand against the blinding sun and recognized a black horse, which was climbing upwards with short steps and sending stones flying to either side.

"God punish me for lying, but I believe it's that dog Nuri!" he muttered, and jumped up. He strode over the space in front of the pen and came to a standstill at the entrance. "He's looking for me!"

With one bound he was inside the pen, and he took his bag from the wall. His wife was still kneeling by the kettle and making up the fire. She did not see him. He pulled out of the bag his broad, short knife and stuck it at his hip, tightening his belt. He picked up his shepherd's staff of oak and went back to the entrance and stood there.

The horseman had now passed the huge oak with the thick leaves, which stood darkly in a hollow. He was wearing a white headband, and the silver pistols glittered in the sun. Manusakas could now clearly make out the very round, very light face of Nuri, with its black waxed mustache.

"He's looking for me!" he muttered again. "Welcome to the dog, if he comes this way."

He called to his wife. "Hey, Christinia, lay the table. We've got a guest."

"Who?" He heard his wife's surprised voice.

"A devil," replied Manusakas. "Get the table ready, I tell you!"

He went to meet the horseman. Nuri saw him and raised his hand. From a distance his drawling, mocking voice was heard. "Good day, Captain Manusakas."

"Welcome, Captain Nuri Bey. Where are you bound for?"

"For Captain Manusakas' pen. Do you know him?" Nuri asked with a laugh. His teeth flashed, his fresh cheeks rippled.

Manusakas' eyes sparkled with rage, but he controlled himself.

"Who has not heard of his heroic deeds?" he answered, and tried to laugh, but only his upper lip moved, laying his teeth bare. "Only a few days ago he brought an ass into the mosque to join in the prayers."

"I heard that too. A mischievous bird flew by and told me. And I've come to see what shoulders they are that can carry an ass."

"You won't see any shoulders, Nuri Bey. Get that out of your head. Manusakas doesn't show his shoulders."

"If he sees danger ahead, he'll show his buttocks as well, I think!" laughed Nuri, and tickled the horse's ears with his whip. The proud beast reared powerfully and leaped forward at Manusakas.

Manusakas did not stir. But the blood throbbed wildly in his wrists. He held himself in. Nuri Bey had come to his house. Patience! He clenched his fist, and could not curb his tongue. "No dog has bitten me yet, unless he was mad, Nuri Bey," he said thickly. "Look out for yourself!"

"But I am a wild beast, Manusakas," the Turk retorted. "So I don't like singing my own praises. I keep silent."

"Well?" Manusakas asked. "Why do you come to my house? What do you want?"

Nuri bit his mustache and said nothing. Manusakas looked at him from the stone on which he was standing, and also said nothing. Both their hearts were storming in their chests.

At length the Bey's voice made itself heard. "Manusakas," he said calmly, slowly, weighing each word, "you have insulted Turkey gravely; you must pay for it."

"I've amused myself. Let the tax collector come and tell me what I owe."

"He has come."

"You?"

"Yes, I. Turkey, flouted by you, has sent me. From the underworld I received a letter from my father, whom your tribe murdered. I have many accounts to settle with your tribe, Manusakas.

Only a day or two ago your brother rode into the Turkish coffee-house and turned the agas out. Megalokastro is shouting and demanding vengeance. I may not touch Captain Michales—he is my blood brother. I'm touching you."

Manusakas stealthily felt around his belt. He found the dagger. "Let's go a bit further on," he said, "so the wife doesn't hear us. My sons are in the hut, too."

Nuri Bey dismounted. He considered it unmanly to ride while his enemy went on foot. He wound the reins round his arm.

"Let's go," he said.

The two moved forward. The horse set stones rolling and neighed uneasily.

The mountain was deserted, for the sun was at its noon height. Outside the pen Manusakas' sons and the shepherd boys had opened the hole, taken out the lamb, now perfectly done and tender, and had posted themselves around it, some squatting, others leaning forward on their knees. Their jaws worked like millstones as they ate. The wooden bottle passed from mouth to mouth. Not a soul paid attention to the mountain. The sheep, too, disburdened of their wool, were lying under the oak trees. Near them the sheep dogs, their tongues hanging out, had stretched themselves in the shade and were gazing in amazement at the shorn flock.

At the tall leafy oak in the hollow the two halted. They glanced at the flat ground about the massive trunk.

"This place will do," they agreed.

Nuri tied his horse to a smaller oak a little to one side, where the animal would not be able to see the two men. Meanwhile Manusakas cleared the space of stones and slender fallen twigs. Nuri came back and was pleased at finding the field swept.

"You've cleaned it up nicely," he said. "We've room enough."

"Yes, room enough," Manusakas replied. "We could have a feast here if we wanted. But if we want to, we can kill each other. What's your choice, Nuri?"

"That we fight," he answered calmly. "Honor demands it, Manusakas."

"The one doesn't exclude the other," said Manusakas.

"Let's fight," Nuri Bey repeated calmly.

"As you will." He pulled his belt tighter and rolled up his

sleeves. Nuri Bey pulled his white headband closer about his hair, drew the pistols out of their leather holsters and hung one of them up on a branch of the tree. The other he held in his hand. Manusakas watched him.

"Hang it up properly," he said, "I like those pistols of yours. As soon as I've killed you, I shall take them for myself as a remembrance."

Nuri Bey cocked the pistol. Manusakas stood motionless in front of him.

"Manusakas," said Nuri Bey, "yesterday afternoon your tribe came past my estate and you halted. You pulled out your pistol, fired in the air and called me out with the cry: 'I'm shooting at your shield, Nuri Bey!' I'm taking up the challenge, even if Charos gets me!" With that, he fired a shot in the air over Manusakas' head, then stood on tiptoe and hung the still smoking pistol by the side of the other.

They took their stand opposite each other with their legs wide apart and firmly planted, and eyed each other. Their blood was not yet inflamed. They waited. They tried by means of crude mockeries to rouse themselves to rage and bloodlust.

"Damn the beard of your Mohammed!" said Manusakas, spitting in the air.

"Damn your Christ, the bastard!" swore Nuri Bey.

They flouted their gods, but their blood would not catch fire. Then they tried with the saints and circumcision, with the Sultan and the Greek race. But that did not provoke them to the desire to kill each other. At last Manusakas thought of something.

"Captain Michales should be here to settle with you. Remember how he caught you by the belt and flung you onto the roof? But I'll throw you in the same way."

He rushed forward to catch the other by the waist. But the Bey eluded him nimbly. He took a step backward and pulled from his sash the two-edged black-hilted dagger. Now both pairs of eyes grew bloodshot.

"Giaour!"

"Dog!"

Nuri sprang forward with raised dagger. But Manusakas bent and instantly stepped aside, so that the Bey nearly fell. Manusakas from his crouching position butted his head with full force into the other's stomach. Nuri nearly fainted with the pain. Then he mastered himself and again gathered his strength. While his opponent was still bent, Nuri plunged the dagger deep in his side. Bones cracked. Hot blood spurted out and spattered Nuri as he wrenched the dagger out. He gave a shout of joy and licked the blade greedily, till his lips and beard were smeared with blood.

"That's for my father!" he cried. "I'm avenging his blood!"

Manusakas leaned swaying against the trunk of the tree.

"Dog," he muttered. "You've got me."

"The account's settled," Nuri answered. His nostrils quivered.

"You just come here. . . . You just come here," muttered Manusakas, who felt his strength going and could not make a rush at his enemy.

The hoarse, masterful voice provoked Nuri. He raised his dagger.

"One more," he bellowed, "one more stroke, to the heart, giaour, for Turkey which you flouted, you and your brother Captain Michales."

He leaped forward like a flash, to pierce his enemy's heart. But Manusakas dodged, and the dagger struck the trunk of the tree. It broke. Manusakas collected his last strength and plunged his short knife deep and low in the Bey's body.

The Bey bellowed like a buffalo. He tore the knife from his enemy's already limp hand. "For Turkey!" he yelled, and plunged it in his heart.

Manusakas collapsed over the roots of the tree. In a flash his wife Christinia, his children, the pen and the half-shorn ram passed through his mind. Then a thick black cloud covered his eyes. He saw nothing more—and fell forward in a pool of blood.

Nuri crouched beside him. Blood was running from his breeches and flowing to the ground beside Manusakas' head. A sharp, unbearable pain tortured him. He put both hands to his wounded testicles and bellowed. He looked around. The sun was sinking. The mountain was again ringing with the bells of the sheep, and a wind arose.

"Allah, Allah, help me to reach my horse and get away!" Nuri groaned, and tried to stand up.

He held tightly onto the trunk of the tree, pulled down the silver pistols, and stuck them in his sash. He picked up Manusakas' shepherd staff to support himself and looked at the dying man, who was rattling and convulsed. He tried to give him a kick. The pain prevented him. He spat on him.

"I've kept my oath," he muttered. "But you've got me too, giaour!"

He put his left hand between his thighs and groaned, "It would have been better if you'd stabbed my heart, giaour."

Manusakas half opened one eye. It was dim and bloody. His lips were dark blue; they moved to speak. But they stiffened and remained half open. Nuri Bey crawled, howling with pain, to his horse. The noble animal heard his groaning and turned around. The whites of its eyes flashed.

Oh, if I could only get on and ride away, thought the Bey. Mustapha Baba knows herbs that will cure me.

Blood made a trail behind him. Darkness was before his eyes as at last he reached the horse and collapsed in front of it. It bent its neck down and sniffed at its master—at his neck, his hair, his back. Finally it raised its intelligent head and neighed, as though calling for help.

Nuri tried to lift his foot as far as the stirrup. He could not. The pain almost made him faint. He fell close to the horse's front legs and clung to them. It looked at him, with lowered head. Suddenly it understood. It moved forward and bowed its knees over a stone until it was kneeling. Again it looked at its master. When he saw the horse kneeling, he stumbled, face foremost, and placed his arms round its neck. Then he heaved his body and both legs up, till he was fast in the saddle. He clenched his teeth, to be able to bear the pain. But he could not open his severely wounded thighs, and so he rode woman-fashion.

"On, on, brother! Away from here," he muttered. "Slowly, slowly . . ." and he stroked the beloved animal's neck.

The horse moved slowly downhill in the evening twilight, watching the ground carefully so as not to stumble, skirting holes and precipices.

The sun had sunk, blood red, over the mountain. A few women were coming up the mountain to visit their men. When Nuri saw them, he clenched his teeth and held his head high. But the blood was running in thick drops over the saddle and the horse's belly and was painting a track on the stones.

185

It was a most gracious hour, now that the heat was past. The face of the earth grew fresh. Two or three big stars already hung in the sky. In a hut at the foot of the mountain a lamp was burning, and a song could be heard from within: a mother was lulling her child tenderly to sleep. Nuri Bey had shut his eyes. He saw nothing, and heard only the awakening insects, loud as bells. He clung to the horse's mane. Where was it going? It knew its way unerringly. He trusted it.

The horse stopped before the door of the Bey's country house. Nuri opened his eyes and shouted. Servants came running and carried him in. The old nurse made up a bed for him on the sofa. Scarcely was he stretched out before the sheets were covered with blood. Nuri moved his hand and whispered, "Mustapha Baba . . . Mustapha Baba." Then he fell back on the pillows.

It was deep night before Mustapha Baba arrived at the house, breathless, with his sack of healing herbs and ointments on his shoulder. The servants brought lamps and candles. He bent over Nuri Bey and shook his head.

Nuri Bey lay unconscious, with his eyes shut. The old man put some drops of rose vinegar into his nose, and rubbed his temples. The Bey opened his eyes, looked at him, and asked in a trembling voice, "Shall I live?"

"You are in Allah's hands," the old man answered. "He can heal you."

"No one else?" asked Nuri in terror. "Can't you, Mustapha Baba?"

"The wound is severe, Nuri Bey, and in a bad place."

Nuri Bey groaned.

"Allah guided the knife where He willed it to go."

"Why, why, why?" whispered the Bey miserably, and gazed with fear at the old man.

But the old man did not answer. He had known since this morning, when he had seen the Bey so radiant on his threshold.

"Keep still," he said. "Don't ask questions, if you want to get well."

Raki was brought. He washed the wound, stopped the blood and put on a bandage. From his sack he took a handful of herbs and gave them to the old woman to boil. This was for a sleeping

186

draught. He turned the servants out and opened his bag again, to take out a small bottle and some ointment. Weeping, the old woman watched him.

"Mustapha Baba, is the master badly wounded? Can he get well?"

"He can get well," muttered the old man. "But what will he do with life then?"

"What will he do with life? Why do you ask, Mustapha Baba?"

The old man looked about him. "He will never be a man again," he said softly.

The old woman shrieked, and covered her face with both hands.

Next day, just as the sun was beginning to set, Captain Michales stood on the threshold of his shop and stared out at the Harbor Gate. Ships were again loading and unloading, while the waves of the sea were a deep red. He stared, but saw nothing: his gaze was directed within. His body had grown slack in the last few days, and his mouth was bitter and firmly shut. Passing Turks cast evil glances at him, and many of his Christian friends avoided him. They guessed at a dark power in him, and dared not come near him.

Captain Michales took his tobacco box from his belt. Neither wine nor a ride on his mare now brought him any relief. Above all, not this wretched cigarette. He lighted it, took a few puffs, and spat furiously. It poisoned his mouth. He threw it to the ground and stamped on it. "To the devil with you too," he muttered, and turned to go back into the shop, to sit there and, as soon as the day came to an end, to shut it up and escape.

But now there appeared, covered with dust and bathed in sweat, his tongue lamed by terror, Thodores, the first-born son of Manusakas. He stopped in front of his uncle, and stared at him. He tried to speak, but his heart was too full. Captain Michales seized him by the arm and shook him.

"Speak!" he told him, and bent over him. Full of evil foreboding, his thoughts rushed to his brother Manusakas.

"They've killed my father, uncle!"

"Who, boy?"

"Nuri."

Captain Michales let his nephew's arm drop, stuck his thumb between his teeth, and bit. He could taste hot, salt blood on his lips.

"When, boy? Where?"

With tears and curses, Thodores told how at noon that day they had found his father lying under the big oak. He had two knife-wounds, one in the side, the other through the heart. Two women who had come up the mountain in the twilight yesterday—Hadzijorgos' wife and daughter—had met Nuri clinging, pale and exhausted, to his horse, and had found tracks of blood all along the cliff path.

For a few moments Captain Michales said nothing and did not move. He simply stared at the ground. He could see the thick-leaved oak in the hollow, and at its roots a majestic body dabbled in blood. When he had had his fill of this picture, he raised his head and seized his nephew by the shoulder.

"Are you a woman, howling like that? The gates are still open, you've time to get back to the village. Tell them to wait and not to bury him. I'm coming!"

When he was alone, Captain Michales went into the shop, and ordered Charitos out. Nobody must see him. He gave the chair on which he usually sat a kick, so that it smashed in pieces, and flung himself upon a coil of rope, pressing his fists against his head. The shop and Megalokastro sank from his sight, and an oak spread itself before him, a darkly gleaming one, surrounded by thorns. At its foot lay his brother Manusakas. He was not dead —that was not blood streaming over him, but wine! He was clapping his hands and singing, "The Muscovite will soon be here!"

He shook his head and stood up. His decision was suddenly made. He shut the shop and stuck the key in his belt. He did not go into Broad Street, but made his way through the narrow alleys. Out of the Greek quarter, he came into the Turkish. The Hags were not yet at their peepholes and did not see him. In front of the green door he halted. Like a falcon his gaze shot up to the high, blind walls and perched on the tiny balcony with its closed lattice. But suddenly he wrenched his gaze away, with rage and disgust in his heart, as though he had defiled himself, and let his eyes once more sweep over the rough walls. This evening he was not concerned with women and balconies. The falcon of his spirit swept over the head of Nuri and longed to strike its claws into his eyes and his brain.

A strange, inhuman rejoicing filled him. His spirit suddenly shook free and rose. It seemed to enter another body—a man's. It did not deck itself, it did not paint itself, it did not smell of musk. It smelled of male sweat. Now Captain Michales went home. His eyes were blazing.

"Manusakas, my brother . . . Manusakas, my brother . . ." he murmured as he went.

Night fell, and the stars appeared, while a doleful, half-eaten moon hung in the sky. The doors in Ai-Janni were bolted, the lamps went out one after another, and the village was plunged into darkness. Only Manusakas' door stood wide open. The lamps were burning, and in the middle of the main room, on a bier, was the corpse of the master of the house, laid out for the funeral ceremony. It had been washed with wine and veiled in a linen shroud. A cross of wax lay upon the lips, and a small icon of the Redeemer had been placed in the crossed hands. Two huge lamps were burning, one at the feet, the other at the head. His eyes had remained open and were glazed: since no one had been there to close their lids when they were still warm, they would not shut. Ever since morning the relatives and friends had been coming. With mourning strokes the bells announced the dread presence of death. From Ai-Janni, from Petrokefalo and all the neighboring villages the Christians had been coming, to kiss the dead man and take leave of him.

His wife Christinia had flung herself over him and was sobbing and beating her breast. The neighbor women had come—the widows, the mothers whom Charos had robbed, and the orphan girls —and at the sight of the family's grief their own had welled up, and they loosened their hair and joined in the keening. Old Sefakas came on foot from Petrokefalo, armed as though he were going to war. He carried old-fashioned pistols, a long knife with a white handle, and his father's heavy muzzle-loader with its wide muzzle. He halted, stood motionless on the threshold, saw his son lying on the bier, came forward and stretched out his huge hands to clasp both the dead man's hands.

"All's well, Manusakas," he said. "Only you've been in too much of a hurry. It was *my* turn. Now greet the people below for me. Tell them I'm coming too."

After these words he sat down on the threshold for a while. Then he stood up and went back, silent and dry-eyed, to his village.

Slowly the keening continued. The bodies of the mourners grew weary and found consolation and sweetness in weariness. One after another, the friends and relatives got up to go home, to eat and sleep. They were still alive, and tomorrow work was waiting for them. Other people's grief still belonged to other people. It could even secretly bring pleasure, because Fate had struck their neighbor and not themselves. There remained in Manusakas' house his three bosom friends only: his brother Famurios, the man of the grasslands; his godson Stratas, a sturdy young man of thirty-five, of healthy stock, with a pointed beard, slender hips and an open forehead. He was a stranger from Kisamo, who five years ago had turned up in the Lasithi district for the Krustalenia fair. There his fate lay in wait for him in the shape of a girl from Ai-Janni whom he saw dancing. His soul desired her, and he took her. Manusakas set the wedding crowns on their heads. Nine months later he had his first-born christened. That was how they had become godfather and godson. The third was Patasmos the lyre player, a bit of ill-leavened bread the witches had licked at. His father had begotten nine sons, and he was the last—a gray-beard's work. But he was a man in whom the wrath of God moved. No one could challenge him when, at the fair, the jeering manti-nades* began to ring out. In the flick of a wrist, there he was with his scornful rhymes. He knew everybody's weakness or secret anxiety. Fear seized men and women when, enthroned in the middle of the dancing space with his lyre on his knees, he stabbed them, one after the other, with his eyes. At last he would open his mouth, and out would dart the mantinade. He lived alone as an old palikar, without a care. He was the first and best at every fair, wedding, christening and drinking bout. Everyone competed to have him as a guest to avoid being sung about. He was known as Patasmos and Beelzebub and Spear and Captain Wasp. Yesterday he had come to Ai-Janni for the christening. Stratas' third child

* Rhyming couplets, usually topical or personal. (*Tr.*)

was to be christened. But now here was an evil reunion with Charos, who had also come for a visit. Patasmos had been an inseparable friend of Manusakas. They had emptied whole casks of wine together, devoured whole sheep to the bones together. He had loved Manusakas and had never made fun of him.

He bent down, looked at the corpse, and sighed.

"Yes, a man's no more than a bladder—it swells and swells and suddenly—poof!—it bursts and goes to the devil—I mean, to Paradise," he corrected himself quickly, for he was ashamed in front of the corpse.

Stratas bowed his head and said nothing. He took his kerchief and flicked the flies away from the dead man's nose and lips. Famurios stood up, put his arm around Christinia's shoulder and raised her to her feet. Then he lifted each of the other mourners in turn.

"Out with you, women, that's enough! Out with you, and be quiet, sisters of misfortune. We three are taking over the watch for the night."

The women united in an outcry and tried to resist. But the herdsman raised his paws and drove them like a flock into the inner part of the house. Then he came back and sat down at the feet of the dead man.

For a while the three gazed at the murdered man without a word. Each had his thoughts elsewhere. Stratas' thoughts were with his wife, and with the mule he had bought the day before yesterday (it had turned out to be very wild: it kicked, and might one day kill one of his children).

Patasmos was building in his mind a new poem, a dirge, a mixture of truth and lies: how Manusakas had fought with seven Turks, and had killed six of them.

Famurios was hungry. He had seen, hanging on the wall of his brother's cellar, some pork sausages, and in the corner a little cask of raki. Also Christinia had done the baking yesterday, and the wheaten bread still lay in the tray, giving out fragrance. His mouth filled with saliva, and while his eyes remained bound to the corpse, his mind was pondering how he could give the conversation a turn toward sausages and raki.

It must be midnight. A light north wind was making the leaves of the lemon tree in the yard rustle. It cooled the brows of the death watchers. Now that the women were quiet, an owl could be heard hooting up above in the loft. And in the neighborhood the dogs had scented Charos and were howling.

Famurios could feel his innards growing tense with hunger. He could not find a subtle way to guide the conversation. So he burst out:

"Men, what do you think? My eye caught sight of some strings of sausages and a cask of raki in the cellar. Shall we drink to his salvation?"

"Why shouldn't we drink?" asked Patasmos, rubbing his belly, which was beginning to rumble. "Only the dead don't drink. Go, Famurios, with God's help! Go to the cellar! What do you think, Stratas?"

"Isn't it wrong?" Stratas said, "in front of the body. . . ."

"In the first place, we'll drink outside, Stratas. And then only to give us the strength, my boy, to go through with the watch till morning. Besides, we'll be drinking to his well-being. . . . Go, Famurios, please, to the cellar."

Famurios had already grabbed the lamp that burned at the dead man's feet, and made for the cellar. He emerged carrying a string of sausages and the cask. Also, in his belt, he brought three tumblers.

Patasmos jumped up, cut off some lengths of sausages and went out into the yard. There he made a fire and roasted them. The world smelled sweet.

"For God's sake, shut the doors, Famurios, so that the women don't notice the smell!" said Patasmos, as he wrapped the morsels in lemon leaves.

Meanwhile Famurios had filled the glasses to the brim with raki. Stratas too had gone to the cellar, to get a loaf of bread.

When he returned, they gripped the glasses, and touched fingers to avoid the clink.

"God bless his soul," said Stratas.

"His health, friends! Ours too!" cried Patasmos.

"Drink it up in one gulp," said Famurios. "The cask—God has sent it to us—is half full. Brother Manusakas, farewell!"

They drank to the last drop. Then they seized the sausages. Famurios pulled out his herdsman's knife and cut the bread into three parts. Appetite was whetted. They roasted the remaining sausages. Famurios brought a white cheese from the cellar. He placed the cask on his lap and doled out more raki.

"Let's drink to the health of the widow," Patasmos proposed. "I'm sorry for the poor thing. I'll make a mantinade for her."

"To her health!"

They drank. "And to Captain Michales' health!" said Stratas. "He will avenge his blood. To his health!"

"Come, friends, to the health of all the people we know," suggested Famurios, "whether they're alive or dead."

They went through the relatives, the friends, the dead parents, the neighbors, all in turn, and drank. Then they began on the great fighters of Crete—Korax, Hadjimichals, Kriares, Daskalojannes—and drank. Next they came to Arkadi Monastery and drank three large glasses to its health. Then they moved on to 1821 and drank to the health of Kolokotrones, of Karaiskakes, of Miaules, of Odysseus Andrutsos. The cask was nearly empty.

"Let's drink to the health of ancient Hellas," proposed Patasmos, who laid claim to a few grains of education.

"Too dull," said Famurios.

"Well then we'll sing. . . ."

"In the name of Christ, that isn't right!" Stratas objected.

"Quiet, quiet! In a whisper. Not a soul can hear us. Like this. . . ."

And he began, imitating the motion of a fiddle bow in the air, to sing softly:

> "Faithless one, in you the red
> Of dawn was at its prime . . ."

The other two quickly sang after him: "Of dawn was at its prime."

> "When I kissed you, and you said:
> 'It's night, and loving time!' "

"Is that the mantinade you've composed for the widow? Have you no fear of God?" cried Stratas. "Don't you know any sacred songs?"

"Is it sacred songs you want? With pleasure!" He turned to the dead man, crossed himself, and began: "Come to the final kiss. . . ." Hardly had he begun when the three took up the hymn of mourning, fell upon the dead man, and kissed him as the tears fell.

The house droned with the litany. A door half opened, and a woman stuck out her hand, wound in a cloth. But Patasmos made an angry sign at her, and the woman vanished.

Then they felt that the hymn of mourning had gone on long enough, and stood up, the three in a row, before the dead man, and looked at him. They felt lightened. There was in them a surge of strength renewed by raki, sausages and weeping. Famurios spat on his hands.

"Friends," he said, indicating the dead man with his eyes, "shall we jump over him?"

"Suppose we do jump over him!" cawed Stratas and Patasmos together. They pulled their sagging breeches well up, so that their legs should be unencumbered, seized the bier and placed the corpse in the door to the yard, to give themselves room for a run.

"I'll go first!" said Famurios, "because I'm his brother!"

He took his position by the street door, spat on his hands, and let fly. As he came up to the dead man he gave a mighty leap. His skull hit the lintel with a crack. But Famurios did not notice. He landed on his feet in the middle of the room.

"I've jumped over him," he said proudly. "Your turn, Stratas!"

Stratas too took a run and, with his supple, slender body, sprang in a low arc without touching the corpse. He landed lightly on the tips of his toes.

"Your turn, Patasmos," he said.

But Patasmos' heart flinched. He gazed at the bier. How the devil could one jump so high? "I'm not jumping," he said, discouraged.

"Aren't you ashamed of yourself, Captain Wasp?" Famurios chided. "Are you a Cretan or a Carpathian? Jump!"

"I'm not jumping, I tell you. I'm a lyre player."

"Have you no sense of the honor due to the dead, you heathen? It's an insult! Is that all your friendship with Manusakas means? Jump, even if you fall down dead!"

Patasmos scratched his bald spot. He remembered how much he had really loved Manusakas. His sense of honor awoke.

"All right, I'll jump!" he exclaimed, then, "Hop! Hop!" to give himself courage.

He began to run and got up speed. But as he came to the dead man, it seemed to him that the bier reached to the ceiling. His legs caught the feet of the bier and jolted the corpse, which rolled to the ground, Patasmos, with his beard flying, beyond it.

"You've disgraced us," said Famurios. "Get your beard shaved off." He gave him a kick. "Come, Stratas, help!"

They lifted the dead man from the ground, wrapped him in his shroud again, bundled him into the open coffin and pressed the icon once more into his hands.

"There, brother, you're dead. It didn't do you any harm. It hasn't hurt you," said Famurios, stroking the dead man's hair and beard.

He bent down, picked up the cask and tipped it up. There was a little raki left in it. They drank. They sat down once more near the dead man and gazed at him. Their eyelids slowly drooped, their heads sank on their chests, and sleep embraced them.

Next day, before the sun was well up, Captain Michales arrived at Manusakas' yard. He wore a black shirt, black headband and black boots, like Charos. He shoved the women aside as they crowded wailing around him, went in, bent down, kissed the dead man and stood for a long time gazing at him silently. That morning the women of the neighborhood had brought from the fields basil, marjoram, mint and yellow marguerites by the armful and had decked the corpse with them. The dead man, too, gazed at Captain Michales with his open eyes. Christinia, the sons and daughters, Famurios his brother and Stratas and Patasmos and the neighbor women stood in a circle and watched how the two brothers spoke together without saying a word.

This mysterious conversation lasted a long while. When Captain Michales had had his fill of grieving, he went into the kitchen, then out into the yard again. He visited the stable, touched the dead man's cattle and his mare; he went up to the bedroom, saw the wide bed and the working gear and the holy pictures; he looked out of the window at the roofs of the village with the little church of St. John in the middle; then over it and beyond at Petrokefalo, his father's village at the foot of the towering mountain.

"Farewell, brother Manusakas," he whispered over and over, as he examined, touched and took leave of the things the murdered man had loved.

The pope came. The bier was lifted high. The women clung to

it and tried to prevent it from being taken out. Christinia fell down in a faint, and while she was being revived with water and perfume, the corpse and bearers had already crossed the threshold and were nearing the green cemetery at the edge of the village.

From Petrokefalo and the neighboring villages they had come —the men armed, the women in black—to take leave of the fallen pillar of the village. No Turk appeared in the streets on this day. The women tore their hair and extolled the virtues of the murdered man. Old Sefakas, dry-eyed, gripping the double handle of his stick, led the procession behind the dead man. He knew what Charos meant, that it was unbecoming to human beings, and could do them no good, to sink so low as to supplicate him. And so, without words or tears, he walked along, striking the stones with his stick. Showing no emotion, he stood before the hole in the earth.

The pope intoned the last words at the grave hastily, raised his hand and gave the blessing. He took a handful of earth from the ground and threw it into the grave. The corpse was lowered. All bent down, each took a handful of earth, and threw it after.

Captain Michales stepped forward to the edge of the grave.

"Farewell, brother Manusakas," he said, in a calm voice. His burning eyes could bring forth no tears. "Listen to what I am saying to you. Don't come into my sleep to accuse me and make me wild. I know my duty. Have no anxiety." He was silent for a moment, pondering. But he could think of nothing else, and repeated: "I know my duty. Have no anxiety. Just be patient!"

His heart swelled. "Farewell, Manusakas!" he shouted.

Before the escort broke up he returned alone to Manusakas' house and mounted his mare. At that moment Thodores, the eldest son, came running to the street door.

"What orders have you got for me, uncle?" he asked, catching hold of the mare's reins.

Captain Michales bent down and looked at him.

"I mean, how am I to avenge his blood?" asked the son.

"How old are you?"

"Seventeen."

"Stay in your nest."

He put spurs to the mare and took the wide main road to Megalokastro.

7

APRIL WAS OVER, and May came with its sunny consequences—
the melons and cherries, the swelling clusters and the first gleaming vintage grapes, still unripe. The heat became oppressive.
Turks and Christians poured out their sweat and dried wherever
they could find a cool breeze. Nuri still lay consumed with pain
on his bed, and Manusakas was still hidden in Captain Michales'
heart. In Megalokastro revolt was brewing, still under cover. At
night the elders gathered in the Metropolitan's residence, to take
counsel about the threatened position of the Greeks, while at midday in the pasha's konak the beys and hodzas discussed measures
for the repression of the Greeks. The fate of Crete hung on a hair.

On the twenty-ninth of May the bells began to toll dolefully in
the dim light of early morning. The Christians rose from their
sleep and set out for church to commemorate that day's somber
meaning for Christendom. In the middle of the church, on a huge
tray, stood a memorial cake, flanked by two great lamps swathed
in black. Inscribed in almond kernels and cinnamon on the thin
sugar coating was the name of the dead man: KONSTANTINOS
PALAIOLOGOS. This was his death day. On a dark morning like
this one the Sultan's myrmidons had laid him low and put Constantinople under their yoke.

The Christians stood around the cake and listened to the funeral service. All the prominent Kastrians had gathered. There
were the three elders: Captain Elias, Hadjisavas and the Rose
Bug. With them had come Captain Polyxigis, Charilaos the
gnome, the learned Idomeneas, Stefanes the ship's captain, Ka-

sapakes the doctor and the grocer, Mr. Aristoteles. Behind them stood the less important people: Demetros Leanbottom, Krasojorgis, Mastrapas, Kajabes, Vendusos, Furogatos, Bertodulos, and Signor Paraskevas the barber. And to them was joined the throng of the insignificant.

Even Captain Michales had appeared, but he had not entered the church. He stood in the narthex, his shirt and his heart black. Since the funeral of his brother he had spoken to no one. Unrest was in his blood. His mind was busy devising a thousand arts of malice, turning over a thousand occasions on which he could catch Nuri and avenge the crime that had been committed. To him Nuri was no longer a blood brother. The red thread which had bound them together had been cut. He had heard that Nuri had been severely wounded and was near death at his country estate. Captain Michales had sent Ali Aga there to spy, to eavesdrop on the servants and find out if Nuri really was seriously wounded. Ali Aga had come back that same day with his tongue hanging out and had brought the news.

"It's true, Captain Michales, the poor thing is badly wounded."

"Where? Have you found that out?"

"In the testicles, Captain. Your brother, it seems, stabbed him with his knife between the thighs. Mustapha Baba has anointed him and bandaged him, but the pain is torturing him and he bellows day and night. I heard him myself from the gate, Captain."

Captain Michales was dismayed. As long as Nuri was ill, he could not touch him. He would have to wait till he recovered strength. How long might that be? He was in a hurry!

When, early this morning he had heard the mourning bells, he had decided to go to church. Tityros is to make a speech; he'll make us all ridiculous, he thought. He dressed impatiently. He pulled the tassels of his headband over his eyes. He did not want to see or greet anyone. Could that cheese of a little schoolmaster have the least idea of what the fall of Constantinople and heroism and struggle meant?

Leaning against the window at the entrance, he could see, over the crowd, the Metropolitan standing, clothed in black, and with a long, black scarf wound round his hat.

The ritual came to an end. The Metropolitan signed to Tityros. Captain Michales grew agitated. He watched his brother mount the high platform and pull from his inner coat pocket a bundle of papers. Tityros began to speak. At first he stammered and coughed, so that he could hardly be understood. But gradually he warmed up, and his voice filled with power. He caused the towers of Constantinople to rise before his hearers, and the bells of Hagia Sophia tolled in passionate entreaty, as in the midst of the church the last, fate-laden battle pursued its course—that battle which had filled the graves of the vast city with blood. And in the incense cloud above the tray with the cake there appeared the bloodstained head of the Emperor Constantine: everyone saw him.

Captain Michales dried his eyes, which had suddenly become wet. He observed his brother thoughtfully. How could such a flame dwell behind those glasses, above those narrow trousers and under those crooked shoulders?

When Tityros had done, he cleaned his glasses and looked among the women, who stood behind the men, for Vangelio, his wife. As he did not find her, he sat down, sighing.

After the ceremony Captain Michales went over to his brother. "You brought no shame on us," he said.

Tityros scarcely heard him. The flame was still burning in his heart.

They walked a few steps together. The schoolmaster was tired. Slowly and listlessly he started homeward. Captain Michales looked at him covertly. How he had changed since his wedding! His hump seemed to have increased, and he was beginning to be bowlegged.

"How are things at home?" he asked softly.

Tityros did not answer at once. Suddenly the sacred flame went out.

"It's no life at all, Michales," he said at last.

"Why? What do they do to you?"

"Nothing. They don't speak to me, they don't swear at me, they say nothing. And when I turn my back, I hear them laughing."

"Aren't you then master in your house? What sort of a man are you? Kick him out!"

"If I throw him out, she goes too."

They had reached Tityros' house. Captain Michales stood still. "Are they both in?" he asked.

"They're inseparable. He didn't want to go to church, so she didn't go. Is that any sort of a life, brother Michales?"

"Listen, schoolmaster. I'll go in with you and play the two of them a tune to make them dance."

"For God's sake!" cried the teacher, in terror. "Don't do that! If you do, I'm done for! I'm going to do something . . . and then we shall see."

"What shall we see?"

"We shall see," Tityros repeated, looking away.

He approached the door and took hold of the knocker.

"What? Have you no key?" exclaimed Captain Michales in astonishment.

"No. They won't give me one. I have to knock."

Captain Michales wrenched the knocker off with one pull and flung it into the street.

"I want you to have a key by tomorrow," he said, and went off with heavy tread toward the Harbor Gate.

In Captain Michales' shop Captain Polyxigis had been waiting since the end of the memorial service. He paced uneasily up and down. What he had to say to Captain Michales was going to be difficult to express. He sent Charitos out for coffee and lighted one cigarette after another. How could he so much as begin, without provoking a burst of fury from Captain Michales? He did not want to lose his friendship; on the contrary, he was anxious to strengthen it. That was why he had decided to speak to him today. He had tied a piece of black crape to his fez, to show that he too was in mourning for the loss of Manusakas.

"Quick, Charitos. Run to the house and see if your uncle's there. Tell him . . ."

Before he had finished, Captain Michales was on the threshold. Tityros' fiery speech was with him still—but even more so was his rage about the key which had been refused to his brother.

He stared at the early, unexpected guest and pressed his lips together.

"Good morning, Captain Polyxigis," he said coolly.

"I'm glad to see you, Captain Michales."

Captain Michales threw aside his headband and took his coat

off. He picked up an account book from the table and fanned himself with it. He said nothing.

"How hot it is!" said Captain Polyxigis, oppressed by the silence.

Captain Michales obstinately continued to say nothing. He took his tobacco box from his belt and began, slowly and clumsily, to roll a cigarette, as if he would never be done. Captain Polyxigis threw his cigarette away, coughed and pushed back his chair.

"Captain Michales," he said, "I've something to say to you."

"I'm listening."

"I ask you, for the sake of our old friendship, Captain Michales, listen to me patiently. I must speak at some length, so that you may understand the whole thing."

"I'm listening," the other repeated.

"I tried to tell you once before, but you went up in flames and wouldn't let me speak. But now, it's necessary. Listen to me patiently, brother."

"I'm listening. I've said so already. Drop the preliminaries!"

"Hey, Charitos, young man, get me some tobacco and some cigarette paper," Captain Polyxigis exclaimed, to get rid of the boy, who had clambered onto a roll of ship's cable and had pricked up his ears.

Charitos slid reluctantly down from the cable and made off.

"I've something to say to you, Captain Michales . . ." Polyxigis began, hesitating again.

"Well, get on with it!"

"About Eminé. . . ."

"Drop this shameless talk, Captain Polyxigis. You know I don't like it. Love stories and women's gossip are your business, not mine. You've come into my shop, so I can't throw you out. But change the subject!"

"I'm not shameless in talking about this. Calm down, Captain Michales. Let me go on . . . Eminé wants to become a Christian."

Captain Michales picked up an almond from the table and reduced it to dust between his fingers. "If you were a Frank, she'd turn Frank. If you were a Jew, she'd turn Jewess. Are you making even christening an amusement?"

"But it's Christian she wants to become, and I am going to marry her," Captain Polyxigis went on.

"Marry her?" Captain Michales gave a convulsive movement and tore the solid leather binding of the account book. "Congratulations!" he said at last, malevolently, and spat on the floor.

Captain Polyxigis took off his fez. Anger made his head feel as though it would burst. He crushed the fez together in his hands. He looked at Captain Michales, whose face had changed color. Storm away, you old boar, he thought. What I have to say you shall hear, whether you like it or not.

Captain Michales stood up, as though to signal his guest that it was time to go.

Captain Polyxigis did not move. "I am here, Captain Michales, to ask you to give the bride away."

"Me?" He clutched at his beard. "You make me ashamed of my beard. Get Efendina Horsedung to give her away. He's just right for you!"

That brought Captain Polyxigis to his feet. He could no longer contain his rage. He picked up the chair and dashed it to the floor.

"You're going too far, Captain Michales," he shouted. "You're a man, that's true; so am I a man. You fought in the war; so did I. You break into the agas' coffeehouses on horseback; I into their houses. And if you never laugh, that doesn't mean you're a brute. And if I do laugh, that doesn't mean I'm a buffoon. When I talk to you about the woman I intend to marry, I expect you to show me some respect." Captain Polyxigis curbed himself. But his anger had not yet spent itself. Rancor still reigned within him.

It was otherwise with Captain Michales. The longer he listened to Captain Polyxigis the more his scorn subsided. When Polyxigis had begun by making wretched requests, calling him brother and flaunting the mourning crape in his face to appease him, he had felt an impulse to seize him by the scruff of his neck and throw him out. But now that he spoke strongly, like a man, Michales' old brotherly feeling for this foolhardy captain reawakened. The memory arose of how together they had charged the Turkish soldiers on horseback, without even looking around to see if they were being followed. The two captains had not resembled each other in those days, either, but they had become friends. "You

want to free Crete with roaring, and I with song," Captain Polyxigis had said to him one day, laughingly.

But after the war had ended, they had parted. Afterward, when
Captain Michales saw him he either avoided him or, if they did
meet, often abused him. But now that he saw Polyxigis with his
head held high he felt the old friendship arising afresh. Michales
put out his hand.

"Captain Polyxigis," he said, "you're a palikar. I know that. I
don't want to quarrel with you."

"Nor I with you, Captain Michales. Only sometimes you force
my soul into my nose, and I have to snort."

"Well, all right," Captain Michales repeated, and pushed him
gently but firmly toward the door.

"You're turning me out?" Captain Polyxigis shouted, and
stamped on the floor. "I've still something to say to you, Captain
Michales. One thing only. Then I'll go."

"Say it, but be quick."

"Eminé herself sent me. To ask if you would please give her
away."

"She herself, that——" Captain Michales broke off. His disgust
returned. He clenched his fist against Captain Polyxigis' chest.
His voice was suddenly hoarse:

"Enough! Enough, I tell you! Not a word more!"

They were standing at the door of the shop. "God grant you
may be sorry for today, Captain Michales!" said Captain Polyxigis, raising his head toward the sky, which glowed white in the
sun's blaze.

That same evening, when the people of Megalokastro had shut
their doors and were at table, a stout hanum carrying an open
parasol, approached with firm tread and knocked at Nuri's green
door. The Moorish woman, who was hiding behind the door,
opened it quickly and let her in.

"Eminé's still ill," thought the Hags, watching at their three
peepholes. "Hamidé Mula has come to doctor her."

Meanwhile Eminé's Moorish woman advanced across the
courtyard. She was gay and sprightly. Her soul was in a garden. The
watchman was at the estate, looking after his master, and the red
and green lamp was not burning. In the dark the flowers and fruits

gave out their scent, and the Moorish woman danced with pleasure because her mistress had now recognized the true light and wanted to become a Christian. One day she would enter Paradise. And if God in His mercy should turn His eye on her servant and let her also through the golden gate, she would be able to serve her mistress through eternity.

The stout hanum threw her mantle, veil and parasol on the divan, and revealed herself as Captain Polyxigis.

"The mistress is upstairs and is longing to see you, Captain. She has something amusing to tell you," the Moorish woman announced.

But this evening Captain Polyxigis did not respond. On other evenings, as soon as the slave woman rushed up to him, he would laugh and joke and give her a gift: a silk headband, embroidered slippers, or a box of Turkish Delight or almond cakes. Tonight he was empty-handed, and his mouth was bitter and tight.

He went upstairs slowly—usually he took the stairs three at a time—and followed the scent of musk to the mistress' small bedroom.

Eminé heard his step. She was lying half-naked on the divan, and had opened the window on the garden to let in a little fresh air. She tossed on the cushions nervously, now sighing, now laughing. What answer would she receive from Captain Michales, the terrible boar? The question made her uneasy; then laughter overcame her, as she remembered the news that had been brought her this morning by Mustapha Baba. He'll not be a man any more, she thought. He'll still wear a beard, but all the same he'll not be a man. He's unmanned. Nuri's been turned into Nurina. Eminé could not stop laughing.

"Will he get a woman's voice as well, Mustapha Baba? And in time will he grow breasts?" she had asked the old man.

"Perhaps," he had replied, disconcerted by her laughter. "All the same he won't be a woman."

"Poor Nuri Bey, you wonderful hunter of women, you lion of Turkey, what has become of you?" Eminé had shouted. "A mule!"

She had gone on laughing. Mustapha Baba had looked at her, horrified. Then he picked up his little sack and was gone.

Now Captain Polyxigis stood before her.

"Welcome, my captain, my evening star," Eminé exclaimed, and unsheathed her perfumed shoulders. "Welcome, my husband. I've something amusing to tell you."

"I have news for you, too," said Polyxigis, and lay down beside her. He embraced her ardently and breathed in the fragrance of her bared breast. For him, the world vanished. But the woman felt his weight, heavy and solid, and rebelled. Forcibly, though tenderly, she pushed his head up.

"First I want to hear your news," she said. "When you came in you were depressed. Does he refuse?"

Polyxigis drew away from her. The world came back, and with it his cares. "Yes, he refuses."

"The damned wild boar! And why?"

"That he wouldn't say. He tore an account book he was holding in his hand, and tried to throw me out of his shop. But I told him what I thought! I didn't spare him!"

"That's not enough!" Eminé shouted. She got up and stamped with her rose-tinted heels on the floor. "No, Polyxigis, that's not enough. You should have killed him!"

Captain Polyxigis shuddered. "Killed him?"

"Of course, killed him! That's what being a man means. Only a woman answers an insult with an insult. Men kill."

"Kill Captain Michales?"

"Is he a God? He's a wild beast, and you're afraid of him. Aren't you ashamed?"

She seized her nightdress and with a single movement tore it from top to bottom. Her firm, erect body gleamed in the lamplight, and a rill of sweat trickled between her breasts.

"That's how I'd tear him, by God!" she whispered, and suddenly burst into tears.

Captain Polyxigis was dismayed. He tried to take her in his arms to calm her. But she stiffened against him and would not let him come near her. She crouched, like a wild beast, in a corner. She was not crying now. Hard, dry laughter shook her body.

"Polyxigis," she said, beating against the wall obstinately with her little fist. "Nuri disgusted me from the time Captain Michales broke the raki glass apart with his two fingers, and Nuri could not.

Take care you don't make me loathe you too. The man who embraces me must be like no one in the world."

"I won't kill him."

"You can't."

"I won't," Captain Polyxigis repeated, and it was now he who stamped on the floor. His face became distorted, his eyes pierced Eminé like a knife.

The woman saw his fury. It gave her pleasure. A heavy smell streamed from the man's sweating, raging body, and Eminé's nostrils quivered delightedly.

"My captain," she said, "my treasure, stamp and be angry— that's how I like you!" And she opened her arms.

For Captain Polyxigis the whole world collapsed on Eminé's bosom. And when, with extinguished eyes and wet hair, the man rose once more, it was as though he had emerged, holding his breath, from the depths of some dark sea.

"My beloved, my husband, my hero," Eminé cooed, reconciled, stroking his hairy thighs.

Captain Polyxigis lay with his back against the wall and observed the woman out of half-closed eyes that were full of profound joy. At the same time he could hear the noises of the town, the barking of dogs, the far-off serenades of nocturnal revelers. "There's nothing in this world above," he thought, "to equal woman."

And so he rejoiced that God had arranged for their bodies to be in such harmony. He laughed with satisfaction, stroking her firm, round arms.

"Eminé," he said, "don't worry. We'll find another, better man to give you away."

"You haven't asked me what the news was I had to tell you. Have you forgotten?"

"How should I remember when you're lying there before me and it will soon be day?"

Eminé laughed. Then she whispered something into his ear.

"God!" exclaimed Captain Polyxigis. "Oh, the poor fellow!" He felt profound sympathy with the wretched man. Eminé's laughter made his heart contract.

She sat up and extinguished the lamp. But he sat upright where he was, and stared into the dark.

Mr. Idomeneas was on his way home from the memorial service. Today he was in black, with a black band on his hat and an even wider one round his sleeve. He was in mourning.

It was almost midday when he came in. He sat down at his writing table and told his servant Doxania, "I'm not eating today, either now or this evening. I'm fasting." Then he sent her out of the room.

He picked up his pen, took a large piece of paper, sighed, and began to write. Today every letter was a capital letter in red ink. The sovereigns in the great cities also wrote in red ink, and today it was as though Konstantinos Palaiologos, in whose memory the service in the church had been held, were himself turning to address Victoria, Queen of England.

"MY DEAR COUSIN VICTORIA,
    Four hundred and thirty-six years have now gone by since I was killed. I lie beneath the earth and await justice at the hands of the Christian Queen of the upper world. Beloved Victoria, how long?"

Two fat tears dripped onto the paper and spotted it. He could not send it to the queen like that. He took another sheet and wrote with one hand, while with the other he held his handkerchief and wiped his eyes to prevent them from dripping. He wrote, and wiped his eyes, and fasted. . . .

When it was time to light the lamps, his friend Tityros came. Tityros had had a bad day. After Captain Michales had left him, he had found his wife and her brother sitting in the courtyard. They had laid the table and were drinking their morning coffee and milk, eating the last of the Easter biscuits, and laughing. He greeted them. They looked at him without answering. His wife did not get up, did not bring him a cup. Brother and sister winked at each other and laughed again.

Tityros shut himself up in his room. The thing had to end. His heroic oration in the church had given him courage. He would turn that parasite out. "This house is my Constantinople," he muttered. "He's the Turk, I'm Constantine."

He ran noisily downstairs and out into the courtyard. "Why are you laughing?" he shouted, and his chin quivered. "Shut up!"

The woman turned and put her hand in front of her mouth, to

stop her laughter. The brother yawned. He was still in his night-shirt, unshaven and barefoot.

"Is laughing then forbidden, teacher?" he asked mockingly.

"You have nothing to say," replied the schoolmaster. "I'm master of the house here!" He stamped his foot. "And I demand the key of the house. The master of the house keeps the key."

"What will you say next, teacher?" said Diamandes in a tone of amazement, putting his long leg up on the chair. He turned to his sister and pointed with his thumb at the schoolmaster, who was standing behind him, his face greenish yellow.

"Just look at him, the fly!"

Vangelio applauded her brother with a peal of laughter.

"What are you laughing at, you shameless creature?" shouted Tityros, beside himself, and he rushed at his wife to stop her mouth.

But the brother, who had kicked the chair aside, jumped up to help his sister.

"Down with your claws, schoolmaster," he bellowed, "or I'll knock you down."

He swung his fist over Tityros' head, and Tityros started back.

"Get out!" bellowed Diamandes, shaking his fist menacingly. "Get out, or I'll pound you to pulp, Tityros. What impertinence, trying to play the master and demand the key. Hey, you snake in spectacles, you leanbottom, take yourself off! If not, I'll give you legs!"

He seized him by the coat, shook him and pushed him against the wall. Vangelio undid her long hair, took out her ivory bridal comb and began combing voluptuously. Smiling proudly, she looked at her brother, at his broad, hairy chest exposed by the open nightshirt, at his cypresslike form, and then, with disgust, at her sickly husband.

Tityros tore himself away from his brother-in-law and ran to the street door. But before opening it he called out to his wife, "This is no life at all! It's got to end!"

"Yes, end," shouted Diamandes, puffing out his chest, "I can't stand any longer to have you stumbling over my feet, morning, noon and night. The house isn't big enough. There isn't room for both of us."

He turned to his sister. "Vangelio, choose."

Tityros held his breath. He stared at his wife and waited. Vangelio was holding a green silk ribbon between her teeth. She smoothed her hair with both hands, tied it up and shook it, so that it fell over her neck and down to her knees.

"I'm not parting from my brother," she said at last, "not if it means the end of the world."

"That means I . . ." Tityros began, and stopped.

Vangelio shrugged her shoulders. Diamandes laughed drily and again stretched himself out with his long legs up on the chair.

"She's given you the go-by, you poor thing," he said. "Don't you understand that yet, teacher?"

It was the sight of the sea that calmed Tityros down. He sat on a rock near the wall and the hours passed as he sat motionless, gazing at the expanse of water.

The sun was already sinking when Tityros got up from the rock. He looked about him in surprise. His agitation had subsided, his eyes were dry. During all the hours he had been gazing at the sea, he had been wholly without thought. But inside him something was stirring. At last he had come to a decision—in his blood if not in his understanding. He had not been able to make it in any way explicit, but he felt himself safe within his own certainty. "All will go well," he whispered, "I am the master of the house."

He turned into the crooked alleys near the harbor, passed through the Jewish quarter and was again in his own part of the town, in front of the grand house of Idomeneas. There was still a light in his friend's window. He's certainly writing to the queen again, he thought. What a waste of letters! I'll go and chat with him for a bit. It will distract us both.

He knocked. Old Doxania's face showed her pleasure as she saw him.

"Since early this morning the master has eaten nothing," she said. "Get him to eat, and God bless your honor for it! God has sent you."

Mr. Idomeneas too was delighted to have a guest. He had just finished his letter writing and had put his seal—Athena armed—on the envelope. Tomorrow the letter would go to London.

"Others fight with weapons," he said, pointing proudly at the sealed letter. "We two—and Hadjisavas—fight with our brains, and we shall set Crete free."

The schoolmaster shook his head. He did not believe that Crete could be saved by writings and letters and marble fragments. Tired and hungry, he sank onto a high, sagging chair.

"And who will save *us*, Idomeneas?" he asked with a sigh.

"Who? Crete, as soon as we have freed her, schoolmaster! Our personal happiness is bound up with that. In the fight for the saving of Crete we are fighting also for the saving of our souls."

But the schoolmaster shook his head. He wiped his glasses, which were spattered with spray from the sea.

Wandering about excitedly Idomeneas continued: "What other way to happiness can you see? To be sure—what's the good of my talking to you now? You're newly married, drunk with bliss. But the first rapture will pass, and then you will follow my way. For men like us there is no personal happiness. We find it only in the fight for the happiness of the community."

He paused. He wanted to roll himself a cigarette. But he remembered that he was mourning and fasting today, and he put his tobacco box aside. He thought with pleasure of the sacrifice he was making to the community.

"That's the secret, schoolmaster!" He raised his kindly, prematurely shriveled face with pride. "In Megalokastro I am the only one who knows it. Perhaps Hadjisavas as well. Later you too will understand."

He paused again. But his heart was overflowing. Today he must speak. The day demanded it. His friend must at last learn the secret which he had been meekly keeping to himself for years.

"Why do you suppose I write to the queen? Why do I stay here in the half-tumbled-down grand house of my father like a living corpse, and cry out? No, not I—Crete cries out! Because she has no voice she uses mine. You carp and say, 'Your crying's useless, no one hears you.' And I tell you, a cry is never wasted! Before the ear came voices. With their calling and crying the ear was first created, Mr. Teacher! All the kings and the mighty of the earth, to whom I write, will one day hear. And if they do not, then their children and grandchildren. And if not these, then God. Why is God there? Why, do you think? To hear! Don't laugh. Yes, yes, I know, everyone thinks I'm crazy. Behind my back I hear them whispering, 'What a waste of letters!' Let them say it. What do they understand about God and Crete and the duty of man? From among these ruins I cry out to God, and one day He will hear. He will bend down from Heaven to Crete. Ashamed of having left her in slavery for so long, He will ask me, Idomeneas, for forgiveness. Suddenly Saint Menas' Easter bells will start ringing loudly, and the Christians will run madly into the streets strewed with myrtle and laurel. Men and women will stream to the harbor, to greet the Greek king's son. As he steps from the ship, they will kiss one another and shout: 'Crete is risen! Really risen again!' "

He wiped his eyes. He had relieved his heart.

But the schoolmaster's mind was elsewhere; his friend's flame did not warm him. "You and I, my dear Idomeneas, will by then be withered leaves. We shall die slaves, and not live to see that resurrection."

Idomeneas laughed at his friend pityingly. "You're still not capable of understanding me. I have no need to see and to test in order to be set free. I am free even in the confusion of servitude. I enjoy the freedom of the future, generations in advance. And when I die, I shall die a free man, for I have fought for freedom my whole life long."

"That I really don't understand," said the schoolmaster, who was thinking of his wife and her shameless brother, and the key of the house which had been refused him.

"But you will certainly understand it one day," continued his friend. "For the moment you are ensnared by small things, which feast on the souls of men. The soul is a lioness, worries are her lice. But you will shake them off!" he said, giggling at his own wit.

Doxania appeared on the threshold. As Idomeneas had his back to her, she made a sign to the schoolmaster, who was very willing to eat now, as he had eaten nothing all day.

"A hungry bear doesn't dance," he said to Idomeneas. "You speak of great ideas, but my mind is revolving round food."

"I haven't had anything to eat either," said Idomeneas. "What harm does that do? Nourishment too is a louse."

"But the lioness would die," said the schoolmaster with a laugh, "if that louse were missing."

Idomeneas clapped his hands. Doxania came running up, delighted.

"The schoolmaster's hungry, nurse," he said. "Bring him a tray."

"With pleasure," exclaimed Doxania, hurrying off.

"We'll eat together, won't we?" said the schoolmaster. "I can't eat alone. You can endure fasting; but now you must also show that you can endure eating. Fasting, bad living and asceticism—these are lice, too, I think." The two friends laughed, cheered by the mixture of joking and great thoughts.

The full tray came, and Doxania's wrinkled face was lighted up with good humor. The hungry Idomeneas had decided he was not breaking his vow, as he now entertained his friend, and besides, the sun had gone down. And so they tucked in the food with a good appetite and drank old wine from a cask that had long been in the house.

"To freedom!" they cried, clinking glasses.

When it had grown quite dark outside, the schoolmaster's thoughts returned shuddering to his home.

"Why are you depressed?" his friend asked him. But the schoolmaster did not answer.

"How do you like your new existence? Is it easy to live with a woman?"

The schoolmaster went over to the window. "It's night. I must go."

The waxing moon under which Tityros had married had already waned, and the fourteen days of mourning for Manusakas were also nearing their end. Manusakas' first-born son Thodores had spent them in violent agitation. His uncle, Captain Michales, had insulted him—he had treated him like a boy not yet capable of using a knife and killing Turks.

"How old are you?"

"Seventeen."

"Stay in your nest!"

Did seventeen years seem to Captain Michales too few? He was a grown man, he could manage the plough with their ox Russos, and till their field. He was a match, too, for Hussein, Nuri's nephew, the young Turkish palikar-leader in Petrokefalo. When they wrestled, he could throw him—and he could easily plunge his knife into his neck.

"Uncle insulted me," he told his mother who, dressed in black, had gone to her husband's grave as usual and there, with her face pressed to the ground, had keened for the dead. Tomorrow was the fourteenth day. She had come like that each day and had called him, scratching at the earth with her nails.

"You're still too young, Thodores," his mother replied. "Leave the revenge to your uncle."

"But when? When, Mother? Tomorrow is Father's fourteenth day, and we still eat and drink and sleep and the deed remains undone. Doesn't Father appear to you in your sleep? Doesn't he complain to you? Every evening he reproaches me."

He bound the black headband round his head and looked across to the foot of the mountain, where the head village, Petrokefalo, shone bathed in sunshine. The sun had burned the young man's powerful body brown. Thick down was sprouting on his cheeks; his chest too already had a pelt. He lived in the mountains with his father's sheep, and seldom came to the village. But since last year his lonely existence had begun to lie heavy on him, and now every Sunday he went to the village church, to come in contact with women. The blood was beginning to drive him. Since the day of the murder he had not returned to the mountains. His brother Konstantes, the next in age, stayed there as herdsman. Thodores had donned his father's boots, jacket and headband, had adopted also his tobacco box and hazel staff, and had left the big oak to be in Ai-Janni. He often went into Petrokefalo, always sullen and silent.

"I'm going," he now said, taking the hazel staff.

"Where, Thodores, my child?"

"To Petrokefalo. Didn't you say you wanted pomegranate kernels tomorrow to strew over the funeral cake? There are some hanging in the loft at Grandfather's."

Out of his black belt stuck his father's knife, with the dried blood still on it. His mother had wanted to clean it, but he would not let her. "Blood isn't washed away with water, Mother, but with blood." He always had that knife about him. By night he placed it under his pillow.

"Give the knife here, my child," his mother had begged him. "As long as it lies under your pillow, your father comes and torments you in your sleep."

"That's just what I want, Mother," the son had replied. "I want him to torment me." And he crossed himself.

Now he left her, striking the stones with the hazel staff.

"Be careful, Thodores," his mother called after him, as she watched him kick the stones aside with powerful strides. "My blessing go with you!" But her son was already out of sight.

A hare ran through the heather. Thodores hurled the staff after it and caught the animal's paws, knocking it over. He picked it up and hit it against a stone, smashing the head. "I'll take it to Grandfather as a present," he said. "A good sign, the hare will bring me luck. That's how I'll pick up Hussein and hit his head to pulp against the cliff. But he's no hare. It'll mean a hard fight."

Two days before, he had challenged him to a fight, in front of the threshing floor. At Thodores' whistle, Hussein had come out to him.

"Hey, Hussein," he called to him, "the day after tomorrow ends the fourteen days for my father, who was murdered by your Uncle Nuri."

"Pitch and sulphur on his corpse," said Hussein with a short laugh.

The gall rose to Thodores' eyes. He trembled with rage and could not speak.

"What are you goggling at me for, giaour? Why did you whistle for me?" Hussein asked. "Have you gone blind? Didn't you see I was busy winnowing?"

"If you are a palikar, come and fight with me. I'll die a Turk if that back of yours doesn't rub the ground!"

"*My* back, you infidel? When and where?"

"At the same place where my father was murdered—at the big oak. The day after tomorrow, his fourteenth day. Early in the morning, so that nobody catches us."

"Do we bring knives?"

"Yes!"

They had separated. Hussein had gone back to his winnowing, while Thodores returned home. He knelt down on the threshold and took the knife out of his belt, to sharpen it. Then he remembered that he wanted the blood to remain on it, and put it back unsharpened. Later he went to the great oak and leaned against its trunk.

Now, at the entrance to Petrokefalo, near the well, he saw a girl, and went fiery red. She was holding a jug by the handle, to lift it onto her shoulder, but when, from a distance, she saw Thodores coming, she stood still, waiting for him. What a radiant girl! Her body was taut, yet supple in its lines. Above her gleaming almond eyes the brows bent like curved blades. She was like an animal that had caught a scent and now sniffed it tensely.

Thodores eyed her from afar. "Everything's turning to good, today," he muttered, his heart leaping. "There's Frosaki!"

He looked about him: nobody. The other girls had gone some distance away from the well with their jugs. The peasants on the threshing floor were flailing, winnowing and piling the corn. In the whole world there was only Frosaki. And above her head, like a crown, the sun.

He felt a delicious weakening at his knees. He stopped at the well.

"Good day," he said in a trembling voice. He lowered his gaze. The girl's slender, bare ankles gleamed as the sun poured over them.

The girl surveyed him boldly and laughed at him mockingly. "Why are you carrying a hare, Captain Thodores? Are you hunting hares?"

"I'm hunting Turks," replied the young man, raising his eyes. "I've been practicing on the hare."

For a moment their looks crossed like daggers, then in agitation the young man again lowered his head.

The girl corked her jug with a wooden peg. Then she looked hastily about her. There was no one to be seen. "Are you thirsty, Thodores?" she said.

"Yes, I'm thirsty, Frosaki. But who'll give me water to quench my thirst?"

The girl looked down and remained silent, but her neck and ears went a deep red.

Thodores whispered, "Tomorrow is my father's fourteenth day. Come to our house and help my mother with the funeral cake. The other girls of the village are coming too."

215

"If my mother'll let me, I'll come," said the girl. And immediately afterward: "Even if she won't let me, I'll come, because you've invited me. Captain Thodores is someone to whom we don't refuse any wish."

She said it with mocking laughter, to hide her emotion. She looked at him, she devoured him with her eyes. She spent her nights awake, thinking about him. She would have liked to be earth, to spread herself beneath his feet. But now that she saw him in the flesh, she teased and provoked him—yes, she would have liked to scratch him, to hurt him.

Thodores rested his chin on his staff and, gazing at the ground, reflected that tomorrow he would have to fight with Hussein.

"Ah, Frosaki," he said, "if anything happened to me, would you weep for me?"

Then the girl could control herself no longer. Tears flowed over her cheeks, as she whispered:

"I've nobody but you in the world, Thodores!"

"Well then," cried the young man joyously, raising his head from off his staff, "you mark my words, Frosaki: nothing bad can happen to me!"

Two girls with pitchers appeared. Frosaki quickly wiped her eyes, bowed her shoulder under her pitcher and pretended to be looking into the distance. But she could not restrain the throbbing of her heart. Thodores ran into the village, whistling loudly and swinging the dead hare in his hand.

Next day—a Sunday—when the liturgy was over and the memorial service for Manusakas began, Gregores the pope stepped on the platform in the forecourt. Beside him stood a black-bearded shepherd boy holding, on a heavy dish, the funeral cake with its thick icing, its almonds and pomegranate kernels. Manusakas' name, traced in cinnamon, was inscribed there. One peasant after another walked up and stretched out his palm, which the pope filled. Each one murmured: "God be merciful to your soul," and, as he moved on, buried his face in his paws to eat greedily and adorn his own mustache with cinnamon and icing.

Because the fourteen days had gone by the virtues of Manusakas were receiving particularly loud praise. He had actually appeared to old Katerinio, mother of the watchman of the pen, the night before. Her dog, too, had seen him, and his hair had stood on end. He had tried to bark at him, but his muzzle had remained open, and it could not yet be shut.

"The man we've lost walks about as a ghost," said one of the graybeards, crossing himself. "He was killed at the height of his strength and still walks. He won't die."

"He wants blood," said another. "Why does Captain Michales hesitate such a long time?"

While they were still chatting, Kokolios, the watchman of the pen, burst into the forecourt with his tongue hanging out. In his trembling hand he held his horn. The distribution of the funeral cake had just ended, and the pope was descending from the platform while, on their knees, the shepherd boys were licking the dish.

The pope came over to the watchman, while the congregation crowded around them both.

"Hey, Kokolios, get your breath! Have you got bad news? God have mercy on us!"

"Hussein, Nuri's nephew, has been found dead!"

"Where?"

"Under the big oak."

"Who . . . ?"

"God knows. Petrokefalo is in an uproar. The gates have been shut. The Christians are arming. They've laid the body in the courtyard of the mosque, and one Turk after another bows down in front of it, firing his pistol meanwhile. And they're threatening to burn down Ai-Janni."

"What can we do?"

"Someone from Ai-Janni is the murderer, they say. Someone of Manusakas' family. They're demanding Thodores as a victim."

"Someone go to the widow and tell her the news!" the pope ordered. "Thodores must escape to the mountains! Quick!"

But Thodores had already taken possession of his father's musket and pair of silver pistols. Also he filled his sack with cartridges and shot and, opening his father's trunk, took from under its double bottom the Greek flag. He quickly folded it together and fled to the mountains. He passed by the pen and gave instructions to his brother Konstantes. Remembering that he had not taken leave of his mother, he left a message for her that all was well with him and she should please give him her blessing. He put a lump of cheese into the sack and set out to climb Selena, the highest of the Lasithi mountains. There would be shepherds there from whom he had often stolen sheep, as they had from him. This had made them fast friends. I'll sleep in their pens, Thodores had decided, and if soldiers come hunting me, I'll raise the flag, place myself at the head of the shepherds, and we'll fight and shout: "For the union with Greece!"

Toward evening two armed agas came to the widow Christinia's door. They knocked. Not a soul! They knocked again, making the house ring. Nobody!

An old Turk, who had gone up to the mountain in search of wood, was coming back with his load. "Welcome, sirs," he said. "You're looking for Thodores? The bird has flown. He's made for the mountain."

"Be careful what you say, old Braimis. Did you see him with your own eyes?"

"Yes, by Mohammed, with my own eyes. The giaour was running as though he was a horse. I fell to the ground in terror. When I looked again, he'd vanished."

The agas cursed and stabbed the door twice with their knives. On their way back they met, in the ravine which divided the two villages, old Katerinio, to whom the ghost of Manusakas had appeared. She had been collecting wild lettuce and asparagus, and had filled her small sack. Now she was going contentedly home to prepare supper for her son.

The two agas rushed upon her and murdered her cruelly.

In the neighboring villages Turks and Christians now collided. The killings began. One time the corpse of a Christian would be found in the middle of the street, another time a dead Turk, hidden in his garden or in a dried-up well. The tidings flew about like sparks and set village after village on fire. And so too they reached Megalokastro.

One midday Suleiman, the pasha's Arab, was drunk. Not of his own accord. He had been pumped full of raki by the agas and then sent out into the Greek quarter. "Do your best, Suleiman, to find Captain Michales and finish him off, if you're a man," they had urged. He drew the dagger which the pasha had given him at last year's Bairam festival, and rushed bellowing through the Greek streets. As the Christian women heard him they snatched their children out of the streets and shut their houses.

"The Arab! The Arab!" they shrieked, banging their doors and bolting them.

Those Christians who met the Arab as they were going home to the midday meal dived for the first door that would open for them.

"Crete, abandoned by all, is catching fire again!" they told one another, some with fear, others with rage. From the cases where they had hidden them they pulled out their rusted muzzle-loaders, and began to clean them.

At Idomeneas' Fountain the Arab stopped. He was heated by raki and by the midday heat, and his brow, neck and legs trickled with sweat. He shoved his head under the fountain to cool himself, bellowing like a buffalo. The whole quarter trembled. He saw Captain Michales approaching from the far end of the street. With a wild shout he grasped his dagger and made a rush for him.

Captain Michales stood still. For a moment he thought of turning back, but was ashamed. To his right a door opened, and Krasojorgis' wife put out her head. "For God's sake, Captain Michales, why are you standing there? Come in!"

But he had now taken his broad handkerchief from his hip and wrapped it about his fist.

The door of Captain Michales' house also opened, and Katerina rushed out.

"Michales, Captain Michales, have pity on your children," she cried, and ran to his side.

She saw a monster facing her husband, with flashing teeth and rolling eyes.

"Now I'm going to gobble you up, Captain Giaour!" the Arab yelled, his dagger raised.

The woman started to come between the two men. Before she could do so, Captain Michales, with all his strength, planted his fist in the Arab's belly. With a roar he fell. Captain Michales wrenched the dagger from his clenched fingers. As he turned, he saw his wife.

"Your place is in the house," he said. "Go!"

Captain Michales, with his wife behind him, went in. She brought him a fresh shirt. As he changed, his body cooled down, and he smiled under his mustache. He gazed at the sharp dagger. "Wife," he said, "give Thrasaki that dagger, to sharpen his pencils with."

That same evening two young Turks, the sons of the muezzin, beat up the harmless Bertodulos in the Pervola and trampled on his straw hat. They were about to tear his cloak too, but he cried out, and they ran. Early next morning, the muezzin was found tied to the great plane tree, frozen blue and stark naked. His mouth had been bound with his green turban cloth, to prevent him from crying out. He was set free, his legs were rubbed, and he was given a hot infusion to drink. As soon as he could speak again, he described how two Christians, one of them with a wild mustache like a mountain goat, the other a lame man, had taken him prisoner, stripped him and tied him to the plane tree with the gallows rope. They had meant to cut off his beard too, but had forgotten the shears. So they merely spat on him and ran off toward the harbor.

The pasha was beside himself. He ordered all the lame in Megalokastro arrested and thrown into prison. A search was also made for Captain Stefanes, but he was not to be found. The police put the lame men in the stocks and dosed them with castor oil. But they all behaved like palikars and revealed nothing. After three days the pasha tired of feeding them and plying them with castor oil (there were some thirty of them), and he let them go. But he had Suleiman the Arab put in irons when he heard of his failure.

The days went by. A strong south wind came from Arabia and flaked the walls of the houses. Noses, ears and mouths filled with thick, hot dust, whirled up by the wind. Megalokastro groaned as in a fever. At noon the dogs huddled in the shade, and the men and women gasped. They did not stir from their shops, where they fanned themselves with straw fans and gulped down cool sherbet. Barba Jannis was at his height of glory. He ran through the heat, selling the snow-cooled drink. The old man feared the fire of summer as little as the frost of winter. His profit making cooled him in summer and warmed him in winter. And so he remained evenly tempered, all the year round. He neither left off his flannel in summer nor put on an overcoat in winter.

In the gardens the watermelons swelled to the point of bursting. Every morning the gardeners brought mountains of watermelons, gherkins and cucumbers to the main square near the great plane tree, and to the Three Vaults. The vine trellises were showing their first colored berries, and the first sour-sweet figs appeared in the market. The earth was exploding with fruitfulness—how could the fruit dealers keep pace with it? Turks and Christians stood before the piles of fruit, and the vendors sang their wares full-throatedly. At evening they gave away what was left over, to the children, old men and destitute old women, who rushed up and collected what they could.

When the sun sank, the earth breathed. It grew cool, and tender shadows settled over Megalokastro. The housewives sprinkled their yards and gathered now in one house, now in another, to gossip.

It was Sunday again. They were in the courtyard of Krasojorgis' wife. While they were enjoying themselves, nibbling dainties and cracking jokes, Penelope rushed in wailing. She was pale, her eyes staring. She wore her patched and spotted house dress. All jumped up and led her to a chair. Krasojorgis' wife gave her a drink of cherry juice. She drank and moaned at the same time.

They asked what was wrong. Penelope swallowed what was left.

"Demetros. . . . Demetros. . . ." she cried.

"For God's sake, is he ill?"

"He's gone off."

"Gone off? Where?"

"With his umbrella!"

"Where, my dear?"

"Into the mountains again."

"But why, Penelope? What's up with him?"

"Ah, I'm so worried! He ran out with his umbrella. . . . He's run away from me once before—with his umbrella that time too. During the 1878 rising."

"Oh, that's a bad sign! You mark what I say, my dears!" exclaimed Chrysanthe, slapping her knee. "That means another rising, God punish me if I'm lying!"

"Don't say such a thing, my dear! May the devil's ear be deaf!"

"God punish me if I'm lying!" Chrysanthe repeated. "How does the mouse get wind of an earthquake and escape? In the same way Demetros gets wind of the rising and runs out with his umbrella."

"He has no money," Penelope whispered. "And who'll cook his meals for him, who'll do his washing for him and his mending, and make his bed and cover him up at night? I know he'll come back to me, like last time, with his breeches in holes!"

"Don't make such a fuss, my dear," said Krasojorgis' wife, "I'm well on the way to being sick of my husband, with his cushions of fat."

But Penelope was not consoled. She again opened her mouth to wail, but the mistress of the house popped a spoonful of halvah with almonds into it.

"What's Captain Michales doing, neighbor?" She turned to Katerina quickly, to change the conversation. "For days and days I haven't seen him."

"Things are well with him, God be thanked," replied the captain's wife. "But he leaves the house at dawn and does not come home till night. How can you expect to see him?"

She sighed and fell silent.

And in truth things were well with Captain Michales. Only the world was too small for him, like a prison. He was rattling his chains. He rode over the fields as far as Nuri's country house. When he saw it lying there among the olive trees and cypresses, his heart growled.

"Patience, patience, my heart, don't be in too much of a hurry. Wait till he's well," he muttered, and turned away.

Every evening, late, Ali Aga came, covered with dust, from Nuri's country house with his news. "Today he tried to get up, but the pain overcame him and he rolled back onto his bed." . . . "Today he got up. His Moor supported him and guided him out to the yard. I stood in a corner behind the water trough and watched him. By my faith, Captain, I didn't recognize him. He's so pale, so thin! And where have those cheeks of his gone, and that well-kept mustache? His skin is full of furrows." . . . "Today he came out into the yard without the Moor. He looked at me, and I went up to greet him. But he waved me away—he didn't want to speak." . . . "Today the Moor got him onto his horse, and he went for a ride. The Moor ran behind, in case he should faint and fall from the saddle. And the horse went carefully, as if it understood everything!"

One evening, after days and weeks, Ali Aga came panting into Captain Michales' shop, where the captain sat waiting in the dark.

"He's well," said the old man. "Today Mustapha Baba left the house. 'You don't need me any more, Nuri Bey,' he told him, 'the rest lies in Allah's hands.' And with that he went. The Bey rode out this afternoon without being accompanied by the Moor."

"What does he look like? In his stride again?"

"He's still pale, Captain. Yellow as a bit of lemon peel. Gloomy. Quiet. He doesn't eat, the old nurse told me, he doesn't drink, he doesn't sleep. He's always sighing. And yesterday, when the old woman asked him when Eminé Hanum was coming to the estate, he caught hold of the stair rail to prevent himself from falling. He nearly fainted. He looked at the old woman with staring eyes, and did not answer."

"You talk too much, Ali Aga."

But Ali Aga stayed where he was. He wanted to say something more, but hesitated.

"Why are you scratching your head? Is there a piece of news you're still keeping back?"

"They say, Captain——" He broke off.

"Speak out, you blockhead! What do I pay you for?"

"They say the poor creature is maimed."

"What do you mean?"

He lowered his voice still more.

"He's no longer a man. And Eminé Hanum has heard it . . ."

"Go!"

Ali Aga reeled back. Stumbling among the ships' cables and paint pots, he found the way out and vanished.

Captain Michales started to his feet.

"That can't be!" he shouted, rushing up and down in the darkness of the shop. "It isn't possible!"

Biting his mustache convulsively he kept saying to himself again and again: "It can't be! But supposing it is? Suppose it's true? How can I take vengeance on a maimed man? What sort of vengeance is that? What does death mean to him?"

Suddenly he made a decision: I'll go and see him myself!

He let a few more days elapse. The man must rest a bit longer, he thought, get back his strength. And one Sunday he mounted his mare. The plain lay in the blaze of summer, the vine trellises were heavy with clusters, the sky burned.

"Summer, vintage, war. . . ." he whispered. "Ah, Mother rich in sufferings!" Full of pity, his spirit embraced Crete. Crete was to him a living, warm creature with a speaking mouth and weeping eyes; a Crete that consisted not of rocks and clods and roots, but of thousands of forefathers who never died and who gathered, every Sunday, in the churches. Again and again they were filled with wrath, and in their graves they unfolded a proud banner and rushed with it into the mountains. And on the banner the undying Mother, bowed over it for years, had embroidered with their black and gray and snow-white hair the three undying words:

FREEDOM OR DEATH.

Captain Michales' eyes grew moist. When he was alone he was not ashamed of tears. "Luckless Mother!" he whispered. "Luckless Mother!"

Between the olive trees gleamed the Bey's country house. Captain Michales put spurs to the mare.

The gate stood open. He rode through it. In the yard he dismounted and looked around. So many years ago, here, in this yard, near this gnarled olive tree, the two of them had kneeled together, and their blood had flowed. They had had the choice between death and brotherhood: they had become brothers. And now that, after all those years, he was returning to that same yard, it looked as if God had repented and they must kill each other. . . .

A servant ran up and recognized him. "Welcome, Captain Michales," he said.

"Where is the Bey?"

"Upstairs."

"Go and tell him I've come and would like to see him."

Nuri's stallion scented the mare and neighed to her. But the mare did not answer, for she was pregnant.

The servant came back. "The Bey says, welcome, Captain.

Would you have the kindness to wait until he is dressed? Shall I give the mare some hay, Captain?"

"No."

The captain went to the fountain and took the brass cup down from its hook. He drank. There was an inscription in Turkish lettering around the rim of the cup, in which their blood had once mingled. On that evening Nuri Bey had translated it: "Raise thy head, O traveler, and drink. Even the hen raises her head when she drinks, and thanks God!"

The servant appeared. "Will you be so kind as to come in?" he said. "The Bey is waiting for you."

Captain Michales pulled his black headband tighter, concealed the bone handle of his knife, and went in.

Nuri Bey was sitting on the divan, in a dim corner of the room, dressed up like a bridegroom. He knew for what purpose his guest had come, and was ashamed to appear before him pale and debilitated. He had put black pomade on his mustache and rouge on his cheeks. His eyelashes too had been colored with charcoal, to make his eyes brighter. He too had pushed his black-hilted dagger deeper down into his sash to make it invisible.

"Welcome, Captain Michales," he said, stretching out his hand. But the other buried his hands deep in his belt; he would not touch the hand that had killed his brother. Nuri Bey, humiliated, leaned back.

Captain Michales remained standing. He was trying, in the half-dark, to measure the strength that remained to Nuri, and to weigh his words accordingly.

"Are you in such a hurry, Captain Michales, that you won't sit down? And you've come all this way. . . ."

"Can't you stand up, Nuri Bey?" Captain Michales asked. "The business that has brought me to your house is not discussed on divans."

"I know. Why do you remind me, Captain Michales? Only don't be in a hurry. Let us first drink a coffee, smoke a cigarette, and talk a little. And then what you want shall happen, Captain Michales."

His voice was tired and full of bitterness.

"Right, Nuri Bey. Since you wish it, I won't be in too much of a hurry," said Captain Michales, and sat down opposite him. He

looked intently into Nuri's face, and involuntarily the Bey drew
back still further into the shadows.

"You were wounded, Nuri Bey—they say, severely. . . ."

"I'm very well, as before, Captain Michales. Don't worry," the
Bey answered defiantly. "My bones are still where they ought to
be."

"I'm glad," said Captain Michales.

The coffee came. Each rolled himself a cigarette, and they both
sat in silence, with bent heads. He has come to kill me, to avenge
his brother's blood, reflected Nuri Bey, without excitement. He's
dressed in black, like Charos. Welcome to him! What good is life
to me now? For me life and shame are one.

"Welcome," he said suddenly. "Day in, day out, I have waited
for you."

"I have drunk the coffee you gave me and smoked the cigarette,
Nuri Bey. We have nothing to talk to each other about. Stand
up!"

"As you decide." The Bey stood up with a great effort. He bit
his pain down. Then he walked with a slight limp to the threshold of the courtyard, where the sunlight fell on him.

When Captain Michales saw him in the light, he drew back,
appalled. So this was the handsome Nuri Bey, the moon countenance, the lion of Turkey? His cheeks were hollow, his eyes
dim; his underlip receded, shrinking as though from a perpetual
pain. Beneath the rouge and the pomade Captain Michales dis-
cerned the complexion of death. He frowned. How could he fight
with this cripple? What a dishonor!

"Nuri Bey," he said, "you're still not right, are you?"

"Do I look pale to you? A cripple? Come! On the threshing
floor the truth will appear."

With trembling knees he limped on. In the middle of the yard
he turned. Captain Michales was still standing at the threshold
and watching him.

A chill overcame Nuri Bey. The giaour sees through me, he
thought. He is refusing me. The Bey tried in vain to speak
strongly. His voice remained plaintive.

"Captain Michales, how long I have been waiting for you! For
no one else, all this time. Only for you. And now that you've
come, do you mean to go away?"

Captain Michales said nothing. His feeling of pity grew stronger. "Why do you keep looking at me? The illness has devoured my cheeks, but my strength remains. Don't listen to people's gossip, Captain Michales. My strength is as before. Come with me."

Captain Michales did not move.

"Shall I have my stallion brought, so that you may see how I ride? Shall I fire my pistols at a target? Draw a circle—I'll shoot at it. Come with me to the threshing floor. There we shall see who is a man."

He pushed his headband to one side and laid his hand challengingly on his sash. But a cold sweat trickled from his forehead and his belly hurt. Captain Michales' heart was full of pity.

"Nuri Bey," he said calmly. "Speaking loudly is a strain for you. Come inside."

Nuri Bey crumpled. Two heavy tears rolled from his eyes. He turned toward the outer door, to hide his pain. He's sorry for me, he thought, so low have I sunk. Nuri Bey, you move men with nothing but pity now.

"Let's go indoors," Captain Michales insisted. "Another time. . . ."

Nuri Bey ceased to pretend. With a despairing look at his swarthy guest he whispered, to avoid being heard by the servants: "Captain Michales, you came to kill me. Why don't you kill me?"

"Let's go indoors, Nuri Bey. We can be heard here."

He approached the Bey, took him by the arm, and felt the weakened body shudder. Nuri made no resistance and followed, hobbling. As he did so, he moaned, "You are my blood brother, don't forget. In this house of misfortune we mingled our blood. I beg you for one favor: kill me."

"Don't be angry with me, Nuri Bey. Some other day. . . ." replied Captain Michales.

"You're sorry for me?" The Bey sat down again on the divan, in the shadowy corner. He asked once more: "You're sorry for me?"

But Captain Michales made no answer. He could bear this shape of woe no more. It was driving him away. What business had he in this Turkish konak? With this poor creature he had no account to settle. What could death mean to him?

He stood up. The sun was already sinking.

"Nuri Bey, good-by. I'm going."

The Bey's hoarse voice now sounded as though it came from a great distance. He said doubtfully, "You're right, Captain Michales. God guard you."

Captain Michales watched this man and thought of how handsome he had been, of his heroic bearing, of the sparks his horse used to strike from the roadway, and of his breeding.

"Captain Michales," came the unearthly voice again, "if ever I was a man once upon a time, give me your hand. If I was not, farewell."

Captain Michales stretched out his hand and softly, so as not to hurt it, gripped the other's hand.

"God guard you, Nuri," he said.

"Perhaps this means good-by forever, Captain Michales. Do you understand what I mean?"

"I understand," he answered, and stepped over the threshold. And Captain Michales, the wild boar, suddenly felt a painful cramp in the back of his neck.

Nuri Bey waited, crouched on the corner of the divan. He listened to the hoofs of Captain Michales' mare trampling over the stones. Then all was silent. The rays of the setting sun penetrated the room turning the walls golden. Soon they vanished, and the walls darkened.

He glided slowly from the divan and went to the mirror. Before it he washed with musk soap, changed his shirt and sprinkled the whole of a small bottle of lavender water over himself. He took a long time combing his hair. Then he went out to the stable and with long, delicate movements stroked the beloved horse from the fine, pointed ears to the slender legs. The stallion bent its neck down and passed its mouth caressingly over its master's head and neck. It neighed joyfully.

"Farewell, my child," the Bey murmured, in tears.

He went up to his bedroom, took a sheet of paper, and wrote: "When I am dead, I wish you to kill my horse over my grave." He placed his seal underneath.

He sank on his knees on the ancient Anatolian carpet on which his father, seven times a day, had made his devotions, facing toward Mecca. He looked through the open window at the starry sky. A strong wind had sprung up. The dog in the stable was barking. In the far distance he heard the song of a passing wagoner, calling with longing to his wife. Nuri Bey thought of Eminé, closed his eyes and sighed.

"Treacherous world, farewell!" he whispered.

From his sash he pulled the black-hilted knife, raised it high in the air, and with all his strength plunged it into his heart.

8

EARLY NEXT DAY, when the Kanea Gate was thrown open, the dark news entered the town: Nuri Bey had been found dead in his country house! In the Turkish coffeehouses the agas hummed like swarms of wasps. Some affirmed at the tops of their voices that the Greeks had murdered him, others said it was a case of suicide. The news had deprived the muezzin in the mosque of coherent speech. Foaming at the mouth, all he could do was to stammer confused words: "Massacre!" "Giaour!" "Mohammed!" The Greeks left their work in the lurch and took counsel secretly by twos and threes in their houses.

The atmosphere was oppressive. The soldiers shouldered their arms and ranged through the streets and over the markets. The pasha appeared in person in the cemetery for the burial of Nuri Bey. Behind him paced the imam and the muezzin, and after them, in a noisy swarm, the armed agas. Even Suleiman the Arab was present escorting the pasha, who had freed him from the irons, having had enough of his bellowing. The servants had brought the body to the tomb. The horse had followed, stepping lightly and neighing. It opened its eyes wide and sniffed the air.

The imam recited the last words in a high monotonous voice and consigned the dead man to the other world. The muezzin took the bloodstained white headband from the dead man's head and stuffed it into his own bosom. With deep obeisances all took leave of Nuri Bey, who was lowered into a grave next to his father's monument. Then the pasha gave a signal that the horse was to be brought to the grave. In his hand he held the paper that

Nuri's Moor had delivered to him. "Agas," he said, "This is the written and sealed last wish of the dead man. Listen!"

He lifted the sheet of paper to the light, and read: "When I am dead, I wish you to kill my horse over my grave."

The agas were appalled at these words. They gazed at the horse. It had bowed its head over the grave, so that the bluish mane hung down, and it was sniffing at the earth. It stamped on the ground with its hoof and called to its buried master with a doleful neighing.

"A pity it is, before God and men," voices could be heard saying on all sides.

"Pity or not," the pasha retorted, "it is the dead man's wish. It rends my heart too, God knows, but it is the will of the dead man to take the horse with him. I would do the same. Which of you will harden his heart and draw his knife?"

All stood as though turned to stone. They looked, horror-struck, at the slender body of the horse, gleaming in the sun. This was no Greek to be killed, no ox or sheep to slaughter to preserve one's own life. This was an ornament of the world, the pride of Megalokastro. Connoisseurs came from Rethymno and Kanea to admire it. Who could raise his knife against such a neck?

The pasha breathed heavily. "Who is ready to draw his knife?" he asked once more, looking about him.

No one stirred. The horse had now crouched over the grave and was sniffing frantically. Its neighing sounded like a human voice wailing over someone who has died.

The pasha turned to his Arab. "Suleiman, you slaughter it!"

The Arab drew his knife and took a step forward. Then he stumbled and fell on one knee. The horse leaped up and gazed at him. The Arab hesitated.

"Courage, Suleiman. Shut your eyes and jump at it!" the pasha ordered, tears welling in his eyes.

All fixed their gaze on the Arab. "If he kills him, I'll pound him to pulp, by my father's corpse," muttered one, his eyes sparkling.

The Arab approached the horse, his knife raised. He began to curse and swear, to arouse his courage. The horse again lowered its neck and neighed dolefully, and the Arab let his arm drop.

"Pasha Effendi," he said hoarsely, "I can't."

"Bravo, Suleiman," came the cries of approval and relief.

231

"I can't," the Arab repeated.

"Take the horse for yourself, Pasha Effendi," cried the agas "save it, if you believe in God!"

"I'm afraid of the dead man," said the pasha, gazing at the famous stallion with longing. He raised his hand to stroke it, but the beast reared threateningly, and would not let him come near. "Let's go," said the pasha. "Let it appease its grief over the grave. It too has a soul. And later, don't worry, hunger will compel it to stop. The dead man's Moor is to remain close by and keep watch. Let him give it fodder and water. And when it has calmed down, he's to bring it to me."

They all moved off toward the town, the pasha contentedly at their head. Allah was great and good and a friend to the pasha. How often had he desired that horse! How often he had longed to grip it between his knees and to remember his youth! If he were to be offered all the women of Megalokastro and then to be given the choice: these women or the horse—he would choose the horse. The devil could take the women! And now, my God, Thou art munificent! Thou killest Nuri Bey and makest me a present of his horse!

They passed the old fortifications outside Megalokastro, where fruit and vegetables were now planted. In the sunset light a Venetian lion glowed red above the stone battlements. A swarm of ravens was returning soundlessly to the ruined towers from the day's hunting. Through the evening stillness Megalokastro was barking, neighing and shouting in the distance, and still farther off roared the sea.

The pasha halted, and spoke to the agas gathered about him: "Remember, the fate of Crete is hanging by a hair. Nuri—this I swear by God—killed himself. Do not make him the banner of a Turkish campaign that would begin the slaughter afresh. By the Prophet, I shall hang not only giaours from the plane tree but— mark my words—Mussulmans as well. Beware!"

Then he cried, "Come, Suleiman," and together with his Arab rode away from them, breathing heavily.

The muezzin shook his head. The great ones quickly exchanged stealthy looks. This pasha was a man with no backbone, a Greek bastard—what business had he in Crete? Was there ever an Anatolian wedding at which no lambs were slaughtered?

The pasha had not yet disappeared through the fortress gate before the muezzin pulled Nuri's bloodstained headband from his bosom and raised it on the tip of his staff as a banner.

"Down with the giaours, children, down with them!" With this shrill cry he placed himself at the head of the crowd of agas.

Down below in the moat two gray-haired Christians were drawing water from the fountain and watering their beasts.

"There we have two of them already," cried the muezzin. "Palikars, at them!" Two palikars drew their knives.

"With my blessing," shouted the muezzin.

The two slid down the slope through reeds and tall sunflowers and reached the fountain. They seized both the little old men and held their heads over its rim.

The two heads rolled into the fountain.

"Forward, brothers!" cried the muezzin. He raised his staff, and the sea breeze swelled the bloodstained headband. Then the troop poured over Megalokastro.

The Christians, who had heard the noise of the returning funeral company a long way off, hastily shut their shops and workshops and ran to find shelter behind the doors of their houses.

The muezzin placed himself in front of the big Turkish coffeehouse at the Kanea Gate and, raising his staff high, cried:

"Allah, Allah, let the giaours taste your knives!"

But old Selim Aga and the other sages led the muezzin into the coffeehouse and ordered coffee, Turkish Delight and a narghile, to calm him down. Then they fetched Efendina and installed him on a stool in the middle of the room. They ordered him to tell a story of women and handsome boys, to deflect the muezzin's mind from blood and massacres.

The days went by uneasily. Hourly the Greeks trembled, lest one noon they find the fortress gates shut and themselves caught in a trap. They were few, and the Turks in their overwhelming numbers could easily finish them off.

Then came fresh Job's tidings. The Turks had broken into Agaratho monastery and murdered the brave Abbot Agathangelos. They had come on him at night, sleeping on the roof. He had been to Thrapsamos to consecrate a church, and as he lay full of food and drink in a heavy slumber, they hacked off his head. One murder led to another. Four days later Agathangelos' cousin, a

233

monk from Vrondisi, the monastery at the foot of Psiloritis, came down to the rich Turkish village of Suros and killed its bloodthirsty aga, just as he had bound two Christians to the treadmill of the well in his garden and was making them turn the wheel.

The Turks in the Greek villages took fright and loaded their asses and mules with all the household goods they could carry—clothes, coppers, cradles, cooking utensils—and their hanums, children and babes in swaddling clothes, and fled to Megalokastro, to the protection of the military. The peaceful and fearful among the Christians, for their part, fled with their families and household goods into the mountains.

The pasha was at his wits' end. For the first time he found himself in a Cretan revolution. He was not the man for such an upheaval. The good-natured Anatolian loved amusements, fine cooking and sleep. Why the devil were these Cretans brawling with one another? And why just now, when he had taken possession of Nuri's famous stallion? He wanted to feed it with sugar and give it water to drink out of his hollowed hands, to win it over. And now this damned Crete must go and have a revolution! He did not know what to do. He went to the Metropolitan and implored him: "Metropolitan Effendi, pronounce an anathema, say that anyone who kills a Turk will find no peace in the grave." He rushed out to the Turkish villages. "Don't run away and leave your houses, you idiots," he told them at the top of his voice. "I swear, not a nose shall bleed. I have already sent a report to Constantinople, and soon troops will arrive and restore order."

But he did not succeed by these means in stamping out the fire. There came another piece of news: "Captain Thodores at noon today set fire to a Turkish village in the Lasithi."

The agas, full of rage, went armed to the pasha.

"Pasha Effendi, the mischief is spreading, the giaours have lost all shame. They're burning our villages. Have you heard what has happened in the Lasithi?"

"Who is this Captain Thodores? It's the first time I've heard of him," the pasha said, playing peevishly with his beads.

An aga from Petrokefalo jumped up.

"A young stripling from an accursed stock! It was his father, Manusakas, who maimed Nuri. His uncle is Michales, that Captain Wildboar. This downy-chin has the impertinence to attack

234

us! If you don't have him caught and pilloried, we shall set fire to the Greek quarter of Megalokastro. We wanted to tell you that, Pasha Effendi. You just think of how you can put it right with the Sultan afterwards!"

"In the name of the Prophet, don't commit such an outrage, you devils!" yelled the pasha. "My head's whirling! When the Sultan hears of what you've done, I shall be finished!"

"Then catch Thodores and put him in the pillory. If not, we'll lay Megalokastro in ashes."

"How can I catch him? Where is he?"

"In the Lasithi. Send soldiers."

He sent soldiers, who tramped through the Lasithi mountains. Thodores gathered his friends about him, young men with adventure in their blood.

Thodores had been luring the agas of Petrokefalo from mountain to mountain. They had sworn his downfall, to avenge the blood of Hussein. For the most part Thodores had been alone; sometimes he had had a few daring comrades with him. They had begun shooting, and when things got too hot they escaped over the precipices. He carried his father's gun and wore his father's boots and torn, sweat-stained headband. He felt that his father's manhood had passed to him from his clothes. His father had risen again, father and son were now one, and Thodores grew stronger and riper from one day to the next. His words, too, acquired weight, and his opinions were respected.

More and more Greeks gathered around him when the soldiers began to thrust into the mountains. About twenty palikars had followed his call.

"Turkey is out for our blood," Thodores cried, "that is why I appeal to you, brothers! Do you know what has happened? From our villages the spark has now flown to Megalokastro. From there it will reach Rethymno and from there Kanea. Soon all Crete will be burning. Don't lose courage! Remember that those dogs are not just hunting a murderer. Even if they catch him, they won't lay down their weapons. They're hunting the whole of Christendom! Our grandfathers and our fathers knew that before us. Now *our* time has come. He unfolded the flag he had taken from his father's trunk, and they saw the inscription: FREEDOM OR DEATH.

When the pasha heard, he was seized with rage. He hurried out to seek the Metropolitan. The giaours' pope would have an account to settle with him. He took the Arab with him and growled about his ill luck all the way. The anxiety about Crete was not the only one. This morning he had had another piece of bad news. Nuri's servant had come running from the cemetery to tell him that the horse was lying dead on the grave. He had refused both food and water.

"I gave it to him, Pasha Effendi, but he wouldn't touch it. He wanted to die."

The sun was high. The muezzin craned his neck from the minaret and announced the great virtue of prayer and the mercy of God.

The Metropolitan sat on his broad divan, with his rosary between his fingers, conversing with the learned Hadjisavas in low tones. In his thoughts he was back once more in the years of his youth, when he had been archimandrite in Kiev and Representative of the Holy Sepulcher. His head was full of Russia. What a blessing of God that country was! what a soil, what corn, butter, smoked fish and caviar it possessed! And then the golden domes on the churches, and the silver icon-shrines, and the pearls, sapphires and rubies on the Gospels!

"As long as Russia survives, Hadjisavas, I am afraid of nothing," he said. "One day Russia will open her mouth and swallow Turkey. And then Crete will see freedom. We have no other hope."

But Hadjisavas was looking absent-mindedly out of the window. A sultry bora was blowing. Hadjisavas had recently been on his father's land near Aja-Irini, an hour's distance from Megalokastro, and—whether it had been a message from God, or put into his mind by the old times he had been studying—the idea had occurred to him that this soil might be concealing a celebrated ancient city. And there, as he scratched about with the iron tip of his stick in the field, by the bank of a brook, a glittering thing had rolled out from the moist earth. A golden ring!

He had just shown it to the Metropolitan. Two figures were engraved on the ring: a woman with exuberant hips, holding a double ax in her hands, and near her a naked man of slender build —just like the Cretans of today—with his foot poised to dance. Above them both was placed a seal, a half moon.

He now laid it in the Metropolitan's palm and said: "In God's name, Bishop, hide it. No one must hear of it. What treasures that soil must hide, what golden ornaments of the dead! But we are slaves. If we reveal the treasure now, Turkey will rob us of it. Let us be patient. As soon as Crete is freed, may some other Greek dig up the ancient city and win the renown."

The Metropolitan shook his head. All that was very nice, but he had many, many souls to care for. What concern of his were things which the earth had swallowed up thousands of years ago? He listened politely, but tried to lead the conversation back to present-day Crete and to Moscow.

Hadjisavas was put out. "Your Reverence expects freedom from Moscow, the people expect it from guns, and I from this ring, which you, Bishop, despise."

Murzuflos opened the door. "The pasha, most reverend Bishop," he said.

Hadjisavas rose with a laugh. "The Anatolian has not done with the Cretans yet?" He kissed the Metropolitan's hand, and made his escape through a concealed side door.

As he entered, the pasha began immediately to shout.

"Metropolitan Effendi—the Cretans have raised the flag and are demanding freedom. What freedom? I don't understand. If you obey God, in Whom you believe, and do what He commands you, do you then complain of being a slave and raise a banner and demand freedom? No! Isn't it the same with God's representative on earth, the Sultan? What devil's game is going on here in Crete, to rob me of peace?"

"What happens, though, if you obey a god in whom you don't believe, Pasha Effendi?" the Metropolitan replied. "The Cretans don't believe in the Sultan. That's why they feel they are slaves and seek freedom."

The pasha put his hands to his temples; he could not understand. He kicked the door open and went out. When he reached home, he sat down at the window and gazed through a small telescope at the sea, to see if the Turkish ships with more soldiers were coming yet. The soldiers would make everything clear and restore order. . . .

Behind his door Captain Michales waited with two loaded pistols. Each evening he sent his wife with the baby in her arms, accompanied by Thrasaki and Renio, to spend the night with one of the neighbors' wives. He remained alone in the house. But after a few days he said to Thrasaki, "You will stay here with me; you must get used to it." After that, father and son kept watch together. For several days nothing happened. This Sunday, Captain Michales was even enjoying a rest in bed. While he was entangled in reflections, there came a heavy knocking at the street door. He heard screaming and howling, and he recognized the voice of old Marjora, a relative, whom Tityros had recently brought in from the country to help his wife with the marketing and cooking. He had also thought it would be a consolation to have one of his own people in the house. Captain Michales peered through the little window. Old Marjora stood in the middle of the yard, shrieking and tearing her hair.

"Hey, Marjora, what's all the screaming about? Come up!" he ordered.

With trembling jaws she stood before Captain Michales' bed. She tried to speak, but her words were unintelligible.

"What are you saying?" Captain Michales shouted. "Diamandes? What the devil's the matter with him?"

"He's dead!" shrieked the old woman. "We found him just now in his bed. Stiff! Vangelio is screaming and beating her breast. She's shaken him, taken him in her arms, rubbed him with oil of roses and with vinegar. But he remains stiff! He's been poisoned. He's dead."

"Poisoned? How do you know that? Who poisoned him?"

"He's dark green in the face."

"I'll go back with you."

"Don't you breathe a word about it!" he told his wife, as he followed old Marjora through the street door.

At the end of the street, close to Idomeneas' Fountain, lay his brother's house. He went through the door, which was standing open. From the bedroom Vangelio could be heard wailing and beating her breast. Tityros, his teeth chattering, cowered in the lower room, on a corner of the divan.

Captain Michales went up to him. The schoolmaster raised his eyes and at once lowered them again.

"Schoolmaster," said Captain Michales, "look me in the face!"

Tityros raised his head. Frightened eyes flickered behind his glasses.

"You killed him," whispered Captain Michales. "It was you!"

"I?"

"Yes! If a man had killed him, it would have been done with a knife. But you've done it with poison, like a coward."

"I couldn't bear it any longer."

"I don't blame you for killing him, but I do blame you for killing with poison, woman fashion."

"I couldn't bear it any longer," the schoolmaster repeated. "I couldn't have done it any other way. He was the stronger."

"Does your wife know?"

"She may. She doesn't speak to me, and when I go upstairs, she pushes me away. I'm sitting here and waiting."

"What for?"

"Nothing. I'm waiting."

Captain Michales went out into the yard. The sound of Vangelio's lamentations was monotonous, like running water. He re-entered the house.

"Why are you waiting?" he asked again.

Tityros became suddenly more cheerful. "Come what will! Come what will! I'm not afraid any more."

"But your wife may denounce you."

"Let her do what she will. I've done what I wanted. Now it's up to her."

"Stand up. Keep calm. If she does denounce you, tell the truth, even if it means prison for life. If she doesn't denounce you, say nothing! And don't let the dead man weigh on your conscience. Are you listening? A proper man kills when it is necessary! Stand up!"

He helped his brother up and said, "Let's go and arrange for the funeral."

Next morning, when the mourners came to view the body, no one could see the dead man's face. It was covered with flowers. Vangelio had pillaged her small garden. The neighbors' wives too had sent armfuls of rosemary, basil and roses. Only Captain Polyxigis pushed the flowers aside to look. At the sight of the swollen face, he hastily covered it up again and cast a dark look at Tityros.

When Vangelio saw the pope enter, she came down from her bedroom and, with her hair loosened, threw herself upon the corpse. She lay stretched out over her brother's body motionless, soundless, as though asleep. But when the four bearers came to take him away she offered no resistance. She stood up and cut off her tresses near the roots. She wound them into two thick braids and knotted these around the dead man's hands. Then peacefully she let him be carried out and at the threshold raised her hand as though to bid him farewell. Going back into the house, she brought out her brother's clothes, heaped them in the yard and set fire to them. Then she cleaned the house, made herself tidy, and sat down in the yard, her staring eyes fixed on the flames.

After the interment her uncle came and sat down beside her. He took her by the hand and asked her if anyone suspected murder. She looked at him without answering. She merely shook her head and pressed her lips together defiantly.

Tityros was afraid to sleep either in his own house or in his brother's. He spent the night talking with his friend Idomeneas about death and the immortality of the soul.

Three days went by. Vangelio paid no attention to Tityros when he passed her as he moved like a shadow in the house. She bolted herself in her brother's room, lighted the lamp of the dead, and placed near it a glass of pure water, in case his soul should be thirsty. She knew that a dead man's soul roamed the house for fourteen days. She could feel its presence on her hair and on her neck and on her shriveled hands. At night it fluttered like a butter-fly over her lips. The world had never given her anything more beautiful.

For three days she did not speak and her gaze remained fixed and tearless. She wore black; only the ribbon that she bound about her hair was yellow.

Her aunt Chrysanthe begged her to come to her small country house by the sea in the hope that it would make some slight change for her, but she shook her head and remained bolted in her brother's room. She did not go to the grave. Quietly she rummaged in her trunk among her scant possessions. Then she cleared the house, as though she were going on a journey.

On the third evening she said to old Marjora:

"Lay the table. Get out the white embroidered cloth, and the good dishes and knives and forks, and tell your master that I will eat with him this evening. Don't light the lamps, except the two lamps for the death watch."

The schoolmaster was ready to faint with fear when he saw the burning death lamps. He sat on the edge of his chair and dared not look his wife in the eyes. She sat opposite him, pale and stiff as a corpse, barely tasting the food. She said not a word. A thick coating of powder lay like chalk on her skin. She had put on her white wedding dress and had stuck the faded lemon blossoms in her hair.

They sat there, neither of them making a sound. From time to time Tityros would open his mouth, but the words remained stuck in his throat. Sweat poured over him. Through the open window facing the courtyard the night breeze came in gusts, making the two plumes flicker.

Suddenly the woman stretched out her hand and filled the two glasses to the brim with wine. The wine was a red throat-scraper from Kissamos, a wedding present from the blessed Manusakas.

She raised her glass and with a violent blow smashed Tityros' glass. "I drink to your health, you murderer!" she said in a deep, almost masculine voice.

She left the room, stepped out into the yard for a short while, and once again locked herself in her brother's room. In the morning they found her hanging from a clothesline attached to the roof beam.

Early in the morning the news reached Captain Polyxigis as he lay in Eminé's bedroom. The widow was ready to be christened, but had decided to wait patiently till Crete was calm again, in order not to provoke the agas. She was delighted at the thought of becoming a Christian and going into the streets without a veil. She looked forward to being able to gaze about her in church, and to being seen. Air and sun would play about her freely, she would wear Greek blouses and ruched skirts, and would show her raven-black hair for the world's pleasure. Christ for her was a door which she could open, through which she could walk, without a veil, into the streets.

While she mused, stretched out on her bed beside Captain Polyxigis, about all these advantages of Grecian life, her black nurse entered, disheveled and breathless. She had run across, first thing, to the Hags, to learn the day's news; and now she was back.

"Captain," she stammered, "your niece Vangelio has hanged herself."

Captain Polyxigis let go of Eminé's hand. He stood up.

"Hanged? When? Who told you?"

"The Hags. Last night, in her house. With the clothesline."

Meanwhile Eminé had pulled out her little round mirror from under the pillow and was examining tongue, teeth and eyebrows.

"Hoo! my tongue's not red today. Where's my mastic, Maria?"

"She's left her husband, they say, to follow her brother," the Moorish woman went on, while she searched for the mastic.

"How my race has fallen—and I have no children," thought Captain Polyxigis, sighing.

He bent over Eminé, who, without a care, was admiring her beauty in a mirror, and caressed her body tenderly.

"Our son will be half Cretan, half Circassian. That means he will be immortal!"

As if he had realized this for the first time, his breast filled with confidence. He had been about to leave, but his knees were trembling, and he sank back onto the bed. That he should produce a wild son, drunk with Circassian blood, who would ride horses before he could spit!

He had long ago ruled that brother-and-sister pair out of the book of his race. They had been degenerate: the one a good-for-nothing and swiller, the other a sour, aging, infertile maid. He had no other nephews and nieces. The line was near extinction. But from this Circassian who chewed mastic in front of her mirror and whose mouth smelled of musk his son—the immortal man—would come, to glorify the seed of the Polyxigises to all eternity.

Then he remembered the Moorish woman's tidings and felt ashamed. He murmured, "Eminé, my child, I must go," stood up, put on his belt and donned his fez.

Eminé raised her naked arms and stretched. "Go," she said peevishly, and looked at him out of half-closed sickle-curved eyes. She yawned.

During the three days between the death of Diamandes and the suicide of Vangelio, events in Crete grew more turbulent. In the

villages the Christians killed several agas and the Turks in Megalokastro retaliated accordingly. For one man killed in the country
two Greeks fell that same night in the alleys of the town. The
reins had slipped from the pasha's hands. All he had left was his telescope, with which, from the window of his seraglio, he searched
the sea for Turkish frigates.

On the third day, suddenly, at noon, the fortress gates were
closed. No one could go in or out.

And with that day began Ramadan. The Turks touched neither
bread nor water nor cigarettes all day. But as soon as night came
and the first star shone, they made up for everything. A big
drum stood in front of each wealthy aga's konak. Dully and
heavily it sounded, like a signal for war. The Christians, gathered
in their houses, trembled at it, lest the agas after their evening feast should rush into the streets and beat the Christian
doors in.

All his neighbors came to Captain Michales in the evenings,
hoping for protection. Since it was summer, the men lay in the
yard and on the veranda, while the women stretched themselves
in the bedroom. Captain Michales kept watch in his little room,
with his gun above his head.

One night there was a secret gathering of the spokesmen and
leading people in the Metropolitan's residence. Captain Michales
was there, and so was that bear of the sea, Stefanes. He had put
on his sea boots, as though he were going on a voyage. The Metropolitan spoke briefly and cautiously. Crete was once more passing
through dark and uncertain days. Christendom was in danger.

The Rose Bug again had a suggestion: "Go, my lord, to Athens,
seek out the king. They must send us supplies and munitions. If
not, we are lost. But go yourself. The face of a man is a sword."

The Metropolitan shook his head.

"I do not leave my lambs when the wolf breaks in. Let Captain
Elias go."

But Captain Elias said angrily, "My dice still roll, Bishop. I'm
not an old man. I can still command in war. I'm not going. Let
the quill-driver Hadjisavas go." His bushy eyebrows still twitching
with wrath, he turned to Hadjisavas.

"Let us not drag our poor, unhappy Mother Greece into this
with us. It will only hurt her," said the Metropolitan. "Let us

243

trust in the great powers, above all in Russia, which is of the true faith."

"Let's trust in the small powers—in our own strength," said Captain Michales. "That is my opinion."

"Mine too!" shouted Captain Elias. "Why has the wolf a strong neck? So that he can seize his prey by himself!"

"Let's each of us throw a stone into Suda Bay," suggested Mr. Idomeneas. But nobody was listening to him. They separated at about midnight without arriving at any decision.

Day and night alternated, each with its terrors. All day the hungry and excited Turks ran out of the mosques inflamed by the muezzin's harangues, and rushed about with the glassy eyes of the blind. At night they reeled, well fed and drunk, into the coffeehouses, then swirled into the Greek part of the town and fired shots into the air, terrifying those who crouched behind closed doors.

Each night, when the agas were still at table, Ali Aga slid along the walls to Captain Michales' house and brought the news. . . . This is what the imam said today in the mosque . . . those are the words uttered in the coffeehouse . . . the muezzin demanded violence, but this or that bey opposed him—all the news was scalding hot, evening after evening.

One night there were three soft knocks on Captain Michales' door. In came Ali Aga, very depressed. He sat down on his stool near the water trough, and all the neighbors gathered around him.

"That damned telegraph!" said Ali Aga with a sigh. "It's a dog with its head in Crete and its tail in Constantinople. Someone pulls its tail in Constantinople and an hour later it barks in Crete and causes trouble."

"Trouble, Ali Aga? Speak plainly! What do you mean?" asked Krasojorgis anxiously.

"The pasha received a telegram today, saying that tomorrow soldiers will arrive in Megalokastro! With cannon, they say, and cavalry, and the green flag of the Prophet!"

"O my Demetros, what hole will he creep into, so the soldiers don't catch him?" screamed Penelope, flinging herself down on her swollen knees.

Ali Aga then described the jubilation in the coffeehouses. There it had been decided to go down armed to the harbor next day and pay homage to the flag of the Prophet. The longer Ali Aga spoke, the more his depression disappeared—he was carried away by his news. He was no longer the humble old man in the corner to whom nobody paid attention; he had become a person of consequence.

"I shan't set foot outside, tomorrow," said Mastrapas, whose kindly eyes looked frightened.

"Neither shall I," said Chrysanthe. "Not even to evening service, God forgive me." She had placed herself under Captain Michales' protection, like the other women, since her brother now spent every night with Eminé. Instead of making her a Christian, he has turned Turk, God forgive me, she thought, but never said it aloud.

The neighbors slept that night like hares; they hardly shut their eyes and pondered how they could force the bars of their prison and get out.

In the morning trumpets sounded from the harbor. The Turks stood there, fez to fez, covering the walls with red. Thrasaki, who had escaped from home, climbed up on the rocks at the harbor entrance and let his insatiable eye range far and wide. The rusty steamer lay at the quayside and disgorged from its entrails bristling Anatolians with pock-marked faces, cannons and horses. At the end came a swarm of clamoring dervishes wearing green skirts and pointed white hats, and with daggers in their belts. They clambered onto the mole, unrolled the green flag of the Prophet in front of the Harbor Gate, and began dancing around it slowly, clapping their hands.

Thrasaki drew nearer. Suddenly the dance of the dervishes became wilder, as they spun like tops, and their robes stood out like bells. Their eyes began to redden. They drew their daggers and wounded themselves, so that blood spurted out, and they howled. Gradually their wildness subsided, they stuck their daggers back in their belts and moved more calmly. Their bellowing became half song, half speech, then a whispering, a soft and tender moaning.

At noon Thrasaki came home in great excitement and told his astonished listeners what he had seen.

"Weren't you frightened?" his father asked him, frowning.

"I wasn't frightened of the soldiers."

"The dervishes?"

"Not of them, either."

"Of what, then?"

Thrasaki hesitated.

"Go on, say!" his father urged, tilting the child's bent face up by the chin.

"Of the green flag, Father!"

Megalokastro sank into darkness. In the first days after the landing of the troops a disquieting stillness reigned. The Christian elders went in and out of the Metropolitan's residence, the agas held secret councils, now at the pasha's porte, now in the noise-filled barracks. For one hour a day the three fortress gates were opened, and in came Turkish peasants with their hanums and worldly goods, excited and fearful. There was no more room for them in the mosques and tekes. They broke open the doors of Christian houses, threw the Christians out, and took possession.

The Metropolitan sent Hadjisavas to Athens with letters in which he adjured the Greek brethren to send ships and save the Christian Cretans from the knives that had already been drawn by the Turks.

One evening the neighbors gathered early at Captain Michales', to come to a decision. No one was missing. Even Captain Polyxigis, Idomeneas, Tulupanas the baker, the black-clad gravedigger Kolyvas, and Dr. Kasapakes with his French wife, had put in an appearance. Only Archondula and her deaf-mute brother were absent. Archondula was under the pasha's wing, and had no need of Captain Michales. Her brother had just done a portrait of the pasha in oils. He purposely kept the window on the street open, so that the passers-by might admire the pasha in the gold frame on the wall. It was an unsurpassable likeness. Nothing was missing. Not even the wart on his nose or the pig's bristles in his ears.

The gathering was taking place in the house rather than in the yard, so that they would be secure from eavesdroppers. Captain Michales was sullen. It displeased him to see the Circassian-Turkish Captain Polyxigis in his house.

Thrasaki was among them. "You sit with us," his father had told him. "You're a man."

246

All waited for Captain Michales to speak. Captain Polyxigis could bear it no longer.

"To what end have we come here this evening?" he asked, with an angry glance at his sister, who had dragged him along. "We are going to decide," she had said, "what we should do to save ourselves from the Turks." But he, after all, could decide nothing without Eminé. What these people did here was no concern of his.

Captain Michales wanted to say: "Why are you here, Polyxigis Bey? Your friends live in the Turkish quarter, your home is at the green door." But the man was a guest in his house. It was against good manners to provoke him like that. So he kept silence.

Tityros stepped in the breach. His strength and courage had grown since the death of his wife. He no longer felt inferior to other men. He had proved that he too could kill, and kill properly, so that the murdered man did not visit him at night. His dead wife too never troubled him in his sleep. The schoolchildren had been the first to perceive his new strength; he took no nonsense from them and beat them soundly. So now he spoke in place of his brother:

"Three courses lie before us. Either we stay quietly in our houses, and perhaps in that way prevent a massacre. Or we escape through the fortress gates and distribute ourselves among the villages. Or we wait to be taken away by the Greek ships that the Metropolitan has sent Hadjisavas to Athens to ask for. Let us therefore examine which of the three courses is the most hopeful. And then let us adopt it, and may God come to our aid!"

Their chairs creaked, their heads bent, each one weighed his opinion. But they saw obstacles in each course.

The first to break the silence was Kasapakes the doctor—the fat, pock-marked peasant's son who had gone to Paris to study medicine. There he had attended lectures on law for three months, because he mistook them for lectures on medicine. When he had discovered his mistake and frittered away his father's vineyards, he had returned to Megalokastro with a broad-brimmed hat and the daughter of his Parisian landlady, and had opened a grocery. Now he talked down at Tityros.

"There is a fourth course also, schoolmaster: that we should take refuge in the consulates of the Great Powers!"

"Where will there be room enough for us, doctor?" retorted

Krasojorgis. "You say 'consulates' and seem very pleased. But even a consulate is only a house with four walls. How many people will it hold? Perhaps two families. And what becomes of the rest?"

Mastrapas opened his mouth to speak and hesitated nervously.

"Speak out, neighbor," Tityros encouraged him.

"What you decide. . . ." stammered the bell founder, flushing.

Krasojorgis stood up. He had sweated with anxiety all day, and now his body reeked of every smell a man can exude. His wife gazed at him with pride. She liked to see her husband excited like that.

"We're listening, Krasojorgis," said Tityros.

"Listen, then, to what I think. The safest course leads to the villages. Are we to squat here as though we were in a mousetrap? The Turks have slaughtered Greeks before now. Why wait for the ships? Or shall we look for a four-leaf clover? I put no trust in Athens. They'd like to, but they can't. They're afraid of Turkey, they're afraid of the Franks. How often have the Greeks not been . . ."

"But how escape, neighbor? Tell us that!" snorted Kolyvas. "We've a heap of children."

"I put no trust in Athens," Krasojorgis continued. "But I do trust Krasojorgis. Let me take command and, by the bread I eat, I'll bring you all into the mountains, with your wives and children, your beds and pots and pans!"

A murmur arose. All drew closer to Krasojorgis. He observed with pride the excitement his words had provoked among the group. Just look! They had always despised him, because he was awkward and had no training and wore patched boots. Now he would show them!

"Let's hear your plan!" said the doctor, who was injured because not enough consideration had been given to his proposal. "Those are big promises, neighbor. I don't like that."

"Neither would I, doctor, if I couldn't keep them. But listen: I'm on good terms with the soldiers who guard the Hospital Gate. A tiny bit of smuggling—two or three demijohns of raki, two or three packets of tobacco, a string or two of sausages that I present them with so they'll keep their eyes shut. . . . Let's not go too

248

deeply into that. I'll grease the wheel again, and out we all slip, unmolested."

"Long may you live, Krasojorgis!" exclaimed Kolyvas. "I entrust you gladly with my children."

"I, too," said Mastrapas, peering uneasily at his wife, to see if she was in agreement.

At this moment there were three soft taps at the door.

"Ali Aga," said Tityros, and got up to open it.

But Captain Michales raised his head. "Throw him out!" he said.

Tityros opened the door. "Ali Aga," he said, "don't be angry with us, this evening we're having a meeting. Come tomorrow."

Ali Aga, however, remained standing in the street door.

"I came to tell you that the agas are planning to kill you all."

"For God's sake! When?"

"During the Bairam festival."

"Come in."

The little old man crossed the yard and leaned against the door-post.

"Good evening, neighbors," he said, in arrogant tones. Today he was breaking a fearsome piece of news and was preening himself. But suddenly he saw Captain Michales on the corner of the settle, and collapsed.

"Forgive me," he said, "I'm in a hurry. But it was necessary to come. If you believe in God, neighbors, look out! The agas are planning a massacre before the Bairam festival is over. They've already allotted the different parts of the town. The best palikars will come to ours, on account of Captain Michales."

"Good. Go," said Captain Michales, raising his hand. Here Mastrapas interposed. "Try to find out what you can, Ali Aga, and come here again tomorrow evening. Good-by!"

The old man went across the yard and out through the street door, and glided off to the Turkish coffeehouses.

Captain Polyxigis stood up. "Excuse me, I have business this evening. My sister will tell me what you decide. All I wish to add is this: I shall go to the mountains—that is what honor demands."

"A good thing you remember it," growled Captain Michales.

Captain Polyxigis ran off at high speed. It was late. Eminé had certainly gone to bed already and was chewing mastic to keep herself awake while she waited for him.

Now all turned to Captain Michales, to hear his opinion. He felt better, now that the air was free of the scent of musk and Turkey.

"Neighbors," he said, "all of us here are men and have weapons. It would be shameful to leave Crete in the lurch in these most difficult days. Let us take the women and children into safety. Krasojorgis has spoken well. And after that, there is only one course for us: to arms! The schoolmaster, Mr. Idomeneas—all!"

Old Tulupanas had been twiddling his thumbs, and thinking about his son, whose face now had no nose, no ears, no lips. Where was he to go? Who would take him along? His appearance caused terror. And whoever touched him might be infected. The day before yesterday police had come to take him away to the lepers' village. The poor mother had screamed, and the old man had pressed some silver coins into the hands of the sergeants to make them go away again.

Against his will a deep sigh escaped old Tulupanas, so that all turned towards him, to ask what the trouble was.

"Nothing. . . . What should be?" he answered, while tears streamed from his eyes. "I'm not going out with you. Where can I go? Who will have me?"

He got up. No one raised a hand to hold him back. Stumbling, he found his way to the street door and disappeared.

"Agreed," said Tityros. "We've come to a decision. What is your view, Mr. Idomeneas? You haven't opened your mouth yet."

"You know my view. You all know it. I've expressed it again and again: everything you are saying and doing is froth and frills, as long as Suda Bay remains.

"Agreed!" exclaimed the doctor, suppressing a laugh. He grabbed for his enormous hat with a view to leaving, for it was nearly midnight.

"Doctor," said Captain Michales, "you are coming with us to the mountains."

"But—"

"There's no 'but'! You're coming. That's what you're a doctor for. There'll be wounded."

The doctor looked at his wife. She sat at the other end of the divan, not understanding very well what was being said. She pressed her handkerchief to her mouth and coughed. The poor woman had become shriveled and yellow. Paris was now no more than a far-off legend to her. Ah, if she could only get aboard a steamer, a pinnace, a nutshell—anything to get away, anything to get away. . . .

Captain Michales rose. "What has been said will be respected," he said, and went up to his small room. He had spoken too much and longed for solitude.

The neighbors breathed with relief. Tongues were loosened. The women, too, joined in the conversation. Renio appeared and brought the salver with raki, conserve and coffee.

"God guide this thing aright," said Krasojorgis, raising his glass. "To your health, Captainess. May you have joy in those you love. And your health, Renio!"

They clicked glasses. All drank. Renio poured out again. They were happy.

"What a drop of drink can do!" exclaimed Krasojorgis, smacking his lips. "A glass of raki, no bigger than a thimble, my soul upon it—but the whole of Turkey drowns in it! I can see, at the bottom of my glass—there lies the fat Sultan, dead!"

"It's not the raki that does it, it's the company," Tityros suggested.

"You're right, schoolmaster," said Mastrapas, his tongue too loosed at last by the drink. "Men are like bells. If they are in tune, death has no terrors for them."

The bell founder's ear was sensitive. One night last summer he had been unable to sleep: the bells of a flock, outside on the mountain, were not properly in tune together, and this set his soul jangling. At dawn he got up, climbed the mountain, found the flock, tuned the bells, went home, lay down and slept.

"Like bells, so are men," he repeated. "Whether they're wooden rattles, or sheep bells, or church bells, small or large—each one has his own sound. A joy it is for the flock when the bells are in tune, and it no longer fears the wolf."

But Mr. Idomeneas shook his head. What concern have I here? he thought, what sense has this talk?

He got up and beckoned to Tityros: "Come, godson. Sleep in my house and keep me company."

He felt a strong need for some elevated conversation. The two of them would again discuss the stars and the immortality of the soul. No other questions existed for him in the world, only these two. At most Suda Bay could be placed beside them. All the rest was noise and smoke.

The meeting broke up. Some, made brave by raki, returned to their houses like palikars. Others stretched themselves out in the yard and on the veranda at Captain Michales', and the women lay down in the bedroom. It was after midnight.

Thrasaki had listened intently all through the evening. The personalities of his father's guests had stamped themselves deeply in his brain—the frightened ones, the calm ones and, after the raki, the happy ones. The deepest impression was made on him by his father, who, unlike the garrulous company, sat quietly with bent head, speaking only when necessary. Through all these observations Thrasaki was ripening, without knowing it, into a man.

The schools had closed. Thrasaki rose early and joined his father in the shop. He liked to watch his father's every movement. He was beginning to understand why Captain Michales was so sparing of gesture, speech, and laughter. One day, the boy thought, he too would be just like that: not like Captain Polyxigis, or Krasojorgis, or Tityros. His thoughts churning darkly inside him, he ran toward the harbor. There he heard shouting and cursing. He quickened his pace and came to the barbershop of Signor Paraskevas. A crowd of Turks stood outside it. In their midst Thrasaki saw the man from Syra. The Turks were abusing and spitting at the unfortunate man, as they drew their knives. He stood there trembling, with his shirt torn and bloodstained, his face covered with rotten eggs and tomatoes. He was assuring the Turks that he would flee, go back to Syra and never set foot in Crete again. Only they must have mercy on him and on his daughter, for whom he had to find a husband.

Thrasaki ran back to tell his father. Captain Michales was writing a letter to his nephew Kosmas who had turned Frank: ". . . If you are a man, if you have any feeling of shame, leave the land of the Franks and think of your own country. It needs you, the hour has come. Why were you born? Why are you called a Cretan? Come at once, take up arms like the other young men. There is another thing I must tell you, nephew . . ."

Thrasaki burst in. "Father," he shouted, "they're trying to kill Paraskevas in front of his shop. Save him!"

Captain Michales rose and saw what was happening from his doorstep. A crowd of raving dockers had now pinioned Paraskevas. Not a Christian was to be seen in the street. The Greek shops were shut, their proprietors had vanished. Captain Michales saw several knives gleaming in the sun.

"Father, help him! You're not afraid?"

Captain Michales stared soberly at the scene. The Turks were overwhelming in number; to attack them meant certain death, and the captain did not admire rash deeds. But he was ashamed before his son.

"Aren't you going, Father? Are you afraid?" his son asked again.

"I'm going," said Captain Michales and approached the knot of men.

He walked slowly and calmly forward, his dispassionate face showing neither anger nor fear.

When the Turks saw him coming they stood still. What did the giaour want? Had he no fear of them?

Captain Michales reached them and raised his hand to bid them let him through. They moved aside, amazed. What was he going to do? They lowered their knives.

Captain Michales went up to Signor Paraskevas and seized him by the ear. "March! Home! Don't let my eyes catch sight of you any more!" he said peremptorily.

Paraskevas ducked his head between his shoulders and staggered forward. Captain Michales went with him, still twisting his ear. The Turks let them pass without a word.

"Back home!" Captain Michales repeated. "Quick!"

Paraskevas began to run, turned at the first corner and vanished. The Turks, motionless, stared after Captain Michales as he proceeded slowly, with the same calm stride, back to his shop.

Thrasaki watched him in astonishment. He wanted to ask his father a question, but dared not. Captain Michales sat down again at his table, picked up the pen and bent forward to finish the letter: ". . . nephew, that your Uncle Manusakas. . . ."

9

At the end of the month of fasting came the festival of Bairam. The agas put on their best clothes and filled the coffeehouses, where they sat enthroned on soft cushions. The Turkish boys craned their slender necks and sang their long-drawn-out melodies. Because of the great heat Barba Jannis had ordered three assloads of snow from Psiloritis and now ran up and down with his bronze can to bring refreshing coolness to the agas.

In the barracks near the Three Vaults the soldiers' trumpets resounded and salvos were fired at the sky. The pasha and the profusely braided officers betook themselves to the New Mosque to pray. The rings of lamps still burned on the minarets. In Hamidé Mula's teke the Saint's tomb was adorned with rosemary and basil. In front of it sat Efendina, cross-legged, singing verses from the Koran and swaying to and fro. Gray-haired worshipers knelt on mats around the Saint. They had brought their narghiles with them and were smoking as, with eyes half closed, they took up the responses from the Koran in a soft, beelike hum.

These old people were profoundly happy and had already entered Paradise. They lacked none of the good things of life. The noise of Megalokastro came like a murmur of water through the cracks in the door and the latticed window in the wall, and in the distance the sea roared. Old Hamidé Mula ran tirelessly hither and thither on bare feet, bringing now a piece of Turkish Delight, now a small heap of glowing charcoal with which she carefully warmed the narghiles, so that they bubbled cheerfully like cooing doves in a circle round the Saint.

But while they were all sunk in this paradisiacal stupor, sud-

254

denly loud shouting rang out, doors creaked, women screamed and pistol shots tore the air. Fled was divine blessedness. The graybeards jumped up.

Efendina laid the Koran on top of the flowers and rushed to the door to open it. Turks with knives between their teeth ran bellowing past, their chests and arms spattered with the blood of giaours.

Suleiman, the pasha's enormous Arab, hurtled along at their head, his chest and feet naked. A yellow burnoose waved about his shoulders. His eyes flashed, his full hanging lips foamed.

"Down with them! Down with them!" he bellowed, and his scimitar whistled through the air.

"Where are you off to, brothers?" cried Efendina, peeping fearfully out of the door.

"To slaughter that wretched rascal, to drink his blood!" roared the Arab.

"Who, Suleiman?"

"Captain Michales."

Efendina blenched and cried, "Have you no fear of God?"

But his voice was lost in the din that rose from all the Christian courtyards and houses. Doors were being battered in, women were climbing onto the flat roofs and some, in panic, threw themselves off, with their children in their arms.

Captain Michales was standing armed behind the street door. He had sent his family up to the bedroom and had kept only Thrasaki with him.

"Come here," he said to the boy, "and listen carefully to what I say. If they manage to smash our door and force their way in, I shall kill you all, so you won't fall into their hands. And you first, Thrasaki. Do you understand?"

"I understand, Father."

"And do you agree?"

"I agree."

"Don't tell the women. They'll be afraid."

"I won't tell them anything."

The two stood behind the door and listened intently to the noise from the street.

Some of their neighbors had already escaped. Krasojorgis, Mastrapas and Kolyvas, with all their children, had left a few days before. Next were Penelope and Chrysanthe. They had disguised themselves as hanums. Tityros, too, had dressed up as a Turk, in baggy breeches and a white turban. He had stuffed his glasses down his chest and reeled out to the Hospital Gate. Tulupanas had stayed with his son. The doctor had hoisted the French flag, and Idomeneas had declared that he would not run away: he had placed the flags of the Great Powers above the fountain.

"When are we going, Father?" Thrasaki had asked, only yesterday. He longed to get out to the fields and mountains.

"We're staying to the last."

"Why?"

"Think it out for yourself," his father had answered, and had said not another word.

It was now midday. The cries of Megalokastro grew more and more hoarse as it shrank under the Turkish knives. The muezzins climbed the minarets for the midday prayer and announced the loving-kindness of God.

Five or six Turkish dockers came running to the Pervola Garden and rammed Signor Paraskevas' door with an iron bar. They stormed into the house and found his daughter under the divan. They hauled her out and threw her on her back. . . . Later they discovered the unhappy barber hidden behind some jars, dragged him by the neck to the threshold and slaughtered him. Then they bundled up Pervola, who was streaming with blood, and rushed out with her.

Captain Michales heard shots from the direction of Idomeneas' Fountain, at the end of the street.

"Here they come," he muttered, and cocked his gun. He turned round and looked at his son.

"Here they come," Thrasaki repeated, and he too cocked his little pistol. In the last few days his father had taught him to shoot.

"You're not afraid, are you," said the father, gazing hard at his son.

"Why should I be afraid? I've learned to shoot."

He straddled his legs, planted them firmly on the stones of the yard and waited.

More and more shots went off. The Turks had now halted at

Idomeneas' Fountain. They leaned with their shoulders against the decayed door of the grand house, to burst it open.

Mr. Idomeneas had been sitting at his writing-table since early morning, composing a letter to the Great Powers:

> "O ye Mighty of the World! In this moment, as I commit these lines to paper, the Christian population of Megalokastro is being slaughtered. Once more the air is ringing with shots. Turkish bandits are breaking open the doors of the Christians; they are dishonoring their women, they are killing the men, they are taking the infants and smashing their heads.
>
> "I raise my voice. I am nothing, a man without consequence, lost on the rim of Europe, far away from you, ye Mighty of the World! Yet God stands close to me! He is angry, He is striding up and down the lonely room in which I write. He does not speak, He presses His lips together and waits to see the answer you will give me. You should know—I shall not send you another appeal after this. I have had enough of crying in the wilderness. If this time you send me no answer, I shall turn to God and——"

Here Mr. Idomeneas broke off. He heard the shots and put his head out of the window. He saw the Turks straining against his door.

"What do you want?" he shouted. "Have you gone blind? Can't you see the flags of the Great Powers over the fountain?"

There were shouts and catcalls. A stone grazed his ear and cheek, then smashed to fragments an old Venetian mirror on the wall beyond.

Mr. Idomeneas jumped back and put his hand to his ear. It was covered with blood. He smeared blood over the whole of his hand and pressed it on the letter.

"There, there, there!" he shouted. "That's how this letter ends. May the blood of Crete be upon your heads and upon the heads of your children and your children's children, England, France, Italy, Austria, Germany and Moscow!"

The door burst in, and the Turks rushed across the yard with their knives between their teeth. They knocked down old Doxania, who stood on the threshold of the house door, with her arms outstretched, trying to bar their entry. They trampled on over her. Yelling, they ran up the stairs. The tottering mansion trembled to its foundations.

Idomeneas, from his study, heard the wild horde approaching. The moment is come, he thought. Idomeneas, do not dishonor me!

He looked about him—he wanted of his own free will to choose the manner of his death. No weapons hung on his walls. He needed none. He would not fight with the sword but with the brain. The pen was his weapon. His decision was made. "I shall stay at my post, here," he muttered and struck the table with his fist. "Here's where I fight, here's where I shall die!" He sat down and grasped the pen. . . .

The Turks broke the door in with a kick and stopped short, amazed. They found Idomeneas calmly bent over a large, blood-stained sheet of paper.

"Giaour," they yelled, "where've you hidden your treasure?"

Idomeneas raised his head from the letter. "Here," he answered, and pointed to his forehead.

One of them laughed. "Is your head a money-box?"

"Slash it in two, then we'll see what it's got inside!" yelled another. And before Idomeneas had time to reply, the Turk split his head from brow to throat with one stroke of the scimitar.

They stormed through the house and flung clothes, rags, chairs, tables and mattresses into the street.

As they turned the corner they met Suleiman the Arab, who, with ten barefoot ruffians, was on his way to Captain Michales' house.

"Where are you coming from?" asked Suleiman, breathlessly.

"From Idomeneas' Fountain."

"You leave Captain Michales alone, or I'll drink your blood. He's reserved for me!"

He went to the fountain, splashed himself with water, and drank greedily like a bull calf. His sweating comrades also drank. One of them looked through the splintered door and saw an old woman stretched out on the stones of the yard, keening for the dead and tearing her hair.

"Shall we kill her?" he asked.

"Too dull, Mustapha."

"On!" the Arab now shouted.

They rushed down the street, arrogantly clashing their scimitars.

Behind the door Captain Michales heard the crew approaching and recognized the wild voice of the Arab.

"They're looking for me," he thought, and kneeled down behind the water trough, using it as a parapet. He pulled Thrasaki down beside him. "Christ will conquer," he whispered, crossing himself.

He turned to his son. "Courage, my child."

It was the first time Thrasaki had heard his father speak gently and call him "my child." He flushed with pleasure.

The rabble was now before the door. The Arab was distributing instructions: one man was to climb on the backs of two comrades and so onto the wall, and then jump down into the yard, while the others smashed in the door. "But no one's to lay a finger on Captain Michales! He belongs to me. He's insulted me. I'm going to have my revenge on him—drag him to the plane tree and hack him in pieces and throw his flesh to the dogs of Megalokastro to eat."

Thrasaki heard the threat and looked at his father, who had already aimed the barrel of his gun at the top of the wall.

"Did you hear, Father?" he asked.

"Silence!" Captain Michales whispered through his teeth, without turning.

A scraping on the wall was heard, and heavy breathing. Someone was climbing up. Captain Michales hid himself completely behind the trough. Only his gun barrel showed. He had pushed Thrasaki behind him.

A wild, shaggy head emerged above the wall. Between the teeth a broad-bladed knife flashed. The man glanced stealthily over the yard. Now a hand was stretched out. . . . Captain Michales pressed the trigger. The bullet struck the man full between the eyebrows.

Up above, in the bedroom, crouching behind the window sill, the captain's wife was giving suck to the baby, while through the cracks of the shutter Renio watched her father and Thrasaki in the yard. When she saw the Turk's head vanish, she thrilled with delight.

259

"Hail to your hands, Father!" she whispered, full of admiration.
"Renio, my poor child," said the captain's wife, "our life is
hanging by a hair. Do you know what your father plans to do?"
"If the Turks get in, he'll kill us. And he'll be quite right."
"You ought to be a man," said her mother. "Aren't you afraid?"
"We've got to die sometime, Mother. Let's die without dis-
honor."

Their conversation broke off. Something was happening in the
street—a violent rushing to and fro, fresh shouts, fresh curses.

"Isn't that Efendina's voice?" said Renio, and cautiously opened
the shutter.

It was, in fact, Efendina. When he had seen the raving Arab
rushing in the direction of Captain Michales' house, his heart
had contracted. He loved Captain Michales, though the captain
compelled him twice a year to debase himself; perhaps he loved
him just because of that. What would Efendina's life be without
this monster of a Greek?

What other pleasure have I in the world, wretch that I am? he
wondered. My mother beats me, the people of Kastro, Turks and
Christians alike, pelt me with lemon peel. I've no money, no wife,
no hero's courage, nothing. Nothing, except Captain Michales. I
count the days and the months. Every six months a great pleasure
comes to me again, and a great sin. And who knows? God is
merciful, God is bountiful; perhaps I too may become a saint the
day after my death. And they will erect my tomb by the side of
my grandfather's. God bless Captain Michales! Without him,
would I still be able to become a saint?

His heart rebelled. No, no, I won't let them kill my Captain
Michales! What a noble, what a lusty man he is! What wine he
has in his casks! What sausages, what chickens and suckling
pigs!

Efendina's head caught fire. He leaped up and darted in pursuit
of the Arab. He even forgot that the streets were broad streams,
and crossed them without hesitation to rescue his friend. On
Broad Street a band of booty-laden Turks called out to him.
"Where are you running to, Efendina? Who's after you?"

They formed a chain and barred his passage. Efendina halted,
out of breath and bewildered. The Arab would surely reach the
house before him, smash the door in and kill Captain Michales.

"Do you recognize no God above you?" he whimpered. "Let me through! It's urgent, brothers!"

A flash passed through Efendina's brain. He looked over his shoulder and screamed, "Saint Menas!"

The Turks burst out laughing.

"You godless people, why are you laughing? Can't you hear his horse's hoofbeats? I saw him ride out of the church. Can't you hear him? There he is! There he is!"

The Turks' hair stood on end. Did they really hear the jingle of harness? Was that a horseman approaching?

"There he is!" Efendina screamed again, his eyes popping. "There he is!"

The Turks did not even turn to look. They ran away.

When Efendina saw them running, he stood transfixed with dread. Had he become so powerful that he could make it true? he wondered. Had he not already, in the last rising, seen the Saint chase away the Turks who were trying to force their way into his church? He broke out in a cold sweat. Now he could distinctly hear the horse approaching.

"Allah! Allah!" With this cry he gathered up his clothes and ran for all he was worth.

As he rushed past Idomeneas' Fountain, he found the Turks just on the point of bursting open Captain Michales' street door He rushed up to them.

"Look out, children!" he screamed. "He'll gobble us up! He's coming on horseback."

"Who, you idiot?" roared the Arab.

"The neighbor."

"What neighbor?"

"Saint Menas. There he is!"

They all wheeled round. Everything danced before their eyes. They could distinguish nothing.

"There he is! There he is!" Efendina cried, turning away. He clung to Captain Michales' door like one possessed, as though he wanted to hide from the eyes of the saint riding by. He must already be past Idomeneas' Fountain. He could recognize Saint Menas distinctly, with his never-changing form just as the icon showed him: sunburned, with white hair and beard, on a purple-red horse with a golden saddle. The air round about Idomeneas'

Fountain was filled with white hair, red horse and golden harness.

"There he is! He's in sight!" he whispered, and his jaw quivered.

"Where is he? I can't see properly!"

"There he is! Dark, with white hair and a red horse. . . . He's seen us. Now he's making for us!"

With a leap he left the door and ran for the harbor. Behind him the Turks followed, panting. They too heard the horse now —it was after them—and the Arab, turning round for a moment, made out, on the horse, in the air, a rider.

"Run, children! Run!" he yelled. His yellow burnoose fluttered away from him, but he had no time to pick it up.

Out of breath, they reached the harbor. They wiped the sweat off, crouched down in the shade, let their tongues hang out and sniffed like dogs. Efendina had collapsed with his face to the ground and lay there twitching.

Megalokastro groaned under the knives of the Turks. The Christians raised their hands in entreaty to God. The Metropolitan crossed himself. He could no longer sit and listen to the slaughtering of his flock. "God be with me," he murmured, and stood up. He clapped his hands, and Murzuflos appeared.

"I'm going to the pasha," the Metropolitan said. "Bring me my great robe."

"Are you going out in the streets, Bishop?" asked Murzuflos. "The Turks are raging. I'm coming with you."

"I shall go alone, Murzuflos. Help me to dress."

He wrapped the golden stole about him and set the imperial miter on his lion's head. He grasped the tall crosier with its two intertwined loops. "In God's name," he said.

Murzuflos gazed at him, full of admiration. He was a marvelous apparition with his towering form, the beard a stream of snow, the eyes blue, benevolent and flashing. It would be like the Metropolitan that Murzuflos would paint God the Father, clothed with golden clouds and in the act of plunging down upon Megalokastro to put an end to the massacre.

The main door of the Residence was thrown open. Upon its marble lintel was inscribed in large black letters: "In this doorway the Turks hanged the Metropolitan of Megalokastro in the year 1821. Everlasting be his memory."

"Everlasting be his memory," murmured the Metropolitan, as he crossed the threshold.

Murzuflos' eyes were wet. "God and Saint Menas be with you, my lord," he said in a trembling voice.

"Don't worry, Murzuflos. I am neither the first nor the last," replied the Metropolitan, pointing at the black inscription.

He crossed the forecourt of the church and greeted Saint Menas with bowed head as he passed his door. Then he strode off with masterful bearing in the direction of the pasha's porte.

Murzuflos watched him depart to his lonely battle with death. He was ashamed that he had let him go alone. "This is the moment," he muttered, "when it will be seen whether you, Murzuflos, have a soul in you, or only a stomach." He crossed himself and slipped off after the Metropolitan.

Megalokastro was filled with din. The Christians were screaming, the Turks were roaring and laughing. Among these sounds one could distinguish the keening for the dead.

The Metropolitan strode onward, and his heart contracted at what he heard. "How long will the people of the Hellenes," he sighed, "hang from the cross. We are men, Christ, we are not gods like You. We cannot bear it. Bring the resurrection at last!"

He could feel Megalokastro with its walls, houses and human beings as though it were his own body, and wherever a door was smashed in, wherever a woman beat her breast, his heart hurt.

From the market place a crew of bloodstained, drunken Turks was approaching. When they caught sight of the gold-clad Metropolitan, they halted awed. "What sort of a beast is that," they growled. "Where's he going? Draw aside, God help you, or he'll trample us down!"

The Metropolitan walked with even steps to meet death. His eyes, filled with sorrow and anger and thirst for martyrdom, saw neither streets, nor men. He was dominated by one thought: Oh the sweet happiness, if I should be killed to set my people free! How did it go—that word of agony of Christ on the Cross, of which the Gospel tells? *"Eli! Eli!"* That means: "Joy! Joy!" in the language of sacrifice. *"Eli! Eli!"* the Metropolitan whispered, and the nearer he came to the pasha's seraglio, the more he quickened his pace. Behind him Murzuflos glided like a dog.

He reached the huge plane tree, glorious in cool, rustling green. Its trunk was flecked like a leopard skin. The Metropolitan's eyes blurred and he saw thousands of Christians dangling from it like fruit.

Two soldiers before the pasha's gate lowered and crossed their guns and would not let him through. Then Murzuflos who understood Turkish ran up and spoke to them. They raised their guns, and the Metropolitan entered, Murzuflos going ahead, to open the doors.

The pasha observed the Metropolitan peevishly. He had been leaning out of the window to listen to Megalokastro bewailing the dead. Even he, the good-natured Anatolian, had gone savage. Perhaps it was the ancient Turkish thirst for Greek blood that had awakened in him. And yet he felt ashamed that he, as pasha, had not the courage to order a halt, to strike the knives from the hands of the agas.

The Metropolitan stood on the threshold, filling the doorway. "Have you no fear of God, Pasha?" he shouted.

"Why have you dressed yourself up in gold for me, giaour's priest?" replied the other, angrily. "Are you hoping to terrify me?"

"Have you no fear of God?" the Metropolitan shouted afresh, and raised a finger threateningly toward the sky. "Does the shedding of blood not concern you? And where will it fall, do you suppose? Upon your head!"

"Hey, don't yell so, Metropolitan! The plane tree stands before you!"

"God stands before me. I am not afraid."

The pasha moved away from the window, paced to and fro and at last stopped in front of the Metropolitan. He looked him up and down and could not think what line to take with him. He imagined him in all his gold and crosses dangling from the plane tree, but dread seized him. And yet this insolent Greek mouth must be stopped, he thought. It was not to be endured!

He barked at the Metropolitan. "Don't make me lose my temper. Go! I'm telling you out of kindness. I'm not afraid of anybody!"

The Metropolitan left God and brought the Sultan into play.

"Very well, you have no fear of God. But what about the Sultan? You know that Crete causes him anxiety. He means to have peace here, and that is why he sent you. And what has Your Worship done? Allowed a massacre! And the massacre will bring a rising in its train. And the rising will attract Moscow. Forgive me, Pasha Effendi, but I see your head on the point of falling."

The pasha froze. He too saw his head on the point of falling.

"What am I to do, then?" he asked, fearfully.

"Don't lose a moment. Order the soldiers to sound their trumpets, as a signal that the slaughter is to stop. Give orders! Threaten! You're the pasha! Show it!"

The pasha clutched his head with both hands as if it needed propping up. "Cursed be the hour in which I first set foot on this devil's island of yours!" he shouted.

He looked imploringly at the Metropolitan. "My lord Metropolitan," he said, "why are you standing there on the threshold? Come in and sit down, so that we can discuss how to bring this thing to an end."

"While we are talking, Christians are being slaughtered. I cannot sit down. First call the soldiers and give the orders! Until I hear the trumpets I shall not sit down! Neither shall I go away."

"The devil take you! Damn the lot of you Cretans! Bad and good together!"

Furiously he went out into the antechamber. His oaths mingled with the noise of officers rushing past with their scimitars and spurs.

The Metropolitan, standing there on the threshold, sighed. "God has not found me worthy to hang in the doorway of the Residence. Never mind. It is enough that the Christians will be saved."

The pasha came back, mopping his brow. "Now you'll hear the trumpets," he said. "Go! I've had enough of this business. I don't want to see anyone now. Is it earth I'm standing on, or a powder barrel?"

At that same moment Captain Michales turned to Thrasaki. The boy had been kneeling close to his father and listening to what was happening in the street—Efendina's cries, the Arab's curses, the steps of the men running away, and now the sudden stillness which settled over the whole quarter. Only a sound of keening came from Idomeneas' Fountain.

"Are you hungry, Thrasaki?"

"Yes, I'm hungry, Father."

"Then tell your mother to come down and prepare a meal. I think our work's done for today."

He propped his gun against the step of the trough and felt for his tobacco box, to roll a cigarette. He heard the keening again. They've killed poor Idomeneas, he thought, and now his old nurse is mourning for him. He shook his head. What resistance could Idomeneas have put up? He must have been slaughtered like an Easter lamb.

As he put the cigarette in his mouth there was a sound of trumpets and heavy, measured steps. Captain Michales stood up and cautiously opened the door. About twenty soldiers with shouldered arms marched past, on patrol. A crier ran at their head, calling out, "Peace! Peace! Come out of your houses, Christians!"

Next day the pasha issued a command: "What has happened has happened. Destiny so willed it. But now let peace reign; not a nose is to bleed any more! Let the fortress gates be opened, let the Christians come back from the villages and the Mussulman farmers go back to the villages. And those who have gone out into the villages to resist are to lay down their arms and take up their work again. Not a hair of their heads will be touched. The Sultan is merciful and pardons. Mussulmans and Christians, by my good will, listen to the words of the pasha. For in my forecourt stands the plane tree, and the noose is waiting for the disobedient!"

The Turks wiped their knives clean and once more sat cross legged in the coffeehouses, smoking their narghiles and listening with half-closed eyes to the chubby-faced Turkish boy as he sang in his womanish voice. The Christians ventured out from their houses, gathered up the murdered and summoned Kolyvas from his village. Murzuflos, Kajabes, Vendusos, Furogatos and the others shouldered picks, and began to dig long trenches in the cemetery before the Kanea Gate. Graves were also dug in the churchyard of the Sinai Church of Saint Matthew, near the Pervola.

Manoles the pope, panting and with his shirt sleeves rolled up, laid the dead together by fives, spoke the prayers in haste, commended each group of five to Heaven and turned his attention to the next five.

For three days the men dug graves and the women washed doorsteps and bedrooms clean of blood and mourned in silence, so that the agas would not hear and be enraged anew. For in their glance and gait one could discern the after-tremors of the massacre.

On the fourth day Captain Michales called his son into his small room and said to him:

"Thrasaki, the time for the rising has come. Let the pasha say what he will, he's an Anatolian, he understands nothing. Once Crete has caught fire, it isn't easily put out. Do you understand?"

"I understand, Father."

"So tomorrow, first thing, we men must get the women and children out of Megalokastro. I'll go at the head, you bring up the rear. Understand?"

"Can I keep the pistol?"

"What? Do you suppose we shall be unarmed? We're going to your grandfather's. Tell your mother to get ready."

In the afternoon Captain Michales rode to the Hospital Gate and out, and reached the widow's inn. He dismounted and called the lively widow. She appeared, plump, bowing and scraping.

"I'm leaving my mare here this evening. Feed her well. I shall fetch her tomorrow morning. Get three asses ready for me as well."

"You're taking to the open, Captain Michales?" the widow asked, slowly and ostentatiously buttoning her bodice. "Does that mean the massacre isn't over?"

"It's just beginning," he answered, and without lingering strode swiftly back, to reach the fortress gate before it closed.

It was now full summer. A south wind was blowing from the Libyan desert and whirling a blinding dust along the road. Captain Michales kept his face toward the sea, to breathe some cool air. He could see the uninhabited island of Dia, bare, rose-pink and shaped like a turtle swimming in the sea.

Some time ago, in a mood of depression, he had taken a boat, set sail, and after some hours had reached the deserted island. He had landed at the little, stony All Saints' Harbor. He had made his boat fast and climbed upward in the oppressive heat. The cliffs glowed, the air danced. Two sea gulls flew over his head, swooped down, almost grazing him, and screeched in amazement. Between the boulders the frisking rabbits sat up and eyed him. Captain Michales had climbed to the very peak. He had looked about him: loneliness, the island a heap of stones, and on all sides the sea, deep blue, with wild waves. The air was pure—human breath had not yet spoiled it. That's where I'd like to live, he had thought. On those cliffs. I'm sick of fresh water and green grass and people.

Quickening his pace he reached the fortress gate and passed through. A few corpses were still lying in the alleys; there was a stench of corruption. He stopped in front of Furogatos' small house and pushed the door open. He went into the miserable hovel and looked around. No one. "Hey! Anybody there?" he called.

He caught a high, timid little voice, like a bird's. And slowly, out of a large, bulging cloak there arose, gleaming in the dusk, the little bald head of the terrified Bertodulos.

"Who's there? Who's there?" he asked, blinded by fear.

"Don't be afraid, Mr. Bertodulos. It's I."

He recognized Captain Michales, and his heart returned to normal.

"Welcome, noble sir!" he said, raising his hand as though to take off his hat and greet him.

"Are you ill, Mr. Bertodulos? Your teeth are chattering. Are you cold?"

"No, Captain. I'm frightened."

"Aren't you ashamed?"

"No, Captain, I'm not ashamed."

He wrapped himself in his cloak, sat upright and leaned back against the wall. He crossed himself. "Kyrie eleison," he said. "It passes my understanding how a man can take a knife and kill another man! I don't understand it. I couldn't even kill a lamb. Did I say a lamb? Would you believe it, Captain? Cutting up a cucumber makes me shudder."

"Where's Furogatos?"

"God protect him, Captain. What shall I say? A heart of gold. When the massacre broke out, he took me from my room. I couldn't walk for terror. Holding me by the arm, and with his lyre over his shoulder, we set off. In the streets what Turkish ruffians there were, Captain! What mustaches! What legs! I hid my face in my cloak, so as to see nothing. He didn't put me down till we reached the water trough in his yard. His wife rushed out, saw the lyre, looked at me and shrieked like a demon, "They're trying to murder us, and you carry lyres about with you?" She regarded me too as a lyre! But God was merciful to us. Next day she went off to her village and we were rid of her."

Furogatos now appeared. "Welcome, Captain Michales, to my poor hovel. I know what you want from me. I've come direct from your house. When?"

"Tomorrow. Call Vendusos and Kajabes too. War, too, is a feast. I'm inviting you."

"That's fine, Captain. But what about him?" said Furogatos, pointing to Bertodulos.

Bertodulos listened, his eyes wide. He understood what the two Cretans were talking about: guns, mountains and hiding places. His teeth began to chatter again.

Captain Michales looked down at the good-natured old man, who had now muffled himself up completely.

"We'll take him too," he said. "One more won't do any harm. He'll come as a guest."

The count stretched out his head. The last five or six hairs on it stood on end.

"Into the mountains?" he screamed. "With the guns?"

"No. With the women and children. You'll gossip with them and make them forget everything," said Captain Michales, and strode to the door. "Till we meet again."

"Where are we meeting, Captain?" Furogatos asked.

"Up on Selena, above Petrokefalo, in old Sefakas' sheep pen."

He went out and passed through a narrow alley. Barba Jannis was on the way home with his empty bronze can, tired and depressed. When he saw Captain Michales he stopped.

"Captain," he said, "much blood has flowed. Let's think how we are to avenge it."

But Captain Michales shoved him aside. He had no patience now with idiots and half-idiots.

He halted at Captain Stefanes' modest dwelling. The self-willed ship's master was sitting alone on his small sofa, darning. As an old sailor he was well up in all sorts of woman's work.

Every day he swept his little house as if it were a ship's deck, and filled Saint Nicholas' lamp with oil, although in the hour of stress the saint had not stirred a foot to come to his help and save his *Dardana* from going to the bottom. "The poor thing can't always get to all the ships that are in distress at sea! He has a right, all the same, to the oil he consumes," he would say each morning, filling the little lamp to the brim.

Now he raised his eyes from his needle. "Welcome, Captain Michales," he said, bowing. "What wild north wind has blown you here?"

Captain Michales gazed at him in silence.

"I understand," said Stefanes. "You're getting your band together. But if you were thinking of adding me to your list, count me out."

"I think you too are getting ready for action though. Come with me, Captain Stefanes."

"No, I tell you. I'm no good on dry land. The earth requires legs, and I'm a hobbler. I'm going to Syra, to the Cretan Committee. They're giving me a ship."

He turned to the icon. "Are you listening, Saint Nicholas? Don't play me another trick like last time!"

"Good-by then, Captain Stefanes. If I never see you again, forgive me, and may God forgive you."

The sea wolf laughed. "That's just what Polyxigis said to me the day before yesterday. . . . You fool, I'm not going to die yet. I don't need any farewells."

His mocking old eyes twinkled as he called after Captain Michales, who was on his way to the door: "Hey, Captain Michales, Polyxigis has beaten you to it. He has already hoisted the banner and set up his headquarters in Kasteli. He's got his little hanum with him too, so they say."

Captain Michales stood still. His face darkened. The world around him swayed. He gripped the iron latch, and the nails with which it was fastened to the door gave. As if the house was falling, he gave a leap and rushed out into the street.

"Hey, Captain Wildboar, just call: Eminé! and she'll come to you. . . ."

Next morning they started. At their head was Captain Michales, his pistols and knives thrust well down in his leather belt, his thick woolen cloak flung about him. Behind him was his wife, erect and fearless, with the infant in her arms. Renio walked beside her mother carrying a cloth in which were wrapped her best clothes and her mother's trinkets. Bringing up the rear was Thrasaki, straining to appear taller than he was. Ali Aga had gone ahead, an hour earlier, with two asses, and was waiting by the Three Vaults.

The soldiers with dark faces and shouldered arms guarded the fortress gate. Noisy bands of peasants were pressing in, and the vault of the gate rang once more with shouting and neighing. Captain Michales opened his cloak and held it before his face, as if to shield himself from the dust. He slid close along the wall and escaped in the crowd. "Hurry up! hurry up!" Thrasaki ordered the women, and himself squeezed through, whistling and pretending indifference. They made a hurried stop at the inn, to get the mare and the asses.

Toward evening they arrived at the patriarchal farmhouse of Captain Sefakas.

The front yard was a seething mass of grandchildren, male and female. Here, during the bloody days in Megalokastro, they had gone ahead with the vintage and had gathered the grapes into the huge wine press in the yard. And now sturdy lads, naked to the waist, were treading the grapes, tipsy with the smell of the must.

Captain Michales' nostrils quivered joyfully. The scent of grape juice seemed to him sweet as blood. "Greetings, nephews," he shouted, and Katerina turned towards her husband, amazed at the gay note in his voice.

They walked into the middle of the yard. The grandfather came forward, his lean arms in the wide-sleeved white shirt stretched out in greeting.

"Welcome, children, and grandchildren!" he said. "Eat and drink. All is yours."

"I'll hand your daughter-in-law and grandchildren over to you," said Captain Michales. "I'm going into the mountains."

"All right, Michales! You have been a wild colt since you were a child. You still haven't grown prudent."

"I shall grow prudent only when Crete is freed."

"Then," said the grandfather, joking, "it were better not freed.

If you become prudent, it'll make no difference whether you're alive or dead!"

Father and son jested so, with affectionate give and take, until the huge table had been laid inside the house. The old man's daughters-in-law and grandchildren, left him by his sons, dead and living, went in and out. The ground floor, the yards, the bedrooms upstairs and the flat roofs were full of his family. In these perilous days they had all gathered from the neighboring villages under the old man's magnanimous protection. With them came also their asses and mules, cattle and dogs and sheep. Now Captain Michales' mare joined them.

The neighboring villages were astir when the arrival of Captain Michales became known. Next day he rode out on his mare and made the round of his command, to stoke up the rebellion.

"A lot of blood has flowed in Megalokastro, brothers!" he cried in each village. "A lot of blood! Honor demands that we avenge it. Forward! To arms!"

He left the villages behind and climbed up Selena. In front of his father's pen he planted his banner—a piece of black cloth with red letters: FREEDOM OR DEATH. He sent two palikars to the peak of the mountain, to light a fire there. They did not come down until they had passed the signal on to the other crests to the east and west, which took up the message and carried the fire further.

Thodores heard from his sentinels that his uncle had arrived. When they met, he kissed his uncle's hand.

"Thodores, you crazy fool, didn't I tell you to stay in your nest? But you, a beardless lad, were in a hurry and disobeyed me. Take your banner down, fold it up and hide it in your breast. Unfold it only if I'm killed."

The captains of eastern Crete saw the beacons, understood the message and gathered in the sheep pens of old Sefakas. Captain Michales sent his father a message, asking him for permission to slaughter his sheep to feed the leaders.

"It is great luck for my sheep to be fodder for captains," answered the grandfather. "Only don't touch the big bellwether— the black one. I'm keeping him for my funeral."

On the fifteenth of August, the royal festival of the Assumption of the Virgin, the captains sat together in a row in the open space

272

of the large pen, while the sheep were being turned on the spits. That day the grandfather also had climbed the mountain on foot, to take part in the national assembly.

They were fourteen in all. Each one had his story, which surrounded him like an aura. There were three immortals in this assembly. A throne had been erected for them, a wide bench covered with sheeps' fleece. The younger ones—those under seventy—sat on stones, flanking the three.

On the big bench in the middle sat the grandfather. A hundred-year-old lion with a flowing beard that now covered his open, shaggy chest with its wound-scars from the great rising. His eyes were shaded by thick, bristling eyebrows—so thick that he had to stroke them back in order to see. In spite of his many years his cheeks had remained fiery red, and when he grew angry one could see the blood throbbing in his temples. His arteries had nowhere become chalky; tirelessly they gave drink to that aged body. And it was still thirsty and drank, full of eagerness. He had not yet had enough of the world. He touched, heard, saw, tasted and smelled it with the same longing as a twenty-year-old. He saw men and women as tiny creatures swarming about his feet. He was sorry for them and laid his hand on their heads to instill courage into them. Shedding human blood was no pleasure to him. But as soon as it came to a fight with the Turks his eyes grew wild and his hands never wearied of slaying them. He quite forgot at such times that the Turks too were human.

The peasants honored him, and came on Sundays and high feast days to the village square to sit at his feet. In his old age he resembled one of the ancient gods, the immortals. When the elders of Crete assembled to deliberate about freedom and death, they made him sit in the center, and when the captains stood up to speak, they looked at him.

To the right of the grandfather in today's assembly sat another old warrior, Captain Mandakas. His hair and beard were short, his neck thick, his bone structure clumsy, his face furrowed with scars from Turkish scimitars. He had an ear missing, bitten off by a Turk in 1821. Two fingers of his left hand were also missing; when a young man, he had been bitten by a poisonous snake, and had himself hacked them off with an ax, to save his hand. It was a pleasure to him to see Turkish blood flow. Each time Crete had taken up arms, he had hurled himself blindly on the Turkish soldiers. He had stormed through the Turkish villages—plundered, burned and escaped. He killed Turkish women too; during a rising, he had no other interest in them. He had been a tremendous wencher in his day, but in wartime he had kept away from women. He would not even touch his own wife, as long as he was carrying a gun. If he saw her coming to bring him food or cartridges, he would shout at her: "Don't come near me, damn you! don't inflame me! Put it all on a dish and go away!" But when the war adventure was over he would rush from village to village, from embrace to embrace, in festive delirium. Now a graybeard, the one pleasure remaining to him was to swagger out to an assembly of the captains with his silver pistols, and show the scars on his chest.

On the grandfather's left lolled Captain Katsirmas the pirate. Tall and thin like a ship's mast, clean-shaven, sunburned, squinting, he had neither the mighty, lordly style of the grandfather nor the heroic verve of Captain Mandakas. He was a difficult man to get on with and full of bitter accusations against God. He had always played a lone hand and relied only on himself. But his strength too was now gone.

Of the other eleven captains, one was an abbot from the Monastery of Christ the Lord, with blue eyes and a flowing beard. Another was a schoolmaster from Embaro, a misshapen shriveled bit of a man whom nobody could set eyes on without asking: "What's that rabbit doing in a gathering of beasts of prey?" But one had to see him in battle, when his spirit caught fire; or to accompany him to a drinking bout, where he played the lyre to set the stones a-dancing. And when people heard him speak, they felt like praying to God, "Give me ten ears, that I may hear it all." Captain Polyxigis too had come, good-humored and self-contented, with his silver pistols and a silk scarf smelling of musk, a present from Eminé. He sat down next to Captain Michales. Their eyes met, but they did not speak to each other.

Some thought that Tityros also ought to be invited, for he too had become wild and fierce. He had put away his books and now swept through the villages, to speak in the churches on Sundays and set men's hearts on fire. But the grandfather had opposed this. "He's never done a thing in his life but talk," he had said.

"Captain's work is hard. Besides—and that settles it—he's still too young."

All ₹ ₹es were now turned upon the ancient. He rose, stretching out his bony arms in their white sleeves. His voice boomed darkly: "Welcome, captains, to my mountains. Only two things does a Cretan possess: God and his gun. In the name of God and our guns I open this meeting today. Once more we must speak about Crete. Let each man stand up and say freely what he thinks. But first, will the holy abbot of Christ the Lord give the blessing?"

The abbot had already donned his priestly stole. He went over to a boulder, in a hollow of which there was still some rain water. He bent down and plucked a sprig of thyme, with which he performed the sprinkling of the holy water. Then he began to say the prayers, while the captains rose to their feet and took off their fezzes and headbands. It did not matter that they did not precisely understand the words in church language: God, victory over the barbarians, justice, mercy. They had no need of such ideas, for in Captain Sefakas' sheep pen they saw Crete in the flesh: a mother in mourning, barefoot, starving, bloodstained. They raised their hands to Heaven and prayed for their mother and her children.

They crossed themselves and sat down again. For a while no one was able to speak. Their throats were swollen and speech bitter—it would not come forth. Once more the grandfather was the first to speak. Turning to Captain Mandakas he said:

"Captain Mandakas, as a child you ate powder out of your spoon. You have fought right through two generations. Your spirit may have been a bit giddy at first, but with age it's grown clear. Speak, then! Let's know what you've got to say."

"The younger ones should speak," he answered.

The grandfather turned to Captain Katsirmas. "What have you got to say, Captain? You too have been fighting at sea for two generations. You've seen and suffered a great deal. Your opinion has weight. Speak."

"I have no word to say," came the answer, sullenly. "When a man no longer has any strength, he no longer has anything to say. The young ones should speak."

"Very well, then, the young ones!" the grandfather exclaimed, folding his hands over his pistols and preparing to listen.

275

The abbot of Christ the Lord stood up. He was short and square. His cheeks, his forehead, his muscular arms and his throat had been scored with scimitar strokes and pierced by bullets. He directed his gaze at Captain Michales.

"Captain Michales," he said, "I think the first word is yours by right. You escaped from the massacre and you called us together. What, then, have you to say to us?"

Captain Michales stood up. His blood was racing. He leaned on his gun.

"Brothers, captains, you know very well I can't spin speeches. So I'll speak bluntly, drily and soberly; forgive me. Once again the noose is tightening around Crete. Soldiers and dervishes have come by ship; the Turks are slaughtering our brothers in Megalokastro. We are no lambs. The blood of the killed is crying out. Arise, captains! Freedom or death!"

He sat down.

The captains wagged their heads, and put them together by twos and threes. The aged Kambanaros, the first elder of the communes, rose. The murmuring died down. The speaker was well known for his clear reasoning. He was a man whose thoughts were measured. As soon as he stood up in an assembly to speak, the hotheads frowned in expectation of the cold water he would pour over them, while respectable folk breathed more easily.

"Kill the king, but don't threaten him!" he exclaimed, and threw a severe glance at Captain Michales. "When, in God's name, shall we learn discretion? How often have we uttered threats, but never have we had the strength to carry them through and force the Sultan out of Crete! Curses on him! But it's we who pay. Men and women and vineyards are destroyed each time the fire flares up in us. And we, the leaders, bear the responsibility for thousands of souls! And what are you aiming at this time, Captain Michales? Do we want to plunge Crete again into a bath of blood? You are a shrewd man. Tell us, then: how many ship-loads of guns and ammunition and food and tents and horses have you already obtained? How many cannon to storm the fortress? Tell us, please, what understanding you have reached with Greece and with Moscow so that we may all fall upon the Sultan with one blow. Give us the facts! Reveal to us your secret, Captain Michales, that our hearts may rejoice!"

All turned toward Captain Michales, who sat silently, chewing on his mustache. What sort of a secret was the old man driveling about? He had no secret. Neither the Muscovite nor the Greek had sent him as an envoy. He had come. He had come on his own decision, he was sent by Crete, crying and wailing within him.

But at this point the short, pale, bent schoolmaster jumped up from the boulder on which he had been sitting, and the words rolled from his tongue like a wheel:

"Old Kambanaros wants hard facts before moving: ships and provisions and weapons, and the Muscovites to send soldiers to get themselves bloody heads, and our poor mother Hellas to join in too with her three bits of regiments. But when have great deeds ever happened in the world with security, old Kambanaros? When has discretion inspired men to leave their houses and their property and take to the mountains in search of freedom? That is just the art of the palikar: to break out without security. The soul of a man, Captain Kambanaros, is not a dealer but a fighter. Fighters are what we Cretans are, not shopkeepers. The heart of Crete is a warship, that lets fly at the Sultan's fleet and blows it sky high. So forward in God's name, I say with Captain Michales. To arms, brothers! This is what I have to say, you leaders, and he who has ears to hear, let him hear!"

"My blessing on you, schoolmaster," murmured the abbot, and raised his right hand in the teacher's direction. He repeated aloud, so that all could hear: "My blessing on you. The soul of man carries no pair of scales—no, it carries a sword. You are right."

"Better an hour of life in freedom than forty years of slavery and prison," Captain Trialonis of Jerapetra threw in.

Old Kambanaros shook his discretion-filled head.

The leaders had now risen to their feet, excited by the speeches and counter-speeches. They were chattering and arguing together in groups of two and three and five. The prudent were in the minority; the palikars—those who would stake all—outweighed them. With angry, squinting eyes, Captain Katsirmas watched the band of captains foaming around him like the sea. Captain Mandakas sighed, remembering his youth. "Ah! these people here take pencil and paper and add up for and against. In our time we had one cry, Freedom or death!, and our brains reeled, and we charged the ramparts of Kastro to breach them. Man is spoiled, he's grown small, Captain Sefakas!"

But the grandfather looked with warm sympathy at the younger men assembled around him, and he smiled. Everything's in order, he thought, I have confidence. The old go under the earth and come again out of the earth. Made new. Crete is immortal.

He stood up. "Hey, children," he shouted, "this is an assembly of the elders, not a Jewish school. Sit down, and let's reach a conclusion. Captain Kambanaros is on one side, the schoolmaster on the other—there are two courses. We have met together in these mountains to decide. So choose!"

Captain Polyxigis rose. He twirled his musk-scented mustache and bowed his greeting to the three old men. His shirt was open, and a red mark, made by Emine's teeth, was visible on his white throat. Coolly he looked the captains up and down, and paused for a second at the somber countenance of Captain Michales.

"Brothers, captains," he said, "leaders of eastern Crete! Whoever speaks in your presence is in duty bound to weigh his reasons. I have weighed mine. Leaders, listen to me. If we wait, Captain Kambanaros, for the shiploads you demand to be landed and for the Bear to set his bowlegs in motion and bring us help from the north, we shall never free ourselves. And we shan't either—God forgive me!—be worthy of freedom. To judge by my experience in the few years I've lived and worn my belt, freedom is not a cake that drops into one's mouth and is there for the swallowing, but a citadel to be stormed with the saber. Whoever receives freedom from foreign hands remains a slave. So it's fire to the villages, the ax to the trees, the tramp of men at war, streams of tears and blood! And even if we fall with our skulls split, fresh men will stand up in our place. Strife and mourning have far to go in Crete. A hundred, two hundred, three hundred years—I don't know. But one day—there's no other way, don't listen to people like Captain Kambanaros—one day, yes, by the royal sun that circles over us, one day we shall see freedom!"

Captain Polyxigis had taken off his fez, and his head steamed in the sun. The captains, exalted, leaped up and shouted, "Freedom or death!" Captain Michales went over to Polyxigis. With his heart bursting, he said, "A devil has got between us and is trying to separate us. But Crete is again at stake! Here's my hand!"

"Brother, Captain Michales," the other answered. "Here's mine too. And let the devil go to the devil." He laughed. But Captain Michales was already sorry. He went back to his place, his countenance somber.

The meeting lasted another hour. They arranged all the details of who were to meet, and where and how, in order to occupy the crossroads, blockade the Turkish villages, gather the multitudes into the high-lying monasteries.

Wine was brought. They sprinkled it on the ground, taking oaths. The three eldest rose from their large bench. The sun was setting as the meeting came to an end.

In God's name! The leaders dispersed to their realms and gave orders to their companies. Young and old fetched their weapons from the lofts or dug them up out of the earth. Many of the guns were old muzzle-loaders from the 1821 period, which they now cleaned of rust and tied together with cord. The poorest shaped themselves clubs and made plans to fall upon the Turkish soldiers and seize their weapons.

In the courtyards of the monasteries, girls and women tore up old manuscripts and folios and made cartridge cases of them. Skilled monks pounded ointments and balms for wounds in mortars. Roofs of churches were torn off, and their lead turned into bullets. Crete became a workshop of freedom, working day and night. The August moon shone, the cruel sun had already grown a little less harsh. Tenderly it stroked its beloved Crete, which had again given birth to wheat and barley, maize and grapes, and was now longing for the fresh rain. The first autumn clouds were already appearing in the sky, white and downy. A tiny, light breeze urged them along, till they had formed themselves anew and gently covered the face of Crete.

The must was fermenting in the casks. But who will drink it? the Cretans asked themselves. Who will bake the bread from this year's harvest? Who will live to celebrate Christmas? The mothers gazed at their hero sons, the wives at their husbands, the sisters at their brothers, and saw Charos staring over their shoulders. But they said nothing. They knew that they were Cretans, and had been born to die for Crete.

Eminé too had joined the Cretan ranks, and now, unveiled

like the Christian women, helped to make cartridges in the churchyard in front of the church of Kasteli. She put together the cases, but her mind wandered. It was wholly unmoved by the fate of Crete, by Captain Polyxigis, and by Christ and all the saints. It kept flying into the mountains, to the wild man who hunted there. In a few weeks—on the fourteenth of September, Holy Cross Day—she was to be baptized. Fat, heavily moving Chrysanthe stayed at home, in the konak of Ali Aga which the captain had taken over, and prepared the baked meats for the great day when the Moslem woman was to become a Christian.

Seven captains, each with his train of palikars, were to come as godparents. Tityros would be asked to make an oration. The people of the neighboring villages also were expected in crowds, to witness with their own eyes the baptizing of Nuri's wife. It seemed to them a good omen—that Turkey would return to Greece. They took pride in pampering the beautiful new Christian woman. Eminé accepted everything with a smile.

On the evening of the assembly of elders, Eminé was sitting at the window and waiting for the return of Polyxigis. She had washed and combed herself and dyed her heavy eyebrows. How she would have liked to go with him and to see those fourteen mighty captains like eagles on the cliffs! And then she would have met the wild, stiff-necked Captain Michales! At the thought her bosom rose passionately. Why, my God, did she think of him? what did she find in him? He was no man, but a wild beast, lone, ugly—she did not even like him! She had been right to choose the gentle, attentive, sweetly speaking Captain Polyxigis. And yet—if only she could, even for a moment, see Captain Michales up there on the mountains.

She lifted her slanting eyes to the rosy peaks of Selena. Nuri Bey had completely vanished from her mind and body, as if he had never lived, as if he had not been as superb as a lion, as if he had never embraced her. Her flesh was like the sea. A ship would glide over it and scratch it for a moment. Then it would draw together again, untouched as a maiden. How should she still think of the cretinous pasha who had bought her from her father? That had been her father's trade, by which he lived: he begot lovely daughters, fattened them well, displayed them and sold them . . . or should she remember the beardless palikar, the young Circassian, who one summer night had fallen upon her in a garden by the river bank and thrown her down among tall sunflowers? She had thought he wanted to murder her and had struggled against him, but he had not killed her. After the embrace he had become tame, had bent tenderly over her and smiled at her. "What's your name?" he had asked, "mine is. . . ." How should she remember his name? All those men and many others had glided over her and lost themselves in nothingness. Now it was the turn of Captain Polyxigis. Now he was gliding over. But alas! She could feel that, on the day of their wedding, he would depart from her, and a three-masted pirate frigate with black sails would suddenly rise up from the bottom of the sea.

While Eminé, sighing, gazed out of the window, Captain Michales was riding, all alone, down to his father's house. His heart was beating hard with anger and shame. You fool, you're fighting for freedom and yet you're still a slave, he cried within himself. Your lips say one thing, your hands another, and your heart means another! Why do you prattle, you hypocrite Captain Michales, and beat your breast because of Crete? Another demon has fixed its claws in you and is your master, you man without honor! And even if you fall in battle and if you storm Megalokastro and set Crete free, you're still without honor. Your heart is after something else, your purpose dwells elsewhere!

He had sent his best palikar, Thodores, ahead with the flag, and was wholly absorbed in argument with himself. He had seen Polyxigis again and on him had smelled that accursed Turkish musk. He had spied the red bite on his throat, and his blood had shuddered. "Curse her," he whispered, "curse the bitch! As long as she's alive, I am dishonored." He had the picture ceaselessly before his eyes of how the bridegroom had chosen his godparents from the assembly, how he had invited them to the crowning-day, how he had also approached Captain Michales and had started back before his glance.

"I can't stand it any more," Captain Michales cried aloud, "this is no life. I must make an end of it."

Captain Polyxigis, Eminé and Chrysanthe were still at the table, eating their evening meal, when there was a knock at the door and in came Tityros. Captain Polyxigis was astonished. Since Diamandes and Vangelio had met so swift a death, he had not seen the schoolmaster again. At first he had been angry with him, because he suspected him of having poisoned Diamandes out of jealousy. But he had soon changed his mind. It was unthinkable that such a lamb of God could kill. And so he put the blame on destiny. It had been written. . . . He no longer had anything against the schoolmaster. Now that he saw how the schoolmaster traveled through the villages arousing men's hearts for the rebellion, he was willing to forget the whole business. He was delighted at seeing him so unexpectedly.

"Welcome, schoolmaster," he cried, and made room for him.

The schoolmaster greeted him gaily and sat down, so that his face was lighted up by the lamp. Captain Polyxigis was startled by the change in his appearance. Was this Tityros—that half-helping with glasses on a string, tight breeches and a crooked back? Beside him sat another man!

Tityros had in fact become another man. Since the day he had murdered his pretty, boorish brother-in-law he had begun to undergo a transformation. He now knew that the whole secret of manhood did not consist in possessing a great strong body. One must have in one's soul the strength of decision! A horsefly with decision could fell an ox. Manhood was soul, not body. The day he had understood that, Tityros had begun to change. Gradually his body, too, gained strength. He no longer stooped, he ate with appetite and drank wine. His cheeks grew red. And—greatest surprise of all—he caught fire and went after women. Now that he traveled from village to village to speak about the fatherland, he had made himself godfather to various children and had established a family tie with their parents; in this way he could always count on shelter for the night. It happened that one of these new relatives, a woman in Kasteli whose husband was absent, had a sense of fun. One night, after a gay conversation, they found themselves—they themselves did not know how—in bed together and in each other's arms. Since then, Tityros had passed through Kasteli often and had slept with his relative—whom God, he hoped, would protect!

"You too are at war, schoolmaster," said Captain Polyxigis, filling his glass for him. "Your learning is becoming to a captain, and carries a flag with the alphabet embroidered on it."

"I hope I'll soon get hold of a gun as well," answered the schoolteacher with a laugh. "The alphabet is good as an appetizer. But the meat dish is the Turk."

Eminé propped her apple cheek on her hand and gazed at him. That's Captain Michales' brother, she thought. A schoolmaster like that. . . . And she tried hard to discover in his face the fierce, cruel features of the captain.

Chrysanthe got up and went out. She could not look at the schoolmaster. The two corpses rose from the earth and sat down opposite her at the table.

"Will you have the kindness, schoolmaster, to come to the baptism on our crowning-day?" Captain Polyxigis asked. "Eminé is going to be baptized and become Eleni. That same evening there'll be the wedding, too."

"That's just why I've come, Captain—about the baptism. As he was digging in his field near Kasteli, old Mavrolias found a splendid pottery basin. He asked me to come and see it. He thought it was old. And truly, God alone knows how many thousand years old it is. On the outside it's covered with decorations—a grape and coral design. I'm not sure what all the decorations are. And in the bottom of the basin I found a handful of Egyptian beans, which have become like charcoal from the long time . . . by my soul, that basin comes from the time of Minos!"

"Well . . . ?" Captain Polyxigis asked. "What's your idea?"

"Don't you see, Captain? A font! The village pope couldn't think what vessel he was to baptize her in! The church font is much too small. And now God, in the moment of need, makes a splendid basin rise up out of the earth! A good omen, Captain! By my faith, soon Constantinople will be Christian again!"

He stood up, for he was in a hurry. At his godsister's the table was laid and she was waiting for him.

Captain Polyxigis said, with a laugh, "Your brain is pregnant, schoolmaster, it brings forth. Eminé, what do you think?"

But she said nothing. She gazed at the schoolteacher, but her soul had shaken free from her body and had swept far away from Christ and fonts.

The godsister had in fact laid the table and filled the wine bottles and was waiting for her godbrother. She was a man-woman, square, with long white teeth and a thick black mustache. Her broad face was sown with pockmarks. It was just this ugliness that had made the schoolmaster lose his wits. Strange world: if she had not been pock-marked, she would not have kindled the schoolmaster's blood, and he still would have been too timid to embrace a woman.

Tityros wished her good evening. His godchild, still a baby, was lying in the cradle. Another small son was asleep on a little sofa. The husband was a peddler and was now making the round of the villages. Godbrother and godsister were quite alone in the house. They ate hastily, emptied their bottles, crossed themselves, covered up the icons to prevent them from looking on, and hurled themselves into the heaped-up bed.

Next morning the schoolmaster found an excited crowd in the village square with its three gnarled poplars. Hearing the shouting, peasants were rushing barefoot out of the houses. A monk had just arrived. His chest was bare, he was gasping, and blood trickled from his feet.

"Brothers," he shouted, "I've been sent by the fathers of the Monastery of Christ the Lord. Hassan Bey, the general, has marched out of Megalokastro with a strong force of soldiers and invaded the monastery! Where is the captain of the village? Help us, brothers! To arms!"

The captain was lying in Circassian arms. When he heard the noise, he leaped up, dressed and stuck his pistols into his leather belt. Then he ran in the direction of the voices. He seized the monk by the arm.

"Don't shout like that! Don't upset my people!" he said, and pushed him into his house, shut the door and gave him something to eat and drink. The monk regained his breath.

"Now speak," Captain Polyxigis ordered. "And none of your whimpering before me. They're only Turks, you silly monk! The devil will get them!"

10

God brought the day. The heights were touched by the torches of the light. It glided down the slopes and flooded the plains. Then it shot shafts over the indigo clouds and poured down upon the tortured body of Crete. If God had now had the notion to look at Crete, He must have felt pity at the sight of the burning houses, wailing women and orphaned children around the feet of the naked and hungry mountains. And pity for the men who—too wild to pray—clung to the passes and the peaks and, holding up a bit of cloth with a cross embroidered on it, went into battle, barefoot, without bread and without ammunition, with nothing but their miserable patched-up guns. For how many generations had they raised their hands and implored God? When had God ever leaned down and listened to them? Heaven was deaf, God had changed faith. They tightened their grip on their guns.

The first gleam of morning found Captain Polyxigis busy with preparations for war. The evening before, he had sent a runner to Captain Michales with the news that the Turks were besieging the celebrated monastery. Now let him let fly the banner: Freedom or Death! Speeches and debates should be ended; the real voice of Crete, the gun, must speak.

"Hey, Captain Michales," he had added to his letter, "to the devil with our little feuds and concerns. They've eaten into both of us. 'Who are you afraid of?' someone once asked the lion, 'the elephant? the tiger? the buffalo?' 'No,' he answered, 'the louse.' The louse has bitten both of us, Captain Michales. Sometimes we called it pleasure, sometimes worry. But it was always a louse. The devil take it! Crete calls. Give me your hand, brother!"

Eminé came out and leaned against the doorpost. Her eyes were

285

ringed with blue; her lips were bitten. The captain turned to her at last. His mind was still stirred by the proud words he had sent to Captain Michales yesterday evening, and his face was severe.

"Where's your mind strayed to?" the Circassian woman asked fiercely. "I'm here and you don't give that a thought."

He was just hanging a double bag embroidered in colors from the saddle. He had filled one part of the bag with cartridges, oilcloth and balsam, and in the other had put a loaf of bread, a soft cheese and a bottle of wine. How should he answer the woman who stood there in the doorway watching his departure? Since he had written those words to his wild comrade in arms, it had become clear to him, as never before in his life, where woman belonged and where Crete, and where the real duty of a man lay.

"I must tell you a secret," said the Circassian, coming closer to him. She stroked the mare's neck, bending her head so that her hair fell over her neck like the mare's mane and nearly touched the ground. The yard filled with the scent of musk.

"A secret?" asked Polyxigis, and his hands stiffened and remained motionless in the air.

"Yes, and I'm telling it to you so that you won't say afterwards that you did not know. Sometimes I get news from Megalokastro. One of these days Nuri's relatives mean to attack Kasteli with soldiers and seize me. And if I don't return to my faith they'll kill me. So go to the Monastery of Christ the Lord! But keep your wife in mind also, Captain Polyxigis!"

He stood there for a moment, wavering. Outside a multitudinous din was audible. Wives were bidding their husbands farewell, old women wept and men tore themselves loose. "Good-by," they shouted, and gathered around Captain Polyxigis' flag at the three poplars in the village square.

When the Circassian saw that her man remained silent, she said, "A woman's a citadel, too. She has to be taken."

"I'm not forgetting," the man answered at last. "Good-by!"

He folded her in his arms. He felt her firm bosom, and his senses reeled. The world could come to grief, if only this thrilling body might never leave his arms. The woman closed her eyes, raised herself gently on her toes and reached his mouth. His knees gave way.

The mare whinnied. The captain mastered his dizziness and

leaned against the doorpost. He freed himself from her mouth and softly pushed her from him, caught hold of the horse's mane and swung himself into the saddle.

"Good-by!" he said, and without turning rode through the outer door and galloped to the village square.

That same morning Captain Michales stood in the grandfather's huge yard at Petrokefalo, surrounded by his best palikars. He had confided to the keeping of Thodores his banner—the black cloth with the red letters. Beside him, armed, were his sometime drinking companions, Kajabes and Furogatos. Vendusos had gone out to make arrangements for his family. Bertodulos had stayed with the women.

Captain Michales turned to his wife, who stood silently on the threshold with folded arms. "Good-by, wife," he said.

"God be with you, Captain Michales," she replied calmly. "God be with you, palikars!" she added, while her eyes glided earnestly over her husband's young comrades in arms.

The grandfather came out. His cheeks glowed red in the early morning light.

"Forward, children, with my blessing!" he cried, raising his heavy hand. "Go with God's blessing! You're fighting for Crete, and that's no joke! Happy the man who lays down his life in the service of Crete!" He went on: "On this day it seems to me better —I couldn't say why—to be killed in her service than to live in her service."

The noise forced its way into Thrasaki's sleep. He guessed that his father was setting out for war, and leaped from his bed, to appear on the doorstep wrapped in a red embroidered rug. His father looked at the boy, still half encompassed by dream as he bobbed up between his grandfather and his mother, and laughed.

"Good-by, Thrasaki, till you're old enough!" he said, and jumped on his mare. He crossed himself. "In God's name!"

The village emptied itself of men.

The celebrated Monastery of Christ the Lord had been founded in ancient times, before the fall of Constantinople, before the coming of the Venetians to Crete, when the Byzantine emperors still ruled in the East and far into the West.

The story went that it had been built by the Emperor Nikiforos —that great, dark soul who had been led astray by a woman's beautiful body and had missed plunging to Hell by a hair's breadth. But he had managed to grasp hold of God and make him listen. And God had heard him and placed him in Paradise, together with the other sinful and sorely tormented emperors.

He had gained mastery of the world, landed in Crete, stamped down the Saracens, overthrown the Crescent, and set up over the scorched fields and plundered towns the banner of Christ. And one evening, the story went, he was passing through a ravine. Here, under a lemon tree, he thought he would sleep and, as soon as God made day come, press on toward Chandaka (that was Megalokastro's name then). It was the month of May: the moon was full, and the night air quivered with the song of the nightingale. The emperor saw Christ the Lord approaching, barefoot, faint from long journeying. Christ the Lord stopped under the lemon tree. He did not see Nikiforos, and stretched Himself on the ground with a sigh. He took a stone for a pillow and said, "How tired I am." Then He folded His arms, shut His eyes and went to sleep.

All night the emperor felt a sweet, ineffable happiness. It was the gift neither of the moon, nor of the nightingale, nor of slumber. He had entered Paradise.

Waking up at dawn, Nikiforos said, "This tree, where Christ has slept, is hallowed." He commanded that the holy lemon tree be surrounded by a monastery. And that, they say, is how the Monastery of Christ the Lord was founded.

The Byzantine emperors died, the Turks took Constantinople, the Venetians overran Crete, the Ottomans subdued it. The monastery was destroyed, rebuilt, destroyed again. And now, beleaguered by the Turks, its bells rang mournfully and cried their message to the countryside: "All you believers, come and help!"

The abbot was arming himself in the church, the monks were digging up the guns from under the sacred altar. The abbot knelt down before the huge icon of Christ near the iconostasis.

"Lord Christ," he cried aloud, that all might hear him, "forgive me, the fault is mine, I am the one to blame! And now the dogs have come to avenge the blood."

He was in fact responsible. On the first of September, the beginning of the ecclesiastical accounting year, the abbot of Christ the Lord had been on his way back from Megalokastro. He had gone there to be confessed by the Metropolitan and to lay at his feet the monastery's yearly contribution. He had also begged him to take the monastery under his protection, to use his influence with the pasha to make him prevent the Turks from attacking it again. How many more times would they burn the monastery down? "Have pity!" he had pleaded. "I've grown old, Bishop. My wounds hurt. I haven't the strength left for defending it!"

"How old do you suppose God has grown—yet He can still lay fresh burdens on ten saints!" answered the Metropolitan, with a laugh. "Go with my blessing, and stop worrying."

The abbot had taken the Metropolitan's blessing with him as he rode his mule through the Hospital Gate. In the sunset light he looked at the blue, shimmering mountains in front of him, at the harvested fields, the vineyards generous with clusters, the olive trees loaded with fruit, and at the sea. His heart flew upward.

"It's beautiful, this false world," he murmured. "Crete is beautiful, God is great."

He kept close to the shore, crossed the red sand of the river bed, drank a raki at the widow's inn, then started up Cruel Mountain. His mule carefully trod the narrow goat path along the precipice. A light breeze was sighing. The abbot saw the sea down below, darkening as he watched. He crossed himself and repeated out of a heart filled with happiness, "It's beautiful, this false world. Crete is beautiful. . . ."

Three powerful young Turks, who had been lying in wait for him, hidden behind a rock, rushed on him with their knives. They had decided to avenge the many graying hanums still living whom the warlike monk had widowed in the 1866 rising.

The mule started and very nearly threw the abbot into the abyss. He forgot he was an old man covered with forty scars, and leaped to the ground with the suppleness of a wildcat. "In Christ's name!" he shouted, drawing his knife.

Above the abyss the four bodies whirled, entwined. The small, bony but very agile abbot laid about him in all directions. His blood kindled, his youth came back, and all his forefathers who had fallen in battle against Turkey rose up in him. It was not only he doing battle, but all Cretans together.

Night broke over them, and down below the sea lay dark. The stars in the high heavens seemed incongruously gay. A night bird squatted up above on a cliff, watching the four forms in their dance of death.

"In Christ's name!" shouted the abbot again, and with an immense effort he freed himself for a moment from the clutches of the six pairs of limbs. Then he hurled himself with all his strength against the human bundle, to ram it over the precipice. It began to slide. For a moment it held on, but a last mighty push broke its resistance, and the three Turks fell bellowing down the abyss, into the sea.

The abbot leaned against the mountain and crossed himself. Blood was streaming over his head and chest; his monk's habit was torn. He bound his wounds with strips of stuff, and called his mule.

"Give me strength, O Christ," he prayed, "to get to the monastery. After that, do what Thou wilt."

He clenched his teeth and with great pain climbed into the saddle. "God is great," he murmured and rode on.

Next day Megalokastro echoed with the new exploit of the Turk-gobbling abbot. Three Turkish women, new victims of Charos, united in the wailing for the dead. Accompanied by a crowd, they hurried to the place of the fall, climbed down to the wild shore, picked up the bodies and buried them in the sand. The men struck their knives into the mound of the grave and swore that they would build the monument out of the ashes of the accursed monastery. And that was why, one morning, the ravine before the Monastery of Christ the Lord was filled with red fezzes.

On the same morning fresh bands set out from the Hospital Gate against the besieged monastery and against the big Turkish village of Kasteli, which the giaours had occupied. The nephews, cousins and friends of Nuri, with the ferocious muezzin at their head, pressed forward as if possessed. In Megalokastro the Christians through shuttered windows watched them as they streamed by with pistols and daggers and plunged their knives into Greek doors.

That morning, on the other side of the sea, Athens awoke. From the columns of the Parthenon the light gradually spread to the plain, on which the city made famous by intellect and beauty was beginning to awaken, powerfully assisted by the throats of the milkman, the newsboy and the vegetable vendor. From the vacant school buildings, storerooms and cellars where they had been given scanty quarters, the Cretan refugees emerged silently. They held tins and bowls in their hands and took up their positions in front of an open door, through which one could see into a yard containing several large caldrons. They waited for an hour in the queue to get their couple of spoonfuls of lenten soup. At first they had been ashamed, because they were not used to begging but hunger had compelled them.

Mother Hellas, though also haunted by Charos, was going short of food in order to give it to the starving Cretans. Miserly householders opened their purses, newly married couples sacrificed their wedding presents, popes raised their hands to God, and ships put out from places on the near-by coast to smuggle ammunition, food and volunteers into Crete.

On the island of Syra, rich in ships, Captain Stefanes limped about the back alleys of the small town and stretched out his hands in entreaty. "A ship for me, too, Christians, a ship for Crete!"

And God did arrange that, precisely at the time the two leaders who were his friends were marching to Christ the Lord Monastery, Captain Stefanes was hopping on the ship that the patriots of Syra had entrusted to him. It had a cargo of flour, belts, muslin bandages and cartridges.

Captain Stefanes crossed himself, took the icon of Saint Nicholas and placed it well forward in the bows. He whispered to it. "I'm placing you here, Saint Nicholas, my saint, because your eyes see better than two pairs of men's eyes. Never say, after this, that you were in the cabin and saw nothing!" The sea saint with the short beard looked at him in silence. In his hands, eaten away by salt, he was holding a toy—a ship with tiny men on board. He was smiling. Captain Stefanes bent over him and kissed him.

A small cloud like a smoke cloud appeared in the sky to the south. It grew, and other clouds came frisking behind it like sheep, driven along by the hot south wind as by a shepherd. By midday the whole sky was covered. The first lukewarm drops of autumn rain fell, and the first claps of thunder boomed over the sea.

Captain Stefanes turned his flashing eyes to the south and

smiled. "Up, south wind, master of waters, pour your floods down, so that neither sun nor moon appears and I can bring Crete's dowry to land in pitch-black darkness, with a turn of the hand."

Vendusos, too, heard the thunder as he climbed the mountain. He was oppressed by the sky hanging dark above him. "Wait, sky," he muttered, "till I get to my godfather Jorgaros. Then you can let your temper go!"

He quickened his pace, to reach the mountain village of Anapoli. He wanted to ask his godfather to look after his wife and two daughters until Crete should be at peace again.

He arrived in the deep of night. He knocked on the door. Not a soul! He knocked again, and his godfather came to the door, with reddened eyes, disheveled hair and pale face.

"Greetings, Godfather Jorgaros," said Vendusos. "May I lie down in your house tonight?"

"Ask for my head and it's yours," answered the godfather. "Welcome!"

Vendusos entered the house. The wife did not appear. Jorgaros left his godson for a moment, and subdued voices came from the bedroom upstairs. Soon they ceased.

"And Godmother?" Vendusos asked.

"You must excuse her, Godson Vendusos," Jorgaros answered. "She's not been well, these last days. She sends you her greetings and bids you welcome."

The godfather laid the table, brought food and wine and lighted a lamp.

"Excuse me, Godson," he said, "I've not much to offer you. But how was I to know you'd do me the favor of coming this evening? Tomorrow I'll kill you a chicken, God willing."

The south wind raged, the rain slapped against door and steps.

"Tomorrow, first thing, Godfather, I must be gone, God willing," Vendusos replied. "I've given Captain Michales my word. I've come, Godfather Jorgaros, to ask you a favor."

"Anything in my power," replied Jorgaros, nodding his head.

"If you have a room to spare, to shelter my family, till the weapons are silent . . ."

Jorgaros drank a gulp of wine, as though his throat were constricted.

"It happens that a room is vacant," he said, lowering his eyes, "just since the last few days. Take it, Godson Vendusos!"

He stood up to open the door and go out into the yard. He came in again at once, wet through. "God be thanked," he said, "it's raining. The soil will be soft for the plowing."

He pushed the table to one side and made up a bed for his godson on the settle. "Sleep, Godson," he said. "You've come a long way."

Next morning Jorgaros brought him a mug of milk, a dry barley loaf and a large hunk of cheese. The sky was now clear. The cocks of the village were fluttering on the roofs and crowing.

"Good-by, Godfather," said Vendusos. "How can I repay your friendship? Only God can reward you."

"The Almighty pays what is due, don't worry, Godson Vendusos. Good-by!"

The washed rocks glittered in the morning light, and the raindrops on the branches shimmered. Vendusos strode down the mountain, whistling gaily. He had found protection for his family, he was relieved of that nightmare, and he was now in a hurry to get back to Captain Michales, Kajabes and Furogatos.

The door of a hovel outside the village opened, and a little old man appeared on the threshold. Vendusos recognized him. He was old Zacharias, Jorgaros' uncle and a man of skill. He grafted trees and barbered and doctored men and women. Every Saturday he took a clay bowl, some soap, a pair of clippers and a razor, and sat down on the small bench by the church, to shear and scrape as many heads as presented themselves. Close by him he had a small sack, which his customers filled with bread, vegetables and raisins; next to it, there stood two jugs, for wine and oil. When he had done his barber's work, he heaped up the cut-off hair and set fire to it, so that the space around him was veiled in stinking smoke.

"A long life to you, Uncle Zacharias!" Vendusos called out to him, and stopped.

"Welcome to the lyre player!" the old man answered. "What's happening in the world, my child? Where is it going?"

"Don't ask, Uncle! To the devil!"

"And you?"

"I'm going with it. Can I get away from it? Last night I slept at my Godfather Jorgaros' house. We had a good long talk. Now I'm off."

The old man raised his hands to Heaven. "At Jorgaros'," he muttered. "Lord have mercy on me! So that's why the poor man sent a message that no one was to come to his house to mourn for the dead!"

"What's that, Uncle? What mourning?"

"Didn't you notice anything?"

"What should I have noticed?"

"His son was killed, yesterday morning. They had the body in the bedroom."

Vendusos covered his face.

"Hey, Vendusos," exclaimed the old man, "don't cry! Fare you well! We all have to die!"

At Christ the Lord Monastery too it had rained that night. The faces of the monks, who had been kneeling for three days and nights behind their bulwarks, waiting for the Turks, looked fresh.

There were thirty-two of them all told, together with about twenty peasants from near by, who had been ashamed to leave the Christ the Lord in the lurch. When they had heard the storm bells, they had taken their wives and children to a high-lying cave, a citadel made by God, and then repaired to the monastery with their provisions—a sheep or a goat and a woolen sack full of barley biscuits.

Noon was already near when Captain Polyxigis with his palikars reached the top of the pass and began to approach the monastery. From a distance they caught the sound of shots and of Turkish trumpets. Some of the comrades hastily took up positions at the top of the pass, to protect their brothers in the rear.

Captain Polyxigis stood up in his stirrups. "Greetings, brothers," he shouted, and fired a pistol shot. Then he turned to his panting companions. "Let 'em have your greetings, my children! But I don't want a single bullet wasted!"

He pointed at the huge mass of accursed red fezzes swarming about the monastery. Fifteen bullets whistled into the Turks from behind. Some twenty bodies fell to the ground, bellowing.

The monastery echoed back cries of "Welcome, children!" Old Ilarion, the deaf bell ringer, grasped the bell rope and began ringing festively.

The Turks raged as they raised their eyes and saw through the mist that the top of the pass was occupied by Greeks, who were now seeking cover behind the cliffs.

"Allah! Allah!" they bawled.

Most of the Turkish ranks remained where they were, with a close grip on the monastery; the others stormed up toward the crest.

It began to rain heavily. A cloud hid the top of the pass, while the rain beat into the faces of the Turkish soldiers and blinded them.

"God's with us," shouted Captain Polyxigis. "Give 'em another volley."

They reloaded and fired. Shouts and curses rang out. But the clouds now sank lower and protected the Turks too. Their red fezzes and glittering bayonets could barely be made out.

The abbot, who saw through the loophole that the Turkish numbers had divided, called out the news to his people. "Forward, children!" he shouted. "Now! Let's attack them and loosen their grip!"

Monks and peasants leaped up, the bell ringer again seized his rope and rang the signal for attack. They gathered in the courtyard. The abbot ran ahead, opened the big door, and they all rushed out, shouting.

For a moment the Turks were bewildered by the two attacks. Some tried by means of a counterattack to drive the monks back into the monastery, but in the midst of the attack they received the order to withdraw deeper into the ravine. They were pursued by the monks.

Suddenly a trumpet call rang out. The Turks stopped. Immediately afterward, behind the monks, other trumpets sounded.

"The Turks have encircled us," shouted a monk. "We're in a trap! Back, Reverend Abbot!"

"They've broken into the monastery!" yelled another.

The abbot stuck his pistols into his belt, drew a knife and without a word hastened back to the gate of the monastery.

Captain Polyxigis had at once seen the new danger and stormed down with his palikars. The rain had grown heavier. Twilight spread. Turks and Christians formed a huge knot of fighting men, each of them at once attacking and on the defensive.

"Follow me!" the abbot now shouted, and Captain Polyxigis also urged his companions on and pressed through to the gate.

A few Turks had already got into the monastery courtyard and were running toward the church. They were flinging burning tow and rags in all directions.

"You damned dogs!" they heard two wild, hoarse voices behind them. The abbot and Captain Polyxigis had crossed the threshold together, and they now rushed on the intruders. The Turks who were following were driven against the church wall and massacred by the monks and palikars, who now arrived all at once.

For the present the danger had been averted. The heavy outer gate of the monastery was double-bolted. Night came. The fighters broke ranks and silence fell.

"Back to the pass!" ordered Captain Polyxigis. "God will be with us again tomorrow."

The Christians counted their losses. Of the monks and peasants, three had been killed and several wounded. Ilarion the bell ringer was missing. Two of Captain Polyxigis' band had been killed and many wounded. They buried the dead by night at the top of the pass: two doughty palikars, both from Kasteli, uncle and nephew. Captain Polyxigis took two sticks, made them into a cross and placed it on the mound.

"We'll be back later," he said. Then he turned to his comrades. "Now for some food, children! We're still alive and we're hungry!"

They lighted a fire, cooked and ate. The excitement of the battle flickered in their talk. Sentries were posted for the night. The rest folded their arms and slept, exhausted.

Down below, the lights in the church burned till midnight. The monks were praising God, Who had stretched out His hand and saved the monastery from fire and death. The aged Photios mixed balsam and tended the wounded all night.

The Turkish soldiers also were burying their dead, caring for the wounded and thinking, as they stared silently into the campfires, of their wives and children in far-off Anatolia. Who would plow the fields there, prune the vines, and earn bread for the family?

As the first pallid light appeared in the sky, Christians and Turks sprang to arms. Two dervishes, one with a drum, the other with a flute, ran among the Turkish soldiers from group to group, to give them courage and fire.

The monks, too, took up their posts. The abbot's head was bandaged. His wounds were still bleeding, his white beard was full of red drops. He kneeled down before the loophole, and his eagle eye flew over the enemy's position. Wherever a head poked up, his bullet hit it without fail. It's an evil craft, killing men, he thought. But it's not our fault, O God! Make us free, God, then we'll have peace.

Above, at the top of the pass, Captain Polyxigis made his rounds and gave each man his orders. Each was already behind a boulder and aiming his gun at the red fezzes. But Captain Polyxigis was too proud to hide and walked upright from man to man.

Bullets were already whistling over their heads.

"Take cover, Captain, or you'll get hit!" his palikars called to him.

But Captain Polyxigis laughed.

"I'd like to, children. I'm frightened too, God knows. But I'm ashamed. Want to be captain, Polyxigis? Then you must pay for it."

"You carry a splinter of the Holy Cross about with you," shouted a tall lad with a poison tongue. "That's why you're so fearless."

That angered Captain Polyxigis. "The holy splinter, you idiot," he said, "is the soul of a man. I know no other!"

Down below, the battle was flaring afresh. The Turks advanced and the monastery was again in danger.

"Christ will be the victor!" yelled Captain Polyxigis. "Down and at the Turks!"

The palikars leaped from behind the rocks and rushed down. Stones came rattling behind them; the whole mountain seemed to be in motion.

After the guns had done their work, the short daggers came into play in hand-to-hand combat. The guns in the monastery also were silent: it was no longer possible to distinguish the fighters. The abbot ordered his most daring men to join in the melee, while the others stayed behind the bulwarks and guarded the monastery. But the Mussulmans outnumbered the Christians, seven to one. The abbot and the captain moved among their men, putting fire into them. But wave on wave of Turkish attackers fell upon them, and toward midday the Christians began to weaken. The sun seemed to be standing still in the sky, and the rescuing night infinitely far away. The attackers pressed on. In the midst of the confusion the glances of the abbot and the captain met. Each saw the monastery burning in the eyes of the other.

Suddenly a salvo thundered in the lower ravine. The Christians watched with amazement as a dark banner climbed higher and higher and with it, clambering from boulder to boulder, a bellowing horde. At its head, on his mare, rode Captain Michales, wearing his black headband.

"Hail to you, brothers!" he shouted, firing his pistol—and, turned to the enemy.

That day and the next the wounded Turks poured back into Megalokastro.

"What's happened with the monastery? Is it still standing? Do you call yourselves soldiers?" shouted the pasha, tearing his beard.

"It was all going well, Pasha Effendi," answered the wounded, "until that cursed Captain Michales fell upon us."

They were hoarse with thirst and demanded sherbet from Barba Jannis. Efendina too emerged and recited verses from the Koran, to allay their pain. From the great plane tree hung, like a bell, poor Ilarion, the deaf bell ringer. The Turks had taken him alive two days ago. He was still holding in his fist a piece of the bell rope, which he had refused to let go, so that the Turks had had to cut it.

The Metropolitan never put off his vestments, day and night. Each moment he expected that the Turks would force ther way in to the Residence and haul him off to the gallows. He did not want to make that journey half naked and barefoot. He had sent for Pachunios the ascetic from the Kadumas Monastery by the Libyan Sea, to hear his confession. He took communion every day, that his soul might be ready at any time. Murzuflos did not move from his side, and kept him company like a dog. He slept on the threshold of his bedroom, that he might in no case be separated from his master, and that their souls might pass together into the beyond.

At the monastery night came at last. Christ and Mohammed separated. The Christians lighted fires on the mountainside, the Turks around the monastery walls. The monastery remained hidden in deep darkness. Captains Michales and Polyxigis met and discussed the situation. They settled the place and manner of tomorrow's attack, and parted without having exchanged a friendly word.

Captain Michales squatted alone by the fire, deep in a dark colloquy with himself, and rolled a cigarette. His heart was opressed. He was fighting, killing and at every moment exposing himself to death—for Crete. Yet his mind was not with Crete. When, mounted on his mare, he stormed forward with the cry: Follow me, you faithful!, in his secret self he doubted his own faith. And when night came and he withdrew into solitude, he did not think, as in the past, about the freedom of Crete; his spirit wandered elsewhere.

What have you sunk to, Captain Michales? he asked himself, and spat into the fire.

In this bitter mood, he heard light footsteps and a cough behind him. He turned. It was Vendusos, to whom he had given leave to make arrangements for his family's safety.

"What's happened, Vendusos?" Captain Michales asked, and stood up.

Vendusos, who had long suspected what worm was gnawing at Captain Michales, whispered into his ear, "Captain, Captain, Eminé. . . ."

Captain Michales started. Then he seized Vendusos by the arm. "Speak softly!"

"The Turks attacked Kasteli tonight and made off with her."

Captain Michales stretched out his hand to the fire. He wanted the burning pain. . . .

He wheeled around. "Where?"

"Toward Megalokastro."

Captain Michales burst out, "Come with me and keep quiet."

But Vendusos resisted. "D'you mean to leave your post? And suppose the Turks make a night attack?"

"Shut up!"

He picked out ten seasoned palikars. "Come with me! We're going on a raid."

299

He turned to the others. "I'll be back before dawn. Look after yourselves meanwhile."

It was past midnight. The exhausted Christians lay in deep sleep. Inside the monastery the fathers bowed their faces to the flagstones of the church and implored God to protect the monastery. The abbot had bandaged his wounds with oiled cloth, but remained at his post. Through the narrow loophole he could see the Turkish soldiers standing around the fires, and could catch the clink of their weapons. "The dogs aren't asleep," he thought. "They're up to something."

The sky was clear, the stars shone gaily, a sharp breeze came from the mountains. A big star shot in a long sweep. The abbot crossed himself.

"A great disaster is approaching," he murmured. "O God, grant that it is not the monastery."

And while his eyes were still directed imploringly at the sky, suddenly trumpets and drums sounded and a loud shout of "Allah! Allah!" Dark waves of men struck against the monastery, and at the pass, up above, others rushed upon the sleeping Christians. The soldiers were already beginning to place ladders against the monastery walls.

The abbot called his monks together. "Brothers, the monastery is lost. Listen to me. I am the one to blame. It's me they want to take, to avenge their blood. So I'm giving myself up to them. Farewell!"

"Reverend Abbot," said Photios, the healer monk, "they'll kill you."

"What else should they do with me, Father Photios? Of course they'll kill me. But they'll spare the monastery."

"They'll kill you and not spare the monastery. The Turks are treacherous, Reverend Abbot!"

"Let me do my duty. Let what will happen, happen. God is above, let Him do as He will."

He took his abbot's staff, tied a white cloth to its tip, went out and climbed on the wall and waved the staff, shouting. A Cretan Turk bellowed up at him. "What d'you want, Devil's monk?"

"Who is your leader? Go and tell him that the abbot is giving himself up. He can grind me to powder. But he must give his word that the monastery will be spared."

The resounding voices were heard by both sides. They paused, and in the stillness the cocks began to crow from the monastery roofs. Morning had come.

"Lay down your weapons and come out—the monastery will not be harmed," came the voice of the leader, Hassan Bey.

"Swear," the abbot cried, and raised his hand toward heaven, already overspread by a rosy glow.

"Yes, I swear by Mohammed."

The abbot climbed down from the wall. The monks surrounded him, and hugged his shoulders, bidding him good-by. The others also pressed around him and kissed his hands.

"Farewell, great martyr, farewell!"

He approached the church, fell on his face and kissed the threshold. "Lord Christ," he whispered, "farewell!"

Then he glanced over the courtyard, the church, the cells, the storehouses and bulwarks, and with raised hand he said, "Farewell!"

As he stepped over the threshold of the outer gate, the Turks seized him, and he vanished in the crowd. At the same time a horde broke in through the open gate and poured, bellowing, into the monastery.

"They've set it on fire, the perjuring dogs!" Captain Polyxigis shouted. His head had been wounded by a scimitar cut and was now bandaged. With an effort he subdued the pain.

"Where's Captain Michales?" he roared, sprang on his mare and put spurs to her so that she flew down toward the monastery.

But Captain Michales was not yet back. His standard-bearer Thodores took the lead, and they attacked the Turks from the flank. Flames were already darting from the monastery, and through the ravine more and more troops with red fezzes pressed on.

The younger monks swung themselves over the walls and ran with the retreating bands up into the mountain.

"Where the devil is Captain Michales?" Captain Polyxigis asked Thodores when they had reached the top of the pass. His face, throat and chest were covered with blood.

"I don't know. In the middle of the night he went off on a raid."

"A raid? Where?"

"I don't know, I tell you."

From the pass the Christians looked down at the monastery.

The flames were shooting up, and the edge of the smoke cloud obscured the sun.

Captain Polyxigis stood there in dark perplexity. He had forgotten his pain, he no longer bothered to wipe the blood away. His eyes were wet.

"Let's withdraw, Captain," said one of the palikars. "You're wounded. Don't stay here looking at the monastery. It's done for. God willed it so. We've done our duty."

"If only Captain Michales had been with us," the captain sighed.

They dragged him away almost by force and started off toward Kasteli. The other band with Captain Michales' flag made for Petrokefalo. The bitter tidings preceded them, and as they arrived they could hear the wailing for the dead.

A scout, who had been left on the pass to observe the Turkish troops, caught up with Captain Polyxigis' band at midday. The captain lay stretched out in a dried-up river bed under a plane tree, resting in the shade while Photios, the healer monk, cleaned his wounds.

He gazed at the scout. "What's the news, Jakumis?"

Jakumis, a sunburned pygmy with grasshopper legs and lynx eyes, came forward. His eyes had seen so many violent deaths and enjoyed so many feasts and so often watched the world stand on its head that nothing could make them shrink or shine. "The world's a wheel," he was in the habit of saying, "a revolving wheel."

"And who turns it, Jakumis?" people would ask him.

"Sometimes God, sometimes the devil," he would answer. "The two are in league. One destroys, the other builds up. They're neither of them ever out of work."

"May your wounds heal quickly," Jakumis said now. "Don't be disheartened. We've come down—another time we shall go up. Don't worry. The wheel turns."

"What's happened to the monastery?"

"What do you expect, Captain? The devil's got it. . . ."

"Wither that tongue of yours, you blasphemer," cried Father Photios, crossing himself.

"I only meant that it's become what it was before it was built. Dust."

"And the dogs?"

"They have taken the abbot off with them. You mark my words. They'll make tobacco boxes of his head."

And in fact, while the scout was talking about it so bluntly, the Turkish soldiers were driving the abbot of Christ the Lord with their bayonets toward Megalokastro. They formed a ring around him to prevent the native Mussulmans from killing him in their rage for vengeance. Their orders were to bring him alive to the pasha.

The sun was still high as they entered Megalokastro with trumpets and drums. Beaming with joy, the pasha appeared on his balcony to greet them. The abbot was placed before him.

"Bow, you giaour priest!" the pasha shouted.

Dark, thick blood was dripping from the abbot's beard, but his eyes were undimmed. He gazed at the pasha, at the howling Turks all round him, the sky and the slowly setting sun. He felt a strange lightheartedness, and his shoulders prickled as if wings were trying to break out for the crossing to the beyond.

"Have you no fear?" the pasha cried. "Why is your face all shining? Where are you in your thoughts?"

"In Paradise," the abbot answered.

The pasha was furious. It was not the first time his knife had glanced off a Cretan rock as he struck it.

"You're not in Paradise, you devil's monk," he roared, "but facing the plane tree!"

"It's the same thing," said the abbot.

"To the plane tree with the giaour," ordered the pasha, foaming at the mouth.

The Arab and some of the soldiers seized the abbot and dragged him out of the courtyard. Outside in the streets a mob howled. The plane tree was only a little way from the pasha's porte, near the Venetian fountain with the marble lion.

As always, just before sundown, there was a swarm of birds in the plane tree. They were twittering gaily as they settled down for the night's slumber.

A bench was brought and the abbot placed on it. The soldiers called for a Turkish barber. He appeared, with razor and scissors and bronze basin. When he saw the abbot, he laughed. "You're a brave palikar," he said, "I'll shave you without lather."

He grasped him by the beard and began to shear it off. The

abbot bit his lips, so that he would not cry out. The Turks shouted with laughter. Suleiman had meanwhile fetched the rope and was greasing it. Several Christians, hidden behind shutters on the opposite side, watched the preparations with bated breath. The pasha too sank into a chair within view of the abbot.

When the barber had done his work, the scars from the scimitar wounds on the abbot's furrowed face came into view. The Turk now took the scissors and cut off his hair near the roots.

"Hey, you giaour priest," the pasha shouted at him, "the rope's ready and greased, the Arab's standing over you. Acknowledge Mohammed, and you'll save your life."

The abbot stepped off the bench, seized the rope from the Arab's hands, made a noose and slipped it over his neck.

"Answer!" bellowed the pasha, jumping up.

"I have answered," said the abbot, pointing at the noose round his neck.

"Curses on you Cretans!" shouted the pasha, blue with rage. "Hang him!"

The abbot stepped up on the bench again. The Arab made the rope fast to a thick bough of the plane tree.

The abbot crossed himself, looked about him and saw in the air a troop of ancient popes, gray-headed fallen warriors who, like Christ, had worn a crown of thorns and now greeted him with open eyes.

The abbot uttered a cry of joy. He kicked the bench away and hung in the air.

When Captain Michales came back to the monastery toward noon, to resume the fight beside his companions, he found neither monastery nor companions.

The Christ the Lord was ablaze. The cupola of the church had fallen in, the ancient decorated iconostasis was smoldering, the vestments, psalters, icons already lay in ashes. In thick clouds the smoke rose into the still air and hung over the ravine.

Captain Michales tugged at his beard and stared. He could not turn his eyes away from the devouring flames.

"How could I go away? How could I go away?" he groaned, and tore the hairs from his beard.

Last night passed through his mind. The breathless chase, his comrades panting after him on foot, then later, at dawn, the wide, dry river bed and above it, between the white chalk cliffs, the twenty Turks driving before them a mare, on which there sat a muffled woman. . . .

They closed, they went for one another with knives, they bellowed—for how long? An hour? Two hours? It seemed to him to pass as quickly as a flash. The valley whirled about him, became a threshing floor. In the middle of the threshing floor stood an acacia, and under it was the muffled woman. With head erect, sitting motionless on the mare, she waited for the victor. She had turned her face away from the men.

Suddenly the beaten Turks began to flee from the threshing floor, throwing down their pistols and knives and making for Megalokastro. Captain Michales turned his head away, to avoid looking at the musk-fragrant woman, and beckoned Vendusos to him.

"Take this woman and bring her to my old aunt Kalio, at Korakjes. Tell her she's to give her food and drink till we see what happens."

"Shouldn't I take her back to Kasteli?" asked Vendusos. "Poor Captain Polyxigis will kill himself."

"Let him kill himself."

As he gripped the reins, for a moment his soul staggered. Whither was he to turn? He came to a decision. He spurred the mare and stormed down to Christ the Lord Monastery once more. And now here he was, staring at the flames.

"I should not have gone away," he groaned again, and tore hair after hair from his beard.

He dismounted, and picked up a handful of hot ashes. His impulse was to smear them into his beard and hair and rub them into his face. But he controlled himself. He opened his fist, and the ashes dropped.

"Let the one who's to blame burn and perish like that!" he muttered, and leaped on the mare. He spurred her so that her belly bled.

Now Crete was afire from end to end. The mountains, the ravines, the crossroads rang with shots and hoarse voices, and the

305

men had turned into bellowing, biting, murdering beasts. The grizzled champions thought of their youth and took to the mountains, some armed to take part in the fighting, others, weakened by their years and old wounds, to impart advice to the new captains. They taught them the stratagems of the earlier leaders— how to send out spies, trick and encircle the Turks, break into the Turkish villages by night.

Captain Elias came riding out on his old mule. He rode from mountain to mountain and hid in the various captains' nests in turn. "Old age is crippling, children." He sighed. "I can't fight any longer with weapons—I shall make war with my head, until that too drops to the earth and turns into earth!"

Today he had reached Vrisses, the green village rich in springs, and was sitting under an ancient, hollow plane tree. Children, women and old men were sitting around him, listening open-mouthed.

"How often," he said, brushing the darkly luminous foliage with his withered arms, "this plane tree has sheltered doughty captains in its shade. Whoever saw them thought they must be immortal. And yet they too died. Who would have believed it? They have turned into the soil of Crete, and we tread on it."

He sighed again. His heart was oppressed today. The evil news of the burning of the Christ the Lord was flying like a raven, croaking, from village to village. It had reached Vrisses shortly before noon. Around Captain Elias sat many old man, wagging their heads and muttering, and many weeping women.

Captain Elias pretended not to see or hear: he was trying to deflect their thoughts from the great misfortune by reminding them of worse disasters in the past.

Swift hoofbeats were heard, and all turned to look. Among the olive and plane trees they made out—sometimes obscured, sometimes appearing in the sunlight—a horseman with a black headband.

"Captain Michales!" they cried, in violent agitation. Captain Elias scratched the ground with the end of his stick.

"He's coming back alone," screamed one woman who had just given her child suck, hastily buttoning up her bodice. "Where are our husbands? Where's my husband? The wild boar took them off on his neck!"

"He left the monastery when it was in danger, they say. He ought to be burned!" cried another, and turned to go away so that she might not see him.

"Don't spare him, Captain Elias," said an old man. "Nobody leaves his post like that. Rub his nose in it! You're the eldest and the most respected. We're under his orders and can't show him our tongues. You can!"

Captain Elias raised his stick. "Enough!" he cried angrily. "I don't need your advice."

They bunched together, opening the circle that they had formed around Captain Elias.

Captain Michales approached, sweat soaked and somber. His eyebrows hid his eyes. Mare and rider were steaming in the early afternoon sun.

As he recognized Captain Elias under the plane tree, he wanted to turn, but it was too late. He would have to bite the bitter apple. He dismounted.

"Good day, Captain Elias," he said, stretching out his hand.

The grizzled captain pretended not to see the outstretched hand, and scratched the ground again.

"Let's call it a good day, Captain Michales, even if it isn't one," he replied.

Captain Michales' blood boiled. He gripped the mare's reins and looked as if he meant to mount again and ride away. He was not used to having stones thrown at his feet. He observed the faces around him. They know already, he thought, and his face grew more savage still.

He tore some leaves from the plane tree and threw them down. "It's the way things happen in war, Captain Elias," he said. "You know that well. How often in your time Christians were smoked out. Think of Arkadi."

"Don't dare speak of Arkadi!" shouted the old captain, and both his eyes—the glass one as well as the good—sent out sparks. "Were we, at Arkadi, smoked out, or turned into gods? But at the Christ the Lord—forgive me for saying so—"

He broke off and turned to the women and old men. "Leave us alone. Go to your homes."

All stood up. As they went past Captain Michales the old men threw oblique glances at him, and the women cursed softly and

307

gave him a wide berth. Only the young mother who had just given suck to her child stopped fearlessly in front of him.

"What's become of our husbands?" she asked, looking him straight in the eyes. "Answer for them before God!"

"Get away from here!" shouted Captain Elias. "Silence!"

When they were alone, he leaned on his stick, gave a heave and stood up.

"Captain," he said, "when you arrived, you offered me your hand. I refused it. You have disgraced your name, Captain Michales."

"Even if you are the older," Captain Michales retorted, "even if you are a fighter from 1821, I've something to say to you. And you mark what I say! Whoever speaks to me must weigh his words, Captain Elias!"

"I too have something to say to you."

The gall rose in Captain Michales' eyes. But the man before him was old, old as the hills, a relic of 1821, a fragment from the ruins of Arkadi—he could not touch him. He turned away and stood under the plane tree.

"Why did you ride away in the night and leave the monastery in the lurch?—You don't answer? Where did you go? Didn't you know that the Turks would attack as soon as they found out you had left your post? And they did find out, the dogs. I don't know who betrayed it to them, but that's how the monastery was lost. And you're the one who's to blame!"

Captain Michales felt his temples bursting. He lowered his head. "I'm not the one to blame," he said in a whisper.

"Then who is?" asked Captain Elias, leaning against the tall trunk of the plane tree. "Who is?"

Captain Michales was silent.

"Where were you? Why did you go away? You're not the one to blame, you say. Then who is?" the old man repeated relentlessly.

"Don't ask, Captain Elias," said Captain Michales dully. "It's my business. I owe no explanations to anyone."

"You owe explanations to your forefathers, to my forefathers, to all our forefathers who are part of the earth of Crete on which we tread. Aren't you a Cretan? Aren't you one with the soil of Crete? What do you mean, then, by propping yourself up with the words, 'I owe no explanations'? Have you no shame?"

Captain Michales drove his nails into the trunk of the plane tree. It was the first time he had heard a man speak to him so boldly and contemptuously. Was the old man right? But Captain Michales would not give ground.

"I owe no explanations to anyone," he repeated defiantly. "Only to myself. Good-by, Captain Elias. I want to be alone, to arrive at a judgment."

"From the judgment that you pass we shall see how much soul, and what kind of soul, has remained to you, Captain Michales. Go with the blessing and the curse of the Lord Christ. One thing I've still got to say to you—and remember what I say —Captain Michales, Crete still needs you! You understand what I mean."

The thought had come to Captain Elias that the other might kill himself and that Crete would lose that pillar.

"I understand," Captain Michales answered, and sprang on the mare without touching the stirrups.

Instead of turning right, toward Petrokefalo, as he had planned, he took the road to the left, toward Selena. The sun had set. Night rose from the soil. A fresh wind was blowing from the heights. Captain Michales bared his fevered chest to cool it down.

"She's the one to blame, she, the shameful woman!" he whispered, and halted. He took off his headband and dried the sweat. He breathed deeply. His brain grew clear. He knew now where he was going and what he was seeking—why, instead of making for Petrokefalo he had taken the road toward Selena. Captain Elias was right. The desire came over him to turn back, to seize the old man's hands—those brave banes of the Turks—and kiss them. That was how a man should speak to a man. Mercilessly.

A sturdy old man with a sack on his back and a long shepherd's staff passed him. He did not recognize Captain Michales in the dusk.

"Have you heard the news, friend?" he called out. "The Lord Christ's been burned down."

"Yes, burned down," Captain Michales answered, and drove his horse on to avoid a conversation.

"Damnation take the one who's to blame," cried the old man, shaking his staff at the sky.

309

"Damnation," echoed Captain Michales' voice in the darkness. The slender half-moon set, and the stars in herds circled round the unmoving North Star.

Captain Michales did not raise his eyes to heaven. He kept them fixed on the base of the mountain, where a few pale lights twinkled. He was nearing the small village of Korakjes.

The house of his aunt Kalio stood at the entrance to the village. At this hour the old woman would certainly be asleep. All her life she had got up with the cock and gone to bed with the hens. She had married, borne children, acquired grandchildren and great-grandchildren, and was now crinkled like a currant, hunchbacked and deaf, yet her eyes still had a light in them. Charos had forgotten her.

Captain Michales dismounted and sat down on a stone at the curb. He pressed his head down hard between his two fists. Captain Elias' words were like knives in his heart. "You have disgraced your name, Captain Michales!" he repeated again and again, to give himself courage to carry out his decision. In the village he heard a dog howl long and mournfully, as though it scented Charos near.

My aunt has no dog in her yard, he thought, no one will hear me . . . no one . . . no one. . . . But his mind was neither on his aunt nor the dog. He sighed.

He stood up and peered toward the village. The few lamps still burning went out, one after another. Houses and people sank into sleep. He sprang on the mare and crossed himself.

"In God's name," he muttered, and entered Korakjes.

When he reached his aunt's house he tied the mare to the ring on the tottering door and entered the yard. He knew the place well. On the right, the winepress, the vats, the casks. On the left, the stall for his late uncle's mule and ass, and the compartment for the two oxen. Now the animals were dead and the vineyards divided up among the sons and daughters. In the darkness Captain Michales could feel the decay.

He glided forward. His hand groped through the hatch in the top half of the central door and softly pushed back the bolt. The door opened. He listened, holding his breath. From the small settle, he could catch a sound of quiet breathing, then a slight rustling.

Someone was lying asleep there. Captain Michales' heart throbbed. Who?

He drew near the settle with a thief's tread. His hand lay on his belt, and clutched the hilt of his dagger. His nostrils quivered— no scent of musk. It must be the old woman, he thought, and his heart beat more calmly. He could now make out white hair on the pillow and a shriveled limp cheek. He stepped back.

She's in the middle room, the good one with the icon-shrine, he thought, and his heart again began to swell like the sea.

He stretched out his hand and pushed open the small door. The middle room was faintly lighted by a lamp that stood in front of an ancient icon of All Saints. Two other pictures were visible at either side of it: the Archangel Michael and the Martyrdom of Saint Catherine.

He leaned against the doorpost. On his aunt's old iron bed, he distinguished a body lying under the coverlet. He could see raven-black hair spread out over the pillow, and the air smelled of musk.

His eyes grew dim. He breathed hard. He could not control his heart. With one bound he was into the room, clutching the black-hilted dagger. He held his breath, glided forward on tiptoe and pulled away the coverlet. Her bosom gleamed. His eyes sparkled for an instant, but his brain remained black with the blood that flooded it in waves.

The sleeping woman stirred and sighed. Her lips whispered a secret word, and smiled.

Captain Michales bent down. The light from the little lamp flashed on the dagger. It swooped through the air and plunged to the hilt into the white bosom.

Eminé screamed. She opened her eyes, and saw Captain Michales. Surprise, joy, pain, accusation—all were whirled together in that last look.

"Oh," groaned the man. His body shook with pain. He wrenched the dagger out, to avert death. But it was too late. Eminé's eyes were already glazed.

11

THE GRANDFATHER sat in his yard under the old lemon tree, with a slate and a chalk on his knees. Through the open door he looked out thoughtfully at the mountain. It glimmered softly in the misty dusk. A moist south wind announced rain to the earth. It was cool.

"Winter's coming," he sighed.

He thought of the women and children who had been hunted from their homes by the Turks and had crept into the caves without bread, without sufficient clothing, without men to protect them. He thought of Crete, once more rattling its chains of slavery and not knowing where to stretch out its hands for help. The Franks—those dogs—had no heart; Greece, a beggar mother, had no strength; the rebel Cretans were still small in numbers, and their stocks of arms and food were even smaller. How were they to hold out? And now, on top of that, God was sending them winter and so was taking the side of the Turks.

"Thou art a Cretan and thou shalt be tried," murmured the old man, and closed his eyes. The whole island with its mountains, fruits and people was conjured up in the space between his two temples. How many risings had he lived through? How often had the houses been burned, trees felled, women dishonored, men killed! And always God had refused to turn His eyes upon Crete.

"Is there justice and pity anywhere in the world?" he cried, and struck the slate with his fist. "Or is God deaf and merciless?"

At that moment his grandson Thrasaki came out of the house, and the old man's features lighted up. That was God's answer! All would still end well. Keep calm, old man: think of your grandson!

Thrasaki was sunburned and in his few months in the mountains had grown into a wild animal. More and more he resembled his father in eyes, eyebrows, lips—and self-will. He now went over to his grandfather, took the slate from his hand and looked at it, frowning.

"You've still not written it out," he said severely.

For a month he had been trying to teach his grandfather the alphabet. By dint of strong desire the old man had managed, in spite of his years, to learn a wretched letter or two, in order—so he said —to be able at least to write his name. To be sure, he had in mind a higher aim, but he betrayed nothing of it to his grandson. But the old brain refused to take in those letters, and the heavy hand, used to mattock and gun, adapted itself badly to the brittle chalk. Sometimes the chalk, sometimes the slate, would break in pieces, and Thrasaki would grind his teeth in rage.

His grandfather beat his head. "I had things to do, my child. I wasn't able. Don't scold me."

"What had you to do? You were sitting on the threshold all day. I saw you! If anyone came by, you struck up a conversation with him. I know you kept the slate on your knee, but where are the strokes and the curves? At that rate you'll never learn!"

"Don't scold me, Thrasaki, my child. It's hard for me. My hand doesn't obey me—how can I explain it? I want it to go to the right and it jerks to the left. I press just a little, and at once the chalk breaks. Do you see?"

"All I see is that you'll never learn the letters," answered Thrasaki, shaking his head. "Give me your hand, let me guide it."

But at that moment they heard footsteps. The grandfather looked up, pleased to be released from strokes and curves. A pale, tired stranger came in sight. He wore Frankish clothes, which hung loose about him. In his hand he held an old umbrella, tied up with string.

"Good day, countryman," the grandfather called out, "where are you bound for? Sit down and have a rest. And a drink of raki."

The stranger stopped and leaned on his umbrella. He said nothing.

"Where are you going?" asked the grandfather again.

"For a walk," he answered.

"A walk?" cried the old man, surprised. "Haven't you heard the

313

shooting, dear Christ? The world is breaking to bits, and you're going for a walk? Put down your umbrella and pick up a weapon, I tell you. Aren't you a Cretan?"

"Yes."

"What are you waiting for? Throw that umbrella away!"

The traveler looked at the cloudy sky.

"It's going to rain," he said, clasping the umbrella tightly to him.

Thrasaki meanwhile was examining the traveler's face. Suddenly he shouted:

"Aren't you Mr. Demetros? Mr. Demetros Leanbottom, our neighbor? Your poor wife, Penelope, was quite beside herself, because she didn't know where you had gone."

"Where is she?" asked the other, in agitation.

"How should I know? Probably running around to all the villages to find you."

Big drops began to fall. Demetros opened his umbrella and moved off on his way.

"Do stop, in Christ's name, and let me give you a raki!" cried the grandfather. "Where are you going? It's raining."

"I've got an umbrella," answered Demetros. And he was out of sight.

"What's the matter with him? Who's driving him out, Granddad?" asked Thrasaki.

"His wife," answered the centenarian, laughing. "The poor man's had enough of her and has made off."

Bertodulos in his little cloak, with his guitar slung over his shoulder, came out of the house. For breakfast he had eaten a barley biscuit soaked in vinegar and oil, plus a large chunk of cheese, and had drunk a tankard of wine. The wine had made him gay and he now came into the yard, his eyes dancing, to sniff the air.

He was tired of being cooped up in the house with women and children. He played to them on the guitar, to divert their thoughts from the men fighting in the mountains. When the wind was favorable they could hear ragged firing in the distance. Then the women would step out on the roof and listen, and their souls would fly into the mountains, to their men. Their only comfort then was Bertodulos. He played the guitar and sang pretty *canzone* from Zante, till they grew a little calmer.

"May God guard you, my little Bertodulos," a newly married girl, the pope's daughter Christinia, had said to him the day before yesterday. "A song is like a man. It comforts a poor woman."

The goodhearted old man drew himself up proudly. Is song like a man? he thought. And all these years, like a fool, I never knew. I too might have had a wife and children and lived like a human being. . . .

"What do you mean?" he asked the young woman.

"How could I explain, my little Bertodulos?" she answered, laughing mischievously. "Only we women understand things like that. I shouldn't try prying into them, if I were you."

Now he approached the grandfather and his sharp little mouth had a mocking smile.

"Have we already got past Alpha, little granddad?" he asked. "Have we reached Beta? What sunken rocks have we still to sail around?"

"If you want my blessing," said the grandfather, turning to his grandson, "don't let this gentleman make a laughingstock of you by taking guitar lessons from him. That's a thing that's only for prima donnas!"

Bertodulos cleared his throat, but said nothing—he dared not. A few days ago he had answered the old man back, and the old man had at once seized him under the shoulders and with one arm hoisted him onto a high ledge in the wall. He had shouted, while the women cackled with pleasure, until they got him down with a ladder. So now he merely cleared his throat, squatted down behind the grandfather and hid the guitar behind his back.

"Come, I'll teach you to aim properly, little Thrasos," said the old man. "That's a game for men. Bring me the muzzle-loader."

But Thrasaki had already fetched it and had placed it behind the door. "There it is," he said. "I spent all yesterday cleaning it."

"You have my blessing. You'll be even better than your father. Why are you goggling at me? That's what we want. Woe to us, if the son doesn't do better than his sire! The world would go to pieces."

He laid his hand on his grandson's head and said:

"You must outdo us all, Grandson. We Cretans are not like other people. We have twice as much work to do. In other parts of the world if you're a shepherd, you think of nothing but the sheep. You're a farmer and you think of the oxen, the rain and the crops. Or of your goods, if you're a merchant. But a Cretan thinks of Crete as well. And Crete is a great plague! It takes all you have and is always right! It demands of you even your life, and you give it, and are glad. A great plague it is, you mark my words!"

He laid the weapon across his lap and stroked it, like a living, beloved being.

"This is my life," he said, and applied himself with great attention to the loading.

"Now find yourself a target! There, that raven on the top of the acacia—have you spotted him? Hey! put the old girl to your shoulders! Take aim!"

Bertodulos shut his eyes and stopped his ears. A hollow thunder roared out. Smoke rolled from the muzzle, and the raven fell between the leaves of the tree to the ground.

Thrasaki leaped with joy and ran to pick up the dead bird. He threw it at Bertodulos' feet, to frighten him. The poor count drew back, grabbed his guitar and with trembling lips went back to the women.

All the daughters-in-law and granddaughters had gathered in those rambling buildings. In addition, the day before yesterday, Captain Michales' two neighbors, Mastrapas the bell founder and fat Krasojorgis, with their families, had joined them. The Turks had occupied the villages in which they had taken refuge; they had fled with their beasts of burden, and had thought of Captain Michales' father. His house was accounted an impregnable fortress, he himself a generous man who turned nobody away. As they appeared before the outer door, Krasojorgis, practiced in flattery, raised his hand to his breast and greeted the grandfather.

"Hoary royal eagle, I and Mastrapas the bell founder, neighbors of your son Captain Michales, hunted by the Turks, are come to shelter beneath your wings. Hoary royal eagle, do not drive us forth!"

The grandfather, who liked being flattered, answered smiling, "My wings are broad. Come in!"

Bertodulos, too, greeted the newcomers with ceremony.

"Greetings, Captain Sefakas," said Mastrapas. "They are right when they say your house is a monastery."

But the old man held up his hand. "Welcome," he said harshly, "but on one condition: both of you are here to bear arms! So take a weapon, each of you, and go where the men are. I do not give food to shirkers or cowards! The women and children I will take care of, don't worry about that." And with a laugh he added, "Don't point at Signor Bertodulos. He's a woman and a child, both together."

Everyone laughed. But Krasojorgis and Mastrapas looked unhappy.

"We have no experience at all in warfare, old Sefakas," Krasojorgis ventured to say. "If it comes to fighting, we're lost."

"Well? If you don't go, won't you be lost one day in any case?"

"The later the better, Captain!"

"Bad luck to you!"

Krasojorgis jumped.

"All right, don't be angry, old Sefakas. We'll go. God help us!"

They unloaded the beasts. The women got down, and the other women came to help them. In a covered corner of the yard they made themselves a hearth. In the evening all sat together at the big table. But next morning the grandfather took two guns from a cupboard, gave them to Krasojorgis and Mastrapas and accompanied them as far as the end of the village. There he handed them over to his old shepherd, Charidimos.

"Good morning, Charidimos! Take them at once by the path up the pass, to where Captain Michales has his hide-out. Be careful, the poor fellows are new to the game. Don't go and lead them into a village full of Turks."

He turned to the two recruits and gave them his hand.

"Go with God's blessing. Do your duty! Be men. I take charge of your families. Good luck! Greet the mountains for me!"

A few days later, as grandfather and grandson were chatting of the old man's experiences, hoofbeats rang out from the mountain path and a group of men came riding down the slope. Shielding his eyes with his hand, the grandfather looked toward the mountain, but in the misty air he could make out nothing clearly.

Old Mavradis, the village crier, came by.

"What's the news, Captain Decoybird?" (That was what the grandfather called him.) "Who are those men riding in?"

"They say Captain Stefanes' ship has arrived in Aja Pelaja harbor. It's bringing ammunition and food. . . ."

The grandfather crossed himself.

"Poor motherland," he muttered, "you deprive yourself of the best morsels and send them to us.—And so?"

"And so, these are your son's men, to fetch the treasure. Give them a good reception!"

"They are welcome!" said the grandfather, opening both wings of the gate.

At the head rode Vendusos. "You're no use in a fight," Captain Michales had told him, "but you have knocked about the countryside and you're cunning. So I'll make you our guide."

"Greetings, Captain Sefakas," shouted Vendusos, dismounting. "If it's no bother to you, we'll bed down tonight in your house and, if God wills, ride to the coast tomorrow at crack of dawn."

"Welcome, children! First have a drink," said the old man, stretching out his hand to the newcomers.

Blackened with powder and emaciated, the palikars entered the yard. The women hurried to them and asked eagerly after their menfolk. A fire was lighted. The caldron was put on and the table laid. Night fell, and lamps were lighted; by their light the bony, serious faces gathered around the copious meal. They ate like beasts of prey, their jaws crunching, drank like buffaloes, and their harsh man's smell spread through the house. The women stood around them at a breath's distance, and joyfully served the rugged guests. The grandfather too stood near them and marveled at them without a word.

When they had eaten, drunk and crossed themselves, he said, "Now lie down and sleep. Ah! if only I were young enough to bear all the fatigue with you. What a wretched thing I've become. I sleep in a bed every night, eat and drink morning, noon and night, am a useless guzzler, no longer carry a gun, and nobody shoots at me. I don't wish even my enemies such wretchedness."

"God grant us we may live to reach your wretchedness, Captain Sefakas!" said Vendusos with a laugh.

"You're the guide," replied the old man, "you'll go to sleep last,

Captain Vendusos, however tired you may be. We two must have a word together."

"At your service, Captain Sefakas," answered Vendusos, with an effort suppressing a yawn. "It's not for nothing that I was promoted guide."

The palikars stretched themselves out side by side, wearing their clothes and their weapons, and even before the women had cleared the table the house was shuddering with the din of the snorers.

Since it was cool, the women heaped wood on the hearth and kindled it. The grandfather sat down in front of it with the lyre player by his side, and the two warmed themselves. The old man stared silently into the flames, but his brows twitched with wild eagerness. Finally he could no longer restrain himself.

"One thing I must discuss with you, Vendusos," he said in a whisper. "One thing that makes my heart bleed. But tell me, like a man, what you know. I'm a hundred years old and can't stand lies."

Vendusos guessed the question in advance. He became thoughtful. At length he said:

"I will tell you the truth, the whole truth."

The grandfather lowered his voice still more. "Why did Captain Michales go out that night, when the Christ the Lord was destroyed?"

Vendusos poked the fire. Then he crouched back on the bench.

"Leave the fire alone," said the old man and grasped him by the arm. "Where did he go?"

Vendusos gulped. He was afraid that he would betray all, once he began to speak. "Captain Sefakas, it's not my business!"

"Speak!" commanded the old man, and shook him by the arm. "Speak out, and don't try deceiving me. Why did he go out? Where? He's brought shame upon me. And that's why he cannot look me in the face. He's afraid I shall ask him questions. But by my soul, I've a good mind to go one day—yes, tomorrow!—and seek him out in his hiding-place, call his palikars together and accuse him before them all. And if you don't answer me now, Vendusos, I shall certainly do it, by this fire! And if he still has the impudence after that, let him try to go on playing captain!"

This hoary lion is capable of anything, thought Vendusos, and shuddered. Then he said:

319

"Don't get savage, old Sefakas. I'll tell you the whole thing from the beginning. Be patient."

"I'm patient. I'm listening."

"You know that Nuri Bey had a Circassian girl. . . ."

"Oh," the old man groaned, and beat his breast with his fist. "The shame of it! So there's a woman. . . ."

"To be sure there's a woman," said Vendusos, now determined to reveal all. "Oh, you wanted the truth, there it is!"

"I want the truth. Be sure of that. Only speak softly. Sleep too has ears. Don't let 'em hear us. Well?"

"She was called Eminé. Captain Michales saw her one evening at Nuri's konak and became mad for her. On the day of the earthquake, Captain Polyxigis also saw her, and it was just the same with him. He kept hanging about her house. He had completely lost his wits. Finally he stormed into her house, sighed something to her, got into her bed and made up his mind to marry her, the fool! She was to become a Christian. Baptism and wedding were to be celebrated together, the day after tomorrow, Holy Cross Day."

"Go on . . . go on . . . What has that to do with my son?"

"You'll soon understand. God forgive me, but I believe Captain Michales was even more bewitched by the Circassian's beauty than Polyxigis. On the night he fought before the Christ the Lord, I brought him news: Nuri's relatives had broken into Kasteli and seized the Circassian girl! At once he sprang on his mare to go after them and took ten of us with him. In the early morning we came upon the kidnapers near Cruel Mountain. Your son fell upon them like a raging lion. Never yet have I seen such a heroic deed, Captain Sefakas! All praise to you, who have begotten such a son! The Turks left the woman and fled for their lives."

"Oh," the old man groaned, burying his face in his hands. "So that was it: for a woman's sake he left his post, like a man without honor! The shame of it! Call that a heroic deed?"

"Don't curse him, Captain Sefakas! By my father's loins, your son never once so much as looked at the Circassian girl! 'Vendusos,' he said to me, 'take this woman and bring her to my aunt at Korakjes. Tell her to take care of her until we see what happens next.'"

Vendusos paused and gazed into the fire. He continued: "What happened next you will have to know, old Sefakas."

But the old man did not answer. His face had turned into a skull of wax.

". . . One morning she was found dead—a knife in her heart," whispered Vendusos.

The grandfather stretched out his hand, groped for a wine bottle and drank. He became calmer.

"Who killed her?" he asked softly, as though his voice came from a cave.

Vendusos bowed his head. Should he tell that too? He had formed his own opinion some time ago.

"She must have killed herself . . . she herself had hold of the knife . . . that's what people say."

"Let people say what they like. Who killed her?"

Vendusos raised his head. "Now you may put the pistol to my breast, old Sefakas, but you shall hear it: your son."

"Why?"

Vendusos had got it over with. His heart was lightened. He no longer had any need to dissemble. He replied at once. "Jealousy."

The old man tossed a piece of wood into the fire.

"He did the right thing," he said at last. "A bad beginning, a good ending. The worm was gnawing him. He was right."

"You don't blame him, Captain Sefakas?"

"He was only to blame for one thing: that he left his post. But he has paid for it and is still paying, and one day he will be free. I have confidence in my blood."

"What has the woman done to him?"

"Do you think the woman matters? Only Crete matters. But go now and sleep. And keep your mouth shut! Let no breath of this escape you! If it were to get out, the two captains would kill each other. And that would not be in the interest of Crete. Good night! Go! I shall sit up by the fire."

Morning found the grandfather still in front of the hearth. The fire had gone out. He had fallen asleep with his head on his breast. Vendusos and his wolf pack had already consumed their barley biscuits, drunk several jugs of wine, and moved on. When the grandfather opened his eyes, only the smell of their cigarettes, their boots and their wine-laden breath still hung in the air.

Toward midday, when the women in the yard had finished the

baking and the grandfather had at last formed the letters Alpha, Beta and Gamma on the slate and was longing to show them proudly to his grandson, there appeared at the outer door a young fighter from abroad. He was wearing a fustanella*, jacket, pointed shoes and a high fez with a thick tassel. Over his shoulder hung his gun, and his cartridge pouches were slung across his broad chest. His glance like an eagle's swept over the threshold.

"A Liape†, a Liape!" the women shrieked, half scared, half joyful. The grandfather raised his head from the slate.

"Welcome, Hellene!" he cried. "Come in, young eagle!"

The man with the fustanella raised a slender leg and stepped over the threshold. The women took courage, came closer and admired his supple body. "Oh, what a joy for the eyes of the mother whose son he is!" one whispered. "He's like a Cretan."

The young hero stood before the grandfather and greeted him. "Are you, sir, the man they call old Captain Sefakas?"

"From head to foot. Only I used to be captain, once upon a time. Now I'm only old Sefakas. And what good wind has blown you to my house?"

"I come from Captain Stefanes' ship. My name's Mitros and I'm from Rumelia. I've heard that Crete is fighting, and I've come to fight too. In Syra a man in Frankish clothes, who calls himself your grandson, gave me this letter for you."

The grandfather stretched out his hand and took the letter. He examined it and passed his hand over it with great joy. It came from his favorite grandson: the first-born son of his eldest son Kostaros.—The first grandchild he had dandled on his knees, and the first to call him "Grandpa."

"Thanks, my young hero, for the trouble you've taken," he said, stuffing the letter into his shirt.

With a laugh he glanced at Thrasaki.

"I shall give it to another grandson of mine, a learned one, so that he can read it out to me. But later. Now lay the table, women, we've got a guest of noble lineage, a true Greek. Bring him the best chair to sit on."

They brought an old chair on the back of which was carved the two-headed eagle. The grandfather stood with beaming face in

* Long coat.
† A Greek from the mainland.

322

the middle of the yard. The Rumeliot was reluctant to sit down. He stood in admiration before the strong, snow-white ancient. The old man's like a god, he thought, an immortal.

"Grandfather," he said, seizing the old man's hands, "I hear that you have lived like a great oak tree. You have breathed storms, suffered, triumphed, struggled, labored for a hundred years. How has life seemed to you during those hundred years, Grandfather?"

"Like a glass of cool water, my child," replied the old man.

"And are you still thirsty, Grandfather?"

The graybeard raised his hand, so that the wide sleeve of his shirt fell back and revealed the bony, furrowed arm as far as the shoulder.

"Woe to him," he cried in a loud voice, as though he were pronouncing a curse, "woe to him who has slaked his thirst!"

They were silent for a moment, the young man and the ancient, in mutual wonder. Between the two stood Thrasaki, filled with pride at the old man and the young. And in a circle the women, arms akimbo.

At last the old man asked, pointing to the north, "And what have you brought us by way of news, young warrior, from over there, from Greece? You've no more Turks in your land. You're lucky!"

He sat down on the bench with a sigh, and the Liape sat on the carved chair. Thrasaki sat near his grandfather, gazing insatiably at the man with the fustanella.

"We have no Turks, certainly," answered Mitros, "but we have big landowners, police and politicians. Don't ask me about them, old man."

In the yard there was a smell of hot bread, and the Rumeliot felt faint. He had been fasting since morning. He cast an eager glance at the hot barley cakes. The old man caught the glance and laughed.

"Quick, you women, we'll soon have no strength left," he called. "Bring us some warm bread and some cheese and a jug of wine to put power into the heart."

He let his eyes range over the yard, the barns, the horsepond, the outer door and the wine presses. He brought them to rest on the Rumeliot, and laughed again.

"Do you know why I'm laughing, youngster?" he asked. "By

my soul, people's memory, when it grows old, becomes a cemetery. Sometimes, though, the gravestones suddenly tilt up and the dead climb out. Yes, at this moment, when I see a fustanella in my yard once more, I suddenly remember 1866, and how in this very yard, in the chair in which you are sitting, Captain Liapes (God rest his soul!), a Greek, sat. And my wife and mother-in-law, old Malamo (God rest their souls!) pulled the bread out of the oven. It was autumn, like now, on Saint Drunkard Jorgis' Day. In the village they were settling the wine, opening the casks, and tasting the new vintage. And at that moment there appeared Kastanias (God rest him!), a fellow like from the old days, who could over-take a horse running. With him came Surmeles (rest him!), the famous captain of the steamer *Devil Pandelis* (rest her!). And I said to my eldest son, Kostaros (rest him!): 'Bless that youth of yours, Kostaros, bring us a small cask of wine and let's empty it.' And while I was still speaking, who should appear also from the mountain but Pig-Jorgis (rest him!)—his name suited him—my godfather, a rich owner of herds, with a slaughtered ram over his shoulders and behind him his wife, the black-eyed Angeliko (rest her!), with a soft cheese in each hand? 'Hey, now we've got some good things to eat!' they all shouted (rest their souls!) and burst out laughing. From the street the schoolmaster (God forgive him!) Manelaos, the sweet tooth, who was passing by, heard the laugh-ter, pushed open the door and came in. 'Welcome, schoolmaster,' they cried (God rest them!), 'sit down and do your paper work while we eat and drink.' 'Devil take schoolmastering,' he answered. 'I'm going to eat and drink with you too, and I'll call old Maliario the rhymesmith over, so that he can amuse us with his verses.' With one bound he was outside and fetched Maliario (rest his soul!) with his lyre. He brought, as well, Andrulis from Sfakia (rest him!) with his bagpipes, and Purnaras (God rest him too!—when he opened his mouth to sing, the stones shook). Ah, God rest them all, what's become of their lips and throats and hands?

"I jumped up, took the pipe which I used for filling casks, and made it fast to the bunghole of the cask. 'You wild beasts,' I called out, 'what d'you want glasses for? Do bull calves drink out of glasses? We'll drink straight from the cask—you take a pull, then I take a pull. You start, Captain Liapes, you're the eldest!' I'd hardly finished saying it when he'd grasped the pipe and begun gulping the stuff down, so that there was a gurgling from the cask like from a narghile. God rest him, he drank and drank—we began to think he'd drink the cask dry. Finally we took the pipe away from him, and all the others (God rest them!) had a swill in turn. I wasn't left out either, God be thanked!

"Yes, by God, what a feast that was! Ah, God rest them, how they ate and drank, how they filled their hands with cheese! While we were at it, the ram was roasted, and Liapes, God rest him, got hold of the pipe again. 'You seem to be doing nicely, friends,' came a voice from the door. It was Nechtaris the pope (God rest him!), with the abbot of Our Lady with the Myrtle (rest *him!*). Both of them were as full as sponges with drink. They began dancing in the yard, kicking their legs up high, and singing the funeral hymn, 'To the last greeting come.' And every time they came to the words 'last greeting' they kissed the pipe and took a pull, and from inside the cask there was already the gurgle of the last drops among the lees! Ah, God rest them! what a laughing and singing and mocking of Charos that was! 'Stamp on the earth that's going to eat us,' they cried, and planted their wide soles firmly, some in boots, others barefoot. They had hitched their breeches well up. What bones were those, and what calves, and the hairs on them—real bristles!"

The grandfather fell silent. He stroked his beard thoughtfully. His clear eyes stared into the air, alive with forms. Dread had seized the young man in the fustanella as he listened to the grizzled Cretan peopling his yard with the departed. He could hear the soles of the dead men's feet stamping on the ground, he could see their bristly calves. The women stood some distance away, smiling, and Thrasaki struck the ground happily with his small feet and laughingly challenged Charos. Only poor Bertodulos, who joined them in order to admire the fustanella, shrank back into the house as soon as he saw the apparition of the departed.

The grandfather began to speak again. His eyes were moist.

"I started by laughing," he said, "but now that I've reminded myself of all those people gone under ground, I am sad. No, not sad, but angry. Yes, angry. There's something here that's not right at all! Let God do anything else He likes, but He's done this wrong—may He forgive me! There are men who ought not to die. Why don't the mountains die? These men shouldn't die either.

325

They should remain where they are on earth like pillars and support the heavens. There, there, I'm stamping on you, earth, damn you! Gobble up the fools, the cripples, the crooked mouths! Gobble 'em up! Get rid of them! But not of Captain Liapes and Kastanias and the abbot of Our Lady with the Myrtle and my eldest son Kostaros!"

The grandfather stamped on the ground, and two fat tears welled from his eyes.

"Hey, Grandfather," said Thrasaki, catching him by the hand. "The table's laid. The Liape's hungry."

The old man looked at his grandson, felt the cool little hand on his bony, burning fingers and once more made his peace with God.

"Forgive me, children. I was remembering the ones that have gone and I lost my bearings. But we're still alive. So forward! To table, all the living!"

With these words he sat down on the ground and pulled the table between him and the Rumeliot. He made Thrasaki too sit near him.

"Welcome, countryman! God bless us and keep us always close together!" he said, piling his guest's plate with food.

Meanwhile Vendusos and his wolf pack were approaching the coast. The sea breeze was in their faces, making the tassels on their headbands flutter. Joy gave them wings; they were going to land weapons and load their mules with provisions and give the revolt fresh nourishment. It was all theirs. Greece had sent it for them. And yet—is there any fun in receiving something peacefully and sharing it justly and reasonably? What did they do over the wives? When the parents had come to an agreement, the bride was combed and adorned and the tables were laid; but did meat which one had not stolen taste good? So the bridegroom would storm in on horseback and seize the bride. She would pretend to resist. He would lift her onto his saddle and make off with her like lightning, shooting in all directions and yelling, to his home.

Captain Stefanes' corsair ship, the *Miaulis*, had managed in the darkness to elude the Turkish patrol vessels. She had run the blockade and landed in the small remote harbor of Aja Pelaja, under its mighty cliffs. The sea was gentle as milk. The neighboring villages had not yet noticed that a loaded ship was anchored off their beach. So Captain Stefanes had had time to unload his freight undisturbed and to spread it out on the cliffs.

The sun today was mild, autumnal. The sea mews circled over the ship or squatted on the rocks and watched. Captain Stefanes had come ashore and was hobbling up and down over the thick-strewn flints. He had also brought Saint Nicholas ashore and made him fast to a rock so that his face was turned to the ship. The saint could sun himself, but he was also to keep watch.

"Hurry up, children!" the captain called out to his sailors, "don't let the Turks catch us. Don't give the Christians time, either, to find us and start plundering. They're the ones I'm most afraid of. Be quick, children! Captain Michales' palikars will turn up, wherever they may be."

"There they are already!" shouted the ship's boy, who had climbed to the top of the mast. He pointed at the ten palikars, who came riding down on their mules.

Captain Stefanes turned round and recognized Vendusos at their head. With a laugh he called out to him, "Have you too joined the warriors?"

"That's what I've been condemned to," answered the other, jumping off his mule and embracing the captain. "You've come in the nick of time. We'd no powder left, and hunger was beginning to worry us. A thousand times welcome, Captain Stefanes!"

But the seaman was in a hurry. "Help us unload," he said. "so that I can sail away promptly, as soon as it's night. I've been caught once, and that's enough. Go at it, get going! Pretend you're robbing us, to make it more fun."

Vendusos took him by the arm and led him aside. "Greetings from Captain Michales," he said to him in a low voice. "And if you've any message . . ."

"What message?" asked Captain Stefanes, scratching his head.

"Entrust it to me. No one except Captain Michales shall know of it."

Captain Stefanes bent down, picked up a big pebble, and threw it into the sea. He threw another and still said nothing. At last he plucked up courage and said:

"Vendusos, you're a good lyre player, I know. But, forgive my saying so, I've no trust in that little tongue of yours. As soon as you've had a drop too much . . ."

Vendusos sighed. "Where am I to get a drop too much? Don't worry. . . ."

Captain Stefanes looked at Vendusos searchingly. The sun had browned him. His body was taut, the fat had vanished from his neck and cheeks, and his eyes now shone with something other than wine.

"Open your ears then, Vendusos," he said, in a muffled voice. "Report to Captain Michales my exact words—do you understand? Don't soften them, and don't blow them up."

"You needn't worry, Captain. Speak out."

"I've no good news to send him. I've knocked at some important doors, spoken with leading men and urged them to tell me the truth: whether they had any hope that Crete would be freed, or thought that all our pains would again be thrown to the winds. Some of them beat about the bush, others talked a lot of high-sounding nonsense, and only one man spoke out honestly. And who was he? Captain Michales' nephew Kosmas, who had just landed in Syra—he'd come from the Franks' country. 'You must be brave, Captain Stefanes,' he said to me. 'Crete will not see freedom this time either.' 'Will our blood be shed in vain, then?' I asked. 'Blood is never shed in vain,' he answered. 'Don't you know that freedom is a grain of seed that needs blood in order to sprout? So we're sprinkling the seed now, and it's certain that one day the plant will come up—but that day hasn't arrived yet.' Then he pulled a letter out of his pocket and gave it to me. 'Send it,' he said to me, 'by a trustworthy man to my grandfather, old Sefakas.' It's been sent to him already, by a Liape who was on board our ship. Captain Michales can learn the rest from that letter."

Vendusos listened while his feet kicked the pebbles about violently. When Captain Stefanes had finished speaking he burst out, "Is there no God, then? What do you think, Captain Stefanes?"

"What's a poor wretch like me to think? I don't even know if there's a Saint Nicholas, and are you asking me about God? And Saint Nicholas is sometimes there when he's wanted, and sometimes he's not there when he's wanted. I've learned that much, in the many years I've been beating up and down the sea. So let's not talk about God, but see what happens."

328

The sea was growing dim as the sun sank. The hull of the ship had been emptied, and guns, cartridges, leather equipment, flour and salted fish were now loaded on the backs of the mules— sheer gifts of God to the Cretans.

"I'll bring you more powder and food yet," cried Captain Stefanes to the ten corsairs by way of good-by. But as he was about to jump on board, he remembered the icon.

"Oh mercy, I've forgotten Saint Nicholas!" he said, and limped up the cliff as fast as he could. He carried the icon down and dipped it in the sea to refresh it. Then he kissed the hands of the saint, still dripping with salt water.

"On the journey here you managed well, Nicholas, my captain!" he said to the icon. "Good luck to you, and now mind you don't disgrace us on the return journey. And I vow, by the sea, that I'll order a picture of you from the holy Mount Athos, with short breeches and a black fez and a telescope in your hand, like the sea-hero Miaulis. Miaulis and Saint Nicholas in one—that would be safest. . . ."

He leaped aboard. Clouds were now gathering in the sky. The world grew dark. A light breeze was blowing from the land, and a swell was beginning. Captain Stefanes picked up his telescope. The sea seemed dead. He crossed himself.

"In God's name," he said. "Weigh anchor, children! Saint Nicholas, we're casting off!"

After he had eaten and drunk and the table had been cleared away, the Liape leaned against a doorpost. He was feeling the effect of the rough sea, which had turned his insides upside down. It was the first time he had come down from the Pindus Mountains and boarded a ship. His hero's courage had melted away when he had soiled his fustanella. Even now it seemed to him as if the earth were swaying under his feet like the ship's deck. He smelled horse dung and felt better. He remembered that tomorrow morning, early, Charidimos, the old shepherd, was to take him to Captain Michales' citadel. He gave himself up to sleep with a feeling of security.

When the grandfather heard him snoring, he beckoned Thrasaki, and sat down with him under the old lemon tree in the middle of the yard. The women were no longer working at the oven and had gone indoors. Silence reigned over the yard. It was a good opportunity to have the letter read. The grandfather expected grave news; his grandson Kosmas would not have written unless it was important. The old man pulled out the letter and tore open the envelope.

"Come, Thrasaki," he said, "read it slowly, word by word, so that I can understand."

Thrasaki read:

"Honored Grandfather, I have returned to the sacred soil. Perhaps I shall soon come to Crete and kiss your respected hand . . ."

"He's a flatterer too," muttered the old man, shaking his heavy white-haired head. "But what sort of a letter is this? He doesn't begin by asking after our health. All right! Go on, Thrasaki."

". . . But before such a pleasure can be vouchsafed to me, I find myself compelled to write you this letter. As soon as you have read it, be sure to send it to my uncle Michales. I hear he has raised his banner and is once more fighting in the mountains against the Turks. It is good that he should know how things are, and not grope forward blindly. Afterward let him do as God enlightens him."

"A long yarn. Still, read on. But slowly, Thrasaki, there's a good lad."

". . . So then: from Greece no hope is to be looked for. She is too weak. A poor beggar of a country without a fleet and—what is worse—without the slightest support from the Franks. Crete is a good morsel. And the mighty of the earth are interested in its remaining on the Sultan's plate. If he comes to grief and the heritage has to be divided up, each of the Great Powers hopes that Crete will fall to it. If, on the contrary, Crete became united with Greece, neither God nor the Devil could separate them again."

"Oh," groaned the old man, "this grandchild of mine has learned a lot. Go on!"

". . . Realize, then: this time, too, Crete is condemned to failure. We can have success only in one way: by starting negotiations to get the Sultan to enlarge our rights. This, I know, is merely a bone, but it has some meat on it. Let's gnaw it till the good moment comes."

"We're reduced to dogs, mangy dogs. People throw bones to us! Go on."

". . . I have spoken with many official personages among the Franks and in Greece. Tomorrow I am going to Athens to see some men who are very highly placed. If necessary I shall come to Crete, to help save what can be saved. This time again, unfortunately, the pen will be mightier than the sword. The sword-bearers have done their duty and prepared the way. But they could not reach the goal. Now the pen-bearers are going into action— don't be angry with me, Grandfather. . . ."*

"These quill-drivers!" the grandfather shouted, and spat. "Glasses, tight breeches, hats, swallowtails and stockings! Ugh!"— and again he spat.

He turned to Thrasaki. "Finished? Is there any more?"

"One sentence, Granddad: *'I kiss your hand with deep respect, Grandfather. Give me your blessing! Your grandson, Kosmas.'* "

The grandfather's head sank. He closed his eyes and saw Crete, bewildered and bloodstained, standing before him in the middle of the yard. Was it Crete? Or was it the Virgin, coming from her Son's cross? Large drops of rain fell.

"My little Thrasos," said the grandfather at last, "you have learned a secret. You're a man. Don't betray it!"

"Don't worry, Granddad. Not a soul shall know. Only we two, and a third—my father."

"And a fourth—God. That's enough."

While grandfather and grandson were still talking, Tityros, red-cheeked, appeared on the threshold with his staff and his sack on his back. The grandfather still sat under the lemon tree, now wet with rain, and raindrops glittered in his beard. He himself was like an old tree trunk as, without stirring, he let himself be sprinkled. The old man's leathery skin gleamed wetly. For a moment he did not recognize his son, who looked stout and sunburned and without a stoop.

"Is it you, Janakos?" he called out, and raised his head to see better. "You've changed, thank God. Aren't you a teacher any more? Come in."

"Don't you know me, Father?" asked the teacher, delightedly.

"How should I? I'd be ready to swear you've given up paper work and fashioned yourself a neck, a pair of shoulders and good, healthy cheeks. Didn't I tell you? Those letters are leeches, twenty-

331

four leeches that suck a man's blood. I too have been trying hard to learn that damned alphabet. A stony road! A torment! I stumble from one letter to another. But I've got a definite aim. What about you?"

Tityros laughed. He seized his father's hand and kissed it. "Father," he said teasingly, "it was your fault that I became a teacher. Do you remember?"

"Of course I remember. Do you think I've grown feeble? You were no good for anything else. But really, I was wrong."

The old man looked him up and down, pinched his arm, squeezed his hand and pulled up his lip, as they do with cattle, to examine the teeth. He was satisfied.

"By my faith," he said, "this one's beginning to be a pleasure to me. Of course, you were my child, I was fond of you—but how shall I put it? You were no pleasure to me. You seemed to me like the lather from soap, with your book learning and your stoop. You didn't fit into our family. All our forefathers had worn full breeches and high boots, and carried a gun. But you dressed in the Frankish style, wore glasses and carried a pen. That's that, I thought, the blood's exhausted and is going to the devil . . . But now here you are, coming back to the natural way of men, thank God! And my name isn't Sefakas if I don't give you some full breeches and high boots and hang a gun over your back! Did you hear what I said? Why are you laughing?"

"Are you a prophet, Father? Can you read my mind? That's just what I've come to the house of my fathers for, I swear! You're bound to have an old suit that you or one of my dead brothers used to wear. And surely there's a gun left in your storeroom. We'll burn my Frankish clothes together, here in the yard, like they burn Judas, and I'll dress like a Cretan. Then I'll take a gun on my shoulder and go into the mountains. I too have a special aim."

The old man embraced his son. "Take my blessing," he said. "I'm going to kill a goat in your honor, and this evening we'll celebrate. I had thought of you as lost. Welcome, Janakos!"

The old man forgot his grief over his grandson's letter. He opened an old chest and brought out the finest clothes he could find: an embroidered jacket, full breeches of thick wool, a silken linen belt and a fez from Tunis. He chose boots of the smallest size, and brought a gun from the storeroom. He placed all these on top of the chest, to deck out his youngest son on the morrow like a bridegroom.

There was great rejoicing in the house. For the rumor had been spread that the Turks had set a trap for the schoolteacher in the course of his wanderings through the villages and that they had taken him prisoner and spitted him like an Easter lamb. And now here he was, in full health, devouring with his father a whole small kid and drinking wine out of the jug. Beside the two of them Thrasaki felt quite small! He could hardly bring himself to eat. He simply stared in bewilderment at the schoolmaster. Was this the same man under whose feet they had strewed shot so that he fell full length and broke his glasses?

"Off with you, Thrasaki, to bed with you," said the grandfather. "I've still some things to say to your uncle. And never call him schoolmaster again, do you hear? Always Uncle Janakos now!"

"What was the truth of that business with your wife?" he asked, when they were alone and seated on the low sofa. "Why did she hang herself? Can you explain it? I've asked the others, but they all put me off with talk."

"God forgive her. The poor thing was sick with fear and ran away."

"She did right," the grandfather said. "There was strength in the woman. It takes courage to kill oneself. She was running away from you as well, that's sure. And now what do you mean to do? Won't you marry again? Won't you beget me a little grandson? My last? You must hurry up. My days are numbered."

The schoolmaster's face beamed as he said, "What a miracle, Father! The nearer you come to death, the more you resemble an immortal. Yes, you've discovered the second purpose that brought me here."

"Well, tell me, Janakos! Has a girl dazzled your eyes?"

"Yes, she's dazzled me, and I ask for your blessing."

"Who is she, by Saint Onufrios? Is she all right? Strong bones, broad hips, a good family with lots of vineyards and fields? Has she her thirty-two teeth?"

"She's all right," the bridegroom-to-be answered. "She's got all her teeth—thirty-two and more."

"No, not more! That would not be good. Then she could ride

333

you. A thing that's unnatural is against God's will. Thirty-two are enough. But let's hear who she is. Who are her parents?"

"She's a grandchild of Captain Elias. Her name's Pelaja. And I've come to ask for your blessing."

"Ah, bravo, Janakos! You have my blessing! That's a fruitful stock with sons, grandsons, vineyards and fields. And will she have you?"

"She'll have me and has spoken to her father. He answered, 'We'll ask the old man—he's head of our race!' At first Captain Elias looked sour. 'A schoolmaster,' he said, 'I know him. A lean-bottomed weakling. All the same, his family's all right. Fruitful, with sons and grandsons and vineyards and fields. Wait till I've had time to think it over.' But the girl was in a hurry, and she talked to the grandfather and was nice to him and won him over to our side. 'Good,' he said. 'I give my blessing, but on one condition—he's to put off that Frankish suit of his and dress like a man.'"

Old Sefakas clapped his hands. "God protect you, old Elias! It was a great worry to me too, but I said nothing. And now, into the fire with that suit, tomorrow, first thing!"

The schoolmaster slept well, close to the chest with his bridegroom's outfit. Pelaja came into his dreams and he had no wish to wake up. But the grandfather did not close his eyes. He watched at the window impatiently for dawn to come. The black cock crowed, then the white, and the bright day had arrived.

The old man sprang up and gave Tityros a kick. "Wake up," he called out, "the clothes are lying on the chest. May they bring you happiness! And bring that Frankish suit into the yard. I'm going to light a fire."

He had always disliked the Franks. Now, after his grandson's letter, they made him furious. He went downstairs. The women were not up yet. He lighted the fire. Then he went to wake Thrasaki, who slept in one of the big vats that was like a cradle. He shook him awake.

"Get up, Thrasaki! Come into the yard with me. We are going to burn Judas!"

The schoolmaster appeared, a Cretan from head to foot. He placed his old breeches, waistcoat, jacket, hat and shoes together in a pile in the middle of the yard. They poured petroleum over them, so that the devil might receive them that much sooner. The grandfather handed a piece of burning wood to his grandson and said:

"Come, my child, send 'em to the devil! The Franks have burned us, now we're burning them. Fire for fire! Wind for wind!"

Thrasaki grasped the burning wood and threw it onto the oil-soaked clothes. They flared up at once, lighting the three faces. The grandfather's soles tickled him, and he wanted to dance. When the fire had done its work, he took a handful of ashes, opened the outer door, stood in the middle of the street, raised his hand and strewed the ashes in the air.

"You Franks," he cried with passionate scorn, "may the eyes of my children or of my children's children live to see the day when your houses and factories and kings' palaces burn and dwindle into the air as ashes. As you have burned us, you Franks, may you too burn!"

Toward noon Mitros of Rumelia, sweating from the climb, arrived at the headquarters of Captain Michales. On the highest of the mountain plateaus about a hundred palikars were quartered in a dozen stone huts. Far below them stretched a plain ringed by mountains, on which the villages showed like white flocks. Two of them were burning, and in the stillness the smoke hung above them like some friendly, protecting cloud.

Captain Michales was standing high up on his lookout post, holding a pair of field glasses. These were a present from a Frank, a philhellene who had climbed up to the mountain camp a month before and had not had the heart to leave it.

"Where should I go?" he had said to Captain Michales. "Why should I go down to the towns again? I like it here. Nowhere have I eaten more delicious bread, nowhere have I drunk more immortal water, nowhere have I seen men more like the Greeks of old! I shan't call you Captain Michales, but Captain Achilles. My name's Erikos."

He wore a domed hat, which resembled an ancient helmet. His pockets were full of papers and pencils. He carried on conversations with the Cretans in his modern Greek gibberish and eagerly and continuously made notes.

The Cretans laughed. "He's cracked," one said.

"He writes for the papers," was another's opinion.

"Hey, countryman, what do you think you're doing in Crete without a weapon?" they asked him. "Where's your gun?"

"Here!" he replied, pointing to his pencil.

He had a fair, pointed beard, and his cheeks were rosy. Two of his front teeth were gold. On his head a thick tuft of hair stood on end, and when the Cretans heard that his name was Erikos the tuft made them twist it into "Kukurikos."

One day when Captain Michales' palikars gave battle to a band of Turkish soldiers on the plain below, he had accompanied them, yelling, "Forward, Captain Achilles!" He himself had no weapon. He stood up all the time and took notes furiously. A wild Cretan who was very fond of Kukurikos ran up to him bringing him as a present a Turk's head, which he carried by the hair, while the blood dripped from it. When Kukurikos saw the head, he gave a cry and fell down in a faint.

The Cretans laughed. "What a cotton-wool bottom the man is!" they said, and flung a jugful of water over him to bring him to himself.

When Captain Michales came on the scene, he shouted at them, "Do you think all men are Cretans? Stop acting like fools!" He turned to Furogatos. "Help the poor fellow make the climb back."

From that day Kukurikos had lain in a fever. He was pale and could not bring himself to eat meat. He had bad dreams. Life with the ancient Greeks no longer seemed rosy, and he decided to go. One gray, rainy morning he took leave of Captain Michales.

"The ancient Greeks are wonderful, Captain Achilles, but it's difficult to live their life. I'm a professor—that's to say, a school-master—a good man but made of paper. You're made of flesh and blood. I can't stand up to you. Good-by, and take this to remember me by!"

He took from his neck the cord with the field glasses, and hung it around the neck of Captain Michales. "You're a captain, so you must see further than your palikars."

And now Captain Michales held these field glasses to his eyes and examined the plain. Behind the clouds of smoke over the burning villages he thought he could see the movement of red

fezzes. Fresh troops had come from Megalokastro and were form-
ing to attack the heights. "The dogs are short of nothing," he muttered. "Our position's weak, and there are only a few of us. And
Captain Polyxigis keeps us waiting. I must send him another message."

As he lowered the field glasses and was about to ask whether
Vendusos was back from the coast, he beheld in front of him
Mitros in his fustanella.

"Greetings, Captain. I'm from Captain Stefanes' ship," Mitros
said, holding out the letter.

"Welcome, countryman," said Captain Michales, shaking hands
with him. "Go and join the other palikars, while I read the letter."

Hastily he tore open the envelope. Inside he found an opened
letter and a small piece of paper. On this he recognized his son's
handwriting, and his somber face lighted up for a moment. "I,
Thrasaki, send you greetings, and here is a message from Granddad:
'Read the letter, and do as God enlightens you. There is no hope
for us, and this time too we are threshing empty straw. So take
counsel with your heart and weigh your decision.' "

He frowned, and drew his upper lip back so that his teeth were
bared. "God forbid," he growled, "I should take counsel with my
heart. The world would be blown sky-high."

He unfolded his nephew's letter. Syllable by syllable he read on,
moving from word to word as though he were climbing up a mountain. From time to time he paused and groaned; then he continued to read. When he reached the end, he tore the letter into
a thousand pieces and put a match to it. "I alone must know this,
nobody else," he said, stamping on the ashes.

. . . No hope then! The motherland weak, the Franks treacherous, the Cretans too few. . . . No, in spite of everything, I'm not
stirring from my post. I'm not giving up my eyrie! God cannot
desert me and order, "Give it up!" I'm not giving it up!

He grasped the field glasses again and looked down. Still more
red dots showed on the plain, and from the ravines more and more
troops were emerging. The pasha had sworn to thrust Captain
Michales' band from the eagle's nest where it had dug in its claws,
into the abyss. Exhausted, wounded Crete was gradually returning
to peace: only isolated shots were now heard, and only isolated
blockheads still held their refuges above the precipes and refused

obedience. The Sultan was angry. He sent the pasha a shipload of chains and ordered him to capture the rebel Cretans and send them in chains to Constantinople. If not, he might come in person and tackle them himself.

This command made the pasha's blood race. He felt that his head was no longer firm on his shoulders, and decided to give up his agreeable life in Megalokastro and lead his soldiers against Captain Michales. The Metropolitan heard, and sent a secret message to the captain: "Escape! Take ship and escape! The pasha has sworn your downfall."

But Captain Michales stiffened in his defiance. I'm not escaping, he thought. There's a heavy guilt weighing on my neck. There's a monastery burning day and night in my heart. I must pay for my guilt. Even if all the others leave, I'm staying here on the cliffs, and I'd rather pour oil over my clothes and hair, to burn as you did, Christ the Lord!

He swept the plain with his field glasses. On the slopes more Christian villages were beginning to burn.

"Captain Polyxigis is late," he said again, examining one mountain path after another. "He'll come, all the same. He's given his word. This is war, and in war I trust him."

Since the terrible moment when he had plunged his knife into the Circassian woman's heart, Captain Michales had felt the old friendship returning. He now thought of Captain Polyxigis without hostility—indeed, with compassion. The villages had echoed with the funeral, and Polyxygis' friends had had to prevent him from killing himself. He now went everywhere dressed from head to foot in black. Wherever there was fighting, he flung himself on the Turks blindly, seeking death. He was convinced that the Turks had killed Eminé to prevent her baptism, and he had sworn to build a tower of Turkish corpses upon her grave.

With joy Captain Michales heard voices and the hoofbeats of mules. He bounded from rock to rock down to the plateau, and reached it just as Vendusos and his ten booty-laden palikars arrived. Everyone fell on the mules and unloaded them. Fires were lighted. For days the men had lived on dry bread, and they were longing for a hot meal. They stowed the supplies away safely in their chief's stone hut.

"Thank our Mother," cried Vendusos, firing a pistol shot into

338

the air, "thank our beggar Mother, who's hungry herself and sends us food!"

"Vendusos," shouted the captain, "don't waste your bullets. Come here. I want you to do something."

The lyre player went over to him and listened intently to what he said. Then he balanced on tiptoe, ready to run off.

"D'you understand, Vendusos? It's very urgent! And take care they don't kill you on the way there! On the way back it doesn't matter so much."

"I shan't give you that pleasure," said Vendusos with a laugh. "Not even on the way back. By the Virgin with the bunch of grapes, I've still got a lot of casks to drink dry. And drink them dry I will."

He started off toward the valley. Furogatos caught hold of him by the breeches as he came by.

"Brother Vendusos, did you see my friend Bertodulos? What's the poor chap doing? Do you know, I think more about him than about my wife? Extraordinary, isn't it?"

"He's all right. Hasn't any worries. I saw him at old Sefakas'. He stays with the women and will soon be wearing a skirt."

"What's become of our drinking parties in Captain Michales' cellar, Vendusos? Did I only dream them?"

But Vendusos had already hurried on.

Bent over the slate, old Sefakas held the chalk as loosely as he could, so as not to break it, and anxiously wrote the letters, one after the other. In the last few days he had felt a strange weakness, as if his strength were leaving him and flowing back to the earth. He had grown pale, he could not sleep, and his knees trembled.

I must hurry if I want to learn in time, he thought. And now he used all his strength to force the reluctant hand to move. In spite of the difficulties he formed fine, clear capitals.

"I don't need the small letters," he told his master Thrasaki, who wanted to push him on to fresh efforts. "My work can be done with the capitals."

Grandfather and grandson sat on the threshold.

"Today, Thrasaki," said the old man, "you're not going to scold me. I've got my lesson at my fingers' ends. Look here!"

339

With pride he displayed the slate full of capitals.

"The whole alphabet," boasted the grandfather, "from alpha to omega."

"Bravo, Granddad! You get high marks today! How did you manage to learn it all so suddenly?"

"I haven't much time now, Thrasaki, so I took myself in hand. And now the time has come. Listen, and I'll tell you my secret. Do you think I wanted to learn to read at my age? Why should I? With my hundred years, I know everything and I know nothing."

"What did you want then, Granddad?"

"I simply wanted to learn to write one thing, Thrasaki, before I die."

"What?"

"A Cretan saying. Put your hand on my hand and guide it. Only three words." And now he whispered, "Freedom or death."

"Oh," cried Thrasaki, "that's it! Now I understand."

"You don't understand yet, my Thrasaki. Don't be in too much of a hurry for that. . . . Now guide my chalk."

With both hands the child grasped the grandfather's hard, callused hand and guided it slowly and patiently, until on the slate in large letters there stood the words:

FREEDOM OR DEATH.

12

Icy winds were blowing from the snow-covered peaks. Crete froze. On the slope of Selena, below Captain Michales' camp, there was a large cave, filled to overflowing with women and children. It was here that the Christian women had taken refuge in all the risings, to escape the knives of the Turks. In the 1821 rising the Turkish soldiers had flung burning branches into the cave and suffocated those who were crowded inside. Their bones still glimmered in the damp and frosty air of the cave; and now, once more, women and children stretched themselves out on these same old bones, shivering with hunger and cold and in danger of being killed by the Turks, to leave their bones too to whiten here. By day they would go out to gather a handful of grasses, roots and acorns; they lived on these like cattle. To give themselves courage they kept glancing up at the cliffs where Captain Michales was entrenched. As long as he held out, they were not afraid.

Yet already Turkish soldiers had climbed up the slope and were nearing the narrow ravine which led to the cave. Alerted by the shrieks of the women, Captain Michales came down from his eyrie. In the bitter battle that followed, some of the women had the courage to rush to the help of the men with knives and clubs. The rest knelt wailing in the cave and cried out to God.

The Christians were outnumbered and starving, while more and more Turkish soldiers came up from the plain, driven on by the raging pasha. He had sworn to send the head of Captain Michales, embalmed and wrapped in a turban, to Constantinople as a present to the Sultan.

Toward afternoon the Christians began to waver. The Turks gave a howl of delight that drowned the wailing of the women.

But God intervened. To the rear of the Turks appeared Captain Polyxigis with his men, to spread confusion among the redhats. Some were already fleeing to the plain. Together the two leaders hunted the enemy on their mares. In the heat of the slaughter neither noticed that he was wounded. In the evening they went back to their citadel and had their wounds bandaged. They felt their hunger more violently than their wounds. The palikars opened the newly received treasure: bread, olives, onions, cheeses.

In the stone hut over which Captain Michales' banner waved, the two captains sat side by side on the floor, feasting. Through the holes in the rude walls a cutting wind whistled its way in. Snow was whirling outside. Thodores entered with an armful of brushwood. He lighted a fire for the two wounded and freezing men. Then he went out again, to leave them alone. From the few words of their conversation that his ear had caught, he felt certain they wanted no one else present.

"Blessings on you, Captain Polyxigis," said Captain Michales. "God sent you. The dogs already had us by the throat."

As he spoke he gazed at his comrade with pity and affection. Captain Polyxigis, dressed in black and with a black cloth wound round his head, appeared suddenly aged and pale. He ate but his thoughts were elsewhere.

"Your health, Captain Polyxigis," said Captain Michales, raising the bottle to his mouth.

"Yours, Captain Michales. Mine's gone. . . ."

Captain Michales' heart contracted. Not for the sake of the woman he had killed. She had had to be killed, so as not to divide the two men. Since the night of the murder his heart had been lightened. He was no longer ashamed when he was alone. His spirit had shaken free of the Circassian, and he fought for Crete single-mindedly. He was sorry only for the good palikar, who was pining away for the loss of a woman.

"Captain Polyxigis," he began, "I have something to say to you. Forgive me, but it is shameful to be thinking of a woman while Crete swims in blood. I tell you, on my honor, if a woman stood in the way of my fulfilling my duty, I would kill her with my own hand."

"Captain Michales, you're a wild beast. I'm a man," answered Captain Polyxigis, and threw away the piece of bread he had

342

been holding in his hand. He felt as if his throat were in a noose. He turned to look at his friend. He felt ice-cold.

The two huddled over the fire, gazing silently into the flames. Thodores came in again, added some brushwood and tiptoed out.

The voice of Captain Michales broke the silence, choking, hollow, as though from a long distance. "Do you know who killed her?"

He was overcome by the desire to stake all on one throw: heads or tails.

Captain Polyxigis stared at him. He had not the strength to answer. He waited.

"Do you know who?" the voice asked again.

"Do *you* know?"

"Yes."

Captain Polyxigis seized Captain Michales by the arm. "Who?"

"Not so fast. Don't go wild! You can't hurt a hair on his head! He is beyond death."

"Who?"

"Wait, I tell you. First I must reveal to you a secret—a bitter one. Listen quietly. And when you've heard it, you'll be ashamed, I swear, and not think of women any more, or of their murderers, or of yourself either."

"Who?" the other asked again, with burning eyes.

"I've received a letter—which I've torn up and burned—from my nephew Kosmas. Captain Polyxigis, our labor is once more in vain, our blood will have been shed senselessly. This time too Crete will not see freedom. Greece is weak, the Franks have no honor, the Sultan has the power."

But Captain Polyxigis was not listening. Leaping up, he hit his head with a dull thud against the stone wall.

"Who killed her? Who? Everything else later!"

"I did," answered Captain Michales, standing up and meeting his friend's glance calmly and firmly. "I did, Captain Polyxigis."

Captain Polyxigis leaned against the stones, and his brow darkened.

"No, no!" he shouted at last. "That's impossible! You? You!"

"I had to kill her or you. I thought of Crete. You are a good fighter. Crete needs you. So I killed her. It lightened my heart. Yours too will grow light again. Don't fumble for your knife. If

343

you like we can bar the door, put out the lamp and fight it out here and kill each other. But think of the women and children in the cave. Their lives depend on us. Think of our forefathers. Think of Crete. Then decide."

Captain Polyxigis reeled and fell. He buried his face in his hands. His chest was heaving. He could no longer control his sobs.

"When I read that there is no more hope," Captain Michales went on, without paying any attention to his friend's tears, "I don't know what demon it was rose up in me, Polyxigis. Instead of letting it press me down, I felt a new, savage courage. So that's how it is with you, Great Powers, I thought, you refuse to give Crete freedom. Shame upon you! I, Captain Michales, I, a little Cretan porcupine, don't need you! And let God leave Crete in the lurch if He pleases—I'm not!"

He touched Captain Polyxigis lightly on the shoulder.

"Captain," he said gently, "aren't you ashamed of yourself?" The other mastered his tears. The murderer's words bored into his head.

"Since the hour I lost all hope, Captain Polyxigis," Captain Michales went on, "I've had the feeling, by the soil on which we tread, that I'm immortal. Who can do anything to me now? What can death do against me? Even if all the Turks come storming at me, my ear lobe won't twitch. I am like Arkadi: my clothes, hair and guts are full of powder, and when I see that there's nothing else for it, I'll blow myself sky-high. Do you understand?"

And it was true—only defiance and pride now found room in him. Was it a demon, a God or some wild idea as old as history? He himself did not know. He knew only one thing clearly: whatever might happen, he would not stoop to curse his destiny or to bewail it. He would come to terms with neither the devil nor God nor the Sultan. He would blow himself sky-high like Arkadi.

Captain Polyxigis stood up. Violently he tugged the heavy cloth straight around his head.

"I cannot sleep in the same house with you, Captain Michales," he said, "nor do I want us to kill each other as long as our country is at war, nor will I desert you in danger. But we two will have our reckoning as soon as Crete is at peace again. For you have turned my heart to ashes, Captain Michales."

344

And without another glance at the murderer, he walked out the door.

The women had climbed onto the flat roof, to scour its dangerous burden of snow. With sighs they gazed out at the mountain. What, O God, was happening to the Christians up there? Katerina raised her eyes to the snow-covered peaks and thought of her fear-inspiring husband.

Today the sun was shining brightly, the sky was deep blue, the air icy. The grandfather sat by the hearth and stared into the flames. For some days he had not spoken. He grew paler and paler and remained sunk in dark thoughts.

As Thrasaki entered, the grandfather stood up. He had ordered a tin of red paint and a brush brought him from Kasteli. He beckoned to Thrasaki.

"Take the paint, little Thrasos. Let's go. And give me the brush."

"Where are we going, Granddad?"

"You'll soon see. Be quick, while it isn't snowing."

They reached the street door. Grandfather and grandson looked out at the village, which lay as though dead, swathed in snow. The gleaming, intact snow made everything beautiful. Thrasaki could not marvel enough at this overnight transfiguration of the village.

The grandfather pulled a large, many-colored handkerchief out of his belt and began to clean the snow from the door. Then he took the lid off the tin and dipped the brush into the paint. "In God's name!" he murmured.

"What are you doing, Grandfather?"

"You'll soon see."

He raised the brush and began, slowly and carefully, to paint on the door—first an "F," then an "R," then an "E." . . .

"Ah," said Thrasaki, "I understand!"

The grandfather laughed. "Now you see why I took the trouble to learn to write. In the whole village I'm not going to leave a wall —I shall even climb up the bell tower, I shall go into the mosque, and before I die it will be everywhere: 'Freedom or death!' "

After each letter he put his head back and admired his work. He wondered at the mystery of how one could put together little strokes and curves and out of them raise a voice—a choir of voices. How could those signs speak? Great art Thou, O Lord!

Now his street door spoke. He had given it a voice. "Have I written it well, Thrasaki?" he asked anxiously. "No mistakes?"

"I give you good marks, Granddad. Excellent," said the grandchild with a laugh.

"Then let's go on!"

At the street corner there was a piece of wall free from snow. The grandfather again dipped his brush and wrote. Then he moved on. The paint splashed over his beard and boots, it spotted his waistcoat, but he did not notice. A sacred flame had enveloped him. Wherever he found a flat, clean wall or a large door, he stopped and painted the magic signs. The walls and doors, which before had stood dumb and forlorn, now loudly voiced their longing.

His hand had now acquired the knack of writing and flew along. He reached the village square. Here were the school, the church and the mosque, and a little farther on, the coffeehouse. He dipped the brush into the paint and set to work on the school door. Freedom or death! Two old men came out of the coffeehouse.

"Hey, Captain Sefakas, since when can you write? What are you painting there? What's come over you?"

"It's my farewell," replied the grandfather, undisturbed. "Take it, to remember me by."

The old men shook their heads and moved on.

"An angel has visited old Sefakas," they said. "Charos is near."

The grandfather now stood before the mosque. The walls had been freshly whitewashed, the door was painted yellow.

"Here's where I'll do my best work," said the ancient, "and adorn each letter with a flourish. Just look!" He moved the brush firmly up and down on the yellow door.

"Now let's go home. I'm tired. The church another day. I'll climb up the bell tower on a ladder."

"I can't have you falling down, Granddad. I'll do the climbing."

All over Crete the captains had put water in their wine. They now took counsel and debated this way and that. The Greeks and the Franks and the Muscovites—all were holding themselves aloof. Only a few captains still resisted.

"I have subdued Crete," proclaimed the Sultan, "not a gun is now to be heard on the island. The privileges which in my goodness of heart I had extended to the Cretans, I withdraw, because they have showed themselves treacherous and rebellious."

On the crest of Selena the guns had not been silenced. Captain Michales did not surrender. His shots sounded in Constantinople and the Sultan was enraged. He sent an order to the pasha of Crete: "Bring me Captain Michales' head! If not, your own!"

And the pasha jumped up and down and swore. "Yes, by my faith, I'm going to crush the giaour!"

He girded on his scimitar and looked out toward those accursed Lasithi mountains. He sent a message to Captain Michales: "Go, Captain Michales, take your palikars and leave, with your weapons and with your flags flying. By Mohammed, I will not hurt a hair of any of your heads!"

Captain Michales had answered: "As long as I breathe I shall not leave. Let all Crete submit if it will, I am not submitting. I spit on the beard of your Prophet!"

"Damn Crete, damn all Cretans, damn my lot!" muttered the pasha, and unbuckled his scimitar again. "How am I to clamber up the mountains in the snow and hunt this devil's own fellow! I shall send still more soldiers."

He clapped his hands. The Arab appeared.

"Bring me some chestnuts and a raki. I'm worried . . . do you see the message from the Sultan?"

Without a word the Arab brought a glass of raki, then knelt down and put a row of chestnuts on the glowing cinders in the brazier. The pasha stretched himself out on the divan.

"Tell me some pretty tale, Suleiman, even if it's untrue. By Mohammed, I don't care!"

The Arab's teeth showed in all their width and whiteness. "Today as it happens, Pasha Effendi, I'm able to bring you a piece of good news that will turn your heart into a garden."

"Tell it, you liar, with my blessing! Has Captain Michales laid down his arms?"

"That's not the news, Pasha Effendi, but something better!

You've heard of Hamidé Mula, the sorceress, who has the saint in her yard. I made her cast the beans today and tell your fortune. She squatted down in the middle of the yard, took a sieve and brought out her little bag with beans and shells and pebbles and bats' knuckles. She shook them into the sieve, rattled it and bent over it. Then she muttered the charm. Suddenly she gave a cry, threw off her shawl and began to dance. 'What can you see, Hamidé Mula?' I shouted to her, 'what have the beans got to say?' She became calm, sat down again and stirred the beans with her fingers. 'I see a red fez clapped down over the whole of Crete from Garbusa to Topla Monastery! I see the pasha—that small, dead snail—receiving a firman from Constantinople, with a gold seal, gold lettering and gold cord. The Sultan is sending him gold pounds and gold braid.' 'Yes, isn't he also sending him his daughter, to make him his son-in-law?' 'By the saint who is listening to us, I can't quite make it out.' 'Tell me exactly, Hamidé Mula,' I said to her, 'when are all your deeds and wonders going to happen, that I may go and announce them to the pasha and receive a small baksheesh and you too, my poor woman.' Again she bent over the beans, mixed them and threw them this way and that. 'In three periods of time,' she answered. 'Tell the pasha that. He's not to worry.' And just as you clapped your hands, I was coming in from Hamidé Mula's yard to bring you the news."

All this time the pasha had been playing with his amber necklace and listening openmouthed. His face had become gentle and peaceful; through closed eyes he saw the Sultan's messenger enter Megalokastro, followed by caravans of camels with the dowry from his father-in-law: sacks full of gold pounds, emeralds and opals, and others full of musk, almonds and cinnamon. And a little hanum, the Sultan's daughter, dressed in silk, stepped down from a white camel and with supple movements swept up the marble steps of his seraglio.

At length Suleiman stopped talking. The pasha started, as though awakening. He yawned. "Have you finished, silly Suleiman?"

"I've finished, Pasha Effendi."

"Now stick the pot into the fire and make me a coffee, a foamy one, to wake me up. Are the chestnuts roasted?"

348

"Aren't we going to send any baksheesh to poor Hamidé Mula?"

The pasha laughed. "Silly Suleiman, we're going to take care not to let our mind be puffed up with wind! First we're going to let two 'periods of time' go by!"

"He's not such a fool as I took him for," the Arab muttered sourly as he put the pot into the fire.

As the day was nearing its end, the Metropolitan kept pointing his telescope fearfully toward the restless surface of the sea. Today he was expecting, with the steamer that touched at Megalokastro every week, the secret messenger who was coming to him with instructions from Greece. In the mountains the captains still negotiated with the Turks. They had made up their minds to come to terms, but had not yet laid down their arms. "In God's name," cried the more reasonable ones, "let's harden our hearts to stone, bury our weapons once again, and collect our strength until even the mourning mothers gain strength once more. And then we can raise the banner again. Pretend to kiss the hand you cannot hack off." Still the more fiery ones retorted: "Freedom or death!"

Greece too was undecided: sometimes she uttered vague threats against the Turks, sometimes she fell at the feet of the Franks. The Metropolitan did not know to which opinion he should give his allegiance. His understanding advised him to be measured, patient, and to yield; but his heart, with its crazy courage, shouted, "Freedom or death!" Today, thank God, the secret messenger would arrive from Greece and show him the right course. But darkness was already falling, and there was no sign of the ship.

I must be patient, he thought. God will bring another day tomorrow. Then the news will come.

He went downstairs and into the church, to pray God to calm the sea.

The night passed; the sea grew smooth. At daybreak the soft fragrance of thyme floated over the sea from the mountains, and Kosmas, the eldest grandson of old Sefakas, standing on the bows of the steamer, breathed in the fragrance of his native land. Crete lay before him. Wild cliffs, mournful trees, distant rose-colored mountain peaks. It was a spring day in the heart of winter. Kosmas could not gaze enough at the flesh and bones of his country. How had he set out, twenty years ago, a child with downy cheeks and downy soul? and how was he now coming home? He turned. A young woman, small and pale, came up to him and also looked, with large, terrified eyes.

"Crete," said the young man with a laugh, gently touching her shoulder.

The woman shuddered. "Yes."

"This is where you'll bring our son into the world," he said softly. "This is now your country. Forget the other," he added tenderly.

"Yes, Kosmas, dear," said the woman, and she gripped his arm and pressed it fearfully, as though to make sure that it was there. She became a little calmer.

Crete's mountains, olive groves and vineyards drew nearer. Megalokastro appeared in the white scintillation of the early morning. The scent of thyme grew stronger. The full light had now glided from the peaks over the slopes down to the plains. The trees could be distinguished from one another, the cocks were audible in the sweet moment of morning, the world was awakening.

The man bent toward his wife. "Please," he said softly, "now that you are entering my father's house, keep your heart firm and don't be afraid. Remember that I'm always with you. Remember that you're carrying our son. My mother is a Godfearing woman; she will take you to her heart. My sister, I must tell you . . ." He stopped, frowning.

"What?" she asked, looking at her husband anxiously.

"When she was twelve, her father gave her this order: 'You are not to cross the threshold of the street door any more, and you are not to appear before me any more. Go!' From then on, the poor thing remained shut away from her father and the outside world. She sat all day weaving and knitting for her trousseau. When the old man came home in the evening, she fled to the inner part of the house to hide. When she was twenty, my father noticed that day after day a young man passed by and watched for my sister. One evening a woman of the neighborhood brought her a note from the young man—and later several more. He was in love with her, and he wanted her to meet him one night so that they might get to know each other, with a view to marrying later. After many letters the girl was moved by sympathy and one evening told the neighbor to say that she would be standing at the door at midnight."

Kosmas stopped short. The veins on his brow were swollen. Hatred, fear and admiration of his father reigned in him once more. Crete had vanished. Instead, the terrifying shade of his father swept through the air.

"Be quiet!" whispered the young woman. "That's enough."

"No, you must hear it all," he replied. "At midnight she went down with bare feet, to make no noise on the stairs. But the old man was watching. He glided behind her without a sound. The poor girl went out into the yard, and just as she started to open the door, the old man rushed upon her, seized her by the hair, bored his nails into her and flung her, fainting, into her room, which he locked. Year after year passed and my sister never once dared to go to the window. The old man was killed at Arkadi. Twenty years have gone by since then. But my sister's brain is shuttered tight. She works all day in the house, washing, cooking, and still weaving and sewing, poor thing, at her trousseau. At night she doesn't go to bed. When midnight draws near, she opens her window, leans out, and if some nocturnal wanderer comes by, calls out to him timidly, 'Is it nearly midnight?' "

Kosmas paused. The fair hair, the blue eyes, the charm of his sister, her laughter when she was young. . . .

"Please don't be frightened," he said to his wife.

He took several steps along the deck and looked down into the hold, where Turkish soldiers lay stretched out. "Unlucky Crete," he murmured, and felt the lining of his coat, where he kept hidden the letter with the secret information.

Kosmas could now clearly distinguish, behind Megalokastro, the celebrated mountain Iuchtas with its human shape: a gigantic head lying on the ground among olive trees and vineyards, with a high, bold forehead, a bony nose, a wide mouth and a beard of bluffs and boulders. It lay there, a dead, pale-blue marble god.

The giant is not dead, Kosmas thought, as he looked at the reassuring mountain. As long as he's alive and rumbling inside me, he hasn't died. As long as I'm alive and thinking of him, he won't die. The others may have forgotten him. His life depends on me. He holds me, but I hold him too.

He could feel that his father had struck roots within him that would not be destroyed. Abroad, he had often thought of him, and a trembling would come over him at these times. But never had he felt the dead man so near as at this moment—or so menacing. He knows, he thought, why I'm coming back to Crete and what my secret mission is. Relentless fighter that he is, he'd like to silence me.

Kosmas turned again to his wife. It seemed to him that his father had cast a glance filled with hatred at the foreign woman. But the young man's love for this woman grew still stronger and bolder in the presence of his father. He pressed her to him and defended her and would not give her up to the dead man.

They entered the harbor. On the right gleamed the stone lion of Venice with the open Gospel in its claws. The harbor rang with the din and reeked of rotten lemons, oil and turnips. Kosmas jumped onto the mole and grasped his wife's hand.

"Step with the right foot first," he said softly. "It's a jungle you're coming into! In God's name!"

She stepped on land with her right foot and hung exhausted on her husband's arm. "I'm tired," she said, as cold sweat broke out on her temples.

"The house is close by. Be brave. We've arrived."

They advanced. Kosmas gazed insatiably at the houses, the people, the streets. All had grown old—the black hair white, the cheeks shriveled, the colors washed out, the walls flaky, many of them crumbling. Weeds grew on many thresholds.

He squeezed his wife's hand. "This is my country," he said. "This is the earth where I was born."

The woman bent down and picked up a bit of earth, and let it trickle down between her fingers. "It's warm," she said. "I like that." She thought of her own distant, cold country.

They lost themselves in the narrow alleys. Kosmas, who had let go his wife's arm, strode hastily forward. His heart beat violently. He turned into a small street. From afar he made out the parental door, which was shut. The window above it was also shut. No one in the street, no voices. It was as in a dream. He approached the old arched doorway with the thick iron ring. His knees were trembling. Then he plucked up courage and knocked. In the yard, steps became audible. Someone sighed. Then silence. He knocked again. The door opened. A short, lean old woman, quite white and clothed all in black, appeared. As she looked at the newcomer, she cried out, "My child!" and leaned against the doorpost for support.

Now the sister came too, short and lean like her mother, with gray hair and eyes dimmed by hopelessness.

Joy, tears. Hands grasped eagerly at the beloved body. Even as the mother pressed her big son again and again to her bosom and spoke to him as though he were still a child, she noticed the young woman on the threshold.

"Is that—?" asked the mother softly.

"Yes, my wife."

The sister turned curiously to look at her. The mother whispered to her son, "Why did you marry her? A foreigner!"

"Mother," said the son softly, kissing the shriveled hand, "I must ask a favor of you."

"You're my one and only son. Need you ask? I hang on your words, command me!"

"I entrust my wife to you, Mother. Love her. And my son," he added, more softly still.

The mother started. She gazed at her son speechlessly, asking, imploring.

"Yes," he went on, "she is carrying your grandson."

A delicious warmth rose to her throat and cheeks. But suddenly a shudder overcame her. "Have you asked permission of your father?" she said, muffling her voice. "Does he know? He decides. You must ask him. I'm afraid of him." She whispered, so that the dead man might not hear.

"What can he do to us?" asked the son, his heart faltering.

"How should I know, my child? Has he still a body, so that one can know where he is? Perhaps he's in the yard at this moment, forbidding her to cross the threshold."

The son cried furiously, "He's no right to do that! He's no longer in command here. I'll bring her in!" His voice was suddenly rough as he said, "Chrysula, come!"

He took her by the hand. "Mother, your daughter," he said. The young woman bent down to kiss the mother's hand. Then she stood there and waited.

The mother looked at her closely. She caught sight of the little golden chain around her neck.

"You're baptized?" the old woman asked.

"She is baptized," answered the son. "Here is the cross. She bears your name, Mother. She was called Noëmi, now she's called Chrysula."

He took the chain and pulled from her bosom a small golden cross.

"She is welcome," said the mother and, hesitating slightly, touched her head. They went into the house.

Kosmas walked about with heavy heart. He paced up and down, silently caressing the doors, the old furniture, the heavy clock and the silver pistols of his ancestors, next to the icons.

"And how's Grandfather?" he asked.

"In his village. A hundred years old, but full of vigor. Charos doesn't touch him. He always asks after you."

The two women sat down on the very old, wide divan. The mother looked at her son, who had ripened into a man. He was like his grandfather, Captain Sefakas. The same eyes, which looked at things with warmth and tenderness, the same attractive, eloquent mouth. She cast a sidelong glance at his wife. What am I to say to her? she thought. Another race. Another God created her. I don't like her.

And the young woman saw the stony yard, the pots of basil, the wintry bare vine trellis above the trough. . . . And beyond the yard, behind the tendrils, limitless plains under snow and forests under ice and dark towns and cossacks with naked sabers who broke the doors in and fell upon the Jews . . . and the snow, melted and stained by hot blood . . . and the shrieks of fleeing men, women and children. . . .

She turned around. She saw the old woman observing her. She tried to smile and could not manage it. Her eyes filled with tears.

The old woman was touched. "What are you thinking of?" she asked. "Your country? Where were you born?"

"A long, long way from here . . . in a dark town full of factories."

354

"What sort of factories? What did they make?"

"Cannons, rifles, machinery. But my father—" She wanted to say: "he didn't soil his hands with these things, he was a rabbi." But she kept it to herself.

"What was your father?" the old woman asked.

"He was a good man," she answered with a sigh.

The mother stood up, went out into the yard, broke off a sprig of basil and brought it to her. "Do you have basil in your country?" she asked.

"No."

"It grew on the grave of Christ," said the old woman.

Meanwhile the good news had spread. Chattering excitedly, the women of the neighborhood came running. The house filled. They examined the Jewish girl from head to toes as though she were some extraordinary animal.

Kosmas watched his wife with sympathy. She seemed to him like a wounded swan among a flock of geese or ducks.

Maria, the sister, brought the salver with dainties and coffee. She wore a broad black band around her throat to hide the wrinkles. She eyed Chrysula with enmity, for this girl was young and pretty and had snatched her brother from her.

Kosmas stood up. The first joy of homecoming was over. He had no time to lose.

"I'm going on a little round, to greet Kastro again," he said, and hurried off to the Metropolitan's Residence.

The Metropolitan had been waiting for Kosmas since early that morning when he had heard the steamer whistle as it entered the harbor. "Grant, O God," he had murmured, crossing himself, "that he is bringing good tidings for Christendom."

Kosmas went swiftly through the streets. The beloved town had aged and crumbled—it was beginning to fall into dust, which the wind would carry away. One day, certainly, a new town would be built here but it would not be his. Beloved Crete, he thought tenderly, we're growing old.

He reached Ai-Menas, strode across the forecourt, and greeted the old lemon tree, under whose blossoming boughs the Metropolitan celebrated the Resurrection every year. He climbed the staircase of the Residence two steps at a time.

355

The Metropolitan rose, unquiet and impatient. "Welcome, Kosmas," he said. "God sends you in a heavy hour. What are you bringing us?"

Kosmas kissed the Metropolitan's hand. "This letter, my lord," he said, pulling out the paper.

Leaning against the window, the Metropolitan took it and opened it with burning hands.

There was no hope, said the letter. "The Franks are unwilling to antagonize the Sultan," he read. "The Sultan, grown bold again, means to withdraw the few privileges he had granted to Crete against his will; the General whom he has sent to occupy it possesses full powers to root out Christianity. Therefore bury your weapons again, practice patience, and do not plunge Greece into a bloody adventure. She is willing, but powerless."

He read it greedily, then slowly. His lordly head was bowed. At last he tore himself away from the window and dropped, exhausted, to the divan. He buried his face in his hands.

"Unhappy Crete," he murmured.

At last the Metropolitan raised his head. "Do you know what's in the letter, Kosmas?" he asked.

"I know, my lord."

"I shall send a letter to all the captains, telling them to lay down their arms. We can't go on. There's only one captain I'm afraid of—your Uncle Michales. An unbridled, rebellious soul. I already sent him one warning that he was to get out with his weapons and flags. No one would hurt a hair of his head—the pasha had sworn it.—Do you know how he answered me? 'Do I meddle in your office, Bishop? Then don't you meddle in mine either. Never will I kneel before the Turks. I'll blow myself sky-high!' You, my Kosmas, must seek him out and speak with him."

"I'll go, my lord, but without any hope. He's like my father—a wild beast."

Trumpets sounded, and heavy, marching steps and the neighing of horses. The Metropolitan looked at Kosmas anxiously.

"Turkish soldiers," said Kosmas. "They came on the ship. We took them on at Kanea. They have orders to annihilate everything."

"Unhappy Crete," said the Metropolitan again, raising his hand to Heaven. "How long yet?"

Perplexity overcame them both. The Metropolitan, to give their thoughts a new direction, asked: "You've been in the land of the Franks for many years. What's happening there? What have you seen? Here we live in the wilds."

"Many things, good and bad, my lord! Where am I to begin?"

"Are they believers?"

"They believe in a new godhead, a cruel, great-power one, which may some day become all-powerful."

"In what?"

"In science."

"Mind without soul. In the devil, that means."

"We are now under a terrible sign of the zodiac, that of Scorpio —of the devil, my lord."

"The rest of mankind perhaps. Not we Cretans. We have a higher belief than in the individual, the belief in tears and sacrifice. We are still under the sign of God."

Kosmas said nothing. What purpose would it serve to speak? The Metropolitan was old and believing. He had no support other than belief.

"Not we Cretans, nor the Russians either," the Metropolitan went on. "When I was Archimandrite in Kiev, I understood what believing means. What God means, and how He comes down to earth and goes about and speaks with men. As long as Russia exists, I have no fear."

Kosmas rose. "I shall leave you, Bishop, and let you send the letter to the captains. We must not lose a moment."

"My blessing! And come again tomorrow. I'm going to call the elders together. You too must speak with them."

When Kosmas returned at nightfall to his parental house and climbed upstairs to the old bedroom of his youth, he found his wife stretched out on the bed, crying. He took her in his arms, stroked her hair, touched her chin and raised her troubled face to his. She smiled at him.

"What's the matter? What have they been doing to you?"

"Nothing, nothing. I'm tired."

She let her face droop on her arm. Then she said:

"They all sniffed around me. Then they turned away and whispered among themselves. Only your mother had pity on me.

357

She stood up and said, 'My dears, good-by, we're tired. See you tomorrow!'—She took me by the hand and led me upstairs into your room. She made a movement as if to kiss me, but she thought better of it. 'Lie down,' she said, 'don't pay any attention to them. Go to sleep!'—And so I've been lying here and waiting for you."

Kosmas kissed the curly hair on her neck. She closed her eyes, smiling. The moon rose and shone on her face. Kosmas was appalled by her pallor.

"Go to sleep," he whispered in her ear, "you're tired."

She clasped his hand. "I couldn't, alone. Lie down by my side."

She put her arms around him, snuggled against his chest and murmured a few tender words in her mother tongue. Then she went to sleep.

The moon climbed higher, huge and dumb, filled with sweetness. It was the moon of his youth, of those honeyed nights when he had carried on weighty conversations with his friends about the great unanswerable questions—whence? whither? why?—that trouble young men the world over.

The moonlight now spread itself like a white linen sheet over the bed. The honey-golden hair of his wife, spread out on the pillow, gleamed as though it were lighted by glowworms. Her face shone like marble. Kosmas stretched out his hand to caress her, but drew back for fear of waking her.

How much I love this woman, he thought, is beyond telling. How much good she has brought me is beyond telling. She has opened my mind and heart; she has taught me to love foreign races, which I hated, to understand foreign ideas, which I fought, and to feel that we are all of one origin. What good fate was it that took her by the hand that evening and brought her to me? Smiling, he shook his head. "There's no such thing as fate. I myself grasped her by the hand that evening, nobody else."

And he remembered how he had been in a bookshop in a distant town in the north one day, looking for a book he loved: Chinese poems of the Sung dynasty. He could not find it and as, disappointed, he looked out into the street, he saw a girl in an orange silk blouse passing by. For a second she stood as though in the beam of a searchlight—then she vanished. He was stirred to the depths. The girl seemed to him to have an enigmatic, tragic beauty. And her blouse was of the color he loved above all others. Like lightning the thoughts flashed through his mind.—If I want, I shall run after her, and she'll become my wife. If I don't want, I shall stay here and let her go. I do what I want. But what do I want?—And he was reminded of the story of the Cretan shepherd who had never seen the great city—that was how he pictured Megalokastro. It had been described to him as Paradise, where the most precious things in the world were displayed: white boots with double soles, guns and sabers, sacks full of beans and salt fish, and musk-scented women. For years his mind had been obsessed with this paradise, for years he had longed to go down to it. One day he could bear it no longer. He slung his old boots over his shoulder, in order not to wear them out on the rocks, and clambered, springing from stone to stone, down to Megalokastro. He traveled for seven hours. Toward evening he reached the big fortress gate of Megalokastro. There he came to a standstill with a sharp jerk. Perhaps he was suddenly ashamed that he had not resisted the temptation. He struck the hard threshold with his shepherd's staff and cried: "If I want, I'll go in. If I don't want, I won't go in. . . . I won't go in!" And he returned to his mountain.

"But I will go in!" muttered Kosmas, and ran after the girl. In the black throng of human beings the orange blouse gleamed. As he caught up with the girl, she turned and looked at him with terror.

"The moment you went by," he told her, "I thought: If I want, I shall speak to her and we shall become friends. If I don't want, I shall let her go by. I've made up my mind that I do want."

"Either you're mad," the girl answered glancing anxiously about her, "or a poet. But I've no time. . . ."

"Come with me and let's talk. . . ."

"I've no time. I must go."

"Where are you going?"

"I must go away," she insisted, in a voice that trembled.

Kosmas took her by the arm and said tenderly, "Don't go away. Come with me." The ring of her voice had frightened him. She had said, "I must go away" as if she were crying "Help!"

The girl's thick, finely arched eyebrows drew together. At that moment the whole of her life lay in the balance. "I want—" "I

359

don't want—" Her fate was imprisoned in those short syllables.

"Come," repeated Kosmas.

"Where?"

"Anywhere."

"Where?" She spoke like a child who is afraid of being punished.

"Let's go for a walk. Life is short. Let's talk, as long as there's time. . . ."

She bowed her honey-fair head. "All right, let's talk, as long as there's time. Life is short. Let's go!"

They had gone into a park. Evening had passed from golden green to pale violet, and gradually to dark blue. Both spoke hurriedly, breathing rapidly. Kosmas first, to give her courage. He spoke of Crete, that fearful, beloved island, of his dragon of a father, and of his mother, that holy martyr.

The girl's bosom swelled. "Why do you speak to me of such things?" she asked anxiously. "Since I'm going away and you too are going away and we've no time. . . . People need years to reach the point we have reached at one bound."

They had sat down on a bench.

"What's your name?" asked the man.

"Noëmi."

"Tell me. Noëmi, I'm sure your life is hard. Trust me. I'm a Cretan."

"A Cretan? What's that?"

"A man with a warm heart, Noëmi."

It was the depth of night when they stood up. The young man's heart was overflowing with indignation and bitterness. This little girl had drunk the misery of the whole world. Her words had revealed to him the horror, the shame, the madness of the world. He had listened to her with his face hidden in his hands, and had seen the things she described to him: how the Cossacks had ridden through the town, stormed the Jewish quarter, splintered the doors, killed the young men and rounded up the old, together with the women and children. Her father, the old rabbi with the white, divided beard, had marched in the deep snow at the head of the prisoners. After days and nights in the snow, they had become fewer and fewer. On both sides of the road, women and children were left lying in the snow. . . .

Noëmi began to cry. Kosmas put his arm round her. "How did you escape?"

"I don't know. It was like a dream. . . . Don't ask me!" she cried, suddenly.

Kosmas stroked her hair. "I won't. Be calm now." Then Kosmas asked, "Where did you mean to go this evening? Why were you in such a hurry?"

Noëmi raised her head. "I had come to a decision," she whispered.

"What decision?"

"A friend gave me this orange blouse. I washed and did my hair properly and was going—" She paused and added quietly, "—to kill myself. To be out of it all."

Kosmas kissed her hands. "Come with me, Noëmi."

"But where?"

"Trust me. I don't know if I love you, but I won't desert you. Everybody's deserted you, but I won't."

In the darkness of the park Kosmas could not see her face. He could feel that the orphaned girl was questioning her own thoughts. Suddenly Noëmi raised her head and said, quietly and decisively: "I'll go with you." She had given him her hand. . . .

The moon vanished; the bed lay in darkness. The mother and sister were still chatting softly downstairs, and Kosmas listened to their monotonous voices, like running water. A dog howled. From the yard rose the scent of basil, which had accompanied all his youth. Basil, marjoram, gillyflowers and jasmine were old and dear companions. Kosmas took a deep breath.

This is my country, he thought, this is the house where I was born, this is my wife. . . .

He heard the window of his sister's room open. It must be near midnight. He listened. Footsteps sounded in the street; a nocturnal wanderer was passing by. A longing, perplexed voice floated out of the window: "Is it already past midnight? Is it already past midnight?" The footsteps stopped, and the window was violently shut. Kosmas shuddered.

"My God," he murmured. Tears ran down his cheeks.

Now he could not sleep. With wide-open eyes he waited for morning. When at last he saw the sky growing light, he slipped from the bed, so as not to wake his wife, dressed, went down-stairs, and sat on the divan in the place where his father used to sit. He wanted to challenge the dead man, to drive him from the house and courtyard to which he clung, and to bolt the door behind him so that he might never come back and harm his wife.

Ancient dreads had awakened in him. It was in vain that in the land of the Franks he had tried to free his mind from them. His heart was still a dark cave full of specters.

The sister appeared, yellow and sullen in the morning light. When she saw her brother sitting in the old man's place, she started back in terror. Ever since that night when her father had seized her by the hair and barred her from all men, a hatred had been raging in her that had followed her father even into the grave. Each night she opened her trunks and examined the trous-seau she had made with her own hands: the nightdresses with the wide lace sleeves, the embroidered kerchiefs, the silken sheets. Sometimes the impulse came over her to throw the whole lot into the yard and burn it there. *"My winding sheets! Curse him!"* She would also open the cupboard containing his suits and would whimper like a bitch that has suddenly scented a wolfskin; but she never touched these clothes. She reproached her mother for never having resisted him.

She had loved her brother until yesterday, when she had re-alized that he was married. Immediately she loathed his wife.

"Maria," her mother had said to her, "be patient."

"Damn patience," she had replied. "I'd rather kill myself than go on seeing her."

As her brother now greeted her, she could not control herself and burst into tears. Kosmas put his arms round her.

"Keep calm, sister," he said. "Life's going to be different, you too will have joy."

She shook her gray head. "I'm marrying Charos for my joy," she said, pushed her brother away and left the room.

Kosmas went out into the yard for a breath of air. But suddenly disquiet came over him. Had someone sighed in the room up-stairs? He ran upstairs to his wife.

She was asleep. Her slender foot peeped out from under the sheet: he bent down and kissed it. He stroked her hair softly. A

362

warm breath smelling of carnations came from her slightly open mouth.

As he brought his lips close to her mouth, he thought he heard the stairs creak. Slow footsteps were coming up. It was the old man, the dead man! He recognized the tread. As though turned to stone he sat up on the bed. He held his breath and listened. The stairs creaked again, the heavy footsteps came nearer. They had reached the landing.

"The old man," murmured Kosmas, terrified, and spread his hands above his wife to protect her.

The footsteps halted before the door. The son's heart beat wildly. The whole house seemed to be shaking. He wanted to cry out, but his throat was blocked.

At that moment, Noëmi awoke with a shriek. She stared toward the door, and the sweat poured over her. Kosmas put his arms round her.

"What's the matter?" he said softly. "Did you hear something?"

"Someone came up the stairs. Someone's standing behind the door." She was trembling.

"Don't be afraid. You've had a dream. Look, and you'll see it's nothing."

He jumped up. He tried to hide his own trembling. He flung the door open. Nobody. He laughed carelessly, to give her courage. He returned to her, covered her up, and kissed her shaking knees.

"Don't be afraid," he said. "This is your home, Noëmi."

The young woman looked about her, at the table, the chest, the window and the icon-shrine with the three icons: the Creation, the Crucifixion, and Saint Michael.

"Yes," she said, "This is my home. I shall get used to it." Her eyes were full of tears.

Kosmas saw her weeping, and felt a limitless, longing love. Never had he been so strongly moved. Not even on that first night, when he had taken her. He left the door open, to show he had no fear of the dead, took her in his arms and caressed her from her toes to the top of her head.

A day went by—then two, then three. Kosmas saw his mother and sister daily. They said what they had to say to each other.

363

They talked of the house, of relatives and neighbors, of the dead man who still walked about the house and oppressed them, of Crete. . . . Then there was nothing more to say. Only deep affection united them still, so they were silent.

He ranged about the narrow alleys, following the old paths of his youth. Here, in this square, at the Three Vaults, his heart had leaped for love for the first time. It was here that he had seen the first girl he had loved, in a golden evening cloud, holding a yellow rose and sprigs of jasmine in her hand. The world had smelled of musk. It was a summer evening, and the unmarried girls in red, green and blue dresses walked up and down, with firm breasts and quick steps. Their hair hung down, ribbons fluttered behind them, and they made secret signs. They were like corvettes flying all their flags and setting out to sea to conquer the world. Pale and shy, the lads trotted behind them. They pretended to tease and make fun of the girls, but their hearts were trembling. Among them was Kosmas, aged sixteen. . . .

Now he hurried across the square and kept his eyes fixed on the ground, in case he should meet and recognize some fat matron whose eyes might remind him of the ribbon-bedecked girl of that youthful summer evening.

In Petrokefalo, the grandfather sat in front of the blazing hearth, and froze. His cheeks had fallen in, his knees shook. He stared into the fire and brooded over his life.

A drover came in and greeted him.

"Good news for you, old Sefakas. Your grandson Kosmas has arrived in Megalokastro from the Franks' country. They say he's got pen and paper, and writes."

The grandfather started, and raised his staff, but did not reply.

It seemed to him that the coming of his grandson was a secret annunciation of death. My hour has come, he thought, and stood up.

"Take the big ladder on your shoulder, Charidimos," he said to his shepherd, after the drover had gone, "and come with me."

"Where to, old Sefakas?"

"I've told you a thousand times, you're not to ask me questions. Be quick about it!"

Charidimos loaded the ladder onto his shoulder. The grandfather led the way, with the paintpot and brush, hobbling over the cobblestones. When he reached the village square, he pointed at the small, whitewashed bell tower of the church.

"Lean it against the wall there. Hold it firmly so that I don't fall. Where's Thrasaki?"

"He's gone out with his crew and the old gun."

"That's right. He has my blessing."

The shepherd leaned the ladder against the bell tower, shoved a couple of stones under it and held it firmly with both hands. The old man gasped as he climbed up. Charidimos was terrified. "Lord have mercy on me," he muttered, crossing himself.

The graybeard had now clambered to the top of the ladder and had reached the smooth cornerstone just under the belfry. He dipped the brush into the paint, stretched out his arm and began, one after another, to make huge letters. F, R, E . . . his heart beat joyfully. Who would have foretold, he thought, that my life would end like this? With a brush, a paintpot and letters on the wall! When he had finished his work he bent backward to admire what he had written still holding the paintbrush in his hand. He lost his balance and fell.

Charidimos yelled. Neighbors came running. The old man's head was bloody, and he did not utter a sound.

"His eldest grandson has come back to Crete," Charidimos explained to the neighbors. "The joy at the news went to his head. . . ."

The village was convulsed as though an earthquake had destroyed its foundations. All the women with any knowledge of the art of healing hurried to the scene and plied him with ointments. A messenger was sent on muleback to Megalokastro to fetch Mustapha Baba, who was a good man and doctored Turks, Christians and Jews without distinction. "They're all ill, the poor things," he said, "even if they're Greeks or Jews."

Next morning Mustapha Baba arrived, riding the mule. He brought out his small case, opened his little bottles and examined the split gray head with skillful hands.

On the third day the grandfather opened his eyes. He looked about him and caught sight of his daughter-in-law Katerina. He beckoned to her. "What's happening on the mountain? What have you heard from your husband?"

"He will not surrender," the wife answered.

"He's right," said the old man. "Put a cushion behind my back, so that I can sit up. I'm tired of lying flat. Send for Kostandes from the pen, I want him." He shut his eyes again.

An hour later a fellow appeared, half man, half goat, and stood in front of the small sofa on which the old man lay. This was Kostandes. The grandfather's eyes were closed. He saw nothing. Kostandes waited patiently, his chin supported on his staff. Some day he'll open his eyes and see me and tell me what he wants of me, he thought.

The grandchildren and daughters-in-law stood in a ring around the old man. Thrasaki too came in, with the old gun on his shoulder. He had been on the mountain again, playing at war with his friends. He was waiting to know what would happen with his grandfather, and then—all was prepared—he would lead his band in an attack on a Turkish village and challenge the Turkish youths.

"You wake him, Thrasaki. You're not afraid of him," said Kostandes.

"I'm not afraid of him, that's true," replied Thrasaki, "but I'm sorry for him. He's asleep."

The grandfather heard the whispering and opened his eyes. Kostandes moved his huge feet over to him. The old man blinked at the throng that encircled him. He flew into a fury.

"I'm not dying yet, my half-witted heirs!" he said. "Out with the lot of you! Come here, Kostandes. Bend down!"

The hairy fellow bent over and received his instructions. Old Sefakas spoke slowly; his breathing was irregular, interrupted by pain. At the end he asked, "Understand, Kostandes?"

"I understand, old Sefakas."

"And afterwards, when you've made it known in the villages, hurry down to Megalokastro. Run to my eldest son's house, you know the one, to my daughter-in-law Chrysula. Take two whole cheeses and a nice lamb for her. My first grandson, Kosmas, has arrived, so they say. See him with your own eyes, touch him with your hands, do you hear? And say to him, 'Come, your grandfather's dying. He wants to give you his blessing.' Understand, you idiot Kostandes?"

"I understand, old Sefakas."

"Well, be off with you! Run!"

He left, and soon the clattering sound of the nails of his boots died away.

Next morning both wings of old Chrysula's street door flew open at one kick, and a hairy fellow carrying two whole cheeses in a sack and a slaughtered lamb under his arm strode over the threshold. With his furry chest bare, and reeking of garlic and onions, he walked into the middle of the yard. He dropped the presents on the ground and leaned on his long shepherd's staff. The three women were sitting on the sofa drinking coffee. Upstairs Kosmas was getting ready for a visit to the Metropolitan. They had already composed the circular and sent it into the mountains. With sighs the captains bowed their heads as they read. "Since the Mother Country wills it so," they answered, "we obey her command!"

But Captain Michales' answer was still lacking. When he had received the Metropolitan's letter, he had sent for Polyxigis. The two had shut themselves up in the stone hut, and bolted the door.

"I won't submit," Captain Michales stated.

"The Mother Country demands it," retorted Captain Polyxigis. "Let's not pull against her."

"What Mother Country? I've no confidence in the heads that govern there."

"You've more confidence in your own head?"

"What's the good of joking? No, not in my head, but in my heart. It tells me: don't submit. And I'm not submitting. Do what your heart tells you."

"I have decided to obey."

"Then go, and all the best! Leave me as the other comrades have already done. I need no one. Good luck to you and a fair wind in your sails, my palikar!"

Captain Polyxigis hesitated. His heart rebelled against the retreat and was unwilling to leave this man to his death.

"You're perishing to no purpose, Captain Michales," he said.

"In war no one perishes to no purpose," Captain Michales shouted. "Are you feeling sorry for me?"

"There was one human being I loved in the world. You killed her for me. No, I'm not fond of you, Captain Michales. But I

367

don't like to see you perish. Crete—devil take it—still needs you!"
"I don't need Crete any more," groaned the other. "Go, I tell you."

"Haven't you any thought for your wife? Haven't you any thought for Thrasaki?"

"If you value your life, go!" roared Captain Michales, and the veins in his neck swelled. He kicked aside the baulks that barred the entrance of the stone hut and pushed Captain Polyxigis out. Then from the threshold he shouted for Vendusos.

"Off with you, Vendusos, take what legs you've got and run down to Megalokastro, to the Metropolitan's Residence. Tell the Metropolitan that I've received his letter, and have set fire to its four corners. I'm sending it back to him. I will not surrender!"

"At your orders, Captain Michales," said Vendusos, and stuffed the letter into his bosom.

"Run fast. And if you value your life, don't come back, Vendusos. Here it's death."

"I've children, Captain Michales," said Vendusos with a sigh, "I've my daughter to find a husband for, and my wife and the tavern. . . ."

"Then don't come back. You're Vendusos—I'm not asking anything of you. Behave like a Vendusos! Take Kajabes and Furogatos with you, too, and look for Bertodulos down there, and Efendina!" Captain Michales growled, and turned his back on him.

Vendusos clambered swiftly down the hidden path to the plain, sighing and cursing. "You're Vendusos, behave like a Vendusos." The words lashed his back as he ran. He reached the town and climbed the staircase of the Residence.

At exactly that moment Kostandes entered the parental house of Kosmas and stood in the middle of the yard, pressing his hands against his sweating chest. "Long life to you," he cried, in a voice that was hoarse from a life spent shouting at goats and rams. "Long life to you, women. May you enjoy it! All the best!"

"Welcome, Kostandes," said the mother. "Come in. Sit down and drink some wine. What news have you got for us from the village?"

"Your father-in-law, Captain Sefakas, is dying, Madame Chrysula. Nothing's any use to him now. Even the devil's no use

368

to him now," said Kostandes, with a loud laugh. "And I'm to give you these presents from him, he says." He squatted and laid his staff across his bony knees.

"By God, he's led a good life: eaten, drunk, killed Turks, filled his yard with children and asses and mares and oxen, turned wild land into plowland, planted vineyards and olives and built a church for his soul, too. He's insured himself for up there, too. What more could he do with life? He's hoisted the flag for departure too."

Kosmas heard the voices and came down from his room. Kostandes looked him over curiously from head to foot.

"You are the eldest grandson of old Sefakas, sir? Or am I wrong?" He craned his neck to see him properly. And then he got up and touched him. Grandfather's orders!

"No one else," replied Kosmas.

"Then your grandfather asks me to tell you to go to him, but quickly, and close his eyes. Quickly, I tell you, if you want to see him still alive. By the sun that's above us all, I think he's been waiting for you, sir, all these years, so that now he will be able to give up his soul to the Archangel. 'Take a mule with you,' he told me, 'so that he can ride! I have held an ax, my son a gun, but my grandson, they now tell me, holds a pen. So he won't be able to run on foot. Take a mule and show him the way.' The mule's at the inn, waiting. Let's go!"

To the mistress of the house he said:

"There's the news, Madame Chrysula. And the wine you're offering me—I'll drink it so that you will not be upset."

He drank the wine at one gulp, seized a hunk of bread from the table, smacked his lips contentedly and laughed.

"And listen," he said, "to what else I've got to tell you. Captain Sefakas has also sent out an invitation to a feast. As if he was going to the underworld as a bridegroom! It's not yet twenty-four hours since he sent for me. I'm his shepherd, ever since I was born, and his messenger. 'Run, Kostandes,' he said to me, 'take your staff and climb up to the higher mountains and call together the old war leaders. Stand in the middle of each village and cry: Children, Captain Sefakas is dying! You who are of his time, who bore arms with him and are still alive—Captain Sefakas invites you to his mansion! He doesn't want presents, have no fear! You'll find his tables laid, and you'll sit down in his chairs and eat and drink. And afterwards Captain Sefakas has something to say to you, something important. Pick up your staffs and come!' "

"What does he want to say?" asked Kosmas, who had listened eagerly. Only the patriarchs of the Old Testament had died with such dignity, he thought, and he felt a mighty pride at having sprung from such a race.

"What's he want to say?" the shepherd repeated. "How should I know? I wanted to ask him, but I was afraid—he might have hit me on the head with his stick. So I said nothing. With one bound I was outside, running over the mountains and going into the villages. There I cried the message. Only three old men came out. Captain Mandakas, Captain Katsirmas, and the old schoolmaster from Embaros, the lame one. 'Tell him,' they said to me, 'hold out, Captain Sefakas, don't give up that soul of yours yet, we're coming.' They put on their fezzes with the big tassels and girded on their belts. . . ." Kostandes laughed again. "Three ruins, poor fellows!" he said. "Their heads sown with scars like sieves! Their feet can't shove them forward any more. Three hundred years old, the three together—the spittle running out of their mouths, their eyebrows sagging. They picked up their silver pistols as though they were going to war. Then they hobbled forward, leaning on each other so as not to fall. You don't believe me? When we get to the village, you'll see them."

He stood up and said to Kosmas, "Put on your fez, sir, and come with me. Your grandfather's dying, didn't you hear me say? And he wants you to close his eyes."

The mother crossed herself. "He'll go to Paradise," she said with certainty, "he was a good man."

"So will Father go to Paradise," said Kosmas. "We shall all reach Paradise, because we've suffered in this world."

His sister shook her head and said with an angry laugh, "God is just."

"God is merciful," cried the mother. She went to fetch the incense burner and light the incense.

Kosmas turned to his wife, who had come down and was listening silently on a corner of the sofa. "You're coming with me, Chrysula."

But Kostandes struck the ground with his staff. "What d'you

want with women, by God?" he cried. "They're a pest. 'Forward,'
you say, and they say 'Stop!' And sometimes ambition does get
hold of them and the poor things do rush forward, but then they
gasp and make you sorry for them. Can you leave them behind
on the road? That's wrong! Take them with you? A pest! But
you're the master. It's for you to decide. I've said my say."

"Kostandes is right," said the mother, appearing with the incense burner. "Don't take her with you, my child, she'll get tired."

"Take her," said the sister slyly, "she'll hold out."

Noëmi shuddered at the thought of remaining without protection in such a house. The air was heavy, and she would have
liked to become quite small, like an insect, to be able to hide
under one of the basil plants in the yard.

"I'm coming with you," she said, "I want to get to know Crete."

"Go and don't come back!" muttered the sister. She could not
bear the girl, she held her breath when she came near her. She
had prepared special glasses and plates, knives and forks for her.

"I shall hold out," Noëmi whispered, and rose to get ready.

As she rose, suddenly a giddiness seized her. The house spun
around her. With her eyes closed, she leaned against the wall.
Someone touched her softly on the shoulder. She saw her husband standing in front of her with a glass of water. With a smile
she reached out, but faltered and collapsed in a faint. The mother
hastily brought rose-vinegar, to rub her face and neck.

"She's tired," she said compassionately.

"It's nothing," the sister said venomously. "A faint—even I have
fainting fits."

Kosmas supported her up to bed. Noëmi opened her eyes and
saw the mother bending over her.

"Forgive me, Mother," she said, "I'm tired."

"Go to sleep," said the mother, and for the first time laid her
hand caressingly on her hair.

Kosmas kissed his wife on the neck. "Go to sleep, Chrysula.
Don't come with me. Be patient. I shall be back soon."

She nodded her head, and shut her eyes. "Go, and blessings
with you," she said.

Kosmas hurried to the Metropolitan, whom he found in the
highest agitation.

"I've just this minute received the answer from your uncle,

that wild barbarian. He's not submitting, he says, and we're not to meddle in his business. Christ will bless you if you go to him. Tell him that because of him Crete is in danger. Knock some sense into that hard skull of his. Do what you can, my child, it's necessary."

"I'll do what I can, my lord. I'm going."

Noëmi was sitting up in bed and waiting for him. She was now wearing her yellow nightdress, and her honey-gold hair fell in curls over her shoulders. She clasped her knees and propped her chin on them, brooding. What power love had! How had she been led here, to the end of the world, to this bedroom with the icons, with the crucifixion of Christ—she, the rabbi's daughter? "Ah, if I had not seen what I saw," she sighed, "and my soul were a white leaf with no writing on it, what happiness there would be here!" She thought of last night, when she had lain stretched out on the old iron bed, shortly before she fell asleep. Through the open window came the night wind, laden with the scent of basil and marjoram. Not a dog barked, not a human step echoed. The world lay in tender moonlight. From far away, there sounded a soft, unceasing, rhythmical sighing. It was the sea, which, like herself, could not sleep. "How sweet night is, how trustfully the man I love sleeps at my side. And inside me. . . ."

Kosmas came in, shut the door and sat down beside her. He looked at her with inexpressible tenderness.

"Are you going away?" Noëmi asked, clutching his hand. Her head was burning.

"Noëmi," said her husband anxiously, "you've a fever."

"No, it's not a fever, my dear. I think it's the normal temperature of my race," she answered with a laugh. And immediately afterwards: "You looked at me as if this was a farewell." She was on the point of adding, "forever." She trembled and wanted to cry out, "How can you leave me alone in this house?" But she fought the words back.

"I shall be back soon, beloved. I want to close my grandfather's eyes. . . ."

He held his wife's hand, and life seemed simple to him. All of time gathered into this short moment, as he clasped the hand of his beloved warmly in his. This moment was eternity.

Noëmi gazed silently at her husband.

372

Now it was Kosmas who cried, "Don't look at me like that, as if you were saying good-by to me forever."

He kissed her eyes. A bitter taste came upon his tongue.

"That's how you're looking at me," said Noëmi, dropping her head back on the pillow.

From below the angry voice of Kostandes rang out.

"Hey, master, your grandfather's dying. Come on! Your mother's filled the sack. Good luck to her. We'll be off like the wind! We'll eat and drink on our way. But be quick! It's almost evening."

Kosmas bent over and kissed his wife's bosom, purely and trustfully as though he kissed a sacred picture. "Good-by," he said.

"Good-by," whispered the woman, taking his head in her hands.

For a few moments he remained quietly leaning on her breast. Her eyes were full of tenderness, forsakenness and dread. "Good-by," she said again.

Kosmas rose, and would have kissed her on the mouth. But she put her hand over it.

"No," she said, "no. Good-by."

13

THE FACE of Crete is stern and weathered. Truly Crete has about her something primeval and holy, bitter and proud, to have given birth to those mothers, so often stricken by Charos, and to those palikars.

When they had left Megalokastro and reached the olive trees and vineyards, Kosmas rode ahead, while Kostandes trotted behind with his shepherd's staff over his shoulder. Evening was approaching. The landscape was yellowish and purple, speckled like a leopard skin. Psiloritis was wrapped in its mantle of snow, cheerful, strong and kindly, like a grandfather. In the foreground lay the Lasithi mountains: they also looked cheerful under the soft winter sun. Below them spread the newly plowed fields, some cinnamon brown, others deep black. Here and there stood a group of olive trees with silvery branches, a lonely cypress, a leafless row of vines on which one or two forgotten clusters still hung by shriveled stalks.

Kosmas drank it all in. This is Crete, this is the earth whence I came, this is my mother, he said to himself, his heart beating violently. Whenever the thought of Crete had come to him in far-off countries, a severe, relentless voice had sounded within him. "What have you been doing, all these years?" it would ask. "You keep fighting the air and exciting yourself with words. But you leave your flesh and blood in the lurch, and nourish yourself on illusions. I don't like you." And now he roamed over the soil of his island—its scent of thyme was crowding into his lungs. Now he could no longer escape the voice, and he owed it an answer. But what answer? He had accomplished nothing, he was nothing. Were these hands, thighs, and a chest, or were they mere lumps of flesh? He was a disgrace to a hard, irrepressible stock.

And where was he bound now? So low had he fallen: to bury one dragon of his race and to persuade another to surrender. His heart faltered. He turned to Kostandes, to hear a man's voice.

"Kostandes," he said, "tell me about my grandfather, old Sefakas." He gave him a cigarette, which Kostandes stuck behind his ear.

"What am I to say to you, master?" he began. "We're alive, he's dying. What hasn't he eaten, what hasn't he drunk, how many Turks has he not killed, God forgive him! You mark my words: he's filled his life well, very well. Don't you go pitying him! When he used to come up to the pen, he'd swallow a giant of a cheese with two bites. Then he'd kill a hare with his stick and say to me: 'Roast that for me, Kostandes!' I'd roast it for him and he'd make short work of it! Not a bone would be left. He ate and drank, the sinner, and on his wedding night, so I've heard tell, he broke three beds. Don't laugh, master, I'm telling you the truth."

He took off his headband and wiped the sweat from his dark face. He himself was laughing.

"Did you hear what happened when he married your grandmother?" he asked.

"No, tell me, Kostandes."

"Her parents didn't want to give her to him. He was poor; they were powerful, respected, wealthy people. He was a wild spark, and wherever there was a row he was there. If there was trouble anywhere, he grabbed for his gun at once and made for the mountains. And they were dish-lickers, an obedient, well-behaved family. He was not their sort. Your grandfather sent to ask for her hand; the abbot of Christ the Lord also spoke up for him. But 'no! no!' the bride's parents answered, 'we don't want him!' 'Ah, that's the sort of people you are,' your grandfather replied, 'you cattle, now I'm going to show you!'

"One night he jumped on his mare and rode to the bride's village. He took nothing with him, except a can full of gasoline and a box of matches. And one thing more—a gold betrothal ring tied up in his headband. He rushed through the village and sprinkled house after house with gasoline. 'Hey, peasants,' he shouted, 'I'm setting fire to your houses!' Naturally they jumped out of bed to see what was going on. The bride's parents, too, came running.

" 'In God's name, Captain Sefakas, don't be guilty of such a crime!'

" 'Give me Lenio!' he shouted.

" 'Have you no fear of God?'

" 'Don't mix God up in my business. Give me Lenio! Here's the wedding ring!' He undid it from his headband. 'Choose,' he cried. 'Fire or the ring!'

" 'God will pay you for this, you madman!' the bride's father yelled.

" 'Fire or the ring!' he shouted again.

" 'Have pity on the village!'

" 'Fire, or the ring!'

"By now the peasants were furious. Was a crazy fellow to order them about? 'To arms, children!' they shouted. But at this point the pope came up. 'Fear God, brothers, master your anger,' he pleaded. He turned to the girl's father. 'Hey, old Minotes, cross yourself. He's a good son-in-law. Give her to him!' The more cautious ones took the pope's side.

" 'I'll give her to you, you madman!' yelled the father, 'but clear out of here at once!'

" 'I want her now. Bring her to me!'

"Cursing, the father now brought the girl, followed by her mother who was weeping.

"Your grandfather bent down, took the bride under the arms and hoisted her up on the mare's rump. He dug in the spurs. Dust whirled up. The peasants and the pope ran after him, breathless. At dawn they arrived at Petrokefalo, where the marriage was to take place.

" 'Back you march now,' cried your grandfather to the peasants. 'Next Sunday the tables will be laid, and you'll be welcome. I'm busy now. . . .' "

Kostandes took the cigarette from behind his ear. "That's the way men ought to get their wives," he said, and lighted it, using a piece of dried mushroom as tinder.

They reached a deep ravine. A thin trickle of water ran over light-colored rocks.

"Are you thirsty?" Kostandes asked.

"No. Let's get on, Kostandes! It's late!"

"I'm thirsty. Stop!"

He lay down on the rocks, thrust his wedge-shaped beard and his mustaches into the water and began lapping with his tongue like a tiger.

"There'll be nothing left of the brook," thought Kosmas, marveling at the wild man of the mountains. With pride, as if they were his own, he observed the powerful calves, the slender hips, the pitch-black hair soaking up the trickle.

Kostandes leaped to his feet in one movement, wrung out his beard and shouldered his staff.

"Here, on this rock where I lay and drank," he said, "I killed the Albanian, Hussein, the hater of Christians. Pitch cover his bones! I swore, then, that every time I came through this ravine I'd have a drink, whether I was thirsty or not!"

"You killed him, Kostandes! Alone?" asked Kosmas, who had heard about the appalling deed from the Metropolitan the day before. It had been one of the causes of the massacre of the Christians in Megalokastro.

"Of course alone!" Kostandes replied. "What else? Man against man, as things are done between men. I'd heard that the dog meant to come this way, after he'd set fire to one of the villages. You'll see it. We get to it soon. He'd killed all the men of the village. So I swore to kill him. I lay in wait for him and cut his throat." He began to whistle.

The shadows were lengthening over the face of the land. The two men reached the devastated village. Two or three houses had walls that were still standing. Out of the ruins came women in rags; a girl fetched a sprig from a pot of basil and threw it to Kosmas. "Welcome," she called out.

They reached the village square. Graybeards gathered around them. The few women who were in the group held back. A huge, bony old man, the spokesman, came forward and took off his cap. "We've no chair to offer you to sit down on, we've no glass to bring you water in if you're thirsty, we've no bread if you're hungry. The dogs have burned up everything—may God burn them!"

"We've no proper man, either, to talk with you," said an old woman, and began the keening, in which the other women joined.

"Courage, you women!" said the old man. "Didn't the same thing happen to us in 1866? And yet there were a few little children left, and out of them the whole village was renewed. As long as there are still a man and a woman, Crete doesn't die!"

The old man turned to Kostandes. "God bless that hand of yours, my palikar," he said, "and may you enter Paradise with the knife that slew Hussein."

"Come," said Kosmas, who could bear the horror no more. "Good-by!"

In silence the graybeards propped their chins on their staffs and watched the two move on. The old women wiped their eyes. A girl stood in front of the ruins of her house and gazed admiringly after Kostandes, as with youthful vigor he strode from stone to stone.

The sun was setting as they came to a shut-in, desert plain on which a dark group of oak trees mourned.

"We must hurry," said Kostandes, hitting the mule with his staff, "if we want to get to the next village before nightfall. We'll stop there, with old Kubelina. She's my aunt, my mother's sister. She's got no house, but she has a heart, and that'll be enough for us. You won't find a house standing in that village either. The bandits have raged there too. Curse them!"

A barefoot, half-blind old woman, loaded down with wood, appeared before them.

"How are things with you, little woman?" asked Kosmas.

"As they are with dogs, my child," she answered, "if God would only stop loading man with as much as he can carry!"

"Have the Turks ruined you too?"

But Kostandes made violent signs to Kosmas to be quiet.

"What did you say, my child? I'm hard of hearing. God be praised!"

"Good-by! We must go on."

"Are you a Cretan?"

"Yes."

"Take my blessing! Beget children! Crete has grown empty. Beget children, so the Cretans won't vanish from the world. They'll be needed, too."

"Come," said Kostandes. "It's late." He hit the mule. They hurried on.

"A good thing she didn't throw stones at us," he said. "We had a lucky escape. That's old Kostandinia, the pilgrim's widow, as she's·called. When the poor thing sees a man, she loses her wits. She picks up stones and throws them at him. She takes every man for a Turk."

He gathered some acorns off the ground, shelled them and ate them. As Kosmas looked at him with surprise, he said:

"Those aren't acorns, they're chestnuts. At least we call them chestnuts when evening comes and we've had nothing to eat and can't make things out clearly."

At last they left the plain. A pass appeared in the mountain before them.

"There's the village," said Kostandes, pointing. Kosmas could discern only heaps of ruins on the slope of the mountain.

"Where?" he asked. "I can't see anything."

"In front of you, those stones," said Kostandes. "Soon the people too will come into sight. There, the dogs have got wind of us."

The dogs rushed barking out of the ruins. Their ribs gleamed hungrily.

"I don't see a light anywhere," said Kosmas.

"Where would they get oil, master? At sundown they huddle into the ruins, like owls."

"Welcome," cried voices, and five or six heads peered from behind the naked stones. "Where are you going?"

"To old Kubelina," Kostandes answered. "She'll make up a bed for us in her lordly mansion."

Laughter came in answer.

"Have you a bite of something with you?" one of them asked.

"Yes, we've got something."

"Then old Kubelina will have something to eat. Have you got some bits of stuff to keep warm in?"

"We've got that too."

"Then old Kubelina will be able to keep warm," said the voices, and fresh laughter rang out behind the stones.

"They can still laugh!" said Kosmas, overcome.

Kostandes began counting the heaps of ruins. "Four, five, six—ah, here's my aunt's house!" he said. "We needn't knock, it hasn't got a door. Hey, Kubelina, come out on the balcony!"

A frail old woman in rags, leaning on a bent stick, came out between the stones.

"Is that Kostandes?" she asked. "When will you learn reason? And who's with you?"

"Throw open the doors, I tell you!" answered Kostandes. "Kill two hens. Give 'em to the girl to prepare. We'll have one boiled, the other roast, with potatoes. Open the chests too, get out the silken sheets and make up beds for us. We're glad we've arrived. Be happy in your kingdom!"

"All shall be done, you whirlwind," replied the old woman. She groped her way forward.

"Welcome, sir," she said to Kosmas, who had dismounted and was stumbling over the debris. "Welcome, my child! Don't listen to that silly Kostandes. I've roofed a corner with rushes—that's the best room in the house. Come in."

They squatted on the stones. Kostandes collected brushwood and made a fire. Kosmas opened the sack and took out the plentiful provisions his mother had packed for him. The old woman sat down beside them, and they began to eat. The old woman crossed herself and fell upon the food.

"Come every evening, my children, every evening, and then I too, poor thing, will have something to eat. Have you got some wine with you as well?"

Kostandes pulled out a bottle, which passed from mouth to mouth. The old woman drank, and her eyes grew bright. In her youth she had certainly been beautiful; now all she had left were those huge, gleaming, dark-brown eyes.

"Hey, Aunt," said Kostandes, whom the drink had made gay, "may I be allowed to sing something?"

"You have my permission," she replied. "You're still alive, so sing, you idiot!"

The lusty fellow sang, with long-drawn-out notes, while his aunt, her toothless mouth open, listened and giggled.

I took my Aunt Thodora down
One summer evening to the town.

Your beauty's set me in a whirl.
Ah, if you were some other girl!

Child, be a man, and have your way.
I'll be your aunt again, some day.

New life came into the spellbound woman. She clapped her hands and blushed. Kosmas gazed at her thoughtfully. "What strength these souls have in them!" he thought. "That is Crete."

"Poverty must have its pleasures, my child," said the old woman, laughing. "Suffering needs singing and drinking, otherwise it feeds on us. He's a rough customer, but he isn't going to make a meal of us. We'll eat *him* up."

In the morning, as they were taking leave of her, the old woman picked up a stone covered with red stains and gave it to Kosmas.

"It's the only present I can give you," she said. "Keep this stone in remembrance of Crete." She pointed to the dark red spots. "My son's blood."

In the street Kostandes strode along and sang. Kosmas felt that he was now experiencing the lost meaning of his native country for the first time. Hard of approach, rebellious, harsh was this land. She allowed not a moment of comfort, of gentleness, of repose. One could not tell whether she loved her children or hated them. One thing was certain: she scourged them till the blood flowed.

He turned and looked back at the stone heaps which were the village. A few women and children were visible among the stones. He heard voices and laughter. What strength there is! he thought. What souls! For thousands of years they have struggled in this wilderness of rocks, with hunger, thirst, discord and death. And they don't bow down. They don't even complain. In the deepest hopelessness the Cretan finds redemption.

As they came in sight of the grandfather's village, the sun was at its noon height. A hot south wind was blowing from Arabia, and the sea began to rise beyond the mountain.

Old Sefakas' big house stood out at the highest point of the village. It had a stately air, with its wine presses, oil presses, stables and storehouses, where casks and jars lay in rows. It had wide verandas, where in summer the rugs and pillows were stacked in heaps up to the roof. The high bedrooms were on the first floor. The doors were now open; a stream of people went in and out to see how things were with the captain in his struggle against Charos. The old man's daughters-in-law and grandchildren ran busily about, counting the jars, estimating the value of the store of flour and oil, verifying the casks in the wine cellar. How many fleeces hung from the rafters? How many cheeses were there in the cheese larder? They reckoned out loud what inheritance would fall to each one.

It seemed to the grandfather that they were carving him up alive. He called out angrily:

"Put me in the yard, so that I can't hear you!"

The daughters-in-law and grandchildren prepared a bed for him in the yard.

"Put me on the ground under the lemon tree. Here's where I want to draw my last breath—where the earth touches my flesh and I can touch the earth. Prop me a bit higher, so that I can see about me!"

They placed a cushion against his back to support him. Near him they set his stick and a cup of water to drink from.

"Now leave me alone. Away with you!" he ordered. "Only Thrasaki's to come and sit by me."

He now took a good look around him at the stables, the presses, the fountain, the troughs, the two cypresses that flanked the door, and he sniffed the air, which smelled of lemon leaves and dung. The smell delighted him and he stroked his beard in contentment. He heard a sigh and, turning, became aware of a sturdy, curly-haired youth who stood waiting.

"Well, who are you?"

"Konstantes."

"Whose son?"

"Your son Nikolas'."

"And why are you standing here, so close to me?"

"You're a long time dying, Granddad, and I'm in a hurry to be back at my sheep-pen. I want to be off."

"Off with you then, don't wait about uselessly. I shall be some time. And look after the beasts well."

The curly-headed young palikar bent down, grasped his grandfather's hand and kissed it.

"I shan't go," he said, "if you don't give me your blessing. That's what I've been waiting for since early this morning."

"Take my blessing, then, and go. And listen—go indoors and tell them they're to lay the tables in the yard in front of me, so that the three captains can eat here and I can see them. Are they still eating?"

"Yes, still. Since yesterday evening, when they arrived, by my faith, Granddad, their jaws haven't had a rest. From time to time they dropped off to sleep on each other's shoulders, and then they woke up again and the chewing went on. And the schoolmaster's brought his lyre with him to play an accompaniment. And they keep bothering the women."

"What's come over you, you clucking hen? Shut up! Do as I tell you. The tables are to be laid here, so that I can see. And if they can't move, help them, Konstantes! And don't laugh. They're captains. They deserve respect! Go!"

Charidimos appeared, panting. He had been sent by the grandfather to Captain Michales to bring him the news that his father was dying, and to ask him to come down for the leave-taking.

"What answer have you brought me? Will he come?" the old man asked.

"'I can't leave my post, Father,' he told me to say to you. 'Forgive me, but I can't leave my post. Give me your blessing from afar. Farewell! And may we meet again soon!'"

"He's right. He made one mistake, but now he's learned prudence. Let him have my blessing from afar," said the old man, raising his hand and blessing the air.

He turned to Thrasaki. "My little Thrasaki, do you understand what's going on?"

"I understand, Granddad."

"Keep your eyes open, Thrasaki, and see clearly. Keep your ears open, and hear clearly. Let nothing escape you. Now three mountains will be coming into view—the three captains."

While he was still speaking, Stavrulios, the village carpenter, appeared at the street door. The grandsons had sent for him, to take

383

the measurements for the coffin. Stealthily and fearfully he entered
the yard. The grandfather half shut his eyes, and pretended not to
see him. The man bent down and began to make furtive motions
with his arms. He asked, to distract the old man, "How are you
feeling, Captain Sefakas? You're all right today, God be thanked.
You'll have Charos beaten yet!"

The old man saw that the carpenter was unobtrusively trying to
measure him and he smiled under his lusty, flowing beard.
At length he took pity on him and said:

"Don't be afraid, Stavrulios, you idiot, just bring your rule out
and measure me!"

The carpenter started. "What did you say, Captain?"

"Blockhead, get on with your work and measure me!"

The carpenter thought that the old man was feeling for his stick
and was alarmed. He pulled the tape measure out of his belt and
placed it against the massive body.

"How long?" asked the old man.

"Six foot exactly, captain."

"I've shrunk," he said with a sigh. "Measure my breadth too."

Stavrulios measured his breadth as well and then stood by un-
certainly.

"Run along with you, poor fellow! I want it made of good tim-
ber! Have you got walnut?"

"Of course, Captain."

The old man turned to Thrasaki. "Can you tell walnut, Thrasaki?"

"That I can, Granddad!"

"Good! Well, make sure that Stavrulios doesn't swindle us. I
want it made of walnut. Go!"

Meanwhile the women were setting the tables in the yard. They
brought roast meat and dainties, jugs of wine and copper drinking
cups. The graybeard, propped up on his pillow, watched. Two bees
hummed about his huge head of thick hair, and a few ants were
crawling over his naked, furry calves. Their scurrying amused him.

"Where are the captains?" he asked.

"There they come, Granddad."

With their faces askew, their mustaches drooping, and their
broad red belts loose, the three hobbled slowly out, supporting one

384

another. They wore baggy breeches of thick wool. Their boots were trodden down. Each dangled a camomile flower behind his ear.

"Let's walk straight, brothers! If not, we shall disgrace ourselves," they whispered to each other.

"Hold me up or I'll fall," croaked the lame schoolmaster, who was in the middle. The lean, proud little man was half seas over. His lyre was slung from his shoulder, like a cartridge belt.

Captain Mandakas towered above him on his right. The captain's hair and beard were short; he had a strong neck, solid bones and gigantic ears. At his waist flashed the silver pistols. On the schoolmaster's left was Captain Katsirmas the corsair, weathered by the salt air, his face savage, his eyes squinting.

When they saw the old man, they stopped.

"Are you still living, brother Sefakas?" cried Captain Mandakas, roaring with laughter. "And we've been eating and drinking and saying, 'God be merciful to him.' "

"Won't you eat and drink some more, captains?" the old man invited. "Since yesterday, I hear, your jaws haven't rested. I want you to have your fill, so that you can forget your miserable bellies, and we can talk together like men!"

The schoolmaster started to answer.

"Be quiet!" said Katsirmas, and he covered the schoolmaster's whole face with the palm of his hand. "Or they'll see how it is with us." Then he addressed old Sefakas in a dignified voice, placing his hand on his breast.

"Many years to you, Captain Sefakas! We're happy to be visiting you in your mansion. We've eaten and drunk. We'll eat and drink some more to your health. And then, as you say, we'll talk together like men. Don't be in a hurry."

"I'm not in a hurry," the old man replied. "Someone here is in a hurry."

"Who?"

"Charos."

"We're three leaders," said Captain Mandakas, twirling his mustache. "With you, that makes four. He must wait!"

The three swayed in unison like a three-headed, six-footed monster. His two companions held the schoolmaster fast by the neck to keep him from falling. The grandsons and daughters-in-law had

385

come out and were laughing out loud at the spectacle of the drunken heroes. But old Sefakas called out angrily, "What are you laughing at, there? They're captains, strong men! Hold them up, so they don't fall!"

"If anyone comes near me, I'll split his skull!" bellowed Captain Katsirmas. "I can walk without help."

He shook loose from his companions and with great strides reached the tables.

At last all three reached their thrones and filled the cups. The schoolmaster took the lyre from his shoulder and placed it upright on his lap. He grabbed for a piece of meat and wolfed it, to fortify himself.

Just as he took up the bow, Kosmas arrived on the threshold. The grandfather drew his brows together in an effort to see who it was.

"Who's that leanbottom, standing there on the threshold of my door?"

"Your grandson, Granddad," answered Kosmas, going over to the old man.

"Which one?"

"The son of Captain Kostaros, your first."

"Welcome," cried the grandfather, stretching out his hand. "Come, let me give you my blessing. Where have you been knocking about, all these years? What were you after in the Franks' country? What have you learned? Yes, if I'd only time to ask you questions, and hear your answers. But the oil in my lamp's coming to an end. The world's growing dark."

Kosmas bent down, to receive the blessing. The old man kept his hand on his head and would not let him rise.

"You write, they say. What do you write, by the God you worship? You'll come down to being like Kriaras the rhymesmith, who wanders through the villages and passes a plate around for money!"

With his small, piercing eyes the grandfather searched and weighed him. What sort of a grandson is that? Is he worth anything or not? How could his seed have produced a quill-driver?

"Married?" he asked.

"Yes."

"They say you've chosen a Jewess."

"Yes," said Kosmas, looking hesitantly at the old man.

"Nothing wrong with that, you fool. They too have souls. One God made us all. You did right. You liked her, you took her like a palikar! Provided she's honorable and a good housewife, that she's good-looking and bears sons—ask nothing else of a woman."

"She's had herself baptized, Granddad. She's a great soul. You'll like her."

"Has she some flesh on her bones? Tell me that! What should a woman do with a soul? Flesh is what the seed requires to grow. How long have you been married?"

"Two years, Granddad."

"And children?"

"None yet. . . ."

"You're taking your time! What do you do every night, you pair of idiots? I want strong great-grandsons, made of steel. She's to bear Cretans, I tell you, not Jews. And listen to me: beware of book learning!"

"She's got a son on the way, Granddad!"

"My blessing! Call him Sefakas, d'you hear? That's how the dead rise again! And now go, move aside!"

He beckoned to his daughter-in-law Katerina, who was standing behind him with her arms folded.

"Stick another cushion behind my back," he said to her. "I want to sit upright, so I can speak. Pick me some lemon blossom. I want to smell it. And while we captains are talking, not a sound from any of you! Make room! I want to speak to the old ones!"

The old ones had meanwhile fallen to eating and drinking again. The schoolmaster had propped his head against the trunk of one of the cypresses and, with tears in his eyes, kept singing the same mantinade over and over, to the accompaniment of his lyre.

> At larks all day I've blazed away,
> Used every cartridge.
> At last a sight—and my heart's alight!—
> Of you, my partridge!

The grandfather clapped his hands, and cried:

"Hey, captains, are your miserable stomachs still not full? That's enough! Wipe your beards, wash your hands, tighten your belts and come over here. I've a word to say to you. That's why I invited you. And you, schoolmaster, sling that lyre over your

387

shoulder and leave the larks—powder and shot and all. We've had enough of them! Hey! children!"—he turned to the women and his grandsons—"bring them some water to wash in. Bring them some scent, to stop them from stinking so. Wash them and tidy them up, children, before they come over to me!"

The girls brought scent and splashed it over the old men. They brought rose-vinegar for them to sniff, to sober them up. They supported them and brought them over to the grandfather. One of the captains stood on his right, the other on his left; the schoolmaster crouched in front of him, cross-legged.

Old Sefakas opened his arms and greeted the leaders, as if he were seeing them for the first time.

"Captain Mandakas, renowned leader in fighting on dry land; Captain Katsirmas, relentless corsair on the high seas; and you, Captain Schoolmaster, who also have battled among our shadows and composed the papers of the revolt and written what had to be written to the Turks and Franks—a thousand times welcome to my poor house!"

"Our greetings to you, Captain Sefakas," answered the three, their hands on their breasts.

Old Sefakas breathed heavily and drank a gulp of water from the cup. Then he began again:

"Brothers, do you still remember how, at every rising, we captains gathered under an oak tree or in some monastery, and took oaths and kissed one another, because we were going out to meet death? Such a gathering is this, now, under old Sefakas' lemon tree! Know that for days and days I have been on the point of taking leave of you, but still I don't go. I've made confession and communion, but I don't go. I'm not going, captains, before we four old ones have talked together. This too is a sort of rising. Brothers, what are we going to decide? Do you hear what I say? Are your minds clear? Can you hear and speak? Or am I wasting my words?"

"We can hear and speak!" said the three.

"Then hear me! I am a hundred years old. You, all of you, know my life, I've no need to make a written paper of it for you. That I've fought and worked, that I've had joy and sorrow, that I've done my duty as a man, you can all bear witness. Now my hour has come. The earth is opening, she wants, it seems, to swal-

388

low me. Let her swallow me, let her take her revenge! But she's not swallowing all of me! Look what I'm leaving behind!"

He pointed to his daughters, grandsons, granddaughters, and great-grandchildren.

"A whole people! So I'm not worried about death. I've beaten him. The devil's got the best of him. Different anxieties are devouring me. . . ."

With a sigh he paused. Then, in a voice that for the first time trembled, he said: "For a long time now I've been unable to sleep, captains. A worm is gnawing at me."

He looked intently at the captains, and raised his voice. "Do you hear what I'm saying? Pay attention! Your eyes have gone dim, schoolmaster!"

"We're listening," the schoolmaster retorted harshly. "What worm?"

"A worm is gnawing at me, brothers! I look back at my life. I look forward at my death. And I think and think. Where do we come from, children, and where are we going? That is the worm that's gnawing at me!"

The three captains were agitated by his words. The schoolmaster scratched his pointed, bald head and started to reply, but thought better of it. He had no answer to give.

"Has this thing never come into your minds?" asked the graybeard. "Has this worm never bitten you?"

"Never," answered the three.

"Nor me either, all my life, God is my witness. But lately I've not been able to sleep at night. To whom was I to tell what I was suffering? Those of my children who are still with me are young —fifteen, sixteen years old. Their brains are not firm enough. What would they be able to understand? Kostaros, my first-born son—he'd now be over seventy and would begin to understand. But he was turned to ashes at Arkadi. So I decided: Call a meeting, send for the companions of your youth and have a word with them. Like ears of corn at harvest time are your minds, captains —full of seed. You have surely scented something. Speak! Open your hearts. You've been drinking wine, so they'll open easily. Forward! Let us consult together, children! I don't want to die a blind man. You speak first, Captain Mandakas. Next to me you're the eldest. How old were you in 1821?"

"Twenty-two, brother Sefakas. Have you forgotten?"

"I was thirty, just over. I'm eight years ahead of you. You begin. Speak. You've lived and worn a belt for so many years now. What have you learned?"

Captain Mandakas thoughtfully stroked his thick beard.

"Is it for this you've called us, Captain Sefakas?" he said at last. "These are questions difficult to answer. You're making us pay very heavily for the wine and meat you've set before us. What do you think, schoolmaster?"

"Let the schoolmaster alone!" shouted the old man, "and speak to me. Have you come to understand anything in all the years you've lived? Don't turn and twist about! Speak out boldly, like a man!"

Captain Mandakas pulled a tobacco box from his belt and rolled himself a cigarette.

"You put the knife to my throat, old Sefakas," he said. "What am I to say to you? How am I to begin? I've lived the whole of my life as a blind man, just as you say about yourself, and I don't regret it. Blindly I've gone to war, and hurled myself upon the Turks. I married blindly, I begot children blindly, and went to church and lighted candles and kneeled before the icons. Blindly I've sowed, harvested, threshed and eaten my bread. I never asked myself why I ate, why I prayed, why I killed. And now, since you ask me—stop, Captain Sefakas, if you believe in God! Give me a chance to squeeze my brain until a drop comes out."

"All right, I'll be patient. Squeeze your brain, Captain Mandakas," said the grandfather, folding his arms.

Captain Mandakas called to his foster son, who was standing behind him. "Hey, Janakos, bring me my sack!"

All waited in silence. The grandfather beckoned to Kosmas. "Get a stool and sit down and listen. Do you understand what we're saying?"

"I understand, Granddad," answered Kosmas as he sat.

Janakos brought the sack and put it down in front of his foster father. Old Mandakas fumbled in it and brought out a wide-mouthed glass jar sheathed in leather.

"What have you got in the jar?" asked the grandfather, peering.

Captain Mandakas laughed.

"Is that your answer?" the other asked furiously.

"Other people," Captain Mandakas replied, "take bread, wine and meat in their sacks when they go on a journey. I too take them, but I take this jar as well."

"What's inside? I can't make it out."

Captain Mandakas raised the glinting jar close to the eyes of old Sefakas. The last light of day fell on it, and it gleamed red.

"Can you still see nothing?" asked Captain Mandakas, turning the bottle around.

"Bits of meat," answered the grandfather, "swimming in water."

"Those aren't bits of meat, old Sefakas, they're ears. It isn't water, it's spirits. On the day—in the year 1821—when a Turk bore down on me and bit off one of my ears, I took an oath: every Turk I slew, I'd cut off one of his ears and keep it in a bottle. To tell you the story of my life, Captain Sefakas, all I need is to look at one ear after another preserved in spirits and to tell you whose it was. This one here at the bottom of the jar—the hairy one— belonged to that terrible hunter of Christians, Ali Bey. He had killed my brother Panajis and then retired to his estate at Rethymno to hold a feast of celebration with his harem. That evening I went and sat in the Turkish coffeehouse and smoked my narghile. 'Bring me a bit of charcoal,' I said to the Turk who made the coffee, 'my narghile's going out.' I quickly folded up the mouthpiece of the narghile and ran out. With wings on my feet I dashed over the fields to Ali Bey's estate. I ran upstairs to his bed-chamber where he lay in bed with his hanum, fell upon him, cut off his head, took the ear with me and wrapped it in my kerchief. I got back to the coffeehouse just as the waiter was bringing me the charcoal. I unrolled the mouthpiece and went on smoking. No one had noticed my absence. Next day, when the news of Ali Bey's death spread, the pasha yelled, 'It was Mandakas!' But the Turks from the coffeehouse swore: 'Captain Mandakas was smoking his narghile in Hassan's coffeehouse the whole evening.'"

He pointed to another ear. "This thick, dark one with the ring in it comes off a Moor. Remadan, his name was. Another gobbler of Christians, may his bones soak in pitch! I ran into him one evening alone on the beach at Trypiti, outside Megalokastro. 'Remadan,' I asked him, 'have you no fear of God?' 'He's afraid of me,' the dog answered, 'for I'm Remadan!' 'And I'm Mandakas,' I said, drawing my knife. 'Draw your knife, you too!' 'I haven't got

391

it with me. You've come upon me unarmed, giaour.' 'I've got two. Choose!' I threw him the one he chose, and he brandished it in the air. The fight on the pebbles of the seashore began. We fought and fought, until night broke in on us. Blood was streaming over us, the sweat was flowing, we were boiling. We went into the sea, to cool ourselves. It turned red. We didn't speak, we bellowed. A friend of the Moor's came by. The blackguard wanted to help him. 'I'll spit you like a sardine,' the Moor shouted at him. 'You let us alone and clear out!' 'Hey, Remadan,' I said, 'you're a palikar.' 'So are you,' he answered. 'We're two wild beasts.' 'Then one of us has got to be killed!' I yelled and went for him again. He flagged. I sprang astride his neck and plunged my knife through his windpipe, as you slaughter a suckling pig. I took his ear, ring and all. Here it is!"

The memory of his heroic deeds was warming him up, and he went on:

"This ear, the one beginning to turn green, belonged to that butcher Mustapha; this one, here in the middle, to an Albanian; the torn one, there, to an imam. Damn him, he had a voice like a bell. Pity! I ought to have cut out his tongue and preserved that in spirits. Next to it, this little one, rounded like a sea shell, comes off Pertef Effendi. The shameless fellow, handsome as a picture, looked like Saint George! How could I help it? He used to ride through the Christian quarter and seduce our women. None of them could resist the dog. I was sorry for them, and one night I forced my way into his house. We fought in his bedroom. But he was very delicately built and used to women, and didn't put up much resistance. So I cut through that delicate neck of his and took this rounded ear.

"This glass jar contains all the risings of Crete! I couldn't collect the ears of the ones I killed in battle. But here are the risings of 1821, '34, '41, '54, '78. Now I've grown old. The last rising has brought in no ear! Truly I was a wild beast, I did terrible things, God forgive me. Whenever a rising broke out, I left my house, my children, my unpruned vines, my unplowed fields, and rode to join my leader, Captain Korax*."

As he remembered that famous name, he suddenly sighed. "Never will so mighty a man rise in the world again. What are

*Raven (Tr.)

we, compared to him? Figures of fun! No one ever joked in front of him, or heard him laugh. His eyes were round, dark and wild, like eagle's eyes. He had no faults. He didn't drink, didn't curse, didn't run after women. When he went out to battle he plowed his mare with his heels and swooped down on the Turks. He never turned to see if anyone was following him. He never looked ahead to count the Turkish fezzes. No bullet touched him. That was not a man. No, God forgive me, that was an archangel."

He sighed again. "Only the wings were missing!"

Old Sefakas listened patiently as he fidgeted nervously on his cushions, and sniffed the lemon leaves. At last he could bear it no longer and cried angrily, "Put that jar in your sack, Captain Mandakas! There's no limit to the wild-beast ways of men. Answer my question: What have you learned with all these years? Where have you arrived? Since you can now see your life in that glass jar, tell me: Has your course been the right one, or do you regret what you've done?"

"Regret it!" bawled Captain Mandakas, incensed. "No! If I had to begin all over again, old Sefakas, I'd marry the same wife, beget the same children, kill the same Turks—perhaps even more!—wear the same breeches, the same belt, the same boots! Not a hair would I change. And if I go before God tomorrow, I shall take my jar under my arm and say to Him: 'Either You let me into Paradise with this jar, or I won't go in at all!' "

"Was that what you were born for?" old Sefakas shouted, "to kill? Was that why God sent you into the world?"

"No, don't twist my words, old Sefakas. I'm not bloodthirsty. No, I don't kill for the sake of killing. But. . . ."

He scratched the top of his skull reflectively. Suddenly he shouted:

"But I was fighting for freedom!"

His brow cleared. "Yes," he said, "you ask me where we come from and where we're going. When I began speaking, I didn't know what answer I should give you. But while we've been talking this way and that, my brain's become clear. We're coming out of slavery, Captain Sefakas, and going into freedom. As slaves we were born, and have fought all our lives to become free. And we Cretans can only become free through killing. That's why I killed those Turks. That's it! You asked; I've answered you. Now I'm old: I've put away my dagger and folded my arms. Charos can come!"

He called to his foster son. "Janakos, put the sack where it belongs."

"Those were sound words," cried the grandfather. "Blessings on your tongue, blessings on your hands, Captain Mandakas! You were a long time about it, but you've understood. You have found your way. You've reached the end and done your duty. But do you believe there's only one way? Others are possible, as you'll see. You speak now, Captain Katsirmas, you corsair—it's your turn!"

The sea wolf clenched his fists; his squinting eyes grew red.

"I don't like the way you're treating us at all, old Sefakas," he said. "You've made us come here and just because you're a few years older you demand a reckoning from us. No, I'm not saying anything!"

"Don't flare up, you stubborn idiot," cried the grandfather. "No, it's not because I'm older, but because I'm going under the earth first and I've no time to lose. I don't want to die blind. I'm asking for help, children, for light! Don't you understand, Captain Katsirmas?"

"Yes," he answered. "You needn't yell. But you're not a ship in danger, which I can come and rescue in my boat. All my life I've struggled with the sea. That's the only place I know my way about. I can't help anywhere else. So what do you expect from me?"

"I'm drowning, old corsair," roared the grandfather. "And a drowning man has to be caught by the hair!"

"Your hair, old Sefakas, not ours! You are standing on the threshold of Hades, and fear comes over you. You call it a worm, I call it fear. So you summon your old comrades: 'What is this, children? Where am I going? Where am I being taken?' How should we know anything that could comfort you? We live haphazardly, we die haphazardly, rudderless, with sails bellying. A wind blows. Where it blows, there we go. Water rushes into our ship, we work at the pumps day and night. But the water keeps rising and the pumps are rusty. The wretched things won't work any more, and we go to the bottom. That's human life, and you can yell as loud as you like. What's our duty? To serve the pumps

394

day and night, not to fold our arms, not to complain, not to moan. We ought not to give up shamefully, but to work at the pumps day and night. That much I've learned from life, and you can take it or leave it!"

He turned his savage face to Captain Mandakas. "I wasn't like you, sir, nailed to the land, with blinkers before your eyes, so you could see nothing but Turks and Christians—and kill Turks and cut off their ears and pickle them in spirits. I can't bring a glass jar out of my sack and show it around and say: 'That is my life.' I've made voyages, Captain Mandakas, I've seen the whole world. I've slept with women of all kinds, I've pushed far down into Africa, where the bread is toasted by the sun. I've been in great harbors and little ones, I've seen millions of black men, millions of yellow men—my eyes have brimmed over with them! At first I thought they all stank. I said: 'Only Cretans smell good; and of the Cretans only the Christians.' But slowly, slowly, I got used to their stink. I found—I found that we all smell good and stink in the same way. Curse us all!

"And then I threw myself into piracy. I found out that the world is made up of copper kettles and clay jugs, banging against each other. Be of copper, Katsirmas, you wretch, or else you'll go to pieces! I said to myself. And if you get broken, you'll never be stuck together again: it's finished. So I made friends with some Algerians; we hoisted black flags, lay in wait, fell upon trading ships, killed, plundered, fled and hid our booty on deserted islands. And once—you all remember it—I unloaded at Grabusa a shipload of cinnamon, cloves and musk-nuts, so that the whole of Crete had a sweet scent. Have you forgotten, old Sefakas? I even sent a sackful of cloves and cinnamon to Your Grace."

"Go on," said the ancient. "Come to some conclusion. What does all that amount to?"

"It's to show you what you've got to understand. We feared neither God nor man. I was a Christian, they were Mussulmans. But we let no ship through, whether she was bound for Mecca or for Jerusalem. We set upon her and killed the pilgrims. I was a wild beast among wild beasts. Like the Algerians I grew a pigtail and had the rest of my head shorn. I collected a mass of thaler, ducats and Turkish money. I robbed each ship of two or three women, enjoyed them and threw them into the sea. I was a beast,

I tell you, worse than you, Captain Mandakas! And if you ask me, Captain Sefakas, whether I regret it, then here's my answer: I've lived my life well and soundly, and like a palikar, I don't regret it. God made me a wolf and I eat lambs. If He'd made me a lamb, the wolf would have eaten me, and rightly! That's the order of things. Is it my fault? It's the fault of Him Who made wolves and lambs."

For a moment he squinted at his companions in silence, as though he expected an answer. But none was forthcoming. So he went on:

"And now, captains, I'm old. The timbers have sprung, the hold's splitting apart, water's rushing in, the pumps are working badly. And so I've slunk onto dry land, and adopted good manners. I play the part of a human being. Why? I can't do anything else now. My strength's gone. My hair and teeth have fallen out. The wolf's grown mangy and lousy. I act like a human being. I've sunk to that. I don't kill any more, I don't howl, I bleat like a lamb. When I sit at the village fountain and watch the girls filling their pitchers, my eyes eat the fish, but my belly remains empty. Often I find myself in tears. 'Why are you crying, Granddad?' the girls ask me, and giggle. 'Because I've got to die, damn you, and leave such beautiful bodies behind on earth.' By God, if I were King or Ali Pasha, I'd collect for myself a band of the loveliest girls and have them slaughtered on my tomb, to take them with me."

"You're a bloodthirsty wild beast, Captain Katsirmas," cried the grandfather. "Be quiet!"

"You asked, and I've answered. You wanted me to open the trap door, and I've opened it. Has it given you a fright, old Sefakas?"

The mocker with the toothless mouth glared savagely at the grandfather. He screamed, "The trap door is open, the evil spirits are coming out. You wanted to see and hear them! 'Where do we come from?' you asked. Up out of the earth, Captain Sefakas. 'Where are we going?' you asked. Under the earth, Captain Sefakas. What is your duty? To eat, if you're a wolf; to be eaten, if you're a lamb. And if you ask me about God: He is the big wolf —He eats both lambs and wolves!"

"Don't blaspheme, old pirate!" cried Captain Mandakas. "You're drunk, your mind's reeling, you don't know what you're saying. The big wolf is Charos, not God!"

Captain Katsirmas laughed. "God and Charos are the same thing, cousin! But why should I argue with you? Your brain lives on beans and knows nothing but beans."

He turned to Captain Sefakas. "That's what I had to say to you, old Sefakas. You shouldn't have asked me. Now I want some wine."

"Fill up his cup with wine," the ancient ordered one of his grandsons. "He's confessed, let him have communion. . . ."

He bent his head in meditation. "I'm no judge and I give no judgment," he said. "God heard him. Let Him be the judge."

He turned to the schoolmaster, who, all the time the captains had been speaking, had been wagging his pointed, bald head to and fro.

"Speak, schoolmaster. Stop shaking your head!"

The schoolmaster took the lyre from his shoulder.

"All my life," he said, "I've talked. Now it bores me. You ask about difficult things, Captain Sefakas. What devil put them into your mind? I have no words with which to answer."

"Are we to be dumb, then?" asked the ancient, looking at the schoolmaster angrily. "Be dumb, be blind, be castrated, be at peace? Is that what you want? But you fool, that means a man is a head of cattle!"

"A question can be put into words, Captain Sefakas. Don't get angry. Ask questions as long as you're not tired of asking them. You can shape a question in words, but not the answer. And yet you demand an answer from me."

"I want an answer," said the graybeard, throwing back his head.

"You want an answer, old Sefakas. You shall have it. I shall answer you with the lyre. It is my real mouth. If you understand what it says, all is well. If not, I can't help you. Then you'll die blind, as you were born blind."

"Play on your lyre, schoolmaster. God be your helper!" said the grandfather, closing his eyes.

The sky had darkened. Fat drops pattered on the leaves of the lemon tree and fell refreshingly on the cheeks, the closed lids and lips of the grandfather. He licked them thirstily.

The schoolmaster grasped the bow, bent over the lyre, and became one with it. The bow danced over the three strings, the little bells tinkled, the dark yard filled with bright laughter, as if it were

397

a schoolyard in which the children were playing and chasing one another during recess. Or as if birds in a leafy poplar were awaking at dawn and rejoicing in the sunlight.

The fiddle bow leaped, laughed, danced, and the hearts of the old captains became children, birds, gurgling springs. The grandchildren and daughters-in-law moved nearer, the men and maids sat down on the ground together. And in spite of the falling rain, they listened.

The old grandfather felt as though his heavily built body were losing its weight, rising into the air and floating like a cloud above lemon trees and cypresses. Only in dreams had he so felt the joy of floating. In dreams, and one other time: He had been on his way back from war, on a Sunday; he had washed off the blood, put on clean clothes and gone into the church to communion. Then too his body had felt like a lightly flying cloud. And on the way home it had seemed to him as if his feet did not touch the earth at all. . . .

But slowly the voice of the lyre altered. It became wild and furious. The bells on the bow rattled like those on the neck of a trained hawk as it shoots upward in search of prey. Those were men's voices that rang out from the strings. The captains thought of their youth, of war, of the groaning men who lay dying, of the women mourning, of the horses whinnying and standing on the field, bloodstained and riderless. "Give me back my youth or be still, schoolmaster!" Captain Mandakas almost cried aloud. But already the lyre had again changed its tune; it was soft and lulling and the old men listened with happy smiles.

The sound, through the moist air, was like a distant humming of bees, or the murmur of a deep stream. The sound was like a woman's love dirge far beyond the mountains, on the shore of the foaming sea. Or was it the sea itself, lapping at the shore and moaning? Or was it a yet more mysterious, more magical voice from beyond life, from the other bank, sweetly and sadly and lovingly freeing souls from the flesh? Was it perhaps God Himself, hidden in the moist darkness of the night, Who was calling and raising up to Him with gentle allurement His eternal beloved, the soul of man?

The schoolmaster played as one possessed, so that the fiddle bow seemed to strike sparks. Deeper and deeper he was lost in the darkness. It was as if the lyre, alone and erect under the lemon tree, were intoning a funeral hymn. But its wailing was also a seductive call.

A deep, broad smile overspread the old grandfather's lips. His flying, light body rose in one sweep from the lemon tree further into the air, and now lay like a cloud above the house. Soon it would by a soft transformation become a cloud, falling as rain to the ground, to nourish the young shoots.

That is death, the grandfather felt deep down in himself, that is Paradise. I am going to Paradise. I am there, already. Greetings, O my God!

He opened his eyes and saw nothing but darkness. And out of the darkness a soft, tender voice called him by name.

"I'm coming," the grandfather answered.

All night they let him lie stretched out in the yard. He was showered with rain like a great tree trunk. Kosmas, kneeling down, had closed his eyes for him. Thrasaki squatted beside him and watched him. It was the first time he had seen death so close. With shuddering he gazed upon the grandfather whom he had loved so much. It was as though his grandfather had acquired some new power, dark and sinister—as though he were only waiting to pounce on men and drag them with him under the earth. Thrasaki had a longing to run away. But he dared not stir. He remained where he was, spellbound by fear.

His tribe kept watch around the corpse. The door had been left open. The village had been shaken when it heard that old Sefakas had given up his soul, and all streamed past to take their leave. One after another silently kissed his hand, which lay stretched out upon the stones.

Two old women had washed him with wine and wrapped him in a white shroud of fine linen. It was a relic of his dead wife, Lenio, who had woven it for this hour. Two of his daughters-in-law placed a lantern near his head and a second near his feet. Under the soft light the face of the dead man took on a mild expression.

"Shouldn't we take him in?" suggested Katerina. "It isn't right

399

that he should lie here on the ground and be soaked with rain."

But Kosmas opposed her. "The dead man wants to be here and soaked with rain."

A light, compassionate south wind was blowing. The grandsons brought logs and brushwood and kindled a fire in the middle of the yard, to warm themselves. The flames lighted up the yard and attracted the animals. The mule, the two asses, the mare and the two plow oxen stuck their heads out of their stalls and looked with wonder at what was going on in the yard. The three captains had curled themselves up, full of drink and food, against the strong trunk of the lemon tree, and were snoring.

"Good-by, old Sefakas. Greet the dead!" cried the women, loosening their headbands.

"Till we meet again, Captain Sefakas!" cried the old people, pressing his hand. "A happy journey!"

Each woman also threw him a sprig of basil, that he might take the scent of the upper world with him into Hades. One mother stricken by Charos laid beside the dead man the chalk and scribbled slate of her little son who was dead. "Take my child his slate, old man!" she cried. "Do me that kindness! His name was Demetrakis, he was your neighbor's child. You'll recognize him. He wore a red woolen cap with a tassel, and went barefoot."

Katerina got up and spread heavy rugs over the snoring captains, so they would not catch cold. Then she took Thrasaki by the hand. "Come to bed, my child. It's nearly midnight."

But Thrasaki refused to obey. "I'm watching over Granddad," he said. "Father hasn't come. I'm watching in his place."

In the light of the flames his eyes flickered hard and decisive, like those of his father. The mother drew back and said no more.

The rain showed no sign of stopping. Renio and the other granddaughters brought coffee to keep the members of the deathwatch awake. When silence fell upon the yard from time to time, the deep, confused voices of the night could be heard: small animals and insects, night birds, restless dogs, groaning cattle. Suddenly the cocks rose up and crowed. Day broke.

Toward noon Stavrulios brought the coffin on his shoulder. Thrasaki ran up to examine the wood. It was walnut.

Two hours after midday the grandsons raised the coffin, in which the grandfather lay at rest, and bore it out the door. Moving slowly, they carried him around the village. Then they stopped at all the crossroads, and the girls threw basil and marjoram onto the corpse, as if it were a picture of the Crucified One.

The whole village accompanied him like a single family, bareheaded and serene, as though he were really the God of the village who had died. They paced slowly along, so that the grandfather might take leave of his village with his accustomed calm. Suddenly, when they were already outside the village and nearing the graveyard, the sluices of Heaven opened wide and the rain poured down.

The peasants yelled with joy. For months they had longed for a real rain, for the crops threatened to be dried up. And now, God be thanked, they raised their sunburned faces with eagerness toward the streaming sky.

"The grandfather has turned to rain," murmured one of the old men, "he's coming back to our village."

Without hastening they reached the cemetery, wet through. Two stalwart grandsons had dug a grave. The red, loamy soil was full of mussel shells, as if these mountains had once been the bottom of the sea. It rained and rained. The grandfather was lowered gently. The mourners each threw a handful of earth upon him. Then they prepared to return to the house.

Now they ran fast, for they were in a hurry to sit down at the loaded tables and to devour the black ram that the grandfather had marked for his funeral feast, and to drink wine. And to forgive his soul.

Kosmas sat on the broad divan. His soul was troubled, his body tired. He shut his eyes. He wanted to rest for a little before going up the mountain. He had bidden Charidimos find a storm lantern and to hold himself in readiness. Before daybreak tomorrow they must be at Captain Michales' headquarters. His sleep only lasted a moment, but it was long enough to let his dead father in. Kosmas saw him as clear as could be. He stood before the stairway of his house, preparing to go into the bedroom. He had already raised his foot to place it on the first step. Kosmas was terrified. Upstairs his wife was sleeping. The dead man would now go up and frighten her. He leaped up. "Where are you going, Father," he called out. The dead man with the drooping mustache and the wart on his right cheek wheeled around and looked at him sav-

401

agely. On his head he was wearing a black headband with a red, bloodstained tassel. His mouth was a wound stopped with cotton wool.

He stared at Kosmas, frowning. He was clearly angry, for he was grinding his teeth, and a small red flame darted from his nostrils and licked his face. Suddenly he opened his mouth. The cotton wool fell out, and the wound lay bare. He gave a wild moan and moved hastily up the stairs.

"Father!" cried Kosmas. "Don't do her any harm. She's my wife!"

The son fearfully took a step toward the dead man and called out for the second time, "She's my wife. Don't touch her!" He stretched out his hand to stop him. But the dead man vanished in smoke, and Kosmas now heard—without seeing anything—heavy steps ascending the stairs. . . .

With a cry he woke up. He opened his eyes and saw the guests at their funeral meal. A great dish was just being brought in, with the steaming ram upon it. It lay on its back, with its four legs in the air, complete with head and horns, as though alive. The ravening peasants fell on it and divided it up. The grandsons brought in jugs of wine, and now the funeral meal turned into a joyous feast. But it was not only the wine; it was the heavy rain falling on the thirsty earth; it was also because Charos had paid a visit and had not touched them, but had only taken the old man away with him! So they ate and drank, and the joy waxed. Their feet were tickling. They wanted to dance. The wine he had drunk made the good singer of the village, Stavrulios the carpenter, so far forget himself as to strike up a love song. His neighbors hushed him up quickly. To smother the scandal, the pope washed his throat with a mighty swig of wine and loudly intoned a hymn.

Kosmas stood up and took his aunt Katerina aside.

"Aunt Katerina," he said. "Tonight I'm going to visit my uncle up on the mountain. Haven't you any message?"

The woman sighed. "Are messages any good with him, my child? What he's got into his head, that he'll do, and the world may go hang. May God guide his hand."

"Won't he think of his son, Aunt Katerina?"

"To be sure. Thrasaki's the one thing he loves in the world. But he won't turn his head for that. He'll do what he's decided to do.

There's no hope, my child, from a man who's never once thought of himself."

She wiped her eyes and said no more.

Kosmas went over to Charidimos, who had the ram's kidneys in his hand, while the grease dripped from his goat-beard.

"Charidimos," Kosmas said to him, "you've eaten and drunk well, you've celebrated Granddad's death. Get up now. We're going."

The grizzled servant made a sulky face. "It's raining. A cloudburst. I can't see to the end of my nose."

"We're going," said the eldest grandson in a tone of command. "It's got to be done."

"All right, let's go," Charidimos sighed, cursing his fate, which never allowed him to enjoy anything. Just now, as the fun was beginning. . . .

"Forward," said Kosmas. "Got the storm lantern?"

The hymn was over and Stavrulios asked the pope, "Will you let me sing a robber song?"

And without waiting for the answer, he threw back his neck and made the house hum:

"When will the starry sky be clear?
When will February be here
So I can take my gun . . . ?"

14

OLD CHARIDIMOS threw the light from his storm lantern on the narrow goat path that zigzagged up the mountain. He had not yet recovered from his tipsiness; sometimes he stumbled, and once he fell full length. Ashamed, he got up again and pulled himself together. "Damn wine," he muttered, "the devil take water!"

He turned to Kosmas, for he longed to talk with him. He was bathed in sweat.

"Master, won't you open your mouth? I'm nearly dropping. That's why I'm so unsteady on my legs."

"None of your gab, Charidimos! It's pouring. Let's hurry!"

He wanted to be at his destination by dawn without fail—before the Turks could sight them from the plain. The cloudburst continued, the arteries of the land were swelling, the water splashed down in the brooks. From time to time a bright flash split the sky, and the thunder rolled from mountain to mountain. As soon as its echoes had died away, the gurgling of the masses of water could be heard as they streamed down.

"If you believe in God, master, talk to me!" the old man of the mountains begged. "What's happening out there in the world? Are they sick men like us? Or devils?"

But Kosmas had no desire to chatter. Without a word he continued to climb in the darkness and rain, determined not to profane this holy hour with idle words. A strange, new, vital emotion had come over him. He endured the rain serenely, like a rock, a Cretan rock. To the marrow of his spine he felt the joy of the rocks and the earth as they drank their fill.

The rain was mercifully putting out the fires started by

the Turkish soldiers in the Greek villages and monasteries. It was also putting out the flames in the Turkish villages where Christians had begun the destruction.

Turks and Christians went back into the ruins and set themselves to place stone on stone once more and to build their houses anew.

Bleeding from many wounds and gnashing her teeth, Crete bowed under the yoke again. In caves and monasteries the captains had meanwhile been debating. They had read the Metropolitan's circular again and again, until they had at last understood: it was the voice of Greece. They cursed, they cast threatening glances at the sky and clenched their fists. But at last they bowed their heads. They stuck their daggers into their sheaths, buried their weapons and went home to their work.

Sulkily and taciturnly the Kastrians opened their shops and the peasants plowed and sowed. The heavy wheel of the everyday began to turn again.

Captain Polyxigis came back from the mountains, with a new black band around his fez. He went to Saint Menas, the captain of the town, lighted a candle before him and stood reproachfully for a moment in front of his icon. Then he opened his shop. He retired into the back of it, so that he would neither see nor be seen. He ordered a narghile and smoked, sunk in thought. He paid no attention to the farmers as they came in through the Kanea gate, bringing with them what they had saved in the way of lemons and oranges, wine and oil. His lips no longer smiled; nothing but venom trickled from them now. He already regretted his weakness in leaving the mountain.

I should not have listened either to Greece or to the Metropolitan, he brooded. Captain Michales, that wild boar, has done the right thing! I too should have stayed there to die. What good is life to me now? I'd like to join him again.

He coiled the mouthpiece around the neck of the narghile and, sighing, stepped over the threshold. At that moment Manoles the pope passed by. His grease-spotted cassock was bellying in the wind. He had not stirred out of Megalokastro during the trouble. He had buried, baptized, censed people's houses, filled his pockets and added more fat to his neck. Now he was bearing the sacred chalice and patten, while before him, somber and pale, Murzuflos paced, carrying a lighted lantern in the brightness of noon. Captain Polyxigis crossed himself. He had heard the sad news: the pope was on his way with the last sacrament for Captain Stefanes. On the return journey a shell fired by a Turkish patrol boat into his smuggler ship had torn off both his feet.

"God bless his soul," he muttered. "He's borne himself like a man."

He was about to withdraw again into the half-darkness of his shop when he caught sight of Vendusos, wrapped in a rug and shivering with cold. He waved his hands and talked to himself as he walked. For two days he had been running through the streets as though haunted by some curse, and he could not come to a decision: Should he open his tavern and bring back his wife and daughters and engage once more in his old trade? Or should he throw everything to the winds and return to Captain Michales, to show him that he too was a man who would not let himself be knocked about and trampled on? Vendusos could not stop thinking of the captain's parting words as he sent him with his message to the Metropolitan: "Good-by, Vendusos, you won't come back. You're Vendusos, I don't ask anything of you, behave like a Vendusos if you wish!"

A thousand demons surrounded him. Now his honor demanded that he return to the mountain, to show Captain Michales how wrong he was; and now he remembered his wife, his two daughters and the tavern, and this sent him running down the mountainside again.

When he saw Captain Polyxigis on the threshold of the shop, he stopped. Halt! That was a mighty captain, and yet he's put his tail between his legs and kept his mouth shut. Why? Because it was in the interest of Crete. And would you, you no-account Vendusos, think things out and act on your own? Come on, you idiot, leading in battle is heavy work, work for a palikar. But the leaders show themselves to be even more like palikars when they order the laying down of arms! Lay them down, then! Let's have a talk with Polyxigis, to give ourselves courage. I've got children. Poor me, I must keep alive.

"Good day, captain," he said, walking in. "I've come from the mountain. I have many greetings for you—"

"Leave me in peace, the devil take you!" roared Captain Polyxigis. The sight of Vendusos moved him to wrath, because of his own shame. But this made Vendusos wild in turn. Indeed! This great lord thought he was to be knocked about and trampled on, did he? He would show him!

"I'm going back to the mountain. I'm not leaving my post. And if you've any message . . ."

He said it without thinking, simply to sting the other man.

"You're going back to the mountain? You, Vendusos?" cried the captain with a disdainful laugh. "It's madness!"

"Yes, it's madness, captain. I know. But there's no life without honor! Good day!"

Before Captain Polyxigis could find time to answer, he was gone. Suddenly he knew that he had made his decision: he was not going to flinch, he was going to put both captains, Michales and Polyxigis, to shame! And, if God granted, he would then look after his house and marry off his two daughters.

He walked quickly and came to the church of Saint Menas. He paid the saint a farewell visit and lighted a candle. The church was empty and warm and fragrant with incense. Saint Menas, sunburned, clad in silver from head to foot and mounted on his horse, smiled at him as though giving him his blessing. "A good journey to you, Vendusos," he heard the saint say, "you are on the right track. Don't worry. I will look after your wife and children. And I will find your daughters two good palikars. Good-by, Captain Vendusos!"

Heartened, he crossed himself and left the church. Then he heard people talking and caught sight, through the window of the Bishop's Palace, of the fat, hairy face of the dwarf, Charilaos. What the devil was that receiver of stolen goods, that plunderer, doing in the Bishop's Palace?

Vendusos could not know, naturally, what the wily Metropolitan was up to. The gnome was at the Residence by invitation. They were now drinking their coffee together, and this is what the Metropolitan had on his mind: The Christians who had fled to Athens and to the Piraeus were now returning, to find their houses devastated. The Turks had smashed chests, cupboards and chairs for firewood, and had even taken down the doors and burned them. Only the disfigured walls stared at the homecomers. The Metropolitan wanted to awaken some sense of honor in Charilaos and persuade him to lend money at favorable rates for the rebuilding of the ruined town. Charilaos had made thousands of pounds out of this rising, by keeping on the right side of the pasha. Also, in exchange for a bit of bread, he was raking in earrings, rings, necklaces of precious stones and ducats from the starving Christians. His coffers were brimming over with gold and jewels.

Now, over the coffee, the Metropolitan skillfully and with great urbanity brought the conversation around to God. What profit was it if a man should gain the whole world and lose his soul? Then he guided it further—to the Motherland. How many patriots were immortal because they had sacrificed themselves for the Motherland! And such a sacrifice, it must not be forgotten, need not consist only in giving one's life—it could also be a sacrifice of money. Whoever gave his money would also be immortal and would earn the title of "patriot." God would then open His records and inscribe in them the names of the patriots in golden letters; and, against each name, how many pounds had been given for the Christian cause.

The gnome drank his coffee sip by sip, smoked his cigarette and looked out through the window at the ruined houses and, above them and beyond, at the white-foaming sea. The Metropolitan's words went in one ear and out the other. The cleric's trying hard to get around me, he thought, blowing the smoke out through his nose, he wants to shame me in order to plunder my coffers. Ah, I'm sorry for him! I'm more than a match for his tricks!

When he considered that the Metropolitan had come to the end of his beguiling arguments, he stubbed out his cigarette in the bronze cup and turned to him respectfully. His voice sounded subdued and sad.

"Your words are saintly, my lord. How many times have I not accused myself: ah, if only I were a proper man and could take a gun and offer my life for the Motherland! Or, since God has cursed me and made me a weakling, if at least I were rich enough to give my mite to the widows and help the Christian cause a little! God might then have mercy on me at the Last Judgment! But I'm ruined, my lord, I'm lost. My businesses aren't going well, believe me, my lord, however much the people insult me as an exploiter of the poor. A widow comes, or an orphan, and brings me a little ring. I know perfectly well it's worth sixpence, not more.

And yet I give twice that for it, because my heart burns when I see misfortune. I'm ruining myself and I know it. But I'm human and I'm sorry for them! I've sold a vineyard, an olive plantation, I've even had to mortgage the house I live in, my lord, God is my witness! That's where the money comes from. What's going to become of me? My kindness has devoured me, and when you invited me to the Bishop's Palace my heart leaped with joy. God is merciful, then, I said to myself. He is just, and rewards fair dealing. The Bishop is summoning me, he has heard of my good deeds—but also of my suffering. God has enlightened him, and he will grant me support out of the diocesan moneybags, to keep me from going to the bottom. I hear the communal fund is nice and full, thank God!"

The Metropolitan swallowed drily. That God-damned, avaricious monster! he thought. The sight of the dwarf became intolerable to him. He drank up his coffee with one gulp and fingered his rosary nervously. Charilaos had been sitting cross-legged on the sofa. He now stood up on his small legs and rubbed his hands. "It's cold," he said. "What's going to become of us without fuel, without warm clothing, without enough to eat, Bishop? I've been forced to sell all my hens. But for that, I'd have been able to swallow an egg every morning. That's over, too. God have pity on us!"

Kissing the Metropolitan's hand, he took his leave.

"Pray for us, too, my lord. With your leave, I'll go now. I don't feel well—I must lie down."

Out of the school streamed the children, bumping into each other, yelling and whistling. Tityros had kept them late today, because tomorrow the Christmas holidays were beginning, and so he had given them a last-day-of-term address. He was now a Tityros grown strong, filled out and sunburned. The peasant girl he had married was expecting a child, and the schoolmaster was beside himself with joy. It was a far cry from the days when everyone had pushed him to one side. Now he had the upper hand. Woe to his pupils who now tried to make fun of him!

Vendusos let the children run past. He scarcely recognized Tityros.

"Schoolmaster!" he called out to him, "you've been eating

dragon's-wort and have turned into a dragon! I'm going back to the mountain," he went on, proudly. "What message have you got for your brother?"

Moved, Tityros pressed his hand.

"Vendusos, you're a palikar. Forgive me, I never noticed it all the time I've known you."

"I wasn't a palikar, ever, schoolmaster. But how can I help it? I've become one. Who sits with a blind man soon squints. Captain Michales is the cause."

"I too am doing my duty. Tell him that. This is my way. Whole chains of Cretan children are hanging round my neck. I'm awakening Crete in them, to the best of my power. I left the mountain only to be useful to Crete. And that's why he ought to come down. Tell him that."

"Don't worry, I'll tell him. But we shan't come down. You mark my words! Good-by, schoolmaster!"

"Good old Vendusos," Tityros answered, and watched him with admiration as he went out nimbly through the Hospital Gate.

When Charilaos left, the Metropolitan called his deacon.

"I'm very tired, deacon. All the same, I must go to Archondula's —the pasha will be there. We are going to meet again for the first time in months. He would not come to the Bishop's Palace, I would not go to his konak, so we've agreed on Archondula's house."

"Shall I saddle the ass, since you're tired, my lord?" asked the deacon, a stately, dark-haired peasant's son whose voice rang like a bell. He was reputed to be formidably strong. A pillow could have been stuffed with the hair from his head and beard.

"You're right, bless you. Get the ass. That horrible miser has made me weak."

The deacon laid a rug over the ass, spread on top of that a cloth with a border woven in a design of cypresses and crosses, placed the beast close to a step and heaved the bishop's heavy body onto it.

The pasha, meanwhile, had been having a good meal—he had gnawed every chicken bone clean and drunk a jugful of malvasia wine. Now he too called his Suleiman:

"Suleiman, you blockhead, I've got to go now and see the fat giaour parson, to show the Christians and Turks that the fighting's over. Wolf and lamb have forgiven each other. Bring me my horse. It is not seemly that I should go on foot. And come with me. I've eaten too much and I'm sleepy. Hold me as we go through the streets, so that I don't fall off!"

Just as he was about to mount the horse, there appeared before him, locked in a close embrace, the two seers of spirits, the two choice fools of Megalokastro, Barba Jannis and Efendina. The two were well away in the seventh heaven, hooting and swaying and urging each other on.

Barba Jannis was celebrating. One of his granddaughters had borne a son, so now he was able to hold in his arms his first great-grandchild—a sufficient ground for getting drunk. In his tipsiness he had remembered Efendina, and had summoned him. "Sit down, Efendina," he had told him, "eat and drink."

"Swear to me you won't defile my faith," said Efendina, sniffing uneasily and greedily at the food on the table.

"I swear, Efendina. Have no fear. No pig's flesh and no wine, I'll drink that all myself."

"Wine wouldn't be so bad," said Efendina. "I can drink that. Everybody drinks it."

"I don't want to have your reproaches on my head later on," Barba Jannis persisted. "I'll give you some salepi to drink."

"No, no, salepi doesn't agree with me, Barba Jannis. I'll drink wine. It does no harm. Only pig's flesh does any harm."

They emptied a bottle between them and became happy.

"What do you think, Efendina?" said Barba Jannis. "Shall we do something?"

"Whatever you like, Barba Jannis. As long as I don't have to cross any streets."

"I'll carry you over on my back. Don't worry. Well then, listen: you're a Turk, I'm a Christian. D'you want to kill me? There, take the knife, slaughter me!"

"No, by my faith," shouted Efendina. "Put that knife away, Barba Jannis! You're giving me a heart attack!"

"There! I don't want to slaughter you either. Shouldn't all Turks and Christians be like us two? Live like brothers? Haven't you seen how sometimes a bitch will give suck to a kitten among her puppies? Well, that's how it is with Crete. What am I driving at? That the two of us should now go arm in arm to the pasha and

411

say to him: 'Here, look, Pasha Effendi, how Turks and Christians have made it up. Efendina is Turkey and I am Christendom. We've become brothers. Give us something to drink!' And the pasha, who's a good man, devil take him, will burst out laughing and call that Suleiman of his. 'Serve them!' he'll say, 'they have my blessing!' And out of his cupboard he'll take a decoration for each of us. Then we'll bow to him and go off arm in arm—you, Turkey, and I, Christendom—across Broad Street to the church to pray. And afterwards to the mosque to pray. And finally to Hussein Aga's coffeehouse, where the Turkish youths sing and the spirit of man languishes happily. Understand, Efendina?"

"What about the gutters?" asked Efendina, as he broke out in a cold sweat.

"No fear, I tell you. I'll carry you across on my back. I've learned to swim. Just wait while I arm myself.

He took the scimitar from the wall and the tin decoration out of a kitchen drawer. It was a simple piece of tin, such as they hang on trees to keep off the evil eye.

"Forward!" he said, "in the name of Christ and Mohammed! Say the same, Efendina, you idiot, and then you'll be all right."

"But I must put Mohammed's name first. Let's be fair!"

"What's it matter? Well, then?"

"In the name of Mohammed and Christ," said Efendina, and the two stepped over the threshold, right foot first.

In the street Efendina turned and said, "What do you think, Barba Jannis? Shall we go by Ali Aga's and take the poor man with us too? He's neither Turk nor Greek. He's Turk and Greek, the one just as much as the other. So let's take him with us, to be able to show the pasha all the nations."

"Why not?" shouted Barba Jannis, who in his joy would have liked to give the whole world a kiss.

They reached Captain Michales' quarter and knocked at Ali Aga's low door. Wooden clogs rattled in the yard.

"Who's there?" said a high little voice.

"Two friends, Ali Aga. Open!" shouted Barba Jannis. "We've come to bring you luck."

"I'm afraid, children. Go about your business—what friends?"

"It's me, Ali Aga," Efendina announced himself. "Efendina Horsedung."

The little door opened. The old man was all creased and shriveled. Since the flight of his Christian neighbors he had ventured nowhere. Christians mistrusted him, and Turks would have none of him. Every morning he went into the fields and gathered a few leeks, which he ate with oil. He knitted stockings and hawked them, limping. And he waited for men to acquire reason and for his neighbors to come home. Then there would once more be evening visits, with titbits to eat.

Barba Jannis saw how Ali Aga had fallen in the world, and suddenly he felt very fond of this Turk, whose misery frightened him.

"What's the matter with you, Ali Aga?" he asked, and fell into his arms.

"I'm old, Barba Jannis. I can't bend down any longer. . . . I can't shake it off."

"Are you coming with us to the pasha?" asked Efendina.

"To the pasha?" cried the old man, terrified. "What should I do there? I don't go anywhere."

"It's in your interest, Ali Aga," Barba Jannis explained. "You'll get a decoration."

"For the love of God, go about your business and leave me alone!" screamed the old man, slamming the door.

"Leave him, Efendina," said Barba Jannis, no longer interested. "He's only a bit of dead meat. Let's get on!"

They reached the main square and went in through the pasha's gate.

"Pasha Effendi," they cried, as they saw him. "Stand and admire us!"

"What do you chicken brains want?" asked the pasha, laughing. "What sort of a masquerade is that?"

Efendina hitched up his sackcloth breeches, for the string had broken as usual, and Barba Jannis' scimitar got between his legs so that he was riding astride it. The two advanced, and the representative of Christendom spoke first, solemnly:

"Pasha Effendi, think not that I am Barbi Jannis the salepi vendor! I am Christendom. And that man there is not Efendina Horsedung; he is Turkey. We ate the weed of dissension and became enemies. Afterwards we ate honey and were reconciled. Now we are brothers, Pasha Effendi. Do you see? Crete is like a

413

bitch that can give suck to puppies and kittens at the same time. Milk for all is there in plenty, do you see? Then concord, love, well-being and happiness! Today I've become a great-grandfather; up with reconciliation!"

"Suleiman," the pasha ordered, when he had had his fill of laughing, "that man's no fool! Who would believe it? The two of them have more sense, by my faith, than the Metropolitan and me. Give them a raki and something nice to eat besides."

"And a decoration?" asked Barba Jannis, disappointed. "Isn't there a decoration, Pasha Effendi?"

"Hey, you've got one. That's enough."

"But what about Efendina?" said Barba Jannis, pointing to his friend, whose breeches were sliding.

"Give him a bit of string, Suleiman, to make his breeches fast with," the pasha ordered. "That's enough. That's all the decoration there is. Out with you, I'm busy."

When the pasha arrived at Archondula's, he saw to his satisfaction that the Metropolitan's ass was already tied to the door ring.

"There, the priest's arrived before me," he said. "That means he recognizes my seniority."

Suleiman helped him down from the horse. He walked across the big, paved yard with its pots of flowers. The old maid who was mistress of it all came out to greet him. She was laced up in stays and as thin as a bean pole; her nose stuck spitefully out of her powdered face.

The Metropolitan was standing and the pasha bowed to him as he came into the room. They both sat opposite each other and the Metropolitan took out his rosary. The old maid withdrew, leaving the two high authorities alone.

The Metropolitan warmed his hands over the bronze brazier in front of him. He was frozen. The pasha yawned sleepily. When the Metropolitan saw him yawn, he also yawned.

"It's cold today, Pasha Effendi," said the Metropolitan at last, to open the conversation.

"Yes, winter's come, Metropolitan Effendi," replied the pasha, yawning again. He bent over the brazier and continued to speak, but with great difficulty:

414

"The fumes of charcoal, so I've heard, cause dizziness. I feel dizzy."

"If the charcoal isn't red-hot all through, so I've heard," said the Metropolitan, and yawned.

The conversation died. The pasha grew tired of holding his hands over the brazier and placed them on his knees. He looked about him. He glanced at the big clock on the wall. On top of a carved chest there stood a green vase filled with red velvet roses, and near it a plaster Moor with a hollow head full of matches. And above the door there was his own portrait, resplendent with reds, golds and blacks. He stared out of it with great vigor, and not a hair was missing. As he admired his own handsomeness, the pasha gave a start. It seemed to him that the tassel on his fez in the picture had moved.

He shuddered. "Metropolitan Effendi," he said uneasily, "I just saw that tassel move. Is that possible?"

The Metropolitan was tired and depressed. But he gathered all his strength together, to examine the painting.

"Is it possible, Metropolitan Effendi?" asked the pasha again.

"What, Pasha Effendi?"

"There! For the tassel in the picture to move."

"No, it's impossible, Pasha Effendi," the Metropolitan asserted, and leaned his heavy head against the back of the chair. The pasha did the same and closed his eyes. When the Metropolitan saw this, he closed his.

The cuckoo came out of the clock and called out the hour. The north wind outside blew the shriveled leaves violently across the yard. A sparrow hungrily pecked the pane with his beak. Hearing a terrible snore, it flew away in alarm. The gigantic cat belonging to the house glided in and jumped on the Metropolitan's lap. Curling up, it warmed itself at his belly and slept contentedly, purring. . . . The cuckoo again announced the hour.

Archondula anxiously put her ear to the door. She heard only long-drawn-out, comfortable sounds of snoring, one set heavy, like a drum, the other blaring cheerfully, like a trumpet.

I'll make them some coffee to rouse them, she said to herself. She went into the kitchen and put the pot on the fire.

Soon afterward the pasha heard the door creak, opened his eyes, and saw the old maid with the round salver.

"Sleep has overcome him," he said mockingly, and pointed at the slumbering Metropolitan. "The poor man's no longer up to it. He's grown old."

As the scent of the coffee entered his nose, the Metropolitan too opened his eyes.

"Hearty thanks, Archondula," he said, reaching out for the cup. "I was longing for that. A hair's breadth and I'd have fallen asleep."

Both of them sipped loudly and happily. The Metropolitan turned to the pasha. "The wheat promises well this year, Pasha Effendi."

"The barley too, Metropolitan Effendi," answered the pasha in faulty Greek, and stood up. "We have spent our time well today. Let's meet another day and negotiate further."

"With pleasure, Pasha Effendi," said the Metropolitan, gripping the chair and likewise standing up.

A crowd had collected outside. It had become known that the two leaders were meeting in that grand house, for the first time in so many months, to negotiate and to restore harmony in the land. And so the people waited in the cold, to gape at them as they walked hand in hand out of the door.

Kasapakes the doctor came by and stopped. He saw Aristoteles the chemist standing there waiting.

"What's up, Mr. Aristoteles?" he asked. "Somebody died?"

"Bite off your tongue, doctor," answered Mr. Aristoteles. "The pasha and the Metropolitan are in there, holding council. Someone caught sight of them through the window. He saw them in the room, with papers spread out before them. The Metropolitan was writing and the pasha was speaking, making gestures with his hands. Now they're putting their seals to it. How's Madame Marcelle?"

The doctor shrugged his shoulders.

"Always the same. To give her a change of air, I've taken her to my brother Katsabas' country place."

He spoke with contentment, for he had succeeded in throwing her out so that he could stay on alone with the servant girl.

While they were still chatting, Mr. Demetros Leanbottom came hobbling up from the end of the street. For the first time in seven months he had come home from the villages, where he had been wandering about with his umbrella, in order, he said, to get rid of his congestion of the heart. During his wanderings he had seldom opened his mouth to speak. The peasants said that the fairies had robbed him of his speech, and they honored him as one smitten by demons. They would offer him a piece of bread, and he would take it and push on, chewing, to another village. Sometimes he held the umbrella gripped tightly under his arm, sometimes he opened it, depending on the weather.

As long as Crete struggled with Charos, Mr. Demetros had wandered about, full of anxiety. Now that peace had come to Crete, he too wanted to find peace and return to his wife Penelope. His boots were worn out, his clothes torn, he had lost his hat. His breeches, too wide now for his thin thighs, flapped in the wind like a woman's skirts.

"How thin the sad fellow's got," said the fat doctor with a laugh, "his breeches are empty."

"Don't worry, he'll fill them again," replied Mr. Aristoteles, shaking his cucumber head. Ah, that's nothing to compare with my misfortune! he thought, and then of his grocery in Broad Street, and of how he had no son to inherit it; and of his three shriveled sisters and the three peepholes in the door, through which they observed the world—their only pleasure.

"Welcome, Mr. Demetros," said the doctor to the newcomer. "How are things going with you?"

"Glory to God, I've broken my foot," replied Mr. Demetros, and passed on.

"Only the weak in the head enjoy the world," muttered the chemist, gazing after him. "Woe—three times woe—to people of sense!"

"Oh, I'd quite forgotten," cried the doctor, "I must go."

"A patient?"

"Yes. It's the Jewess Captain Michales' nephew brought back. She's had a miscarriage. Pretty, fair-haired girl—have you seen her?"

"So that's his game now," said the chemist with malicious pleasure, and raised himself on tiptoe to see what was going on in Archondula's yard, to be able to tell his sisters. The excited crowd now saw the stately, white-bearded Metropolitan stepping solemnly across the yard between the pots of flowers to the door, arm in arm with the plump, bristle-bearded pasha. Christians and Turks made room for them, to let them through. The pasha, now quite awake, smilingly greeted the waiting crowd. But the Metropolitan was frowning as he leaned heavily on his crosier. He was impatient to be rid of the Turk. The deacon untied the ass from the ring; Suleiman brought the pasha's horse.

Meanwhile, in the house of her parents-in-law, a weight of suffering had fallen on Noëmi. Last night she had not closed her eyes. She kept thinking of her husband, alone on the mountain, and of her son, who was growing in her and pressing her hard. A strange dread kept her awake, a dark menace lay in the air. An invisible body, a soundless voice, a ghost. . . . Was it the dead man? As this thought came to her, the sweat flowed from her pores. Feeling that she would stifle, she sprang up and opened the window. Cutting morning air came in. Noëmi went downstairs and found the mother bent over the hearth, lighting the fire.

"Mother," she said, "I don't feel well. I'm going out to get some air."

When the mother saw her, she shrank back. The young woman seemed devoured by fear; her bones stuck out. Great dark rings circled her eyes.

"Where are you going so early in the morning, in this cold, my child?" she asked, full of pity. "You'll overstrain yourself."

Noëmi hesitated. She was ashamed to betray her dread, and to say where she now planned to go.

"Don't you know where you're going?" the old woman asked.

"I know, Mother. To church. To light a candle."

The mother gave a cry. "Have you seen him in a dream, my child?"

"Yes."

The mother stared into the air. Her chin was trembling. The young woman was right. He was not dead yet. He came through the air. He passed through doors. He still had some evil design. "Child," she said at last, in a muffled voice, as if she was afraid the dead man might hear her, "go, light a candle for him. Pray to him to have pity on you. But in God's name don't tell him that his grandson—that you—"

"No, Mother, I won't tell him."

"Take my shawl and wrap yourself up properly. Otherwise you'll catch cold."

The church was empty. Faint light filtered through the colored windows and awoke the saints in the icons; it shone on the candelabra, the bronze candlesticks and, above the shrine with the prayer books, Saint Menas on horseback. Noëmi picked up a candle from the bench and went over to the big icon of the Virgin, which hung on the iconostasis beside the Beautiful Gate. She dared not speak directly to the dead man; she wanted to call upon the Virgin Mother to act as mediatress between them.

The silver lamp burning before the Virgin softly lighted her stubborn chin, her two sad almond eyes, and the cherry-red band embroidered with gold stars around her head. Noëmi knelt down and looked up at her speechlessly for a long time. The longer she looked, the lighter and milder her heart became. The young woman was holding her Son tightly in her arms, as though she were afraid she would be robbed of Him: she leaned her cheek tenderly against His cheek and held a small wooden cross before Him as a toy. . . .

Noëmi stood up, lighted the candle in the candlestick, put her mouth close to the Virgin, and spoke to her. She did not yet know the prayers: she spoke to her as to a good neighbor at whose door you knock in heavy trouble.

"Mother," she said to her, "I am the Jewess Noëmi. I've come from the other end of the world. I've left my father's faith and become a Christian. I am in great trouble, Mother, help me! Tell him he's not to come at night to torment me, tell him he's not to do me any harm. I wish nothing but good for his house, I love his son, I have no other pleasure. Mother, I will tell you this too, but don't tell him: in three months I too will be a mother. I'm afraid of his doing my son some harm. Don't let him! I fall at your feet, Mother of all the mothers in the world. Have mercy on me!"

She raised her eyes. She saw the Virgin looking down sadly and hopelessly. Her eyes seemed suddenly to be full of tears. Noëmi shuddered. She took from her ear the golden ring, a present from Kosmas, and hung it on the icon-shrine. "It's all I have, Holy Virgin," she whispered. "This ring is for you. Think of me!"

When she came home, Maria saw her and turned her face violently away. The mother went to meet her and asked, "Did you light a candle to him, my child? Did you hear a voice? Did he say anything?"

"Mother, I'll go and lie down. I'm tired," she answered, and breathing heavily she slowly went upstairs and stretched herself on the wide iron bed on which, while he was alive, the dead man had embraced his wife.

The air was heavy. Noëmi breathed hard and kept her eyes open. She was afraid the dead man might enter in the darkness, if she closed her eyes. The clock downstairs struck again and again, and from the minarets there rang out, passionately and harmoniously, the voice of the muezzin. Noon! She had a bitter taste in her mouth. She could not go down to eat; she lay there, her eyes fixed on the tall date palm that rose above the roofs from Archondula's courtyard. A violent wind was blowing, the shutters clattered, and the scimitar-like leaves of the palm clashed against each other. Opposite her, on the icon-shrine, the little lamp flickered—the tiny flame seemed to want to fly away from the wick. But Noëmi had not the strength to get up and fill the lamp with oil.

Exhausted, she closed her eyes. Did sleep overcome her? She did not know. But when she closed her eyes, she felt, with horrible certainty, that someone, without opening the door, had come into the room. Noëmi cowered to the farthest edge of the bed and forced herself to open her eyes. No one! And yet she felt that someone was standing in front of her, between the bedposts.

"It's he," Noëmi whispered, full of dread, staring into the air. The little lamp had gone out. The icon was sunk in shadow.

The longer she stared, the more strongly she felt the air in front of the bed thicken and take on a shape. At first two silver pistols gleamed in the air, then a powerful neck and a black, waxed mustache and two eyes, lowering from behind thick, bristling brows. . . .

"Holy Virgin!" Noëmi screamed. "Help! Drive him away!"

But he raised his hand, seized the coverlet and wrenched it aside. Then he struck at Noëmi's body with his fist.

The girl gave a shriek and rolled from the bed to the floor. The mother heard her, ran upstairs, and found her in a pool of blood.

"Maria," she cried, "the doctor! Quick!"

She removed the stillborn child, rubbed Noëmi's temples with perfume, lighted the lamp again and waited for the doctor. As she waited she made secret lament for her stillborn grandson. And now her daughter-in-law, pale as wax, opened her eyes and cast bewildered glances about her. Where was she? What was this blood? Who had struck her? Whence came this unbearable pain inside her? She pressed her lips together in order not to cry out. She saw the mother bending over her and stretched out her hands toward her.

"Mother," she whispered, "it hurts," and closed her eyes again.

The mother sat down beside her, moistened her temples again with perfume, and thought of her son. When would her dear one learn of this misfortune? Where might he be at this moment? In the grandfather's courtyard?

But Kosmas was already a long way away from the grandfather's courtyard. Through night and rain he had climbed the steep slope of the mountain. The picture of the grandfather, dying as the lyre gave him the answer to his question, soared before his soul in overwhelming beauty.

Kosmas had been followed in silence by the bowed body of old Charidimos. Suddenly Charidimos stopped dead. He could bear the silence no longer. For him a journey meant conversation and jesting, but this man in the Frankish clothes did not talk and did not laugh.

"Why are you in such a hurry, master? To see Captain Michales? Damn him! The best thing would be for you not to see him. But if your destiny demands that you should, then as late as possible. And as shortly as possible. I was sent the day before yesterday by your grandfather, to tell him that he lay dying and expected him to come and say good-by. When he turned and looked at me so savagely, it gave me a turn."

"Don't worry, Charidimos. He's my uncle. His blood is mine. I'm not afraid of him," answered Kosmas, without stopping.

"Are you strong enough to oppose him? I swear you won't be!"

"I shall be strong enough. But don't talk now! Hey!"

Kosmas was still determined not to mar this hour of silent gathering of his thoughts. For he was brooding not only over his grandfather but over that hard, knotty bough on the tree, Captain

Michales, who perhaps held in his hands the fate of Crete. Where could he find him? How was he to speak with him? What was he to say to him? What demon was riding him?

"It was his fault that the Christ the Lord Monastery was lost," the Metropolitan had told him. "And now he wants to wash away the dishonor. That's why he won't give in. Perhaps he wants to be killed, to pay in full."

"But if the well-being of Crete requires otherwise?" Kosmas had asked.

The Metropolitan had hesitated, weighing his words. "God forgive me," he had murmured at last, "but I believe your uncle has a demon inside him, whose name is not Crete."

"There's a dark moment in his life," his other uncle, Tityros, had confided to him. "A mystery about Captain Polyxigis and a Turkish woman. There's a lot of talk about it. His heart is wild, it no longer follows his brain."

"He was jealous about Arkadi," the gnome Charilaos had told him mockingly. "So the rascal took it into his head that he too would blow something sky-high, so that people should sing a song about him!"

Perhaps they were all right, thought Kosmas, as he climbed upward through the rain, sliding on the slippery stones. How could he move his uncle to make use of the pasha's promise to permit him to retire intact with weapons and banners? Should he stress that the Metropolitan desired it? That the King of Greece demanded it? Would he not shrug his shoulders with contempt? Was he not devoid of all trust in people?

Kosmas kept thinking out ways to speak to this wild, proud man, to guide him into the desired course. At the same time he was torn by his own anxieties. What kind of son would the sickly body of Noëmi, to which he had entrusted the terrible seed of his race, bear him? He trembled when he thought of it. Then his thoughts would rush back to the land of the Franks, to the injustice, shamelessness and poverty he had seen there. And finally, what about his own course? Where would his own life's battle take place? His grandfather had had his place, so had his father, and this uncle still had his. But he? Where was he to take up his position and say: "Here I fight, no one's going to drive me out." He felt that he was hanging in the air.

The rain stopped at last. A sharp frost-wind blew, chasing the clouds. Constellations appeared, and Charidimos stopped and looked searchingly at the sky.

"It's after midnight. We've made good time," he said. "If you believe in God, master, let's stop awhile under this cliff. It's out of the wind, and we can light a cigarette."

"Are you tired, Charidimos?"

"Yes, I'm tired. You must realize I'm old. My bones are getting heavy."

The sly fellow was not tired at all. But he was determined to have his talk. They sat down under the cliff, and Kosmas gave him a cigarette. And now, how was Charidimos to begin the conversation? First he looked up at the sky. What could one say about that? He let it go and considered as possible themes, one after another, his village, Megalokastro, Crete. But what there was to say about them, this Frank certainly had at his fingertips. So that was no good. Suddenly there sprang to his mind one of his uncles, a little fellow called Andrulios. What was this leanbottom's uncle compared to him? A midge. Now I'll show him.

He pulled eagerly at his cigarette, and turned to Kosmas.

"Do you know, master, what's the biggest wild beast in the world? The lion, you'll say. Not a bit of it! Man! Why? you ask. Because he fights and kills Turks like your uncle? Or because he invents weapons with the devil's cunning and kills the lions? Not a bit of it! I'll tell you. I had an uncle. They called him, God forgive him, Andrulios. He was only a half-helping. So they gave him the nickname 'Brownie,' because he was no bigger than a pea, poor man. God's refuse, not worth spitting out. He ran here and there —no, he didn't run, he hopped like a grasshopper, and moaned because his kidneys hurt him. The doctors said he had a stone and was sure to die. And he, my child—yes, what a thing a man is!— he took his ax and went out, and knelt down on the mountain outside Venerato, his village. Ping! Ping! Ping! He began breaking up the mountain with the ax. One year, two years, three. The peasants used to come by, see him and shake with laughter. 'Pitting yourself against the mountain, Andrulios?' 'Yes, against the mountain! I'm going to eat it up!' he answered, without taking his eyes off his ax. In the third year he began building a house at the bottom of the mountain. 'Don't build a house, Andrulios, just take

423

our advice. Whoever builds a house gets married.' 'I shall do that too, you sausages,' Andrulios answered. 'I mean to marry and beget children, so that they can help me beat the mountain.' The peasants laughed. 'What woman will take you, Brownie?' 'When there's a crowd in the butcher shop nothing gets left over,' he answered. 'There'll be a wife even for me.'

"He built the house, and one day a peasant's widow, short and fat and ugly, came by. But she was young. She had a good look at the yard, the cellar, the kitchen, the bedroom. She liked the house. 'Andrulios,' she said, 'what do you think?' And winked at him. My uncle understood. To cut a long story short, they got married. He slept with her and made the best use of the night. But next morning, first thing, when he was still sleepy, he looked out at the mountain, took his ax and began hacking at it again: ping, ping, ping. Every day he bit off another piece. When enough fresh stone had been hewed out, he built a house next door, with another bedroom. He enlarged the yard and built a stable. 'Andrulios,' said the peasants, 'do you mean to build a town?' 'Yes a town,' he answered. 'My wife's with child, where am I to put my children?' 'And you haven't any pains in your kidneys any more?' 'What's that about pains, you idle carcasses? I haven't the time.'

"Years passed. The woman bore children, always two at a time. He kept chopping with the ax. There were caves and pits in the mountain—Andrulios was eating it up. He and the mountain could not be parted. My uncle's hair had turned gray, and his body was even more like a hobgoblin's, but his arms now had a mighty strength, and his hands were broader and longer—they reached down to his knees. Soon he had such a stoop that his paws touched the stones. Whoever saw him burst out laughing. He looked like an ape the pasha once brought to Megalokastro. Whoever saw Andrulios laughed, certainly, but he trembled too. The peasants now kept their distance, for one day he had caught one of the laughing louts by the knee joint and squashed his bones so that he limped ever afterwards. As his children grew, they too threw themselves upon the mountain with the ax, ate it up bit by bit, and built. They married and begot children. My uncle Andrulios was now old and weak, the ax grew too heavy for him. And one evening, as he came home from the mountain, he felt his end drawing near. He lay down on his bed and called his children and grandchildren to him. He ordered them to bury him in the mountain, and to lay his ax by his side. Then he folded his arms and departed. If you happen to pass by Venerato one day, master, have them point out to you Andrulios Village. My uncle's buildings are now a model place."

He stopped. He was sure he had properly impressed the Frank. His eyes shone with satisfaction and excitement through the darkness.

"Charidimos, I know another wild beast, bigger than the lion and your Uncle Andrulios."

"Which one?"

"The corpse-worm."

"Heaven preserve us! In God's name, don't think of that! Bad luck to it!" muttered Charidimos, and crossed himself.

He spat, and grabbed hold of his stick. "Forward, master," he said, impatiently.

By dawn Kosmas had reached the peak of Selena. Charidimos hung back. "Go ahead, master," he said, "and when you've done what has to be done, call me, so that we can go back together. I'd rather not see your uncle. Forgive me!"

Standing at his lookout post, Captain Michales had not slept all night. At the first glimmer of light he picked up his field glasses to observe the position of the Turkish posts below. They were dug in a little higher each day. The Turks were not hurrying. From the few salvos the Christians now sent them, they concluded that their supply of powder and shot must be meager. They knew, too, that the rebels had only a little barley bread left to eat. The siege was perfect and let neither man nor beast through. There was now only one concealed goat path by which a native could reach the eagle's nest by night.

The pasha had never stopped sending messages to Captain Michales, to persuade this last of the leaders to obedience. It would be more useful to Turkey, he had been informed by Constantinople, if the rebels humbled themselves than if they were killed. For then Crete would have gone back under the yoke of her own free will, and the claim of the Franks would fall to the ground. Yesterday evening the pasha had once more sent a message to Captain Michales: "I grant you a last respite. Surrender tomorrow morning and retire with all military honors. I shall not touch you. Otherwise I shall pound you all to pieces, by Mohammed!"

All night Captain Michales had weighed which course he should choose—not for himself, for he had already chosen, but for his companions. There was no hope of winning, and he did not want to burden his conscience with their fate. So let each of them be free to go his way. He had told them of the pasha's message. He had asked them to think it over and at daybreak to bring him their answer.

None of them had slept. As the sun touched the mountain, each man separately had come to the captain. Unwashed, uncombed, in torn clothes spotted with blood, they now surrounded him and waited for him to speak. But he stared at the rocks and waited for the wrath in his heart to subside. When he did speak, it must be with a serene voice and not with a roar. Thought after thought flashed through his mind: Thrasaki, the Circassian woman, the Monastery of Christ the Lord. . . . He let out a curse, picked up a stone and gripped it till the blood dripped from his hand.

His lips and his brows contracted. He looked at his comrades, at the Turks far below, at the uninhabited sky. "Freedom or death," he muttered, shaking his head fiercely. "Freedom or death! O poor Cretans! 'Freedom *and* death'—that's what I should have written on my banner. That's the true banner of every fighter: Freedom *and* death! Freedom *and* death!"

As he said this, he grew easier. After so many years this much was clear at last. His heart strengthened. He now turned calmly to his comrades:

"You know what that dog announces to us. You're men, we're struggling for freedom, speak out freely! We've no more powder and shot, no bread, no hope. The Turks are an army, we a handful. Whoever of you wants to leave, let him go: by my saber, which I shall give up only to God, it's no dishonor! But I'm not going."

For a few moments there was silence. The sun already stood a hand's breadth high in the sky, and the drums began beating. The Turkish soldiers were mustering.

"Speak out freely!" Captain Michales repeated. "And be quick about it!"

A dark-haired, haggard man, whose ancient gun was tied together with string, began:

"That I'm a man, you all know. That I never gave way before anyone, you also know. I'm not afraid of being called unmanly, and I mean to give my opinion frankly. Captain, we're foundering uselessly. It brings no profit to us or to Christendom. Soon there will be another rising in Crete, and we shall not be there to strike our blow too. Our life is now much more important for Crete than our death. Honor or dishonor, I don't care. Advantage or disadvantage to Crete—that's what is on my mind."

Captain Michales listened intently. When the voice was silent, he asked, "Have you done, Janaros?"

"I have."

Captain Michales turned to the others. "Your turn, Furogatos."

Furogatos stroked his mustache, turned his face away, and said:

"All night two devils struggled inside me. One of them said, 'Leave, there's no hope of winning.' The other said, 'Stay, because there's no hope of winning.' When dawn came, one of the two devils won."

"And which?" asked Captain Michales, his eyes boring into those of his companion.

"As for you, Captain Michales—damn the hour I got to know you!"

"Well?"

"I'm not going!"

Captain Michales went around the circle. "And what about you, Kajabes?"

"I," he answered with a sigh, "am newly married; I've a wife and haven't had a chance to enjoy our happiness! That's burning inside me!"

"Well," insisted the captain. "Leave the woman aside. What does the man say? We're asking him."

"Curse the hour I met you, Captain Michales. I too say that. I'd like to leave, but you have shamed me. I'm not going."

"And you, Thodores?" said the captain, turning now to his nephew, who, while his companions had been speaking, had cleaned and loaded his gun. "What do you say, beardless one?"

427

Thodores scowled. He stared at his uncle with mingled anger, admiration and envy. "Do you think because you've got a beard, you're the only one with courage? I'm not leaving."

"Nor I!"

"Nor I," two with graying temples exclaimed.

The others, some twenty of them, silently bent their heads.

"We've no time, the sun's already two hands breadths high," cried Captain Michales. "Speak! Do you want to go? You're free. Good-by!"

Krasojorgis whispered with the man beside him. Then he stood up and laid his hand on his breast.

"Forgive me, brothers," he said in a strangled voice. "We have unmarried sisters, sons who are unemployed, wives and children. And our death does nobody any good. We are leaving."

"Forgive us, brothers," Mastrapas said too, "we're going."

"Bless you! Bless you, brothers!" cried Captain Michales. "God is my witness, I have no complaint against you. Greet the people down there. But go quickly, each man in turn, and don't let 'em see you. Quick, before the sun gets higher still."

"Forgive us, and may God forgive you!"

"You are forgiven," answered Captain Michales. "Damn the man who says anything against you! Good homecoming!"

Five remained. Captain Michales looked at each in turn. "There are six of us," he said. "It's enough. It's more than enough. The brain says, 'we want to leave!' But the heart—God help us!—won't allow it. We are not leaving. Here we shall die as a sacrifice for Crete. Let her speak. We who are dying are doing better than they who will live. For Crete doesn't need householders, she needs madmen like us. Such madmen make Crete immortal."

He looked up at the sky. The sun was climbing rapidly.

"Pick up your guns. Keep changing loopholes, so they don't notice there are fewer of us. In God's name!"

The palikars had begun to disperse and Captain Michales was kneeling down at his loophole, when he heard the clatter of pebbles. He turned around and stared at Kosmas.

"Well, who are you?" he asked. "Keep your head down, if you don't want a bullet through you."

"Your nephew, Captain Michales. Kosmas."

The captain frowned. He understood what wind brought this one

428

here. He said, roughly, "A most welcome visit. Why have you come all the way up here? What does the fox want in the bazaar?"

Kosmas bit his lips, to keep the angry words back. "I'm no fox," he said with a dry laugh, "and this is no bazaar. I too am a man, Captain Michales. Your nephew."

"Only someone who fights is a man. Lie down beside me and tell me why you've come. But in a few words—I'm busy."

He glanced again at the sky. The sun was approaching midday height. He shouted to his companions, "Get ready, children! Load! But wait for my signal before you fire!"

Wild shouts came from below. Kosmas peered through a gap in the rock and saw thick masses of Turkish soldiers beginning to climb.

"Speak! Who sent you?" said Captain Michales again. His glance had moved away from his nephew. He was now keeping his eyes sharply focused on the Turks.

"Crete," Kosmas replied. At this word Captain Michales caught fire and bellowed, "None of your big words, schoolmaster! Talk like a man. And don't tell me Crete sends you! D'you hear? I am Crete!"

Kosmas felt at once that before him was a man who would never yield. Even God could not change the mind of this man—he had made an unshakable decision. Why then grovel before him? The proud Cretan heart in Kosmas rose up. He was ashamed of clever tricks of speech.

"Well, what do you want?" roared Captain Michales, still without looking around.

"I want nothing," answered Kosmas defiantly. His mind rejected all the words he had prepared.

"So you've come to pay a visit to your uncle?" scoffed the other. "Greetings!"

"I did come to tell you my grandfather's dead."

Captain Michales laid down his gun to cross himself.

"God be gracious to him," he said. "He was an honorable man indeed. His dealings were good, his life was full. Now he departs, to sleep. . . . As for you: good-by. We're at war here."

"Have you no message?"

"Go."

"For your wife? For your son Thrasaki?"

Captain Michales' veins stood out, his look grew troubled. He cupped his hand, smeared with powder and blood, to his mouth and yelled, "In God's name, brothers, freedom or death!"

He took aim and fired. The mountains echoed. At once Turkish bullets whistled and a small cannon on the slope thundered. The shell landed behind Captain Michales and set the stones whirling.

"Oh," rang out an agonized cry. The comrades turned. Kajabes rolled off the rock onto which he had climbed, and crumpled up at Captain Michales' feet. He opened his mouth and tried to speak. But the stream of blood that flowed out stifled his voice.

Down below, the trumpets brayed, the soldiers and, at the head, the dervishes with the green flag of the Prophet, bawled.

"Let 'em have it, children!" yelled Thodores. "Let fly at the dogs!"

The scraping of Turkish feet came nearer and nearer.

Captain Michales threw himself upon Kajabes, to take him in his arms. In doing so, he fell over Kosmas, who was lying by his side. "Are you still here, schoolmaster?" he shouted at him. "Run away, don't get mixed up with men!"

But Kosmas did not rise. Smeared with powder and blood, he was listening now to his heart, which had gone wild. In his breast his father, the terrible leader in battle, had awakened, and his grandfather, and Crete. This was not his first battle: for a thousand years he had been fighting, a thousand times he had been killed and had risen again. His blood stormed.

Captain Michales hastily felt the body of Kajabes to find his wound. For a second the man's eyes still flashed, then they glazed. The captain laid the corpse back on the ground.

"Remember Arkadi, brothers!" he cried. "Let's all die like men!"

They could hear the gasping breathing of the Turks.

"We're lost," yelled Furogatos, and felt a quivering in his chest and belly.

"Shut up!" cried Thodores, from whose forehead the blood was flowing and blinding his eyes. He wiped it off with his arm, saw the Turks in front and threw his gun away.

"Children," he cried, "guns are no use now. Draw your knives!"

He pulled out his father's black-hilted dagger and fell upon a dervish, who had rushed ahead and was fanatically waving his flag in the air. But he had hardly reached the dervish when a bullet pierced his heart and he staggered backward.

"Health and joy to you, palikars!" a high voice cried behind them. "I've got back just in time, Captain Michales!"

"What, Vendusos?" cried the captain, his eyes gleaming. "Have you really come back?"

"I'm Vendusos, and I behave like a Vendusos. Take back what you said, Captain!"

"I take back what I said. Forgive me, brother. Come here to me!"

Vendusos took a step, but a bullet hit him in the forehead and he fell to the ground.

Captain Michales' eyes were wet. He clasped the dead man and kissed him on the forehead. Then he turned around and again caught sight of Kosmas. He raised his fist.

"Be off!" he cried. "You've still got time. Clear out!"

"I'm not going!" With one bound he seized Kajabes' gun, slung his cartridges around him and tore the dagger out of the dead man's belt.

Captain Michales looked at him in amazement. "You're not going?"

"I'm not going."

Suddenly Captain Michales understood. His face beamed. He took Kosmas' head in both hands.

"Hail to you, nephew," he cried. "So you too mean to sacrifice yourself? Immortal Crete!"

A storm was rising. The sky, which had clouded over, glowed buff red. From afar came the cawing of hungry birds.

Furogatos sprang up. He was ashamed of having been, for a moment, a coward. Death now seemed to him the great Merciful One, who washed away all dishonor. He crossed himself and drew his short knife. "Freedom or death!" he shouted, and rushed from his cover, bareheaded and unprotected, against the Turks. Five of them surrounded him; he fell upon them savagely, but they threw him to the ground. A dervish knelt on his chest and slaughtered him like a ram.

When Captain Michales saw this he gave the order: "No one to leave cover!"

But of his companions only the two gray-haired ones and Kosmas were left. Sheltered behind boulders they carefully took aim, and not one of their bullets went wide.

Captain Michales, too, aimed serenely at the forehead of each soldier who emerged. A bullet had scored his cheek, another had hit his right thigh. Blood was streaming from him, but he felt no pain. From time to time he cast a glance at his nephew, who was beside him, shooting away imperturbably. "Hail to you, nephew," he shouted to him. "Your father has risen again. Brother Kostaros, you've done a good job!"

"Well met, uncle," the other answered, drunk with joy. He was transformed. A dark, unfathomable ecstasy possessed him. He felt light and released, as if at this precise moment he had at last come home to his own country. All Frankish, intellectual ideas had vanished, together with mother, wife and son. Nothing remained except this single, ancient duty.

"Freedom or death!" he roared, as the Turks came on.

A sudden darkness fell. Snow came down in thick, noiseless flakes. Behind the cherry-red clouds the course of the sinking sun could be divined.

"A happy meeting, Captain Michales!" The old muezzin of Megalokastro, with his green turban on his head, emerged suddenly over a boulder.

"My greetings, hodza!" Captain Michales answered, and sent a bullet exactly through his Adam's apple.

A fountain of blood spurted, and the muezzin caved in.

"Kill them off!" cried a Turkish lad with flowing golden hair. He let fly with a long whip at the backs of the soldiers. Bellowing, they rushed forward.

"Don't flinch, nephew," said Captain Michales to Kosmas. "There's no hope. Long live Crete!"

"You're right. There's no hope. Long live Crete!"

They drew their daggers and rushed forward. The snow was already beginning to veil the outstretched dead. Every red fez grew white. Two vultures swooped down and circled the men busily killing one another.

In the tumult of the hand-to-hand fighting, uncle and nephew were parted. Captain Michales saw from a distance that the Turks had surrounded Kosmas. He broke through the chain of soldiers with which he himself was surrounded, and rushed forward to free him.

"I'm coming, nephew," he called out.

But it was too late.

"He's coming himself, Captain Michales," one of the native Turks screamed mockingly, and threw Kosmas' head at his face.

Captain Michales raised the severed head by the hair like a banner. A wild light haloed his face, which was filled with an inhuman joy. Was it pride, godlike defiance, or contempt of death? Or limitless love for Crete? Captain Michales roared:

"Freedom or . . ."

. . . and did not finish. A bullet went through his mouth. Another pierced his temples. His brains spattered the stones.

ABOUT THE AUTHOR

NIKOS KAZANTZAKIS *was born in Crete in 1885 and died in Germany in 1957. He studied at the University of Athens, where he received his Doctor of Law degree, later in Paris under the philosopher Henri Bergson, and completed his studies in literature and art during four other years spent in Germany and Italy.*

Before the last world war, he spent a great deal of his time on the island of Aegina, where he devoted himself to his philosophical and literary work. For a short while in 1945 he was Minister of Education in Greece. His works are numerous and varied—in the fields of philosophy, travel, the drama and fiction. Perhaps the most outstanding, apart from his magnificently conceived novels, is his long epic poem on the fortunes of Odysseus, which begins where Homer's Odyssey ends.

Outstanding Paperback Books from the Touchstone Library: